The Cajun Pirate

A novel by Wilson Hawthorne

Fresh from his adventures in *The Last Pirate,* Harley Cooper is back in another action-packed tale.

Just months after Hurricane Charley, a storm of a different kind blows in.

Harley's friends are kidnapped, his treasure stolen. To get them back, Harley must battle the demented descendants of New Orleans' most notorious pirate, Jean Lafitte. From the shores of Florida to the bayous of Louisiana, the danger never stops. Modern day pirates, a Voodoo witch, and even the sea itself, rise up to take Harley down.

With pirate tales, boatloads of treasure, and tons of excitement, this sequel to *The Last Pirate* is perfect for readers 10 to 100. From the first page to the last, *The Cajun Pirate* is a non-stop page burner, suitable for the entire family.

Looking for a book you can't put down? Pick up

The Cajun Pirate.

The Cajun Pirate, a novel by Wilson Hawthorne

Published by Eyeland Telemedia, Inc.

This is a work of fiction. Names, characters, places and incidents are either the product of the author's mind or are used fictitiously. Any resemblance to actual persons, living or dead, events, or locales is entirely coincidental.

ISBN 978-1-793-98662-7

www.EyelandTelemedia.com

Printed in the United States of America.

Eyeland Telemedia, Inc.
141 SW 56 Terrace
Cape Coral, FL 33914

www.TheCajunPirate.com

10 9 8 7 6 5 4 3 2

For my mom & dad.
Thanks for my birthday,
Today,
And every day in between.

"A pirate I have always been!
A pirate I will be!
For as long as ships do sail the sea,
There be treasure bound for me!"

- Long John MacBlane

The Cajun Pirate

A novel by Wilson Hawthorne

Book of Secrets

Salt yanked the curtain across his kitchen window.

The room went black.

A moment later, a match flared and he lit a hurricane lantern. Shadows swooped across the wall as Salt's parrot, Aruba, flew to his shoulder.

"Raaaaawwwkk!" the bird shrieked, giving me the beady eye while her feet got comfortable on Salt's shirt.

The two of them left the kitchen behind the lantern, trailing a shadow that looked more like a two-headed sea monster than a man and his bird. I followed them into the den.

Even though we were miles from the nearest person, in Salt's shuttered cabin, on a mostly deserted island, that old crabber took no chances, especially when it came to secrets as big as the one he was about to share with me.

More shadows stretched to the ceiling as Salt set the candle on the floor next to a big, wooden chest.

Two words always came to mind whenever I laid eyes on that trunk during a visit to Salt's place on Cayo Costa. The first word was *massive*. I don't know how he ever got it through the door. The thing is so big, carpenters must have built the shack around it. If my boat sunk and I needed a way off the island, all I'd have to do is strap an outboard motor to that old box and I'd have a new boat – with plenty of room for a crew!

The other word that never failed to occur to me was my favorite word in the whole English language – *treasure*. The trunk was shaped like a classic pirate booty bin. And knowing Salt the way I do, it wouldn't have surprised me one bit if Black Beard, himself, designed it three hundred years ago.

He'll never tell. Pirates rarely do.

The chest arches as high as a cat's back, timbers reinforced under straps of iron. I've begged Salt a million times to let me have a look inside. I just know the thing is loaded with shiny gold coins, jewels and pearls.   But, to my constant disappointment, the trunk has always remained shut, as tight lipped about what she holds as her owner.   And, a gigantic, iron padlock made sure she stayed that way.

Salt knelt by one side. I couldn't quite see what his fingers did down there. I just heard a click and then the scrape of wood. I waited for the lid to fly open, for the treasure to finally be revealed. Salt pulled open a hidden drawer, instead. Out of that drawer, his hands lifted a large cloth sack into the candle light.

"Save for me and Aruba," he said in a dusty voice, "not another living soul has ever laid eyes on what I'm about to show you, kid." He paused, leaning in towards me to drive the point home. "Get my drift?"

I nodded. He knew I'd keep my mouth shut.

He carried the sack and the lantern back to the kitchen placing both on the table side by side. When he leaned over the table, Aruba, took the opportunity to hop off his shoulder and click toenails across the boards to her post beside the lamp.

"Rawwwwwk!" she squawked, settling in to watch her master's hands.

Salt carefully untied the strings on the sack, reached inside, and grabbed a hold of something. With his free hand, he pulled the cloth away.

As candle light flickered over the object, I made out a dark symbol stamped on top – a skull and crossbones. Ember eyes glowed red, staring out at me from the cover of what had to be a seriously old book.

And, dude, I'll admit it, although I'm kind of ashamed to, that skull creeped me out! Something about those eyes. No matter which way I moved, they followed me.

"Harley," Salt said barely above a whisper, "it's time for a little family history."

My heart thumped in my ears like a techno tune. I needed to get a hold of myself.

I felt better after Salt opened the book's cover, forcing those skull eyes down to the table.

He eased through a few yellowed pages of hand-written text, words in Spanish. Two pages later the words ended. Drawings started.

"My great grand-pappy, Gasparilla, liked to keep records of everything. Before the Navy got him two-hundred years ago, he had most of his diddies, maps and ship's logs bound together in this leather book," Salt said with his finger tapping a page.

"No way, dude," I said. "Is this what I think it is?"

"Way," said Salt. "You're staring down a whole book of secrets, the locations of the old pirate's buried treasures."

My mom used to have a stupid Pekingese dog. I had always made fun of her big, bulgy eyes. Well, what goes around comes around, I guess, because I was so bug eyed it hurt.

"I've heard books were good for your vision, kid," Salt said, "but I never thought one could make your eyeballs grow."

He thumbed a few more pages. The book held map after map after map, with stories and log entries crammed in between. He stopped again. This time the page was blank.

"Let me have it," he said.

I remembered my hand hung onto an old rum bottle. I pulled the stopper and shook out a rolled up paper. Salt took it from me, unrolling it against the top of the kitchen table.

"So that's where it came from," I said.

"Uh huh," he said. "I figured that sticking this map in your crab trap last summer would be a cool way to let you in on my little secret – *if* you proved your worth and located the gold."

I *had* found the treasure, even though Hurricane Charley had taken it from me and spit it out in the Gulf of Mexico. But that's another story. A little over four months from that August day, as I sat in Salt's kitchen I began to realize that I might be headed into a whole new adventure.

I thought I had seen it all. Boy, was I wrong. I had no idea.

Salt lowered my map onto the blank page and it stuck to the paper. Not just stuck, though, the map actually *merged* with the page. I snapped my head towards Salt to see if he saw what I saw.

"Old buccaneer trick," he said, his eyes crinkling at the corners.

Pages kept turning and my mind kept racing. *All these maps. Each one representing a fortune in hidden treasure.*

How could Salt have sat on that information, pretending to be a simple stone crab fisherman for all those years? He lived in a shack, for Pete's sake! A round, one-room cabin with no electricity or running water on a barrier island with no bridges!

Sure, he had finally come out with it. Now the whole world knew his story, knew he was a ca-zillionaire. Thanks to the national news, everyone in America had heard how the mysterious Salt was actually Joe Gaspar, the great, great, great grandson of the infamous pirate José Gaspar.

But, for decades, he had walked right over tons of gold buried in his yard on his way each morning to a beat up old crab boat to pull traps and claws for a living. I could not have done that day after day.

As if reading my mind, he said, "Just got to remember - money ain't the greatest thing in life. Not even in the top ten. But, if you do find yourself with a pile of loot, even more important than what you do with it, is what it does with you.

Took me over sixty years to come up with a plan that I knew in my heart of hearts was worthy and right. Now, with your help, that plan can become a reality. We just need a little more cash first. Let's see..."

He turned to the last page of the old treasure book.

"There she blows," he said. "The La Paz Map. That should do it."

Before my eyes he just separated the map from the rest of the paper, just pulled it off as easily as the peel from a banana. He laid it down on an empty part of the table and pushed the hurricane lamp over.

"The La Paz Map?" I asked.

Salt's eyes sparkled with candlelight when he spoke.

"Named for the Peace River," he said. "The sixteenth century Spanish explorers named it *Rio de la Paz*, which translates to Peace River. Oddly enough, the Indians had been calling it *Talakchopcohatchee*, or *The River of Long Peas* way before that. Peas sounds like peace, don't it?"

"Yeah, it does," I had to agree. "I'm all about world peas," I joked.

Salt didn't laugh, though. He hardly ever did.

"Anyway, the Peace River runs down the Bone Valley and dumps into Charlotte Harbor." He paused. "Say, you remember the story about how the Navy surprised Gasparilla, don't you?"

I nodded.

"Well, after Gasparilla drowned that day off Boca Grande, his men, the ones left on the beach guarding the barrels of treasure, took off in different directions. One boat headed up the Peace River to an old plantation the pirates had traded with. They stashed their captain's share of booty there and drew up this map."

"The last one in the book," I said.

"That's right, the very last. They stuck it in here before they gave the book to its rightful owner, the fair Joséffa."

"Gasparilla's wife," I remembered.

"That's the one. My grandmother, so to speak."

"So why'd you pull it out today, Salt? I thought we were going fishing."

"We are. We're going to fish up some treasure, kid. Now let's git!"

He rolled up the map and gave it to me to stick in the bottle while he stashed the book back under the trunk. Aruba flew to his shoulder as Salt opened the front door.

Hammerhead sat on the porch, waiting. He woofed, as if to say *it's about time*. Black Labs can be so impatient, but only because they're so smart. I think they may be able to tell time. He's a big baby sometimes when I leave him alone for a while. Thinks he's missed something.

"Don't worry," I told him. "We're going now."

Salt said nothing, just reached into his pocket and tossed the dog a cracker. Hammerhead caught it in mid-air wagging his tail, crunching it down. Still wagging, he followed Salt down the hill under the oak trees – didn't even look at me! And, I'm his rightful owner. Some dog.

The month of December doesn't look much different than the month of July in the southwest corner of Florida, just a bit browner. The gnarly oak trees that formed an umbrella over Salt's weird, round house didn't really lose their leaves in winter. On Cayo Costa island, it never got that cold. Those old trees had taken a beating in the hurricane, but, even at high noon, the grounds around his shack stayed totally shady.

"So, Salt. This treasure map, it'll lead us straight to a pile of gold?"

"Keep your voice down kid." He shot me a look. "The whole world don't need to know what we're up to!"

Salt had the ability to get a little cranky at any given time, even in the woods out on an island where no one could possibly be listening. Still, I always avoided getting on his bad side whenever I could.

"Sorry, Salt."

"Landmarks change over two-hundred years. But these freebooters had ways around it. We'll find what we're looking for."

Hammerhead stopped and stared at one of the tree trunks, cocking his head to one side. The oak was totally massive, wider at the ground than both me and Salt put together. I'd of bet my last doubloon that a fat squirrel was hiding on the far side of that tree. My Labrador loved squirrels.

"Come on, boy," I said. "We don't have time to play."

Do you think that dog listened to me? No. He cocked his head to the other side, then barked.

"Hammerhead! I said let's go!"

At that moment, a full-grown man, not a squirrel, stepped out from behind the oak.

"Well. If it ain't the famous Harley Davidsen Cooper and his side-kick Salt," the man said. *"Bonjour, mes amis."*

He looked mean, bald-headed, covered in wicked tattoos, shiny death-head earrings. And, to top it all off, he was totally cross-eyed!

"You boys sure be hurryin' scurryin' along," he said low and slow. He spoke with some kind of accent, too, kind of like this chef I'd seen on TV once. "Where you headed off to so fast?"

I glanced over at Salt. He stood dead still. His eyes burned holes through the guy.

Hammerhead barked again.

"Better call off the dogs, Joe," the man said. "I'd hate to see him get hurt."

I noticed the big gun in his hand as he aimed at my dog. Luckily, Hammerhead knew when to keep his mouth shut. He sat down.

"Money's in the bank, Skeebo," Salt said.

"I figured you'd say that, Mr. Gaspar. Or is it just Salt these days?" he said with a lopsided smile. "Is that where you put my cut? In the bank? Keeping it nice and warm and safe for me? Making a little interest maybe?"

The smile slipped off his face quicker than a wave sliding back to the Gulf. Suddenly, he looked plain furious.

"What do you take me for, Gaspar?!" he screamed. "A fool? You don't believe in banks anymore than I do!" He swallowed hard, forcing himself to calm down. "Now why don't we act civilized and stroll down to yonder boat and take ourselves a little ride? The kid's got a map. We won't get lost. It'll lead us straight to a pile of gold. Right, kid?" He grinned through teeth as crooked as he was.

Salt charged and head butted the sucker right in the gut. Skeebo fell over backwards onto the tree roots. The creep's gun boomed up at the sky just before Salt knocked it out of his hand. As they wrestled around in the leaves, Hammerhead attacked, sinking his fangs into the cross-eyed man's ankle. Skeebo squealed like a pig in a pan of hot grease and Salt was on his chest with both hands around his throat before I could even move.

I'm not really known for my reflexes.

A red feather helicoptered down in front of my face.

"We're square Lafitte!" Salt yelled into Skeebo's face. "Don't you get that? We settled this thing a long time ago!"

I watched the feather touch down in the leaves at my feet. The end was missing, burned off, just a charred, black line. Where was Aruba? Did she head to the tree tops when Salt jumped Skeebo? I couldn't find her. The cross-eyed creep must have shot her.

I walked over to kick the idiot in the head.

The man's eyes bulged in at each other even more as Salt's hands cut off his air. It was weird, like he was trying to see into his own eyes, through the bridge of his nose. His lips moved as he tried to form words. Nothing came out, though. Salt relaxed his grip and let him talk.

"Got...the...girl," he sputtered.

"What!" Salt demanded.

"Lover boy's...little honey pot," he said. "The Baker girl!"

Salt dropped his hands, but he stayed on Skeebo's chest, knees pinning his arms. The tattooed freak-a-saurus gasped for air.

"I figured you'd try something like this," Skeebo said. "So we picked up a little insurance in Palmetto Cove today. We've got Eden Baker."

Palmetto Cove is a small town on the west side of Pine Island, Florida. My town. Eden Baker lived there with her mom and dad in a trailer not far from my house. She was my girlfriend.

All the blood in my heart took an express elevator down to my toes.

The sound of an outboard got my attention. Down in the canal, a 16-foot skiff idled up next to my old crab boat. Eden sat on a bench near the skiff's bow, her hands behind her back. A man with a shotgun stood beside her. Another dude drove the boat.

My phone rang.

"Ya see, Gaspar," the man under Salt was saying. "Insurance."

My phone rang again.

"Get it, boy," Skeebo snarled at me. "But, you choose your words mighty careful."

I pulled the phone out of my pocket. Hammerhead let go of the man's ankle to see what I was doing.

"Hello," I said into the phone.

"Harley?" It was Mrs. Baker, Eden's mom. "Is Eden with you?"

Mrs. Baker had a mousy little voice, probably because Eden's dad, Jake Baker, was so domineering. She squeaked when she got nervous. She was squeaking then.

"She left the house in a big hurry," she continued. "Left a pot burning on the stove and everything. Even her phone!"

I could barely think.

"Um, yes...Mrs. Baker," I said. "She's here."

"Well, put her on," she squeaked. "I need to talk to her."

Skeebo wiggled an arm out from under Salt's knee to threaten me with a finger.

"She's going to have to call you back, Mrs. Baker. She's sitting in the boat and I'm on shore." I hoped that would work.

"Well...make sure she does, Mr. Cooper," she said. "Make sure she does."

"Goodbye, Mrs. Baker." I hit the end button.

"Well done, Cooper," said Skeebo. "Now. For your next act, encourage your partner here to get off my chest!"

Salt slowly rolled off him and backed away. Skeebo scrambled to his feet, grabbing his gun. He walked over to Salt and, with the tip of his barrel, motioned for him to raise his hands over his head. Reluctantly, Salt did. Skeebo patted him down, removing a gun from behind Salt's back and a knife from his pocket.

"Hunting today, Joe?" Skeebo asked with a smirk. "Season's closed. I might just have to report you." I picked up on the accent again. Sounded southern, but different. "Now move! Take us for a ride, Cooper."

As we boarded my crab boat I glanced over at my girlfriend. Eden was mad, fuse lit and burning. The girl can strike like a snake when she's cornered. But we were out gunned and outnumbered. I really didn't want her to pull anything stupid.

No, I mouthed to her.

She snapped her head around, angry, long, blonde hair hiding her face. It was just a matter of time before that chick tried something.

Skeebo snatched the bottle out of my hand and took it to the stern.

"Start the motor, boy," he ordered me.

He forced Salt and Hammerhead to sit on the deck under the far gunwale.

"A map. In a bottle," Skeebo laughed. "Really, Joe. You're something else. I guar-ron-tee!"

He uncorked the bottle and slid the paper into his hand.

"Old looking, too," he said. "You don't miss a beat, do ya? Even looks like a real treasure map."

Salt just sat there, watching the mangroves slide by as I nudged the *Costa Blanca* up the canal to the bay. Hammerhead settled down with his chin on top of his paws. The skiff followed us about thirty yards back.

The end of the canal opened up to Pelican Bay. Things got brighter as we left the trees. A quarter mile across the water, Salt's sportfisherman, the *Florida Blanca*, floated gently at anchor. A man stood on the stern near the fighting chair with a short-barrel shotgun at his side watching us drift by. Skeebo waved at him. He waved back.

Five minutes down the bay, I noticed a couple of rangers standing on the dock that marked the entrance to Cayo Costa State Park. They knew my boat and were the friendly type, so they waved when we were closer. I waved back, wondering if I should do more. I stole a quick glance at the skiff behind us. The man next to Eden had sat down, his gun out of sight.

"Don't get any ideas, boy," Skeebo warned.

The moment passed.

The rangers grabbed some gear from their boat and carried it up to the office with their backs to us. They hadn't noticed anything odd.

At the open waters of Charlotte Harbor, I gunned the motor and got the old tub going. I couldn't outrun the skiff even if I wanted to so I just plowed the green water towards Punta Gorda. Above the rumble of the motor I heard Skeebo shouting something to Salt.

"La Paz?" he said. "Where's that supposed to be? There ain't nowhere around here called La Paz."

"Upriver," said Salt. "An old farm. Look. Lafitte. None of this concerns these kids."

"Does now," the man replied. "Ever since you done drug them into it. You want to blame somebody, blame yourself, Gaspar. What's right is right. Your grandpappy cheated my grandpappy out of a fortune – a fortune that rightfully belongs in *my* family, not yours. I aim to get it back."

"I doubt that old legend's even true," Salt said. "There's no record of it. Besides. You and I had a deal years ago. You got your money."

"My how history can change," Skeebo said. "All depends on who's writing it, I suppose. Newsman said you're worth a lot more than you ever told me about. What's right is right, Gaspar. What's right's right."

Feeling anything but peaceful, I took us up the Peace River past the town of Punta Gorda and under its three bridges. Occasionally, our wake scared off a cormorant or two, but besides a couple of small fishing boats in the distance, we had the river to ourselves. After a while, the *Costa Blanca* banked through the s-curves of the mangrove estuary that formed the mouth of the Peace River. I dodged a few sandbars until Salt told me to turn at the Lettuce Lake Cut-off.

There, a mangrove creek fed into the river, twisting and turning through a maze of green. Just when I thought we were going to run aground, the water deepened and the narrow channel opened up to form Lettuce Lake. The lake was tiny, just a wide spot in the creek surrounded by more green mangrove branches. At the far side, a single dock stood in the water at the end of a trail.

"Hold her right here, skipper," Skeebo ordered from behind. "I'll be getting off now."

He motioned for the skiff to pull up alongside my boat.

"You two Boudreaux's keep a hunting dat treasure. We'll sit back in the shade and keep your pretty little friend company."

As the little boat came in, the man with the shotgun saw me looking at him and grinned. Slowly, with his eyes still on me, he reached out his big paw and petted Eden's head like she was a dog or something. She jerked away, baring her teeth like she was about to bite.

That was all I could take.

"You do that again and I'll...I'll!" I yelled, rushing across my boat to the skiff.

Skeebo was faster. He jumped between me and the skiff before I reached the gunwale, wrapping his greasy fingers around my throat.

"You'll what, lover boy?" he hissed.

His breath really stunk, like rotten cottage cheese and dead sea horses. He leaned in closer. I didn't know which eye to look at. I don't think it really mattered. The dude's eyeballs were whacked!

"You do what you're told and we won't have no problem, Boudreaux," he said. "You got me? We hold the cards, boy! The game is over. You and Dr. Pepper here have already lost!"

I heard Hammerhead growling low, next to Salt.

"So you just carry your happy butts up to the loot and bring it back to me!" His hand reached around the back of my neck and pulled until my forehead connected with the sweaty tatts on his. "And I mean *all...of...it!*"

His spit peppered my face on that last word.

"Don't get any smart ideas. Don't bring anyone else into it. You're just going to get them hurt. Act natural. Do your job and everything will work out fine."

He let go, tossing me to the deck like an empty beer can. With a smirk on his face, Skeebo slid the map back into the bottle and tossed it to Salt.

"Pirate map," he chuckled. "You are classic, Joe, classic. You've got one hour. We'll be waiting for you. Don't be late. It's not polite."

When he turned to get on the skiff, I saw another tattoo on the back of his bald head - a skull with a pair of bright, red eyes. And, those weren't crossed. He jumped over into the skiff and they shoved off.

Eden's eyes pleaded with me.

"*Harley?*" she said.

She expected me to do something.

"Aww. Isn't that sweet," Skeebo mocked. "See? She wants you to come back quick, too."

"We'll be right back, Eden," I told her. I felt powerless. I felt like a wimpy idiot. I was letting her down.

She lowered her head as the skiff chugged back to the creek. Skeebo lit a cigarette, blowing smoke out of his nose like a dragon.

Isabella

The holidays had arrived and I had big plans. School was out. Christmas was coming. My sister, Tori, and I had just spent the last two days helping Mom decorate the first real house we had ever lived in. Salt had sailed back from a month in the Caribbean to take me fishing in his new Hatteras. I had a girlfriend, someone I could actually give a meaningful present. Man, I was looking forward to the holidays like I never had in my life. Then, in one morning, it had all gone down the tubes.

"Cheer up, kid," Salt said. "This, to, will work itself out."

"We gotta call the cops, Salt!"

"No need for that. I've got a plan."

He looked away. There was something he wasn't telling me.

"I know this cat," he said. "He'll hiss and show his teeth, but in the end, he ain't so bad."

"But, he killed Aruba!"

Salt's eyes steeled over. Aruba was Salt's only full time companion. He loved that old bird so much, I was afraid to even tell him what had happened. I thought it would crush him.

"What are you talking about, Harley?"

"When you tackled that guy, she must have flown off your shoulder. The gun went off. I found this."

I pulled out the scorched parrot feather. Salt took the red feather, rolling it over slowly.

"One thing you got to keep in mind, sonny," he said through his teeth as he examined the burned end. "This old world can turn on a dime. You just gotta have faith, even through the hard parts. Especially then. If you do, you'll understand everything happens exactly as it should. You might not get it, might not understand it at the time, but through faith you'll find a certain strength that'll get you through it."

He stuck the feather in his pocket and left me to figure out what he meant. After a few moments, he reached over to the wheel and corrected my course to the dock.

"So what's your plan?" I asked him.

"Give the man what he wants."

"What?!" I yelled. "Give them the gold?! Are you nuts?!"

"Don't worry. That's just the beginning of the plan. Go grab the rope. I'll ease her up to the dock."

The old crab boat really belonged to Salt. He had given it to me after the hurricane had sunk mine. I could handle it fairly well, but was still getting used to docking the thing.

Salt reversed the prop to bring her in. Hammerhead and I hopped off. I wrapped the forward line around the cleat in a quick figure eight. Salt had already secured the stern rope by the time I walked down to it.

"Who are these people, Salt?"

"Those idiots back in the boat?"

"Yes. The tattooed guy," I said.

"That would be Skeebo Lafitte," Salt said as he grabbed the piling and hauled himself onto the dock.

"I got that much," I blurted out impatiently.

"I'm getting to the point, kid," he said frowning slightly. "Give me time. Skeebo, and this is a bit ironic, is a direct descendant of a pirate named Jean Lafitte, a fellow who lived two-hundred years ago, a privateer mostly. Operated in the waters up around New Orleans about the same time old Gasparilla was plying his trade down here."

"Privateer?" I asked. "What kind of pirate is that?"

"Back in the day, a privateer was a sea captain who had permission from one nation to plunder the ships of certain other nations. The permission slip was called a letter of marque and issuing letters of marque was a common practice among nations at that time. Served two purposes. One, you had to split anything you plundered with the nation that gave you permission to be a pirate, so those nations got richer. And, two, the privateers acted as a second navy to their host country. They had a right to blow enemy ships out of the water."

"What country gave Lafitte his letter of marque?"

"The United States of America," Salt said. "At the time, around the year 1804, we were still a pretty new nation. We barely had a navy compared to Britain, France and Spain. Hardly any ships in the Gulf of Mexico at all. Didn't need them. Spain controlled Florida. And up until 1803, we didn't even have Louisiana. The picture changed with the Louisiana Purchase. We got New Orleans, Louisiana and everything north all the way to Canada. We needed help fast because the British were threatening to take it away from the U.S. That's where the Lafitte's came in."

"There was more than one Lafitte?"

"Jean had a brother named Pierre. They worked as a team. They skirted the edge of the law, but they provided the city of New Orleans with a lot of stuff by smuggling it in. Made a lot of friends that way."

"So what's all this got to do with you?" I asked.

"Oh, there's a rumor that Jean Lafitte had to leave New Orleans for a while to evade a certain governor who was out to get him. They say he travelled down here and hooked up with Gasparilla for a spell. Our cross-eyed pal thinks my ancestor ended up cheating his ancestor. Skeebo didn't get no inheritance like I did, see?"

"So why don't we just call the cops?" I asked.

Salt hesitated, kind of like my mom does when she's hiding something. I've seen her do it plenty of times.

"Well…old Skeebo's got a brother, too. Name's John. They're kind of like Jean and Pierre, except nowhere near as grand. But therein lies the problem. John is the brains of the operation. And he *isn't* all bark. He's got a pretty mean bite. Plus, he's crazy as a pinfish. If we have the law snare Skeebo, big brother will most certainly make our lives miserable." Salt pulled down the bill of his Matlacha Seafood Company cap and tossed me the old rum bottle. "Come on. Let's get up to the big house. Tick tock."

Many times, when I was with Salt, I never knew what to expect next. This was one of those times. I had no idea where that little path through the mangroves might lead – both literally *and* figuratively. I just knew I didn't want Eden to be sitting on that boat with those goons any longer than she had to.

I followed Salt out of the trees onto a grass covered hill. At the top of the rise stood a large house with white siding under three enormous oak trees. Hurricane Charley had clipped a couple of their branches. To the left of the home a planted field spread over flat ground to a clump of trees, looked like tomatoes growing there. Off to the other side, a pole barn covered a car, a pickup, and a johnboat on a trailer. We stepped up to the back porch.

An orange cat sitting at the top of the steps saw us coming. It stood and stretched. On the landing, Salt leaned down and scratched the cat between the ears. Hammerhead met its nose with his own.

"Hello, Tiger," Salt said. "Mama home?"

"*Dios mio, José!*," a woman cried as she rushed the screen door. "Mama think *tempestad* blow you away!"

The door flew open and this short lady ran out to wrap both arms around Salt. She squeezed him hard enough to make him wheeze.

"Harley Cooper, meet Ana Rivera," Salt said over her black hair.

Ana broke away from Salt, straightened up, and politely shook my hand.

"*Mucho gusto*," she said.

"Good to meet you, too," I replied.

"What's this? What's this?" a smiling man was saying as he came out the door. "My friend! My friend! How are you?"

He hugged Salt, too, not as hard, though.

"And, this is César Rivera, Ana's *esposo*."

I shook his hand.

"You no call. You no write," César said to Salt. "Where you been *mi amigo*? You famous now, no?"

"Long story, César," said Salt. "I'll come back soon. You can cook some *arroz con pollo* and *pastelitos* and I'll tell you all about it. Today, I'm here on business."

"Anything for you, José," Ana said. "Please. Come in."

The door opened to a kitchen. César invited us to sit around the breakfast table while Hammerhead plopped down next to my chair and Ana poured iced tea. Salt motioned for the rum bottle. As I gave it to him, César leaned across the table.

"You see, Harley," César said. "Your friend here has done many great things for us. It is not easy for us here in this country. We leave many things behind to come here. Many things! But, José, he make things much better! Yes!" Then he turned to Salt again. "My friend, it is *so* good to see you!"

César laughed, deeply. I could tell the man was truly happy to see Salt. Unfortunately, I didn't feel like yukking it up at the moment. We had stuff to deal with – *right then!* In my mind's eye, I pictured Eden sitting on the skiff with those three losers, having to tolerate all their stupid junk, and it made me furious. We had to get moving.

Hammerhead's wet nose worked its way between the palm of my hand and my knee as I sat there, prying my hand impatiently. He had to be thinking what I was thinking. See? Smart dog.

"Tick tock, Salt," I said.

Salt squinted sideways at me with one eye as he shook the map out of the bottle. He spread the page onto the table. The map looked very similar to the one I had found in my crab trap a few months before, hand-drawn in thick, black ink on yellowed paper. A large body of water, with the words *Bahia Carlos* written across it, narrowed to a river. I knew *Bahia Carlos* was the old Spanish name for Charlotte Harbor. Over the river, the words *Rio de la Paz* had been written. Upriver, a creek snaked in to Lettuce Lake. Drawings of mangroves surrounded the lake except for one small break where César's path connected the dock to his house.

"*Amigo*," César laughed. "You no come to my house for so long you need to make map?"

"My friend, this map was drawn a long time before you and I were even born," Salt said.

"I see me house," said Ana. *"Pero, donde esta nuestra cochera?"*

"She mean, 'where is our garage'?" César added.

"Not built yet," Salt replied.

From the house, a broken line went east. It stopped at a big, fat X. Next to the X, a miniature hand held something I didn't recognize.

"What's that, Salt?" I asked, pointing at the hand.

"Buccaneers sometimes put symbols on the paper to remind them of things," Salt said slowly. "I think this one means they planted something. See that in the hand? It's sprouting leaves at the top. If they were unsure how long it would be before they came back, these guys would plant a tree over the spot to mark it."

"There's a million trees out there," I said.

"You saying you got something buried in me *jardin?*" asked César looking all excited. "I a rich man?!"

"Sorry, César," Salt said. "My relatives didn't have any safe deposit boxes. This was the best they could do. My family has let it set there until the time is right. You got a shovel?"

"But all those trees, Salt!" I said. "How do we know which one?"

"Gumbo Limbo," Salt said as he got up and walked out the door.

The rest of us followed him outside.

"Each one of these here dashes is a pace, the measure of a man's full stride," Salt told us. "People were a bit shorter in those days so I'm going to make my steps closer together."

He marched off towards the tomato field. I figured he might go around it when he got to the edge, but he didn't. The old man just kept walking right through it, tomatoes and all. He stopped at the edge of the trees.

"Pirates used Gumbo Limbo because you just stick it in the ground and it grows," said Salt.

I looked up at the trees. Dude, they were tall – at least fifty feet – spreading out like oaks. The bark was peeling off like skin with a sunburn.

"They also liked these trees because they grow so fast," Salt continued. "Once they covered the treasure, people weren't inclined to dig under them."

"*Dios mio,*" said Ana. "But, which one, *don Gaspar?*"

"Well, I've got ten more paces to go," said Salt, "assuming the house is in the same place."

Salt moved into the grove of gumbo limbos. He had to detour around a couple. He quit walking next to the trunk of a thirty-footer, toeing the dry grass with his boot. Hammerhead ran up and sniffed the spot.

Salt checked his watch.

Somewhere nearby a motor started up. I saw César coming around the house driving a small tractor called a bobcat. A girl in jeans and a t-shirt walked behind him carrying some kind of shovel.

César weaved the bobcat through the trees, stopped near us, and switched it off.

"I bring you a shovel, *don Gaspar,*" he said with a smile.

"Hello, Isabella," said Salt.

The girl looked to be a couple of years older than me, maybe sixteen or seventeen – and smoking hot as well –tanned skin, black silk for hair, and amazing eyes. Oh, and her jeans? They were skin tight.

She smiled at me, and then at Salt.

"Good to see you, Mr. Gaspar," she said without any of her parents' accent.

"Harley," said Ana. "Please meet me daughter, Isabella."

The girl held her hand out for me. I shook it. She was warm, like she'd been out in the sun. She smiled again.

"Pleased to meet you, Harley," she said.

I'll admit it, right here. I'm a sucker for a pretty girl. It does something to me physically when I see one. If I'm not careful, I get kind of stupid and turn into this sort of caveman type guy who grunts, and stares too long. Usually, my best defense in the middle of one of those episodes is to just repeat what they say. That's what happened then, but, at least I managed to say it in Spanish.

"*Mucho gusto,*" I said.

She giggled before turning to Salt.

"Papa told me what you're looking for, *don José*. I brought something that might help," she said.

She held up what I had thought was a shovel. It wasn't. It was a metal detector.

"Perfect," said Salt as he took it from her.

He began scanning the ground where Hammerhead's nose had been. The thing immediately began beeping.

I'm such an idiot, I thought. *A metal detector.*

The summer before, I had spent hours digging through an acre of swamp with an anchor to find my doubloons. Why hadn't I thought of a metal detector? Oh, well. Guess that was the caveman side of me coming out.

"César," said Salt. "Can you swing that bucket around here?"

César was already on it. He fired up the bobcat and pivoted the mini-backhoe over the spot. About ten minutes later, it hit something. César got the bucket out of the way and switched off the tractor. Shovel in hand, he jumped into the hole. Soon he had scooped out enough dirt to uncover the outline of a wooden circle.

"Barrel," said Salt. "She's gonna be heavy."

He took the shovel from César and tapped on the lid of the barrel. It sounded solid.

"In pretty good shape," he said. "I think we can pull her out. Got any chain, César?"

César nodded and pointed to a barn. "In there."

I don't know exactly how long it took us to dig all around that barrel, but it seemed like we were going to miss Skeebo's deadline. I got pretty anxious. César couldn't move fast enough for my liking as he screwed three eye-bolts into the solid wood. He attached them to the bobcat's bucket with chains. Slowly, he lifted the machine's mechanical arm. The barrel made a sucking sound as it pulled loose from the muck. César swung it out of the hole and rumbled off to the field next to the tomato patch.

"Set her down here, César," Salt said.

He eased it to the ground while Salt tapped all over with the shovel.

"Perfectly preserved by the swamp," he said. "I think it's safe to pry off the top."

César took a crowbar off his tractor and tried one of the cracks on the edge of the lid. It popped. He tried another spot. That made another pop. Soon, the whole lid came off. We all gathered around to look inside.

Salt pulled away some tattered cloth. And there, right before our eyes, was a king's ransom. Some of it was tarnished, but I knew right away it was gold. Coins, gold ropes, jewelry, precious stones – a fortune in loot that hadn't seen sunshine for two-hundred years.

"No doubt about it," said Salt. "This is one of the casks that had been set on the beach after old Gasparilla's retirement party, the day he met his maker."

Salt had that treasure gleam going in his eyes. He reacted to gold the way I reacted to pretty girls.

"What's that?" spoke a voice behind us. "Did I hear that poor, old Gaspy-paspy missed out on his, ah...*golden* years," Skeebo Lafitte said as he and another guy walked up. "That ain't nothing but sad, y'all."

They both had guns – but no Eden. Isabella shrunk behind her dad. Ana moved towards César to cover her. The Rivera family seemed surprised, but they acted more wary than spooked, like they had met Skeebo before. In fact, they appeared to be hiding their daughter from the weirdo.

The cross-eyed man rubbed his tattooed scalp.

"Now that's one thing I plan never to miss out on," Skeebo said. "My *golden* years!" He cackled mean, like a hyena. "Hi y'all doing." He waved at the Riveras. "Long time, no see."

Skeebo took a couple of steps towards the barrel. The other goon raised his gun.

"Mind stepping aside, Mr. Gaspar, while I get a little peek?" he said. "I'm the curious sort, you know."

Hammerhead started growling as he approached. I shushed him before it got worse. Salt moved away from the barrel and Skeebo stepped in, practically drooling, over the gold.

"How sweet it is!" he said licking his lips. "*Double* the pleasure for me!" He turned around and showed us his crazy eyes.

"Just take it and get out of here," said Salt.

"Don't mind if I do, Joe. Or is it 'José' in the present company?" Skeebo noticed the Riveras again, staring at them like a wolf. "Who you hidin' from, Isabell? Come out here where Uncle Skeebo can see how much you've grown. Come on. Don't be shy. I don't bite – unless I'm hungry."

When the other man aimed his shotgun at César's ear, Isabella emerged from behind her folks. Skeebo closed one eye and cocked his head sideways, checking her out from top to bottom. Isabella lowered her eyes. Her playfulness was gone. She looked plain scared.

Skeebo stepped back, bringing a hand up to stroke his stubbly chin. Nobody said a word.

"Mommy and daddy must be proud of the way you turned out. I guar-ron-tee!" he finally said. He snapped his fingers at César. "Okay, Chico, let's get this crate down to the dock. Single file, everybody, behind the tractor. Let's go!"

César climbed into the seat, started the motor, and lifted the barrel off the ground. The bobcat rolled slowly down the hill towards the trail with everyone in tow, single file. Skeebo and the other guy brought up the rear.

At the water's edge, I scanned Lettuce Lake for the skiff. It floated dead center, directly behind my boat. Eden hadn't moved. She sat there, as before, hands behind her back, face furious.

Skeebo ordered César to drive out onto the dock and drop the barrel in my crab boat. The stern dropped almost a foot deeper into the water when the boat took the weight. With any luck, the *Costa Blanca* would never make it past the shallow sand bars.

"Alright, Lafitte," said Salt through his teeth. "We held up our end. Let the girl go."

"My insurance policy?" Skeebo chuckled. "Naw. I'm afraid I'm gonna hang onto that a little longer. In fact, I think you might enjoy a boat ride, too, sugar." He pointed at Isabella with his pistol.

"No!!" Ana screamed. She grabbed her daughter, pulling her back. "*Dios mio,* NO!"

"Now, now, Ms., ah, Rivera, is it?" Skeebo said. "Long as y'all don't do nothing stupid she'll be fine. Help the young lady to her quarters, Pedro."

The other guy was big. He easily separated Isabella from her mom and shoved the girl down into my boat while Skeebo covered the Riveras with his pistol.

My cell phone rang.

I looked at Skeebo.

"Go ahead," he said tiredly. "You know the routine."

It was a very squeaky Mrs. Baker.

"I'm serious now, Harley Cooper. Put my daughter on. She hasn't called and I'm worried sick. Something's wrong. I can just feel it!"

I looked around. I had everyone staring at me and two guns pointed at me.

"Um...I know Ms. Baker, but, um, everything's cool, okay? Just a couple of irresponsible kids out on a day at the beach. Heh, heh."

"*Put her on, NOW!*"

The only thing I could think to do was to pull the old "low signal" trick.

"Wha- -ou say, Ms. Ba-er?" I stammered and threw in a little static for good measure. "Can- -ear you very –ell."

"I said to put Eden on the phone!"

"O-ay. –ere she i-," I said, then hit the end button.

"Remind me to cast my vote for you at the next Academy Awards," said Skeebo. "Now, bye-bye everybody. We got a boat to catch!"

His big henchman started the motor and they cast off. Ana started screaming. It was awful.

I caught a glimpse of Eden. She was fuming.

Isabella sat on my crab boat looking at her mom and dad, totally panicked. A single tear wet a trail down her face.

She must have felt me staring at her because she looked over and silently spoke two words – *help me.*

"And, José!" Skeebo shouted as he spun my boat around. "One false move and this one here's back on her way to Cuba before you can say Long John MacBlane!"

I tried to find Eden's eyes again, too late, her skiff had turned around. Both boats gunned it and took off. We watched them round the bend out of the lake and disappear into the mangroves. The motors droned off leaving us with a seriously sad sound - Ana crying like a baby into César's shoulder.

The Frigate

"Don't worry, Ana," Salt was saying. "I'll get her back."

"José," César said to Salt. "Why you no tell us he here?"

"*Isabellaaaaaa!*" Ana cried.

"I'm sorry, César," Salt said. "I didn't think-"

"These men," Ana said between sobs. "You don't know them. They are *animals!*"

"Listen," Salt said, "all this one wants is that gold. He'll dump the girls off somewhere, but he won't touch 'em. He just wants to get his fanny back up to Louisiana."

"Salt," I said. "Level with me. Who are these guys?"

He took off his ball cap and ran a hand over his gray hair.

"They're in the import/export business," he said finally. "But...not wicker furniture or Dutch chocolate. They're smugglers."

"Smugglers?" I asked.

"That's right. They used to run drugs. Now, it's people."

"People?!" I was confused. "People can just hop on a plane to go somewhere. Why would anyone smuggle people?"

"Well, not everyone can travel freely, kid," Salt said. He looked over at Ana and César.

César had been watching Salt, waiting for an explanation. I think he figured out why Salt had done what he did, why he hadn't gone to the police, at the same moment I understood. He quit staring at Salt, comforting his wife instead.

"César and Ana came by boat a few years ago," Salt explained. "They're Cuban, Harley. They can't live here unless they make it to shore and ask for political asylum. Things got so bad where they lived that they risked their lives coming here on nothing but a raft. They washed up on Cayo Costa."

"Señor, Gaspar," César said to me. "He find us. He help us."

The Cuban reached out and took Salt's hand. His eyes softened. Though he still feared for his daughter, he'd forgiven his friend.

"I found them work on this farm," Salt continued. "Ana ran the house for my old friend Rita. César worked the land. When Rita passed away, none of her kids lived around here anymore. But, Rita's kids were kind enough to let César and Ana stay on as long as they liked. There was just one problem."

"What was that?" I asked.

"*Mi hija,*" César said. His eyes had filled with water.

"Their daughter, Isabella, was stuck back in Cuba with relatives," Salt said. "That's where Mr. Lafitte came into the picture."

"You hired that madman?" I said.

"Not him. His brother, John."

"And, just how did you know him, exactly?" I said, sensing Salt was holding back something more.

"As I've said before, Harley, I made a few mistakes in my younger days…"

"Well, again, if these dudes are so bad, let's just call the cops, Salt!"

"Not that simple, kid," Salt said and he began to walk off down the dock to shore. "Isabella is here illegally. She's an illegal alien. If the authorities got wind of her she'd be on her way back to Cuba. Ol' cross-eyes was right about that."

Salt kept walking up the trail, with Hammerhead trotting off in front. I followed them. César helped Ana along behind me.

"But we can't just sit here and do nothing," I said.

"We're not," Salt said. Then he hollered over his shoulder to César. "You still got that johnboat up here?"

"*Si*, José," said César. "It is in the barn."

"Well, help me get her down there."

We stopped at the building that served as both a barn and a garage. In the last stall I saw a little boat on a trailer. César sat Ana down on a step and joined Salt and I at the boat. The three of us rolled the trailer down to Lettuce Lake and lifted the boat into the water.

"Don't worry, César. I brought her here once. I'll bring her back again."

"I trust you, José," César said, his eyes filling with tears again. "*don* José!" he called out.

"Yes?" said Salt.

"Your map."

César handed the old bottle to Salt. He gave it to me. The page from the Gaspar book of secrets was rolled up inside.

César shoved the little boat off the sand. I held my hand up to say goodbye and César returned the gesture. Behind me, Salt fired up the motor. Hammerhead stumbled back into my arms when Salt spun us around, gunning the thing towards the break in the trees across the salt pond.

Everything had happened so fast I hadn't had time to think about it. As we zipped along in the little boat, my mind began to chew on the day's events. A lot of it seemed crazy, but one thing was clear – Salt knew these guys and they knew him. In fact, he hadn't seemed all that surprised when they showed up. That bothered me.

While our boat beat the tree limbs down the creek, a shiver ran up my spine. I wondered if I really knew the man driving the boat behind me. How many more secrets did he have left to tell? And how many were so dark I'd never hear them? I have a very active imagination. And, if I'm not careful, it can easily blast off to paranoid places. The countdown had started.

I just about jumped out of my skin when Salt reached up and tapped my shoulder.

"They're going to steal my boat," he shouted above the motor.

"How do you know that?"

"Just the kind of thing Skeebo would do to rub it in my face some more. They might take the girls, too."

"We'll stop them before they can," I shouted to him.

"No. They got too much of a head start. And this boat's too slow. I *want* them to take my boat," he said. "Got one of those GPS locators on there."

GPS was a cool way to keep track of your boat. After Salt told me about it, I put one on my boat, too. It came with this little handheld electronic doo-dad so I could check on the whereabouts of the *Costa Blanca* from just about anywhere. No one would ever steal my old tub, but for a week or so it was cool to show my friends. Truth is, I had forgotten all about it until Salt said something. I wished the remote had been in my pocket instead of home in my drawer.

But, of course, Salt thought of everything. The man was prepared. He pulled out his device and handed it to me. I turned it on and tapped the pigeon icon. In a couple of seconds a map appeared. I recognized the outline of Charlotte Harbor. On the extreme western side of the bay a red dot flashed.

"Salt," I screamed. "I found your boat! It's out in the harbor near Boca Grande Pass!"

"Let me see that."

I handed the locator to him.

"That other guy must have taken it out there," Salt said after examining the screen. "He's waiting on Skeebo."

With the johnboat zipping along full throttle, I moved to the stern bench and sat next to Salt.

"Still moving, though," he said. "Looks like they're going to rendezvous in Boca Grande Pass. With any luck, they'll head up the Intracoastal and I can gain on them."

"You mean *we* can gain on them," I said looking over at him.

"Sorry, son. I'm dropping you off. This ain't no game. I've put you in enough danger. Your mom would skin me alive."

"Salt. Mom thinks you and I are going fishing on your Hatteras for a week. She'll never know."

"Look, kid," he said. "For one thing, don't lie to your mom. For another, these Lafitte fools model themselves after the old pirates, Jean and Pierre. They think they're the very reincarnation of those old kooks. Like I said, ol' Skeebo, he's too much of an idiot to be a real threat. But his brother…well, he's a different story. I can't let you get any deeper in this mess."

I opened my mouth to say something. Salt cut me off.

"Mind's made up, kid. You're going home."

Our little boat rounded the last bend of the creek and the water opened up into the Peace River estuary. Salt pulled the brim of his hat down tight as the wind picked up. He squinted at the water ahead of us. I knew he was done talking about it. Salt's more stubborn than a clam stuck in mud. Once he digs in, you're not going to pull him out. If you try, it just makes him get mad and dig deeper. And when he's mad...well, I try to stay away from his bad side.

I just stared at his wrinkly face, trying to think myself around the problem.

"Contrary to what I told Skeebo, there is an account of Jean Lafitte's visit to Southwest Florida. He impressed Gasparilla enough for him to write it down in that book of secrets back at the house. Says there that Lafitte left as a wealthy man, though. Apparently, he or his descendants lost it all.

Seems the Cajun pirate showed up in the summer of 1816, right after the United States had defeated the British in the war of 1812.

Lafitte and his men had just helped General Andrew Jackson beat the British at New Orleans. As a result, all his crimes as a pirate had been forgiven. But, he couldn't help himself. He got back into the sweet trade and the governor of Louisiana, a man named Claiborne, was determined to nail him. Lafitte had to run for a while, so he headed south."

Salt guided the boat around another bend, turned out to be the last. The river quickly widened into the headwaters of Charlotte Harbor. I scanned the bay for Eden, hoping she'd bailed out of the skiff and was walking across the shallow bottom for shore. No such luck. The only thing in the water was the shimmering reflection of afternoon sun.

"My old man used to tell me this one diddie about it when I was a kid," Salt said. "Want to hear it?"

"Sure."

Salt cleared his throat and got into what I like to call his diddie voice.

"One day, old Gasparilla sat on Boca Grande counting out his gold when a call came down from the lookout. A schooner had been spotted sailing in from the north. Gasparilla ordered a boat to put to sea and greet the intruders. He waited on shore, with spyglass in hand, for the sound of cannon. Oddly, all remained quiet. The schooner followed Gasparilla's barque back to port behind the island without a shot.

Soon a tall Frenchman in gentleman's clothing came ashore in a longboat. He wore shoulder-length black hair, an equally dark moustache and a black hat folded up on one side. He introduced himself as Captain Jean Lafitte.

Gasparilla was intrigued with the man's manner and appearance. He invited his new guest to the big house and had servants prepare a meal as he spoke to the captain on a veranda in sight of the setting sun. Turned out that Lafitte was indeed an accomplished sea captain, with an impressive store of knowledge concerning the Caribbean and Gulf of Mexico. Over dinner, Lafitte impressed the old pirate further by revealing the plans of Spain's new king, Fernando.

Gasparilla despised the Spanish throne and always enjoyed obtaining any information, or treasure, that belonged to the royalty of his home country.

Lafitte had heard rumors that Fernando planned to reassert Spain's authority in the New World. The king wished to return the country to its glory days with an increased military presence in places that the British, French and Americans were getting stronger. One of those places, Lafitte had heard, was Tampa Bay, a spot that, on a favorable breeze, lay just half a day's sail from Gasparilla's island.

This royal plan to reassert authority disturbed the Spanish buccaneer, but with Lafitte's next few words Gasparilla forgot his worry. The pirate from New Orleans said that in addition to men and armaments, the Royal Navy planned to ship a pile of gold.

A frigate would soon set sail with enough gold bullion to finance the Tampa operation for five years. Lafitte claimed to know the name of the vessel and went on to state that the ship was then anchored in Havana being fitted for the expedition. The only question was when she would set sail for Tampa."

As we slid under the I-75 bridge, Salt paused long enough to offer me a bottle of water. I took it. He opened one as well.

"Lafitte," he continued, "had made a hasty departure from Louisiana. He lacked the men and the firepower to take the Spanish prize. That is why he had sought out the man known as 'The Terror of the Southern Seas.'

Uh, that would be Gasparilla," Salt said.

"Lafitte offered my great-great-great Gandpappy the largest share of the loot if Gasparilla would join forces and help him capture the frigate. The old Florida pirate didn't have to be asked twice.

At once, he sent a trusted lieutenant, Long John MacBlane, to Tampa Bay to learn the hour of the ship's arrival. In one week's time MacBlane returned with the news. The frigate was due by the first day of September.

Gasparilla wasted no time. He ordered the *Florida Blanca* to be made ready for battle. With Lafitte following in his schooner, the barque departed north under the Spanish flag. They reached Eggmont Key at the mouth of Tampa Bay later that day, anchoring in calm water behind the island.

There they sat for two weeks.

One day, a lookout shouted the good news – a small flotilla approached from the south, two schooners flanking a three-masted frigate. Gasparilla and Lafitte had already put their ingenious plan into action.

There were two main ways into Tampa Bay from the Gulf of Mexico. One pass opened just to the north of Eggmont, another just to the south. But, even further south, a third, very narrow passage existed as well on the northern tip of Anna Maria Island. This type of channel existed at the ends of many Florida barrier islands, as most any captain knew. Tidal currents pushed in and blew out around these island tips forming deep water troughs just off the shore, bordered by sandbars on the seaward side. Just such a narrow passage existed off Anna Maria and might serve the pirates as a convenient trap.

The *Florida Blanca* anchored in the main pass to the south of Eggmont Key, forcing the frigate to sail past her if the captain chose to enter that pass or the one farther to the north. Lafitte's schooner lay hidden behind Anna Maria to Gasparilla's south, obscured from the open sea by the island's trees. If the king's ships decided to avoid the *Florida Blanca* and take the easy short cut to Tampa Bay through the apparently unobstructed tidal channel, they'd be caught between the two buccaneer vessels.

An incoming tide, which flowed through the narrow channel like a river, made the Spanish naval commander's decision easier. He took the bait. Not wanting to tangle with potential problems posed by the *Florida Blanca* in the main pass to his north, the captain allowed the fast moving tide to pull his convoy of three ships into the narrow pass off Anna

Maria. They couldn't yet see Lafitte's schooner hiding in the bay beyond.

Gasparilla waited until the ships had committed to the narrow pass. Then, he gave the order to haul anchor, drop the Spanish flag and hoist his own jolly roger, a huge skull and crossbones with gaping holes for eyes.

The old pirate smiled.

His cannons were broadside to the frigate and within easy range, yet he held his fire. The two pirate captains had devised yet another surprise.

When the Spanish navy heard the first cannon boom, the noise didn't come from either pirate ship. The shot came at them from their starboard side, from the bushes on the tip of Anna Maria Island where Gasparilla had hidden two swivel guns. That blast also signaled Lafitte to reveal his ship and attack.

Realizing the ambush, the Spaniards rushed to battle stations and primed their guns.

Though the range of a swivel gun isn't far, those two on the tip of Anna Maria Island had been set close enough to blast grape shot at the uniformed men scrambling to battle stations on the decks of the three navy ships. Meanwhile, Lafitte sailed due north and fired on the naval ships from the east while Gasparilla began spitting cannon balls at them from the north.

The first Spanish ship, a schooner, turned hard to the north to get her cannons broadside to Lafitte. She almost made it, but the sandbar to her port side stopped her just short and her keel ran hard aground. The treasure frigate behind her had no time to react in the fast moving current. Her bow rammed the schooner aft, on her port side. The weight of the incoming tide locked the ships together blocking the narrow pass.

The third vessel, the other schooner, enjoyed the best position for defense at the seaward end of the channel. Her guns thundered noise and cannon balls at the *Florida Blanca*. A molten hunk of lead sailed just above Gasparilla's head ripping a gaping hole in the canvas. The close call only infuriated 'The Terror of the Southern Seas.' He ordered his quartermaster to close on the third ship.

The *Florida Blanca* had two of the new Scottish Carronade cannons mounted in her bow facing forward, a tact that caught the Spaniards off guard once more. Those two guns blasted continuously, as fast as the crews could reload, smashing the timbers and splattering the crew of the king's proud navy. In the head-on charge, Gasparilla's ship offered a slim target to the naval gunners. The royal cannon balls landed harmlessly in the sea on either side of the pirate ship. Soon, the schooner burned out of control, her masts splintered and her hull peppered with ragged holes both above and below the water line. As she sunk, a lone white flag waved frantically on the remains of her deck.

Meanwhile, Lafitte had already launched two longboats crammed with fighters toting pistols and swords. Lafitte himself stood at the prow of the first launch with a musket at his shoulder. Gasparilla enjoyed the show as the Cajun fired and picked a man off the frigate's deck. Lafitte grabbed another musket and again took aim. Another sailor fell from the frigate, splashing into the tide.

Men on Lafitte's schooner fired flaming arrows at the canvas sails of the first schooner as she floundered on the sandbar. Minutes later, her masts crackled and popped inside curtains of fire. Thick, black smoke spiraled up to the August sky. Frightened young seamen left their guns to battle the blaze, all too late.

Gasparilla smiled again when Lafitte flung a grappling hook onto the frigate's rail. The Frenchman, unaware of musket balls ripping past his skull, pulled himself up the rope like a man possessed, leading the final charge.

An officer came at Lafitte with a sword as the pirate neared the rail. The New Orleans privateer calmly reached into his pocket, drew a pistol, and shot the officer squarely between the eyes. Grape shot from the swivel guns had taken care of many more. Dead or dying navy men littered the deck of the boat. Lafitte stepped over them, slashing a path to the helm with his sword. Pirates from both longboats followed him to the fight. The sound of cannon fire echoed away, replaced by awful screams as the cutthroats lived up to their name.

Lafitte hacked his way to the captain.

Gasparilla watched the poor man raise his hands, sword tip at his throat, wondering what Lafitte would do. He didn't wonder long. The French pirate pushed the bloody steel into the captain's flesh and out the back of his neck.

It was done. The Spaniards were defeated.

Gasparilla stood on the frigate's deck alongside his new partner as the men hoisted wooden chests out of the hold. Lafitte singled out one of the stout treasure trunks and, using an iron key that had been wrapped around the Spanish captain's throat, removed a heavy lock and raised the lid. A pile of shiny, gold ingots flashed in the afternoon sun.

The two pirate captains smiled, Gasparilla clapping Lafitte on the back and inviting the privateer to stay in Florida as long as he liked."

We were into Punta Gorda by the time Salt finished that diddie.

"Salt," I said, "Just like Lafitte needed help, you need my help. There's no way you can handle this alone. Let me go with you. Let me help you."

I really didn't think I had a chance. His mind was set.

"Don't make me beg, Salt," I said.

I was right, though. His face told the story.

"Kid. The reason I told you that diddie is to show you how vicious Jean Lafitte was, not according to a bunch of college historians, but directly from a handwritten, eye witness account I know to be very real. Now, that violent streak is a real nasty bug to be passing down in your genes. I know from personal experience that one particular Lafitte in the bloodline's chock full of that critter.

On top of that, this descendant, Skeebo's dear brother John, is so whacked in the head, he thinks he *is* Jean Lafitte. He's heard the stories. Wants to be just like the guy. He's capable of anything." Salt turned and gave me the hairy sea-eye. "Including killing people."

Hammerhead put his nose to the wind and snorted as if someone from Louisiana had left a rotten odor in his wake.

I must have caught a whiff, too, because I snapped back to reality at the memory of the guy, *and* his hostages. A wave of nausea hit the pit of my belly like an anchor. It wasn't seasickness, either. It was sickness over our situation. This whole thing was not good at all. In fact, it was just plain bad.

I choked the bile down and tried to focus on some sort of solution.

"Well, if they're so bad," I said, "what about you? You're related to a nasty pirate, too."

It was the only comeback I had. When Salt jacked the corner of his mouth into his cheek, I thought he was cracking a smile, about to laugh and tell me he was joking, that he needed my help. But then, the other side of his mouth refused to follow suit. His face got caught in a twist of regret, instead. Pain.

"No, you're right. I've had my moments," he said to the wind. "Point is, I'm trying to change. These guys are doing the opposite." He looked at me. "Any smuggler's going to bit a bit nasty. I knew that, kid. However, it was the only way to get that Cuban girl here. I was glad to do a good deed. But, in a lot of ways, it was a big mistake, too."

He didn't elaborate. I remembered Salt telling me last summer how he'd served time in prison for a different mistake. Just how many mistakes had he made? I knew, for him, each one was a big-time regret. No wonder the dude seemed so bummed most of the time.

But then again, I'd definitely made my share of mistakes, too. And, like Salt, I wanted to improve, no, *prove* myself, maybe even more than he did, to get past them. You know, do something good, make something right. I had made a vow after Charley.

Plus...

"I know how worried you are about Eden, Harley," he said to the waves as the motor pushed us past the last houses of town towards the end of the slow zone. "I found her once. I'll find her again."

He *had* found Eden, in the eye of a hurricane, alone and dying. He saved her life that day. I knew he could save her again. I just wanted to help.

Salt nudged the throttle and the johnboat picked up speed. We didn't talk for a long time. My head was working, though. Don't think it wasn't.

Later, I spotted my boat off in the distance, abandoned and floating like a bobber in the middle of Boca Grande Pass. Salt had given me that boat, the *Costa Blanca* after my boat, the *White Stripe,* sank in the storm last August. He noticed the crabber, too. But, did he run to the pass and let me hop onboard? No. He calmly made the turn into the channel that would take me back to Palmetto Cove. I figured he'd decided to borrow his old crab boat after he dropped me off.

"Where she at, kid?" Salt asked, poking the GPS locator into my hand.

In a few seconds, the screen lit up. It showed a tiny picture of Salt's sportfisherman making its way up a satellite photo of the Intracoastal Waterway, north of our position.

"Just like you thought, Salt. Going up the Intracoastal towards Sarasota."

"Good."

Not too much later, my house came into sight, sitting up like a castle on a high piece of ground at the edge of town.

For my whole life, we had lived in a single-wide trailer like almost everyone else in Palmetto Cove. Hurricane Charley blew most of those tin-dominiums away, mine included. Even in December, four months after the hurricane, the place was still a ghost town.

My family was luckier than most. We were some of the first people back. My mom bought the old Rovich place with a cut of the pirate loot Salt had given us. Charley had blown Mrs. Rovich back to Russia, and no one but my mom could even think about buying waterfront property so soon after a hurricane. Money does the thinking for my mom, though. It burns a hole in her pocket so fast it sets her pants on fire. So before we knew it, my sister and I had moved into the mansion that Mr. Rovich's vodka company had built.

The property rolled along Pine Island Sound like a resort. Charley had picked all the coconut trees like weeds, but he'd spared the swimming pool *and* the tennis court. I was still getting used to it. Really, it was too much for me, too big, too fancy. Mom's different, though. She likes "the finer things," as she says. I think she just likes spending cash. I have to watch her like a hawk.

Salt didn't waste time by taking the canal around the jetty to our dock. He just pulled straight up to the seawall and let go of the throttle.

"This is it, boys," he said. "See you on the other side."

I opened my mouth to say something. He cut me off.

"You know the old saying 'after laughter comes tears'? Well, I like to say, 'After tears come laughter.' That's a fact of life. The only thing we're not privy to is when we're going to hear that laughter. In the meantime it's best to stick to your plan in spite of the tears, knowing that at some point the sun's going to shine again. That's faith, kid."

He winked at me.

"Don't try to follow me, Harley. I'll call you when it's settled."

Hammerhead jumped out and I climbed up the seawall after him. We stood there, side by side, watching the old crabber go.

And, that was that. No goodbyes. Salt turned the tiller, kicked it, and hauled butt across the sound for Boca Grande Pass.

The Beast

I stood there on the seawall watching Salt's johnboat get smaller and smaller when the phone rang in my pocket. It was Eden's mom - again. The screen said she'd called three times before. Guess I didn't hear it. I hit the "ignore" button. I could put her off a little longer.

"What are you doing home?" Mom asked as I walked into the kitchen. "I thought you and Salt where gone fishing or something."

"We were. I mean, we are," I said. "Just needed to stop by and get something."

She looked out the window towards the dock.

"Where's his boat?" she asked. Then, with her hands going to her hips, she said, "Where's your boat?"

Mom can smell a rat quicker than a pelican can nail a fish. She brushed back a clump of hair from her eye to get a better look at me. I had to be very careful – and very persuasive. Her radar was on and I had been lit up brighter than the Christmas tree by our front door.

"Where's *your* boat?" she demanded again.

"Well, that's just it," I said, buying a moment more. "Salt has my boat. He needs it to find his boat."

"Find his boat? Where's his boat?"

I hated lying, especially to my mom. I almost never did it. There wasn't any reason to. My mom and I are tight. I can tell her anything and, though she might not like it, she can take it.

She knows I'm human, that stuff happens. She's good that way.

So, I had no choice. I told her the truth.

"Mom...something bad happened," I said, feeling goose bumps run up my spine.

"I knew it," she said not taking her eyes off me. "I could see it all over you. Sit down."

I pulled a chair away from the breakfast table and plopped down. Hammerhead hit the floor at my feet. Mom sat down across the table.

"Start talking," she said.

I blabbed away faster than an auctioneer on truth serum, spilling out the details non-stop, except when she had a question or two. It was exhausting, but somewhere during the process a weight lifted off my chest.

It's good to fess up to your mom.

"Salt's smart for dropping you off," Mom said. "But, he ought to call the police. There's more than that girl...what'd you say her name is?"

"Isabella."

"Well, there's more than Isabella at stake here."

She got up and paced around the kitchen.

"What about Eden?" she wondered.

She glanced over at me a time or two as her brain crunched the details of what she'd just heard, a plan formulating with each step. Before she could say anything, however, my sister, Tori, walked in wearing a pink, terry cloth robe, with matching towel on her head.

"Mooooom," she whined, "I can't find my red sandals. Can I borrow yours?"

My sister was always a pain. She had just turned nineteen in November and, by some miracle she's never been able to explain, she suddenly knew everything, except the location of her red sandals, apparently.

"You lost mine last week, girl," Mom said a little peeved.

"Oh. Yeah. Forgot. Sorry, Mom. Can I borrow your black ones?"

"You can get a job and buy your own," Mom told her.

Tori huffed and rolled her eyes. She always claimed that capitalism and free enterprise were taking our country down a dead end street. She didn't believe in employment. In other words, she was lazy.

"What?!" Tori said. "That crazy, old hermit gave his little crab-boy here a fortune and we can't spend any of it?"

"One, what do you think bought the house you're standing in?" said Mom. "And, two, I told you to quit calling him crab-boy. You ought to be kissing his butt with all he's brought into this family. You have a whole new wardrobe *and* a new car thanks to that fortune. Now, go pick out something from the closet-full of shoes you *do* have, unless that's against your socio-economic principles."

Tori protested with a squeak, but she turned and stormed out of the kitchen. Mom shook her head and blinked her eyes like she was trying to clear out the crazy-bugs. She sighed, folded her arms across her chest, and focused on me.

"Thank God for hair color, Harley. That's all I can say. Because, between the two of you, I'd look like a little, old gray-haired lady without it."

I smiled for the first time all afternoon. Mom smiled, too. I knew at that moment she planned to give me a chance.

"You've got twenty-four hours, Harley. You hear me?" she said. "Twenty-four. And you better check in every two."

I got up and laid a big hug on her.

"Awesome. Thanks, Mom."

"I must be insane to let a fourteen-year-old go out and do something the cops ought to be doing," she said as she squeezed me. "What's your plan?"

I told her. Next, I ran to my room and grabbed some cash and my GPS locator out of the drawer. Mom was waiting for me by the garage door with a couple of granola bars when I got there.

"At least eat something," she said handing the bars to me.

I stuffed them into my pocket and hit a garage door button. One of the four big, steel doors started up. I snatched my bike off the rack and rolled it outside before the door stopped moving.

"You better call me, Harley Davidsen Cooper! You hear me?!"

"Love you, Mom!"

And there it was, the conditional release.

I peddled up the driveway to the street, Hammerhead trotting alongside on the grass. He's pretty good about keeping up. He even uses shortcuts through people's yards to head me off at the pass. Fast dog.

A few minutes later I leaned my bike against a tree trunk in Bill's yard. His Chevette was parked beside their new trailer. New to them, I should say. Bill's uncle had a single-wide parked in LaBelle he had lent to Bill's dad after the storm reduced Bill's old trailer to I-beams.

Bill's fifteen, a year older than me, but still too young for a full-fledged driver's license. He had a learner's permit. His folks let him drive anyway as long as it's just around Pine Island. Pretty cool, huh?

I saw his dad's Angler on the lift over the canal. Though it was too low to see, Bill's inflatable boat was probably pulled up onto the dock. I walked to the front door and whacked my knuckles against the metal a couple of times, then quickly stepped back.

The door exploded open inches from my body. Bill always tried to hit me with it. Almost broke my nose once. Some friend.

"Dude! I almost *nailed* you, man," he laughed. "All that coin in your pockets must be slowing you down these days."

"Nice try, funny guy," I said, "but I think you need to get rid of some of that lard between your ears, dude. It's slowing *you* down."

He bypassed the steps and jumped straight to the ground.

"Ready to go down to the Hut and scope some hotties?" he asked.

The Burger Hut was one of our hangouts down the road in Matlacha.

"No, dude," I replied. "Need a favor."

"Sorry, man. Eden would kill me if I took your collar off."

He got a good laugh out of that one, too.

"Ha, ha," I said flatly. "No, seriously dude, I need to borrow your boat."

"There's no way my dad's going to go for that."

"Not your dad's boat, *your* inflatable," I said.

"Oh, that. She's a little low on air. What's wrong with your boat?"

"Salt's got it. Got a compressor?"

"Been using a bicycle pump," he said. "What you need it for?"

"Need to go get my boat back. I'll tow yours home once I do."

"Salt's not bringing it back?"

"Look, dude," I said. "It's complicated. Tell you when I get back. Can I have it or not? I need to haul, like, right now."

"Suit yourself, dude. I'm meeting Matt down at the Hut, but I think there's gas in the tank. Let me grab the pump."

He walked over to a small shed between the trailer and the canal.

The inflatable boat sat on the dock, one of the pontoons sagging a bit, definitely in need of air. Bill had found the thing after the hurricane, washed into the mangroves. The numbers had been scraped severely, so bad that you couldn't even read them. Bill had tried to find the owner for a few weeks. When he couldn't, he kept the boat for himself and stuck an old Johnson 9.9 on the back. He named it *The Beast*. Funny. Bill's always the comedian.

After that, he cruised the water as much as I did. He even started fishing for blue crabs like I used to. Since Salt had given me his old stone crab boat after I'd lost the *Stripe*, I didn't go after blues anymore. I gave Bill all my gear, and all my secrets, and off he went in that ridiculous twelve-foot boat. I had to laugh every time I saw him out there. That crazy excuse for a boat barely floated. It had more patches than clown pants! Now, that was truly the funny part.

However, as I stood there, wondering how big the latest leak was, it wasn't so funny anymore. Strange how the tables can turn. One minute you're laughing at something, the next, you're in the very same boat – literally, in my case.

"Here, dude," Bill said handing me the bicycle pump. "You might want to keep this handy. I think I got a hole in one of the patches."

I just shook my head, stowing the pump under the seat.

"Other side's fine," he said. "She'll look better in the water."

He helped me shove the boat off the dock into the canal. Hammerhead jumped right in, tail wagging, all tongue and smiles. He loved the water, even in a clown boat. He should have been a circus dog, I suppose.

"Seriously, dude," I said. "Why don't you get an upgrade? How do you crab in this tiny thing?"

"Never underestimate the power of *The Beast*, my friend," he said. "She won't let you down."

The motor started on the first pull. That much was a blessing.

"Just give her a little love, dude," Bill called over the outboard's putt-putt-a-putt. "And she'll love you back."

I waved at him with one hand over my head as we drifted by his yard on our way to Pine Island Sound.

I still hadn't got used to the way our town looked after Charley chewed her up. Many of the pine trees had no tops. The other trees, the oaks, mahoganies, and banyans stuck into the sky lopsided, missing branches, big bites taken out. Most of the major mobile home wreckage had been cleared off the lots. Areas that had once been cozy yards with shrubbery and swing sets stood vacant like scars. A lot of my old neighbors still lived in the temporary FEMA trailers set up in Punta Gorda, checking their mailboxes everyday for insurance checks that never got delivered.

After the hurricane devastated our coast, Salt let me in on his secrets, telling me everything about his ancestor, the pirate king Gasparilla, and how much of the old buccaneer's treasure still remained. Salt wanted to do good things with that loot, and he had done a lot. We both had. But, there was so much more to do, here and out in the world. The loot we'd just dug up, the loot Skeebo stole, was supposed to go to all the residents of Palmetto Cove in the form of interest free loans. That way they could afford new trailers, new homes, until those slow moving insurance companies made good on their policies. Then, we planned to re-use the money to build a new library, a park and a whole list of things the town needed to become a real community again.

Hammerhead whined and I looked over to see our old home sliding by. I say home, but all that resembled home was gone. Beyond the dock and seawall, bare dirt stretched all the way to the street. The storm had taken what it wanted and bull dozers had scraped off the rest. The only things left besides the dirt were the dozer tracks on top.

Of course, we had to get the girls back, but we had to get that money back, too. It wasn't right. The people of Palmetto Cove, my friends, my neighbors, deserved better than to live in limbo on a gravel parking lot in a bunch of tin cans.

Before, whenever I'd heard about a flood or famine in some far off place, I'd always feel sad for those people. I'd also feel helpless because there wasn't much I could do except send them prayers and a few dollars. But, this disaster hadn't happened far away and the people it affected were folks I knew by their first names.

Ironically, this catastrophe brought another twist. This time, I wasn't helpless. For once in my life I actually had the power to do something about it. Floating down that canal in the middle of my broken town, I became more determined than ever to keep climbing and reach the summit of that mountain I'd vowed to conquer.

I aimed to save Palmetto Cove.

And, I wasn't about to let some cross-eyed, son of a pirate stop me.

At the canal's mouth, I cranked the throttle. The tiny boat took off into the Sound, skipping across the surface like an inner tube. The right side pontoon was a tad low on air, good enough for a few miles, though. I had to make some distance fast, no time for the pump. Salt had a good head start, but he might pull over. And, he'd have to slow down in the manatee zones. If I blew through those slow zones, I'd have a chance. I figured that once Salt knew I had my mom's blessing, he'd let me help. I just had to catch him. That was plan A.

With one had on the tiller, I grabbed my GPS locator and hit the power button. Salt's boat, which was actually my boat, flashed as a red dot on the electronic chart, already across Charlotte Harbor going up the Intracoastal north towards Tampa. He looked to be about even with Little Gasparilla Island. Since he was running the Intracoastal, I assumed his Hatteras was still running it, too. I had some serious catching up to do. I pushed that Johnson outboard as hard as she'd go.

Hammerhead sat in the bow with his chin resting on the air-filled rubber like he'd found a pillow. Circus dog in a clown boat. Nose to the wind. I wondered how he'd look with a red clown nose on his snout.

Above us, clear skies covered everything like a blue dome. To my left, the chop split the afternoon sun into a million tiny stars that twinkled for miles across the sound. To the right, clumps of mangroves dotted the bay with green specks for miles. Boat traffic wasn't too bad, a few flats boats and bay runners fishing here and there, but the bulk of seasonal tourists hadn't shown up yet. All seemed calm and serene out on Pine Island Sound, the exact opposite of conditions in my brain.

We left the smooth water behind and bounced the inflatable boat across the top of Charlotte Harbor. With each hit, the right pontoon seemed a little flabbier, but it was hard to tell. I figured the air pressure would probably last until I reached the north side of the Harbor, so I just kept going.

I ran all the way to Gasparilla Sound before the air got seriously low. Forced to make a pit stop, I left the deep channel of the Intracoastal Waterway for some shallow flats to the northeast. Just in time, too. The boat started to look like a half-inflated beach ball on one side, a beach ball made of patch-covered clown pants, that is.

I cut the motor and coasted up to a mangrove island. I don't think Bill had an anchor anywhere. I just let the tree limbs hold the boat while I grabbed the pump. A bird or something got Hammerhead's attention and he splashed into the water next to the boat.

"We're not staying long, boy," I yelled to him. "Go take care of your pees and poops."

He acted like he hadn't even heard me. He had. He just wanted me to think he didn't. He wouldn't go far.

I clamped the pump nozzle onto Bill's makeshift valve-stem and started pumping with both hands. Air hissed in with each stroke, though you couldn't tell by looking at it. Gradually, the dents and dimples straightened out. She was getting air. It just took a long time with that stupid pump. My arms started to ache. I'm a crabber, though. My body's used to aches and pains. I kept going.

"How come it's always your dog that recues me and not you?"

The voice scared the crap out of me and I fumbled the bicycle pump into the water. When I jerked up to see who had spoken, I saw a mirage - Eden Baker splashing through the water following Hammerhead back to the boat. I gaped like a mute caveman, mouth hanging open and all.

"Scared of getting your feet wet?" she said when she came closer.

"Eden!" I finally burst out. "What! How!"

She was soaked. Her t-shirt stuck to her bones like shrink-wrap, her hair all matted to her head. There she was...alive, safe, and cracking jokes. I stumbled out of the boat, tripped, fell, splashed into the water, jumped to my feet and slogged into her arms. By then, she was laughing.

"Oh, God," she said. "Am I glad you came along."

And that's all she said until I finished kissing her.

"Eden, what happened? How'd you get away?"

"Could I sit down first?" she asked. "I need a little break from the saltwater."

I helped her into the inflatable. Hammerhead hopped in next to her flashing a grin. I just stood there looking at her. Even drenched, she was beautiful. Hammerhead licked her face, reminding her who the real hero was.

"Good job, boy," I said patting his head.

"I dove off," Eden said.

"What?! Are you for real?!"

"Yeah," she said. "We were on Salt's boat and I told them I had to pee. When they untied me, I took off. Ran out the back. Knocked one of the guys down and dove into the water."

"And they didn't shoot you?" I asked.

"They didn't even slow down."

"You jumped off a Hatteras while it was cruising?!"

"Dove off, sir," she corrected. "Nice form, too, I might add. I waited until the channel was narrow. Dove in, swam under water as long as I could, and then got up on the flats. I knew that thing couldn't follow me there. The big chickens didn't even try."

"Eden…did they…um, hurt you?"

"Don't worry, Harley. They never touched me," she said.

She pulled her hair into a pony tail and tied it with a piece of trap cord.

"What about Isabella?"

"Who's that? Oh, that girl? She's fine, I guess. I told her to come with me. Didn't have the nerve, I suppose." Eden shrugged her shoulders. "Anyway, they ditched your boat and their skiff in the pass," she said.

"Did you see my boat go by?"

"I did," she said. "I *thought* it looked like Salt in the wheelhouse. I only saw one person. I started yelling as he passed but he never heard me, because by then I was already up here making my way along these islands, trying to get to a phone."

When she said "phone", my cell rang. Freaky. It was her mom again. I answered it.

"Hi, Mrs. Baker," I said looking at Eden.

Mrs. Baker was squeaking away like an over-caffeinated mouse.

"No. Everything's good," I told her. "Just out of range. Here's Eden."

I handed Eden the phone and shook my head from side to side. We couldn't tell Mrs. Baker what was going on, not yet. Eden nodded at me. She got it.

"Hi, Mom," she said still looking at me. "Yep, everything's fine…I just spaced, I guess. Sorry…Yeah, I left in a real hurry. Forgot my phone and everything…No. It wasn't Harley's fault…yes, Mom. Everything's good. I'll call you later…Love you, too, Mom."

She handed the phone back to me and I ended the call.

"Why'd you make me lie to my mom, Harley? She could get help."

"It's complicated, Eden," I said.

"Is it about that girl? Isabella?"

"Yep," I said.

"I knew it!" Eden searched my eyes for a second before she said, "I knew something was up with her. Did she say anything to you?"

"Say anything? Like what?"

"Like, I don't know. Anything. I don't trust her."

"Don't trust her?" I said. "She's been kidnapped! What's not to trust?"

"I don't know. Girls know things. Besides, I saw her looking at you right before they took us. And, she said something to me."

"Said something? Eden, what are you talking about?"

"Don't worry about it, Harley. Just…if you see her again, stay away from her."

"Can you give me a hint?"

"Don't worry about it," she said.

She'd already given me a hint by not telling me what Isabella had said. I was sure it involved me. Eden was jealous. Oh well, I was pretty sure she'd get over it. We were tight.

I told her what Salt had told me about Isabella and her family. I also gave her a brief rundown on Skeebo and John Lafitte.

"So what's Salt going to do about it?" she asked.

"He never got around to telling me," I said.

"What're *you* going to do?"

I explained plan A. She thought she could help persuade Salt. Then, I told her plan B. She thought I was crazy.

"Well, I guess I'm going on a boat ride," she said.

"I guess you are," I said knowing full well I wouldn't be able to talk her out of it anyway. That was fine. If we couldn't hook up with Salt, I'd have to go to plan B and I'd need someone to steer.

I climbed in and pulled the start rope. We had about a half tank of fuel. With any luck we'd make the marina in Englewood before they closed and get some more.

I idled the boat over the turtle grass until the water dropped off deep enough to punch *The Beast's* mighty 9.9. Even with the additional person, the freshly pumped inflatable rode better. Hopefully, the air would outlast the fuel and we wouldn't have to stop for a while.

I guess Eden got tired of the wet shirt. She peeled it off, holding it open like a parachute over her head to let the wind dry it. She obstructed my view, but I didn't complain. There were worse things to look at, than a chick in a bra.

Although the sun settled down in the west, the day had just grown brighter.

I couldn't believe it. I had her back. Thanks to Bill's leaky, old clown boat. I patted her patches with my hand. Good *Beast.*

Costa Blanca

I checked Salt's position with the GPS locator. The *Costa Blanca* sat dead in the water in Englewood, probably taking on fuel at the marina. We buzzed along in Bill's clown boat eating granola bars and wishing *The Beast* could go faster. Thirty minutes later, Salt still hadn't moved. We were getting close to Englewood ourselves, close enough to have a chance if the dot on the locator didn't start moving.

Just before sunset, with a fuel tank full of fumes, we turned into Slack Pearl's Marina in Englewood – right behind my boat, the stern of the *Costa Blanca* staring me right in the face. This was either very good news or very bad news. I quickly tied off and all three of us scrambled up on the dock.

My boat was deserted. The marina was deserted as well. The lights in the ship's store were dark and no one was in sight.

"Hey," said Eden. "There's a dude down there."

She pointed towards the dry storage building where the marina stored boats up on racks. I looked over in time to see a forklift drive into the building.

"Come on," I said.

We took off running across the pavement. Inside, a huge metal grid held boats four levels high, bigger boats on the bottom, smaller ones up top. The forklift shut down in the far corner.

"Hey!" I called over to the operator as he climbed down.

He heard me and started over. We met in the middle under a bright cone of light.

"Hey, dude," I said. "What happened to the guy who brought in that crab boat out there?"

The guy chuckled. He took off his cap, wiped his forehead, and put it back on.

"He's a funny one, that guy," the man said, rolling a toothpick across his teeth. "Let me guess. Your name's Harley Cooper. Am I right?"

"How'd you know that?" I asked.

"He said you'd be by to get your boat," he told me, smirking.

"Well, where did he go?" I asked again.

"Paid me not to tell you."

The man stuck both hands into the pockets of his jeans.

"Oh, brother," I said. "Well how did he leave?"

"Can't tell you that either," the man said.

I remembered a scene from a movie where a detective found himself in a similar situation. Salt said movies are a waste of time. I beg to differ. Sometimes, they can be very educational.

The cash in my pocket felt damp from the boat ride. I didn't think a dock hand would mind.

"Maybe you'll tell Mr. Franklin," I said waving a hundred-dollar bill under his nose.

He shifted the toothpick from one corner of his mouth to the other and back again.

"That's funny, kid. Me and that Franklin guy speak the same language," he said snatching the money out of my hand. "Must be my lucky day. He took off north in a Donzi."

"Donzi?" I said.

"Yeah. One of our rentals. Nice one, too. Brand new 38ZX."

"Oh, man," I said. "That sucks!"

"Is that bad?" asked Eden.

"Come on, Eden," I said. "He's in a Donzi! You know how fast those things are. Plus, I can't track him anymore."

"Look," the man said. "I'm closing up. You taking your boat or what?"

"Man!" I snapped. "I guess a hundred bucks doesn't buy much hospitality around here! Could you at least give me some fuel?"

The goober rolled his eyes and huffed before walking towards the fuel pumps.

"Gotta pay cash," he said over his shoulder.

He's going to keep that, too, I thought.

After I paid the dude for the fuel, he just took off. I don't think he cared one way or another what we did. I tied *The Beast* to the back of my boat and plopped down into one of the chairs on the deck. Eden sat in the other chair. Hammerhead laid down at her feet. He wagged his tail and eyeballed me like a hungry orphan. He was starving. Night had come and it was well past supper time.

"What now, Einstein?" Eden asked.

"I'm calling Salt," I said.

"Think he'll answer?"

"Only one way to find out," I said and pulled out my phone.

Salt's number was in my "favorites" just under my mom's. I tapped his name. The phone rang once. It rang twice.

"Thought I told you I'd call *you* when this was done!" said a rough voice on the other end.

It was Salt. I heard the Donzi's motors wailing in the background. Those go-fast boats are super loud.

"Salt! I've got Eden," I said.

"How'd you manage that?"

"She jumped off your Hatteras and I found her across from Gasparilla Island," I said.

Eden slugged me in the thigh.

"Hammerhead found me," she said into the phone.

"One down, one to go," Salt said. "Thanks for saving me the work. You've done your part. Now go home!"

"Are you tracking them on your GPS?" I asked.

"Still headed up the channel towards Tampa," he said. "Figure I'm about an hour behind. Lot of slow zones, but I don't want to raise any eyebrows in this hotrod, so I'm keeping her inside the law. They got to deal with drawbridges, though. I don't. I'll catch 'em."

"Then what?"

"Then me and Mr. Lafitte's going to have a chat," he said.

"Salt, it's four against one, man. You need our help."

"Ain't risking no more lives," he said. "You got families back home. They're starting to worry, I'm sure."

"Mom's cool," I said.

"And your girly there? How's her mom? Better yet, how's her old man?"

"We can work on that."

"How 'bout you *work* on getting her home. I assume you tracked down your boat."

"We're in it now."

"Then get going back to Pine Island. Fishing trip's cancelled."

And, he hung up.

"I get the feeling he doesn't want us," said Eden.

I thought for a moment.

Eden was right. My back-up plan, the one I'd decided to follow if I didn't re-join Salt, was completely insane.

I just couldn't think of anything better.

I grabbed a pad of paper and a pen out of the wheel house. I wrote down Bill's name and number, and a message saying *The Beast* belonged to him, mentioning that the dock master ought to call him. Bill wouldn't be happy about it when he learned his boat was a couple of hours away. Oh, well. Under the circumstances it was the best I could do. I stuck the note in Bill's boat half under a seat cushion and hitched the inflatable to the dock, praying it would stay inflated until the next day.

"We going somewhere?" asked Eden.

"We're going to head them off at the pass," I said as I jumped back in the *Costa Blanca.*

I started her up and, with Eden's help, we cast off. I backed the stone-crab boat into the channel and turned south.

"I thought you said we were going after them, Harley," Eden said.

"We are," I said. "They're crawling up the Intracoastal. Salt's about an hour behind the dork patrol. I figure they'll stay on the inside until Tampa Bay. Then, if they're really going back to Louisiana, they'll run across the Gulf to the Mississippi."

"We'll never find them out there," Eden said.

"They won't get that far," I said. "We're going to jog back to Stump Pass and shoot up the coast to Ana Maria."

"Shoot up the coast," she said. "In this tub? You think we can actually outrun them?"

"She'll do fifteen knots easy," I said. "And they've got to stop for a bunch of drawbridges. Look, it's not perfect, but what else can we do?"

"And if we do get there first?"

"I told you."

"You're nuts."

Eden protested by turning to the window and watching the Christmas lights slide by. I figured a little music might cheer her up, so I cranked up some of her favorite stuff, Avril Lavigne. It worked. Her hips started swaying three notes into *Nobody's Home.*

The Intracoastal Waterway runs up and down most of the eastern coast of the United States from New Jersey to Mexico. Congress created it in 1919 to protect small boats from the open sea by providing channels through bays, behind barrier islands, and down man-made canals. In our part of Florida we have a ton of barrier islands just off the mainland that shield the Intracoastal from heavy seas and weather. There are plenty of passes that open between these islands to the Gulf of Mexico. Stump Pass, to the south, was the nearest.

The Intracoastal has a great series of red and green markers to outline the channel. Sometimes, they're on buoys. More often, they're up on poles. I switched off the interior lights and, with the help of a nearly full moon, I spotted a piling ahead.

A captain has to be careful on Florida's west coast, especially in a long, clunky crab boat. The water can get very shallow outside the channel. Sandbars and oyster beds lurk everywhere. I had no time to get stuck.

Stump Pass is narrow and tricky at night, at least for me. I'd only been through there a few times. That was during the day. I pulled out a chart to check the positions of markers and sand bars with a flashlight. My boat had a spotlight over the cabin. I switched it on, swiveling the beam to find the marker we needed. Once we spotted it, I eased the boat to the right and followed the red and green signs around sandbars and shoals out to the Gulf.

The fresh air of the open sea washed over us, a welcome change after the mangrove swamp funk. The wind came in from the northwest, building small seas that rolled into our portside bow, slowing our forward progress a little. With those conditions I knew it was going to be close. I shoved the throttle forward as far as it would go.

"There are pig feet in the ice chest, Eden," I said. "Mind pulling a few out for Hammerhead to munch on? You can thaw them out with some water in that bucket."

I used the pig feet for stone crab bait. They lasted a long time in the traps. To keep them from spoiling I stored them in a cooler packed with dry ice.

One of Salt's stipulations for sharing his wealth was that I continued fishing. He said it built character and kept a guy honest. I didn't care what it did. I loved fishing for blue crabs in my old boat before the storm, and I loved fishing for stones in Salt's boat even more. I don't care how much money I had in my pocket. I'd always fish for something.

Oh, yeah. And one of the best things about having an office like mine was jamming the tunes. Avril was done singing, so I cranked up some *AC/DC* for the ride north. Hammerhead loves dinner music.

Eden and I dined on succulent peanut butter crackers, a double dose of delicious delectability, as my food-loving friend, Smitty, always said. I even had two cans of cold dew to wash them down. After we finished feasting, Eden curled up next to me.

Life is good.

"Harl? You ever try and count the stars?"

"You're wasting your time," I said.

"I mean, like, how many are there?"

"Billions and billions," I replied, trying to sound like that old science guy on TV.

Out on the Gulf, away from city lights, the stars did truly pop at night.

"Makes me feel so small," she said. "Like a flea on a dog."

"Hammer-dude could relate," I said.

Hammerhead whined on the deck at our feet.

"I mean, if aliens travelled through all that galaxy to our tiny, little planet they wouldn't care about all our petty problems, right?" she said.   "They wouldn't care which political party controlled the White House, or what kind of car was the most fuel efficient, or which TV show had the highest ratings. They wouldn't care about any of that stuff."

"They'd probably see us like we see ants when we kick open an anthill," I added. "Just a bunch of ants. All the same."

"Exactly," she said.   "Like this morning.   Those guys snatched me from home and threw me in their boat! All for a bunch of shiny metal? That's just *so* ridiculous in the grand scheme of things."

That was a big jump from the ant thing, but I got her point.

"Very valuable metal," I added.

"Just because we say so," she said. "So what. Why are people so eaten up with greed? That's the point."

Okay, so I missed her point. I kept listening, though.

She continued. "Why can't we get past the hording and the me, me, me, and quit acting like a bunch of rats chasing each other for cheese?"

"Mozzarella, please," I said.

She punched me in the arm. I turned down the tunes.

"I'm serious," she said. "Aren't there better things we could be doing with our time than chasing cheese?"

A wave rocked the boat, tipping her into me. I wrapped my arm around her and got serious, too.

"Here's the thing, Eden. Everybody is busy doing what they think they need to be doing. Even if they happen to be doing nothing, what they are doing makes sense to them at the time. Most people think the best thing to do is make a lot of money. Then, they can start living like they truly want to. In the mean time, they worry. In the end, most never get to that point, that stage of living like they want to. Even if they do make the money, they're still not satisfied. Even worse, they're empty. They forget the dreams they had when they were our age. And, like you say, they only end up wasting their time."

"Thanks, Plato, but that isn't exactly practical information."

"Sure it is," I said. "If you can chill about scrambling for all the stuff you *think* you need, and know that if you work hard you'll get what you *actually* need, you can relax and truly focus on your real mission in life."

"And that is?"

"And that is…different for everybody."

Eden gasped like she got it, but once again, I misinterpreted her point.

"A falling star!" she said.

"I missed it."

"I'm making a wish," she said and closed her eyes.

"Careful what you wish for," I said.

Eden crossed her arms and bowed her head. For the next few moments, the only sounds were the last notes of *Highway to Hell*, the motor, and the splash of saltwater breaking around the boat.

When she had finished, she faced me again, smiling, zipped her lips closed, turned the imaginary lock, and tossed the imaginary key over her shoulder.

Tampa Bay

As we slipped around the north end of Anna Maria Island, the stars blurred, dimmed, and then, winked out altogether. Our boat had motored straight into a fog bank, thick as oatmeal and damp as a wet sock. Visibility shrunk to less than twenty feet, forcing me to slow our speed by two-thirds.

I could not have been happier.

The conditions were perfect for what I had in mind.

I switched off the navigation lights, making the *Costa Blanca* all but invisible.

In his story about Gasparilla, Jean Lafitte and the Spanish navy, Salt had mentioned a narrow channel off the north shore of the island. It still existed. The tide sucked us down the channel and I steered using the depth finder, keeping the boat centered in the deepest part of the trough. The flow tossed us along like a log ride at an amusement park until it spit us out into the bay behind the island. The current spread out. The water calmed. The boat stopped rocking and settled down.

I let her drift for a while, still watching our depth, until I thought we'd gone far enough to reach the Intracoastal channel. Eden spotted the flashing green that marked the waterway's western edge, hard to do in fog that thick. I revved the motor and headed over to it.

My wristwatch glowed 11:45. I hoped we weren't too late.

"I still think your idea's insane," Eden said.

"You got a better plan?" I asked her.

"Yes. Call the cops."

"You know we can't do that," I reminded her. "It'll work out. Remember, Salt said this guy's just a big, misguided pussy cat."

"And you believe everything that old man says?"

"Look, he's known this Skeebo character for a long time. He didn't seem overly concerned about him," I said, trying to put her at ease. "We're in position now. I'm going to shut the motor down. Let's listen."

That was her cue to be quiet. Once the motor was off, silence swallowed us whole. I missed the engine. At night, in the fog, the lack of noise seemed kind of creepy.

I opened the dry storage console to grab my night-vision binoculars, a gift from the U.S. Coast Guard for rescue work we did after the hurricane. The case was gone. I could have sworn I'd left it there. Oh well, plan B -- use my ears. The sound of Salt's Hatteras would give her away.

I cupped my ear, strained to listen, and heard absolutely nothing. Hammerhead shuffled towards us to sit down. Eden and I stood together just outside the wheelhouse, my arm across her shoulder, waiting. Nothing. No boat motors, no car horns, no dogs barking. Nothing.

"Do you think we missed them?" asked Eden finally.

"Anything's possible," I said, getting grouchy. "I don't know. Maybe they anchored for the night."

"If you were in a stolen boat, with stolen treasure and a kidnapped girl, would you stop for the night?"

"Good point," I said. "They could've headed out to sea through another pass."

"I guess we just wait," Eden said.

"All we can do."

My plan relied on surprise. The *Florida Blanca* was rigged with a night vision camera that could spot structures ahead of the vessel with infrared. If they used that, they'd see my boat sitting there, even at night in the fog. We had to remain completely still, like we were fishing, until the last possible moment.

"Shouldn't you turn on your navigation lights?" asked Eden.

"Yeah," I said. "I guess it doesn't matter at this point. They've got infrared in front."

I flipped the lights on. I could make out Eden's face in the glow. She was a tough girl and I was lucky to have her aboard. Her dad, a stone-crabber with a boat similar to mine, had taught her well over many seasons of fishing. Eden Baker could handle a boat with the best of them. I was going to need that skill.

My life was about to depend on it.

Hammerhead pricked his ears. I kept my eye on him as he hopped up and walked over to a crab trap near the rail. Stepping on top of the wooden slates with his front paws, my dog peered off into the black fog and whined. Then I heard it, too.

The motor sounded far off, growling low, but definitely growing louder every second.

A shiver shook a bunch of goose bumps onto my back. Was I ready for this? I'd soon find out.

"Hear it?" I asked Eden. "Could be the Hatteras."

"I don't know...maybe," she said.

"I'd better climb up there just in case," I said.

I don't think she heard me. She looked out into the night, a million miles away.

"Eden? You with me?" I said, "Remember, when she's even with us. And, don't forget the wake."

Eden turned to face me, like she wanted to tell me something, her mouth half open. I waited. Her eyes got all misty, but she didn't say anything.

Instead, she blinked, before wiping one eye with the heel of her hand.

When she lifted her face again, her expression had changed.

"Harley," she said. "Be careful."

"Shhhhh," I said to her. "I'll be back."

She stood on her toes and kissed my cheek.

I scratched Hammerhead between the ears."

"Be good, boy," I told him.

He cocked his head, panting, tongue out.

I threw on a life jacket and climbed onto the hard roof over the wheelhouse. Eden started the engine below me. At first, the motor drowned out the rumble of the approaching sportfisherman. That didn't last long. Those diesels aren't shy. Soon enough, I heard them coming, loud and clear.

I flattened out on the roof so Skeebo and company wouldn't see my profile in the night camera, holding onto one of the small rails that ran along the edge of the roof. I pressed my head onto a coil of rope.

As hum of the big boat grew, Eden stood at the gunwale below with a fishing rod hanging over the side. She turned towards the sound of the chugging diesels just as the sportfisherman emerged from the fog. Salt's huge boat looked like a mountain shaking off a cloud.

It was the *Florida Blanca*. I would have recognized that Hatteras anywhere.

Salt's boat was a Hatteras 77C Sportfisherman. That meant it was a big boat, almost seventy-seven feet long and twenty-two feet wide. The 77C has three decks with a tower on top. It's powered by two huge diesel motors. Salt had bought the upgraded package, so the *Florida Blanca* was rigged with twin MTU diesels to push it even faster. The boat cruised at thirty-miles-per-hour or more, pretty good for a tub that big.

Big, plush, designed for comfort, a trip in the 77C was like taking a luxury hotel suite out to fish. The massive salon featured a wrap-around bar and cushy furniture. Out back, through the sliding glass doors, the big stern deck had a fighting chair capable of handling the largest marlin.

The captain could drive the 77C from one of three locations – up in the tower, inside the cockpit on the third deck, or from the outside on the third deck via a flip-down control panel on a small balcony overlooking the stern.

I hoped the driver would be inside at the helm and that everyone else would be asleep below.

Details began to stand out against her white paint job, dark, tinted windows, an outrigger folded up at her side, the tower high above.

I combed the darkness behind her for a Donzi.

No Salt. No nothing. I had to do this alone.

I got ready as she drove closer.

I waited.

I waited…

"Now!" I yelled.

Eden dropped the fishing pole and ran to the wheel. She gunned the motor full throttle, angling towards the sportfisherman. I couldn't tell if we were going to catch her or not.

"Faster!"

I held on.

After the rise and fall of the *Florida Blanca's* wake rocked our boat, I scrambled to my feet with the rope in my hand.

I slipped on the dewy roof and almost fell overboard, but steadied myself at the last second and put the shank of the big treble hook inside my fist. I used the hook to snag the buoy lines of my stone crab traps. I had decent aim most of the time.

That night, I had to be perfect.

Eden was awesome. She got us close, almost too close. Both decks on the rear of the Hatteras were empty. Nobody ran out screaming or waving guns. I took that as a good sign.

I heaved the big grappling hook at the boat, landing it cleanly on the aft deck. For a moment I thought one of the points would snag the base of the fighting chair, but at the last second it slipped around, flipped up, and hopped over the rail to fall harmlessly into the wake behind the boat.

Eden had seen what happened. She hammered the throttle again and my old crab boat lurched forward. I frantically coiled the rope, but the Hatteras was pulling away. I held the hook by the rope a few inches above the knot. I didn't even have time to aim. I just whipped it around a couple of times and sailed that sucker.

It landed on the deck again. That time it snagged something good. The rope started to go taut. I doubled it around my hand, took a deep breath, and jumped off the roof into the foaming water behind the Hatteras.

Before I had a chance to swim to the surface, the rope almost jerked my arm out of its socket. I fought my way to the top. When I got there, I heard a horrifying sound. The twin diesels aboard the Hatteras revved up as the guy aimed the boat at the open sea.

I could barely hang on – or breathe, for that matter. It was like trying to swim up Niagara falls.

I was about to let go when a weird thing happened. The increased speed forced me up on plane like a water-ski, well, like a ragdoll imitating a water-ski. My legs might as well have been made of cloth or rubber. They were useless. I gritted my teeth and put one hand over the other, climbing the rope to the back of the Hatteras. It was not pleasant, seriously. The prop wash stung all over. I breathed more water than air. And, my arms ached like I was being stretched in some sort of medieval torture machine.

I moved at a snail's pace, hand over hand, inching my way up the rope until the boat hit a wave and the rope came free. I lost forward momentum for a split-second before the hook snagged something else. A bone-jarring, tendon-tearing shock ripped through my arms. My hands lost their strength and I slipped down the rope a couple of feet.

That burned bad, dude.

Crazy thoughts ran through my brain as I hung there trying to compose myself. For one, I remembered that Tampa Bay was famous for having more species of sharks than anywhere else in the world. I imagined myself like this big hunk of tuna with an "Eat Me" sign taped to my back.

I got my mind right and started up the rope again. I guess adrenaline had something to do with that.

After an eternity, I could read "FLORIDA BLANCA" across the stern, upside down. I was flat on my back with the water shooting under me at mach 10. Exhaust pipes thundered out diesel fumes like twin rocket engines. My nose burned. My ears were about to explode.

The final few feet were the hardest.

Somehow, I had to flip over on my belly so I could crawl up the side, easier said than done. I tried to torque my body over a couple of times. It didn't work. Then I tried lifting one leg over the other and digging into the water with my toe. The wake grabbed my foot and flipped me over so fast I didn't have time to close my eyes. Water crashed against my eyeballs like a fire hose. I thought it had dragged my eyelids down to my ankles. God that stung!

The good news was that the maneuver had put me on my belly in a valley between the thrust of the two propellers. Like a crab in a hurricane, I inched towards the stern and hauled my torso out of the water up towards the rail.

The water wasn't done with me yet. The prop wash spun me around, a complete 360. I didn't lose ground, though. I pulled myself higher and tried planting a sneaker on the stern. Of course, my shoe, and the whole back of the boat for that matter, was completely wet and extremely slick. My foot slid back down into the wake. I curled my toes to keep the sneaker from getting ripped off and begged my arms to pull me even higher before trying again.

On the second try, I got some leverage and, all in one motion, heaved myself over the rail onto the deck.

Ship of Fools

I must've looked like a fish fresh out of the water. All I could do was flop onto my back and suck air. I was soaked to the gills, but never so happy to be aboard a boat in all my life.

I didn't move a muscle until the pain died down and I got a little strength back.

When I could manage, I rolled my head over to check out the deck. The only other item besides the fighting chair was one large, wooden barrel which I knew was filled with treasure. A single gold rope hung over the edge to remind me.

Laying down, watching treasure flap in the breeze was nice and all, but I had to hide, and quick. I fished the grappling hook out of the rail and tossed it, with the rope, into the Gulf of Mexico. I unfastened my life vest and flung it out behind the boat. On the far side of the fighting chair, the sliding glass door closed off the salon. I needed to get through that and inside before somebody spotted me.

I went to the door. Through the tinted glass, I could make out an old episode of *The Munsters* airing on a flatscreen TV but the glass was too dark to see who was watching. With a little pressure, the door easily slid open an inch or two. One of Skeebo's cronies sat in a chair in front of the TV. The sound on the TV was off. The guy had ear buds stuffed into his skull. He couldn't hear anything except the death metal that blasted from the mp3 player he held at the end of a white cord. The stuff was cranked so loud, I heard it, too.

I opened the door wider and looked right. The long wraparound couch was empty. So was the rest of the room.

So, I made my move.

In one fluid motion, I slid the door just wide enough to get through, and then closed it fast. I froze. The guy remained glued to the set. Immediately to my left, a set of stairs came down from the cockpit. Suddenly, a door opened at the top of the stairway and somebody started down.

I had one place to hide - a storage compartment under the stairs. I swung open the small door, crouched down and dove in. The footsteps continued down the stairs above me. I listened and waited. The steps stopped at the bottom.

The compartment was black as midnight. I waved my hand around and found the walls and a few cardboard boxes big enough to crawl into. I remembered they were full, though. I had helped Salt load the supplies onto the boat the day before.

I sat still, not wanting to make the slightest noise. As my eyes adjusted to the darkness, I noticed a ribbon of light outlining the door. A form moved across the crack and the light dimmed. The slider to the outside deck scraped as someone pushed it open. Motor noise and sounds of rushing water flooded in from outside. The door slid shut again a few moments later, sealing off the clatter. The shadow fell across the crack of light once more, and stayed there.

My heart beat in my ears.

The shadow moved again and I distinctly heard a hand slap someone across the head.

"*Dude!*" a man's voice cried out. "What'd you do that for, man?"

"The next time you go out to eyeball my loot, Boudreaux, *wipe off your feet before you come back in!*"

I could tell right away – that second voice was Skeebo Lafitte.

"I didn't even go outside, man" the other guy said.

"The carpet's soaked next to the door," said Skeebo. "Who did that? The tooth fairy?"

"Dude, I -"

"Just shut up," Skeebo said. "You're starting to give me a headache. Don't let it happen again."

"Where are we?"

"Just left Tampa Bay," Skeebo told him.

My body leaned into the boxes next to me, like the boat had just rolled with a big wave.

"Jeez. You feel that? What's going on out there?"

"Just the sea," Skeebo laughed. "Don't worry, *mon petit chu*, this old tub can take it. What's the girl doing?"

"Not crying anymore. I fixed that."

"How would you know? You couldn't hear an elephant stampede with those things in your ears!" said Skeebo. "What am I paying you for? Maybe you want to swim back to the bayou!"

"Okay, okay," the man said. "Jeez. Calm down. I'll leave them out."

Things quieted down and I couldn't hear a sound except the hum of the motors and the splash of sea, both of which seemed far away. I stayed put in my hidey hole biding my time.

My thought was that Salt would make his move at some point. I planned to surprise these goons from the inside when he did. With any luck, Eden had gotten through to Salt on my phone and told him I was aboard the *Florida Blanca*. I told her to trail the sportfisherman just out of sight until she spotted my life jacket floating in the wake. After that, she was supposed to call Salt and go home. I figured the Hatteras would out run her if even she tried to follow.

I knew I had just jumped into the frying pan, but I felt better knowing Eden and Hammerhead were safe. That had been the smart part of my plan. I wasn't so sure about the rest.

I tried putting an ear to the door. That didn't work. The motors vibrated the wood too much. I had no way of knowing what the Cajuns were doing on the other side of the door. I really wanted to get to Isabella and let her know help was coming. Was it worth the risk of easing the door open? I decided against it. I continued to sit there like a mushroom in the dark.

My sense of time got distorted in the storage hold. The next time I checked my watch, it was almost 2 a.m. A minute later, the engines died. The rhythm of the bow's collision with the waves changed as the boat lost forward momentum. I felt her slow. The motors turned over a few times, but they didn't re-start.

"Boss, we got a problem," said a voice over the intercom.

Then I heard the guy who had been watching TV say, "Boss. Boss! Get up! We got engine problems!"

"Wha-? Huh?" said Skeebo as if he just woke up.

"The motors," the guy said. "They just stopped."

Two sets of feet stomped up the stairs over my head. I waited for a few seconds, then cautiously cracked the door. The room was empty. Time to go. I rolled out of the hole and sprinted to the stairs that led down to the lower deck staterooms.

The 77C has four staterooms, plus crew quarters. When I landed at the bottom of the stairs, all the doors in the short hall were closed. Isabella could have been behind any of them. I guessed that the cross-eyed maniac upstairs probably wanted the big master suite for himself so I skipped the door to my left for the moment. I tried the knob to the first door on my right. It opened into a cabin with a double bed. A man sleeping on that bed grunted and rolled around under the covers. I held my breath and eased the door shut.

The next cabin door waited on the left side of the hall further towards the bow. I hesitated, not knowing exactly how many men Skeebo had brought with him. After I finally worked up the nerve, I opened the door just enough to see inside. The room was dark, like the first. I pushed the door wider. Light from the hall spilled in on two twin beds. They had not been touched. The cabin was empty.

Before I could pull the door shut, the sleeping man's cabin opened. Instinctively, I darted into the empty cabin and closed the door.

I kept my grip on the door knob with both hands, leaning my shoulder into the door just in case the creep had seen me. He hadn't. His footsteps took him back up the stairs to the salon.

As soon as I couldn't hear him anymore, I swung the door open and crossed over to the bow cabin. The door was unlocked. Isabella laid spread-eagle on a double bed with her hands and feet tied to the corners and her mouth gagged. I clearly saw the whites of her eyes as she spotted me.

"Isabella. It's me, Harley."

At first, I don't think she believed me, but then the wrinkles in her brow relaxed. She recognized me. I untied the bandana they had knotted behind her head. She spit out another handkerchief balled up in her mouth.

"We've got to be real quiet," I whispered to her as I worked to untie her. "The guys are dealing with engine problems for the moment."

"Harley," she said. "They will kill you!"

"They've got to catch me first," I said, trying to say something brave.

"Where are we?" she asked.

"Gulf of Mexico. Salt's on his way in another boat. We've got to find a way to get to him when he shows up."

I jumped over to the cabin door and locked it.

Free of the ropes, Isabella hugged herself, rocking back and forth kneeling on the bed. I don't think they had hit her or anything. Her clothes weren't ripped. I didn't see any cuts or bruises. Still, she looked pretty traumatized. I knelt down and wrapped my arms around her. The girl was shaking like a leaf.

"Listen, Isabella," I whispered. "We're going to get out of here. I need you to understand that. Okay? There's always a way and we're going to find it."

"But, we're trapped in here, Harley," she whimpered. "And, they...they have guns! I know this man. I have seen what he can do. Our lives mean nothing to him."

"Forget that. Okay? Forget that." I lifted her chin. "Isabella. Think about how we're going to get away. Okay?"

She closed her eyes and nodded. Tears slipped around her nose. She wiped them on her shirt and sniffled. She barely had the courage to look me in the eye.

"Okay," I said. "Now, look over your head."

She looked up and saw the hatch.

"When the time is right, we're going through that. It leads to the bow."

"They'll see us!"

"When the time is right," I repeated.

Even scared and miserable, Isabella looked like a super model. I found myself staring at her again.

"Harley," she said, "you've got to promise me something."

I listened.

"If I get sent back, back to Cuba, promise you will go to my parents and tell them how much I love them. Okay?"

"I'm telling you, we're getting out of here," I said.

"Tell them that some way, somehow, I'll come back to them. Do that for me, Harley. Promise."

Her dark eyes pleaded with me. She hurt, but not for herself, for her parents, for what they would go through.

Her hands gripped my arms like two vices, squeezing her desperation into me.

"Promise me!"

"I promise," I said.

Heavy boots thumped down the stairs to our deck. I scanned the cabin for a weapon. The doorknob clicked twice, then rattled back and forth. A fist banged on the wood.

"Open up!" one of Skeebo's guys said outside.

"Time to go!" I said to Isabella.

She nodded. I stood on the bed and unscrewed the hatch. Something crashed against the door.

The paper-thin plywood bulged in.

Unfastening the hatch took forever. At last, the thing popped open. Wind and sea noise howled into the cabin. I threaded my fingers forming a step for Isabella. On a bare foot, she stood in my hands and I boosted her up.

The man smashed against the door again. I pulled myself up as he came flying into the room.

We had no way to secure the hatch from the outside so we ran, aft, towards the black rise of the superstructure. I don't know if the guy in the fly bridge saw us or not. I really didn't have time to think about it. We just flattened our backs against the sloping wall.

I knew the dude in the cabin was going to pop his head out of the hatch any second. We had to keep moving. Hugging the smooth fiberglass with our backs, we felt our way around one side along a narrow ledge towards the stern.

Sure enough, as we rounded the corner, the guy popped up in the hatch and spotted us. He sounded plenty mad, too. I won't repeat what he said.

Salt's Hatteras rolled sideways with the waves like a slippery seesaw. The ledge seemed way too narrow. One bad move and I'd be swimming again.

Hatch man disappeared below, probably on his way to the back of the boat or to call somebody on the intercom to surprise us there.

Halfway down the ledge, we stopped.

The bow was no good. The guy could pop up again at any moment. The stern deck would soon be a death-trap, too, if it wasn't already.

Where was Salt?!

In all directions, the sea remained dark, empty, no help in sight.

I had a thought.

Between our position on the ledge and the stern, an aluminum pole went straight up – one of the outriggers. When you're fishing, the captain puts them out like airplane wings. When you're not, he stows them up. I wasn't sure they would support our weight or not, but I didn't really waste time doing the math. I just pulled Isabella down the ledge to the pole.

"We got to go up!" I said to her. "Keep going all the way to the tower."

I didn't have to say it twice. Up she went, like a trapeze artist, reaching the small deck behind the fly bridge in no time. She kept going. Good girl. I followed. On the fly bridge roof we let go of the outrigger pole and grabbed the ladder that led to the tower.

Skeebo charged out of the salon level two decks down with his pistol raised. He didn't think to look up, though. He walked over to the ledge and aimed his gun around the corner hoping to catch us there.

The motors started running again. The boat lurched forward and came around, accelerating directly into the surf. About that time, Skeebo figured out we weren't on the ledge anymore. The cross-eyed clown looked up and spotted us immediately; probably even saw four of us. He yelled something foul and ducked back into the salon.

I had another thought. The tower had a set of controls. If Salt couldn't get to the Hatteras, I'd take the Hatteras to Salt.

"It's only a matter of seconds before he comes out onto that deck below us," I told Isabella. "Hold on! I'm going to whip this sucker around."

The tower's controls would override the helm. I turned around and twisted the steering wheel hard to port without trimming back the throttle. The Hatteras changed course in a hurry, rolling to the left as she went. I let the compass spin until it pointed due west, then straightened her out.

The water that way was just as empty as the water the other way. No Donzi. No Salt. No rescue.

Skeebo popped out directly below us on the fly bridge deck.

"I don't know what pigeon pooped you out of the sky, boy, but you better get your grubby, little paws off them controls right now!" he shouted, that big pistol aimed right at my head.

I squinted into the dark once more. Nothing.

Below me, Skeebo had closed one eye. The other sighted me down the gun barrel.

"You got the treasure," I yelled at him. "Take us back."

"You want to go back?" he said. "Come on down. I'll take you back."

The Gulf of Mexico was a long ways down. From that height, the water didn't look very inviting either. Jumping was out of the question.

Where was Salt?!

"Now, son!" he screamed.

His gun exploded -BOOOOOM!- ear shattering, like the air split in two. I checked for blood. Everything was intact. Isabella was okay, too.

"*Move it!*" he bellowed. "Or the next one don't miss!"

I learned something right then. Bullets speak a lot louder than words.

My hands jumped off the wheel and we climbed down to the fly bridge deck. A man grabbed Isabella from behind. Skeebo stuck that big gun into my chest. I smelled gunpowder.

"Well, well," Skeebo said snickering. "Old Joe don't have the guts to come see me hisself, huh? Hired a helicopter to drop you out here? He always did run scared." He whipped around, waving the gun into the darkness. "Where are you, Gaspar?!" he yelled. "I know you're out there hiding. I can smell you." He fired the pistol two or three times into the dark.

Before I could run, Skeebo grabbed me by the hair and pulled me inside the cockpit after him.

"Give him a show! That's what we'll do," he said. "He's out there watching, well, we give ol' Boudreaux a show!"

The fellow at the helm sneered at us from the captain's chair as he turned the boat around. Lafitte dragged me down the stairs into the salon and out the back sliding door. I lost track of Isabella.

"Get up on that rail, boy, or I'll blow a hole in you the size of Texas," Skeebo said.

The railing on the back of the boat was slippery and bouncing around pretty good. I didn't have a clue what he was going to do, but I didn't have much choice, either. I climbed up on the rail. Skeebo wrapped an arm around my legs, holding me in place like a set of pliers.

Adrenaline shot through my veins. I got wobbly, light headed. I thought I might pass out.

"How do you like me now, Gaspar!" he screamed into the wind before firing two more rounds over the Gulf. Then to me, the lunatic said, "Sorry. We ain't got no plank to walk, son. But you *can* go back to Tampa now. Do you still want to? Huh? Do you? Well, SWIM BACK!"

He let go of my legs.

For a moment or two, I stayed upright, spinning my arms like a pinwheel while Skeebo laughed.

That didn't last, though.

The boat rocked. My shoes slipped. And, I cart wheeled backwards into the pitch-black Gulf of Mexico.

Fins

I will tell you something I learned about Jean Lafitte because it relates to the predicament I suddenly faced as I fought for my life in the Gulf that night.

In May of 1822, an American brigantine sailed out of Baltimore bound for New Orleans. Her name was the *Aurilla*, a two-masted vessel that carried passengers and cargo. On May 16, as she rounded the tip of Florida in a stretch of water known as the Florida Straits, she was attacked by two schooners commanded by Jean Lafitte.

By this time, Lafitte had been run out of America. He'd been holed up in a cove on the island of Cuba preying on shipping in the Gulf of Mexico and the Caribbean Sea. Apparently, he had also run out of manners. While around New Orleans and Texas, the pirate had gained a reputation as a polite gentleman, even among his victims. Something had changed, though, because what happened aboard the *Aurilla* was not the act of a gentleman. It was downright vicious.

A surviving passenger named Tom Sunderland gave the following account.

Sunderland said the pirates attacked just after dawn on that day in May. They must have been scoping out the ships the night before. One schooner sailed in from the east, the other from the west, trapping the *Aurilla* in the middle. The *Aurilla's* captain surrendered immediately understanding that pirates who frequented those waters usually took some cargo and then hastily sailed away leaving the passengers, crew, and ship unharmed. Having this reputation also benefitted the pirates since it lessened the need for fighting and firing cannons.

Well, the pirates lashed their ships to either side of the brigantine and came aboard. They ordered the crew and passengers to their cabins, keeping the captain at the helm. Sunderland listened in shock as the buccaneers took turns beating the daylights out of the captain one deck above. The poor captain finally gave the pirates the location of the ship's cash and Sunderland thought that would be the end of it.

However, his ordeal was far from over.

After they located the loot, the buccaneers called everyone out onto the deck. They separated the men from the women. They sent the women back to their cabins. They forced the guys to haul the *Aurilla's* cargo over to the two pirate schooners. When they had finished carrying the bags of flour, bundles of cloth, crates of tea pots and all the other merchandise to the pirate ships, the outlaws threw the men in the hold and locked the doors.

The male passengers and crew began to hear women scream in other parts of the ship. Sunderland said they went crazy down in the hold, yelling, banging on the walls, trying to get out and rescue the girls. Eventually, Lafitte hauled one guy out and made an example out of him to quiet the rest. That guy was Sunderland.

The pirates grabbed Sunderland and forced him around one of the masts while they tied his hands together. A big, burly guy brought out the cat-o-nine-tails, a nasty whip with nine separate whips at the end. The dude ripped Sunderland's shirt off his back and whipped the fire out of him with that thing. All the other pirates laughed at Sunderland as nasty welts rose on his back. They placed bets with each other on how many lashes he could take before he passed out. The welts popped and started bleeding as the beating continued.

After a while, he did pass out. He came to on the deck when the pirates threw a bucket of sea water on his face. While the beaten man lay flat on his back, Jean Lafitte grabbed Sunderland's arms and another pirate grabbed his feet. They swung him in the air to the count of "one...two...three!" At three, they threw him over the rail into the sea like a sack of potatoes.

He said the water stung so bad he thought his back was on fire. He tried to scream but ended up choking on a bunch of sea water. By the time his lungs cleared he found himself near one of the pirate schooners. He swam to a rope hanging over its side. The buccaneers let him climb all the way up the rope and, when he finally reached the top, kicked him in the face. He splashed into the Gulf again.

Sunderland struggled to stay afloat. He didn't dare to swim back to the *Aurilla* with the pirates still there. Unfortunately for Sunderland, the current carried him out to sea. When the pirates departed hours later he was too far away to try and swim back, and way too small a speck in the water for anyone on the *Aurilla* to spot him.

By sunset, Sunderland was exhausted. He thought he would surely die that night, either by sharks catching the scent of his bleeding back or by drowning. All he could do was lie still and float face up under the stars.

Sea water is a lot more buoyant than fresh water, especially in the salty Gulf of Mexico. Sunderland floated through the night without another scratch.

The next day he drifted along on his back, occasionally treading water to look for any ships that might be passing through the shipping lane around the Florida Keys. Later that day, a shark did get him, but not the swimming kind. A schooner named *The Shark* fished him out of the sea and sailed on to find the *Aurilla* after they heard his tale.

As Salt had tried to tell me, the apple doesn't fall far from the tree. Skeebo's core was just as rotten as his pirate ancestors. I had just learned that fact the hard way.

I tried to remain calm, thinking Salt had to be nearby. I even thought Skeebo might turn the Hatteras around and pull me out. He didn't. Each time a swell pushed me up high enough to catch a glimpse of the *Florida Blanca*, she had moved farther away. Before long, I lost sight of her altogether.

And, no Salt!

I tried yelling every now and then, but I ended up feeling lonely and stupid each time no one answered. Things got bleak. To tell you the truth, after about thirty minutes, I began to lose confidence. The water felt really cold. My arms and legs hurt. I kicked off my shoes. It helped a little, but not much.

Then, I remembered a trick my friend's brother had told me about one time. He was a navy SEAL and said they were trained in something called "drown proofing." What you had to do was roll up in a ball and quit fighting the water. That brought your heart rate and breathing down so you didn't need much air. You'd work your way to the surface with minimal movements and snatch a breath like a manatee, then float, just let the sea take you. He said you'd pretty much stay near the surface. Navy SEALs survived that way for hours as part of their training.

And, they did it with their arms tied.

So, I grabbed a breath and rolled into a ball. Of course, I couldn't keep an eye out for Salt anymore, but what else was I supposed to do? I'd just give out of steam and drown if I kept flailing around like I had been.

I became part of the sea, rolling along inside the swells as they marched to the coast. I figured I was about twenty or thirty miles off shore. I imagined the waves pushing me back to Florida. I thought calm thoughts and, when I ran out of air, I paddled my hands like little flippers, moving my body into position at the surface for another breath. As my heart slowed and my muscles relaxed, I needed to do this less and less. Eventually, I fell into a rhythm.

The waves had their own rhythm. They came in sets, three big ones, then a bunch of choppy stuff, then three more big ones.

I was a tumble weed, a sea tumble weed, rising to the top where the wave crest collected me, carried me, spun me over before leaving me for the next. I slid down into watery valleys and rolled around until hitching another ride to the peak.

My eyes closed tight, I imagined that I floated at the edge of two worlds. Each realm had its own noises. Above was air, whistling wind, whitecaps curling over, ripping, like giant sheets of paper, hissing foam. Below was the water, the underworld, bubbling, churning and growling. It was cold, hungry, a rumbling belly that swallowed everything.

I lost track of time. I had a waterproof watch. I just couldn't seem to bring myself to turn on the light and look at it. I lost my sense of direction at times. I felt my mind slipping.

I tried to focus on positive thoughts.

I remembered a day at the beach with Eden last September on Upper Captiva. It was still summer, and hot. We sat on the sand just high enough so that the surf reached our toes. My boat was anchored outside the breakers. Hammerhead ran along the water's edge scaring up sandpipers. We had the place to ourselves.

"A dolphin!" Eden said.

I squinted through the sun towards the horizon. A pod of six dolphins broke the surface maybe thirty yards past the boat. They reminded me of whales, shooting up at the sky and splashing down on their backs, just playing, having fun. It was sweet.

"Come on!" Eden said as she took off down the sand and dove in.

I was up and running before her bikini got wet. I couldn't let her beat me.

We swam until the sandbar brushed our knees and we could stand. The dolphins were so close, a few yards away at the far side of the sandbar. One of them stopped chasing the others. The water was clear enough to see the animal turn and come our way. It stopped and slowly lifted its head out of the water to give us a full on peek-a-boo with both eyes. The animal was actually checking us out!

As Hammerhead splashed up on the bar, the dolphin got nervous and dropped below the surface.

"Harley, I'm going out there."

"Eden!"

"What?"

"Be careful. They can get aggressive."

"How can something with a permanent smile be mean?" she laughed.

She slowly waded off the sandbar and began to tread water. Worried, Hammerhead whined and cocked his head.

"It's okay, boy," I said rubbing his wet fur. "I think she's related to them."

A dolphin launched itself at the sky again, only a few feet from Eden. At that distance I understood just how huge those suckers are. It turned in slow motion, slick, smooth, and shiny, hanging weightless for a moment, before crashing into the water like an Orca in Alaska.

"Eden!"

"Relax. I'm okay. This is cool, Harley."

A dark blur shot around Eden in a tight circle. I held my breath. It sped off out of sight, returning in an instant, slower. Then, the most amazing thing happened. The creature coasted to a stop directly in front of her. Eden calmly lifted an arm out to the dolphin and slid her fingertips along the entire length of the animal's body.

Hammerhead barked, but this time the dolphin didn't mind. It nodded its head up and down like it wanted Eden to pet it again. She looked at me over her shoulder with this can-you-believe-this-is-happening grin plastered all over her face. She petted the dolphin a second time with her full palm.

The dolphin drifted forward allowing Eden's hand to trail over its tail flukes. It lifted its head, turning back to watch her with one eye before sliding below the surface, slowly circling her again. Eden treaded water with her arms out by her sides. The dolphin swam under her right arm and stopped. Do you know what Eden Baker did? My crazy girlfriend wrapped that arm around the dolphin. I felt my jaw go slack.

I watched in amazement as the dolphin moved off. Eden's other hand gripped the dorsal fin and, with two hands now, she held on for a ride. The dolphin didn't go fast, just slow and steady. It took her to its pod. The others didn't mind. They kept on jumping and playing in the Gulf as if they hung out with humans every day.

Eden was laughing. Another dolphin jumped over her in a perfect arc against the afternoon sun.

"See, buddy," I remember telling Hammerhead. "She's in her natural element."

The warm memory popped like a birthday balloon when my elbow bumped into something. Spooked, I instantly un-balled and clawed to the surface.

Something floated beside me. I felt it, hard like wood, long, like a log. I latched onto that thing for dear life.

It could have been a palm tree, I guess. I didn't care. It floated and that's all that mattered. I slung a leg over it, riding it like a bare back horse. That didn't work. It slowly rolled me back into the water, so I held on, squeezing the wood under my armpits.

It wasn't a boat, but it was better than nothing. At least I could breathe normally again, except when a wave washed over top. The forecast had called for winds out of the northwest. That meant the waves were headed southeast. That was a good thing. If managed to hang on, I'd be pushed back to Florida.

I checked my watch. 3:57 a.m. I'd been drifting for hours. The sky shined with stars. From behind a bank of clouds, the moon slipped out to join them.

That's when I saw the first fin slicing through the water.

It cruised by about ten feet from my face and angled off out of sight. Another replaced it heading in the other direction. Single fins. They glistened with moonlight as they chased around the log. Another and another.

I was too beat to worry about it. I held on and watched. Let them eat me. I didn't care.

The sea was full of them, so close that I heard them cut the water. Single fins, but no tails. For some reason, my mind became slightly optimistic. Then it dawned on me. *Of course!* Sharks have vertical tails so you see *two* fins when they swim on top of the water. These weren't sharks. These were dolphins! I heard the first blowhole just as I figured it out.

One of them brushed my feet, gently, as if to say "hello." I hung onto the log and waited. The fins slowed down, coming closer. I sensed something to my left. When I turned, I found myself staring into two intelligent eyes five feet away.

Another set of big waves rolled in, doing their best to separate me from my log. I put a death grip on it, fighting to hang on, rising and falling, the world of water, the world of air. It went on like that for several exhausting minutes.

In a way, it seemed like a dream. I've heard it's possible to dream while you're awake. You just have to be tired enough. I was one tired tumbleweed.

After the set of breakers passed, the dolphins returned. One swam up next to my back. I felt him just sort of floating against me, hanging out, warm and friendly. Dream or not, I felt a strong urge to forget the log, let it go, and grab the dolphin.

I guess that's just what I did. I don't remember releasing the log. I just found myself on top of the dolphin.

The dolphin moved off with me on his back, swimming with the waves. He gained some speed, enough to catch the last wave in the set. At the crest, he matched the water's speed. The other dolphins did the same, on both sides of us, breaching and diving. Phosphorescent sea life streaked past, lighting up the night like tiny lasers.

Maybe I was dreaming. Maybe I was dead. Or maybe I was actually getting rescued by a bunch of dolphins! In any case, I certainly didn't feel alone anymore. Of all the ways I thought I'd make it out of that mess, I hadn't seen that one coming.

Those dolphins swam with me like it was the most natural thing in the world. And, from what I could tell, they enjoyed it, too. They all wore permanent smiles. I was smiling, as well.

No, I was laughing.

I laughed until I cried.

Skyscraper in the Sea

The dolphin kept my head just above the water line as we rode the wave tops back to Florida. From that vantage point, I figured I'd see lights along the coast eventually. The other dolphins stayed close, clicking and whistling to each other, jumping and diving along the wave's crest.

Maybe dolphins travelled that way all the time. Who knew? But, it made sense. They let the wave do most of the work. Basically, they were surfing. Surfers are the coolest.

A shooting star streaked over the horizon. I spotted it out of the corner of my eye. Funny how you always look at the spot where a meteorite just flashed, like the thing's going to rewind and zip across the same piece of sky again. Well, as I stared into that same dark corner of sky, to my complete amazement, the thing *did* shoot by again. Then again, and *again*!

Between the dolphins and multiple meteorites, things weren't making a whole lot of sense. I wondered for the second time if I was dreaming.

As if one of them had given a command, the dolphins turned in unison toward the shooting stars. They swam faster, outpacing the wave and we picked up even more speed by falling down its face. On the crest of the next roller I strained to see the meteor shower again, but the sky was dark.

That didn't stop the dolphins.   They swam full tilt, chattering away like crazy. I had to hold on tight. They cut across the waves at an angle, up the peaks, down the valleys, in the water, out of the water. I caught a breath, held it, spit it out and grabbed another like I was one of them. It gave me an appreciation for rodeo riders, only I had to ride this bronco underwater. Dude, it was sick.

We were sandwiched between the next two waves, down near the bottom, when another beam of light streaked by, slicing through the green top of the next wave. It kind of looked like a laser.

I heard my name, as if someone was calling from far away.

I had always heard that when you die, you go to the light. And, when you get there, somebody you knew, somebody who had died before you, called your name. The dolphins, or maybe they were angels, were definitely taking me to the light. Maybe one of my dead relatives, was about to welcome me to the Pearly Gates.

We cruised up the backside of the next breaker and, at the top of that wave, I did see Heaven – in the form of a Donzi 38ZX.

A man stood in the cockpit waving a searchlight. Salt!

With me still on his back, the dolphin shot into the air and splashed down like a boulder. The impact knocked me off.

And, as mysteriously as they had arrived, the dolphins dropped out of sight without even giving me a chance to thank them.

Salt spun around and spotted me treading water.

"Mother of pearl!" I heard him shout as a wave washed over.

Hands tugged at my shoulders and Salt hauled me into the boat. I collapsed in a soggy heap on the deck.

"I was beginning to get worried, kid," he said, as I lay there on my back. "Let me get you something to wrap up in."

He went away and came back with some big, fat beach towels. As I sat up, I realized I was shaking all over. I couldn't stop.

"Hypothermia," he said.

"D-d-dolphins, S-salt, dolphins" I mumbled.

"Slow down, kid," he said. "Wrap up in these." He put a towel around me. "Drink some of this."

He handed me a bottle of lemon/lime sports drink. It never tasted so good.

"I ran into your girly friend back there. She told me the stunt you pulled. Either you're the gutsiest kid I ever knew, or the dumbest. I still don't know which." He sounded a little angry.

I buried my head in the towel so I wouldn't have to face him. Sometimes Salt seemed more like my dad than my real dad.

"Anyway," he continued, "when I didn't find your butt floating in the pass, I figured you'd made it. We found your jacket. Eden said that was the sign. That girl of yours begged me to let her *and* your dog into my boat. But, I got nowhere close to her. Didn't want *her* jumping overboard, too."

I had to smile to myself in the towel.

"So, I took off after the Hatteras. The tracking device lit her up and I followed. When I got a visual, I cut her motors. Check this out."

I dropped the towel from my face. He held up a small remote control device of some sort.

"Another little failsafe I thought might come in handy one day. Figured turning off them diesels would stir things up and give you some sort of chance."

"I was waiting for you, Salt. I had Isabella."

"And, I almost pulled up there. Saw the whole thing with those."

He pointed to a pair of night-vision binoculars on the seat, the ones I had been looking for on my boat.

"Saw Skeebo's pistol again, too. Had to hang back out of sight. Dern fool almost took my head off before he threw you into the drink."

Salt turned his head and I saw blood crusted all over his ear.

"Salt! You're hurt," I said.

"Aw, the bleedings already stopped. Just an ear. But, it did back me off a little more. After ol' Skeebo tossed you in, I had to wait 'til they pulled off. Lost track of you. Then, I lost them, too. They must've ripped out that GPS system."

Salt had been chattering away like a mocking bird. I think he was nervous or something. Finally, he quieted down and leaned in close to my face.

"You okay, kid?" he said in that gravelly voice of his.

I wanted to tell him about the dolphins. I barely had the strength.

"The most incredible thing happened, Salt," I began.

He was looked at me, waiting for more. That's as far as I got. I was wiped out.

"World's full of mysteries, eh?" he said, with his eyes crinkling at the corners.

Salt had that twinkle in his eye, like he knew something I didn't.

I was fading, though, no energy to try and figure it out. My thoughts started to swirl.

"Well," he said after a moment or two, "we best get going."

"Where...we...going?"

"Why, after them, of course."

He put me below. I didn't argue. I just fell onto one of the bunks and passed out under a pile of beach towels.

The next morning I didn't just wake up, I jolted up, you know, heart beating fast, like after a nightmare. At first, it did seem like everything was part some kind of crazy dream. Then, I saw the Donzi cabin around me, not the walls of my room. The hatch above my head was bright with daylight. I laid back down for a second. The boat was still rocking, though not nearly as much, no motor noise either. It felt like we were sitting dead in the water.

I rose to a sitting position, putting my feet on the deck. My shorts and t-shirt had dried out pretty much. My body ached all over, like someone had beaten me with a 2 x 4. Hunched over, sore, I shuffled to the cabin door and opened it.

"Salt?"

Donzi's have a pretty small cockpit. It didn't take long to notice that Salt wasn't there.

I squinted into the daylight as I stepped up, my hand shielding my eyes like a visor.

"Salt?"

Nobody answered. I turned to check the bow. Instead of seeing Salt, I saw a seriously large structure rising straight out of the sea, a metal tower supporting a bunch of buildings and pipes way up in the sky. I heard machinery and people shouting. I looked around. The Gulf stretched to the horizon in every direction, no land in sight. I guessed we had docked at an oil platform.

"Hey, kid!" a man hollered.

I looked up. A guy in a hardhat one level up waved at me.

"Climb the ladder!" he called.

I ducked back inside the Donzi's cabin, crawled across the bunk to the forward hatch and popped it open. After climbing out onto the deck, I grabbed the line and pulled the boat over to the floating dock, hopping off as I got close enough. A set of metal stairs took me to a platform where the steel ladder followed a column straight up.

Dude, that ladder was long. My bare feet ached even more by the time I made it up to that guy.

"Welcome aboard, son," he said. "Follow me."

"Is Salt…uh, Joe Gaspar up here?" I asked.

"That old geezer?" he laughed. "Yeah. He's waiting on you."

The man led me through a maze of hallways, across scaffolds, around pipes, and in and out of several doors before we finally came to some kind of dining room. It smelled awesome! Salt sat at a table on the far side with a red-headed lady, drinking coffee. Salt's ear, the one ripped by Skeebo's bullet, was covered with a white bandage.

"Rise and shine, morning glory," Salt called out from behind his cup.

I joined them at the table. The guy in the hardhat waved goodbye and walked out.

"Sit down, Harley," Salt said. "I want you to meet somebody."

"We're on an oilrig, right?" I asked them.

"Not just any rig, son," said the lady.

"Harley Cooper, meet Red Charles, O.I.M. of the Petronius Platform."

I shook Red's hand, nodding to her. "O.I.M.?" I asked. "What's that?"

"Offshore Installation Manager," said Red.

"Head honcho, big cheese," said Salt. "This here's the boss of the world's tallest structure."

"For the moment," Red said. "Those folks in Dubai are working on a *new* skyscraper that's going to take away our crown." She sipped her coffee.

"That's cool," I said. "But, I don't get it. You live in New York, or someplace, but you work here, too?"

They looked at each other and Red laughed.

"No, sonny boy," Salt said. "This here oil platform *is* the world's tallest man-made structure."

"Whoa!" I said. "I *knew* that ladder was seriously long!"

"Oh, the top of this shed's only about two-hundred fifty feet above the Gulf," Red said. "The business end goes down another seventeen hundred feet below the surface."

Red pulled her hair back and put a rubber band around it. The stuff was long, thick and wavy, and so bright her head looked like it was on fire. She caught me watching her and smiled. I got embarrassed. I could feel my face turning the same color as her hair.

"He's so cute," she said to Salt.

"Careful, darlin'," he said. "He's got a girly friend back home."

This idle chit-chat was killing me. I needed to talk to Salt about Isabella, the Lafitte's, the treasure that was getting away. Sharing laughs over a cup of coffee was the very last thing we needed to be doing, but I didn't know how much Salt had told Red, or how much we could trust her.

"Uh, Salt," I said. "Why are we here?"

"Ran out of gas," Salt said.

"Son," said Red, "could I get you some grub?"

A few minutes later I had a tasty plate of eggs, bacon and toast in front of me. When I smelled that food, I forgot all about talking to Salt. I gobbled down another full plate after the first one was empty.

"Joe," the red-haired lady said, "I'm going to check on the pilot."

Salt nodded as Red stood to leave.

"Bet I can find you some shoes while I'm at it, cutey," she said to me. "What size are you?"

"Eleven," I said. "Thanks."

"Big feet for a young pup. You're going to be a tall one."

She left us alone in the dining room.

"Salt, we've got to get going, man!"

"Simmer down," he said. "First, we got to know which way we *are* going. Red's graciously offered to have one of their helicopter pilots look around for the *Blanca* while he's ferrying some roustabouts to shore. We're waiting to hear back.

Why don't you use this little lull to make a phone call. I bet there's somebody back in Palmetto Cove who's wondering where you are right about now."

Mom! I had forgotten all about her. I was supposed to call her every two hours! She'd be calling the Coast Guard any minute. And, Eden! Man, she was going to kill me, too.

"Aw, man! You're right! They have phones out here?" I asked him.

"Sure. The whole place is covered by the cell tower on top." He passed his phone to me.

Mom answered on the first ring. I convinced her I was okay. She told me that Eden had dropped my boat off just after daybreak. Hammerhead was home keeping her company, although he was spending most of his time out on the seawall waiting for me to come back.

Next, I called Eden.

"You dried out yet, cowboy?" she answered on the other end.

"You wouldn't believe me if I told you, Eden."

"Just try me, then," she said.

"Ended up hitching a ride with Salt."

"Salt?! How? Harley, I want to be there with you guys. That was a pretty sneaky way to leave me behind!"

"Eden, it's way too risky. We're still after those guys. And...they still have Isabella. I don't know what's going to happen. Besides, your mom would never let you go."

"Bock, bock!" she said like a chicken.

"Seriously," I said.

"Where are you, Harley?" she said. "I'm coming."

"Eden. Look, forget about it. This is the last thing you need to get mixed up in. Just stay there, be cool, and I'll be back in a couple of days. Christmas is coming. Don't you have some shopping to do?"

"Yeah, I've got to go buy some coal," she said. "Harley Cooper's on my naughty list."

Red walked back into the galley waving a pair of boots at me.

"I've got to go, Eden. I'll call you as soon as we get to land."

"Get to land? You're still out at sea?"

"Pulled over at a gas station. Call you later! Running out of battery! Bye!"

I hit the end button.

Red set the boots at my feet.

"Try to hang onto them, cutey pie," she said. "I had to pay twice what they're worth. Now you owe me." She laughed.

I checked my pockets for cash. The Gulf had taken it all.

"Don't worry about it," she said. "Consider them a gift from the oil company."

The boots were a little worn, but they came with fresh socks and fit perfectly.

"Pilot's getting close to Grand Isle now," she told Salt. "Hasn't spotted your boat yet, but he's got his eyes peeled. And, I got a guy pumping some fuel into your hotrod."

"Now *I* owe you," Salt smiled.

"Shouldn't be a shock to your system, sugar," she said. "You been owing me forever." She turned to me. "Want a tour of this junkyard?"

"Awesome!" I said.

"Call you when I hear, Joe."

Salt nodded, then headed off for another cup of coffee as Red handed me a hard hat and led the way out.

"Almost four thousand oil and gas platforms in the Gulf of Mexico," she said as she took me across a narrow catwalk. "Out of the ones bolted to the sea bed, this is the tallest."

"What's it called again?"

"The Petronius Platform," she said. "Named after a Roman writer."

"Cool," I said. *A writer like me.*

"Well, he ended up killing himself."

"Bummer," I said.

"Anyways, we're about ninety miles due south of Mobile, Alabama, standing in seventeen hundred feet of water."

"How'd they build this thing?"

"Watch your head," she said.

We ducked under a hissing pipe and up an even narrower passageway.   Every now and then, guys in oil covered jumpsuits squeezed passed us.

"Took them about three years to put it together," she said. "Wound up costing five hundred million dollars."

"Whoa! That's crazy."

"Well, on a good day, we can pull out fifty-thousand barrels of oil and another seventy-million cubic feet of natural gas. Running 24/7 for four years? Well, do the math. We've done okay."

Anyway, this platform has twenty-one well slots," she continued. "Some pump oil and gas out of the sea bed, but most of the active ones are busy pumping water *into* the ground."

"Why in the world would you do that?"

"Oil reserves are pressurized. When we tap them, the oil naturally squirts out. As we drain those big pockets, though, the pressure decreases. We pump in water to keep the pressure high."

"Doesn't that mess up the oil?" I asked.

"Oil and water don't mix, sonny."

My new boots clicked up another metal staircase. On the landing, a blast of fresh salt air hit me in the face. We stood out in the open on a wide, flat platform. A fat, yellow strip of paint ran across the deck from our feet to the middle.

"Helicopter landing area?" I guessed.

"Yep."

The Gulf of Mexico rippled off to the horizon in every direction, deep blue. No boats, no birds, just water as far as I could see.

"From the bottom of the sea, we're twice as high as the Empire State Building," Red said. "Tallest free standing structure in the world. Most people don't count it though, since we're only a couple a hundred feet off the surf."

"Don't you worry about hurricanes?" I asked, thinking about what Charley would have done to all that exposed metal.

"This is a compliant tower," she explained. "That means it's built to move with the wind and sea."

"Move? That's crazy. How far can this thing move?"

"A lot farther than you might think, kiddo. Most buildings sway only a half-percent of their total height. Any more than that and people start to get motion sick. This rig? She moves a full two percent of her height. Two percent of two thousand feet is forty feet. Trust me, when you're on top, you can feel it."

I closed my eyes and tried to sense the motion. Hard to say if I felt anything or not. I still had my sea legs from the night before. I was already weaving around.

Red's cell phone rang. She cupped her hand over it, holding it to her ear.

"Get Joe. I'll meet you there," she said after a moment, snapping the phone shut. "Come on. Something very interesting just happened."

In the dark control room, Salt already stood hunched over a computer monitor. A man sat in front of him with a hand on the mouse.

"Morning, Sully," Red said.

"Red," the man seated at the computer answered.

"What we got here?" asked Red.

"I'll play it again," he said.

"Is that a video?" I asked while trying to squeeze in for a better view of the screen.

"Yes," said Red. "A lot of the choppers are equipped with video cameras. The company uses them to assess damage on unmanned platforms. Our pilot filmed your boat and sent the video to us. Where's that water, Sully?"

The movie started on the screen. A boat, a sportfisherman, moved slowly across a bay. The camera zoomed in to the name across the stern – *Florida Blanca*.

"They're in Barataria Bay, near the north side," said Sully. "Now, let me speed it up a bit."

The boat moved twice as fast through the bay, into the next bay, and up a creek.

"Okay," Sully said. "Right about here something funky happens. You see the shoreline? Watch."

He switched to normal speed. The *Florida Blanca* followed the channel into the bayou. She turned to starboard... and simply vanished.

"Roll it back," Red ordered.

"You won't see nothing," Sully said. "I'll even slow it down."

The boat re-appeared and reversed its course in the creek. It froze. It sailed forward, this time slower than before. Then, before our eyes, the boat drove directly into a grass island and disappeared, as if someone with a giant eraser rubbed it right off the picture. Gone!

"Our guy flew around for a while looking from different directions," Sully explained. "He never saw the boat again."

"How odd," said Red. "Any ideas, Joe?"

"All I need to know is that she's there, in Barataria," Salt said. "We'll figure out the rest when we get there."

"Good luck with that one," chuckled Sully as he pushed back from the console. "Aw, man," he said a moment later.

"What's that, Sully?" asked Red.

"My fat finger accidently hit 'delete' just now," he said.

"No big deal, man. You showed me all I need to see," said Salt patting him on the back. "Thanks again, Red," he continued. "You've done us another huge favor."

"I'll add it to your account," she smiled. "So, you're headed to Barataria Bay?"

"Eventually," Salt replied. "First, we need some inside info on these eels."

The Crescent City

I stood in the Donzi's cockpit next to Salt waving goodbye to Red and the guys on the oil rig while Salt pointed the boat northwest and kicked the throttle. We jumped up on plane faster than a mackerel after baitfish.

Seas were calm that day, allowing Salt to make good time, around forty miles-an-hour in fact. The Donzi felt solid, a good boat for open water. Nice choice, Salt.

"Why don't we go straight to that bay?" I asked Salt over the engine noise.

"That's Barataria Bay, kid," he said as he watched the water in front of the bow. "The Lafitte family has a lot of history in those waters. It's just west of the mouth of the Mississippi. To get in there, we'd have to use the pass between Grande Isle and Grand Terre. The island of Grand Terre is where Jean Lafitte headquartered his pirate kingdom about two-hundred years ago."

"So what. You and your family's been on Cayo Costa for the same length of time and he just strolled right in."

"Didn't know he was coming," he said. "These guys'll be expecting me. Probably got that place rigged with cameras or even a few hooky-do's."

"Hooky-do's?" I repeated.

"That's pirate-ese for booby trap," Salt said as he drove the boat. "No. Barataria's their warehouse. We need to hit 'em somewhere else, find where they live, surprise them."

"How're we going to do that?"

"With a little help from my friends," he said.

Salt pushed the throttle, shifting the Donzi into over-drive. That thing definitely had some giddy-up. The ride was bouncier, but I didn't mind. We had comfortable seats. I settled into one and watched the sea roll by.

When you're offshore, out of sight of land, you might as well be on another planet. I loved that alien seascape. Out there, the water was as clear as the air almost, and way more blue. If a fish broke the surface, it was usually some cool kind of ocean going type that didn't swim around inside Pine Island Sound. The ones out there are bigger, faster, and ultimately more wicked.

The oil rig shrunk on the horizon behind us. I hoped that the people who worked there actually had time to appreciate their awesome backyard. I know I would. I'd be on top of that tower every day, just staring out to sea. I don't think it would ever get old. Of course, I'd probably get fired for goofing off.

I wondered if any kids got to go out there and hang out while their parents worked the rig. They'd still have school and homework, sure, but think of the fishing!

After Salt told me he was related to a pirate, showed me the buried treasure in his yard, and made me his partner, he also told me to live my life no differently than I had been living it. He said to work hard in school and to keep fishing for crabs. Well, I had done both. And you know something? The harder I worked in school, the more used to it I got. I won't say it got easier, but it did get easier to set aside the time to study *and* to focus on the books while I was studying. Salt said that was the result of practice. I think it was the result of having my mind set on a new goal – running a business with Salt after I was done with school.

Salt had convinced me about the importance of a good education in the business world. If we wanted to set up a world-wide charity foundation, we needed to know more than how to fish. It motivated me to have a dream. I ended up getting the best grades I'd gotten in a long time. And you know what else? It felt good, too.

Salt also thinks learning about stuff doesn't stop at the front door of your school. He's right about that. Keep your eyes and ears open no matter where you are, no matter how old you are, and you'll just keep growing smarter and smarter. No one had ever put it to me that way before. I was glad Salt did.

The fishing part of the equation was no problem. I loved that. End of story.

High overhead, a frigate bird sailed around the stratosphere, all alone, just a beak with black wings and split tail against the sky. I bet he had a good view. He looked pretty relaxed, too, wings locked, like a glider, coasting the currents.

For a little while, I felt just like that bird, carefree, gliding over the waves. The sea will do that to you if you're out there long enough. Even though we had a bunch of problems to deal with, being out in the Gulf really put me at ease. It was a perfect day for a boat ride.

The Petronius Platform stands about one-hundred thirty miles southeast of New Orleans, so it took a few hours to reach the mouth of the Mississippi River. We passed a lot more oil rigs on the way. I wondered how far down they went and how many wells they controlled. Red had told me that some rigs connected to wells as far as five miles from the main platform.

Under the Gulf, a spider web of oil and gas pipelines connected the rigs to terminals in the sea and on shore. One even ran all the way back to Tampa! I had no idea.

It seemed like an awful lot of oil traveling around down there. I hope those big oil companies are careful. The Gulf of Mexico deserves that much after giving all she has.

I'd always heard how powerful and majestic our nation's largest river appears. I had never seen the Mississippi before, but it sure didn't look very impressive at its mouth. Salt said the river actually had many mouths that spilled into the Gulf, that if you added them all up, the opening truly would be enormous. The one we took rolled out between two low, sandy islands, slick calm. Salt opened up that Donzi and we flew across the brown water like a fighter jet with afterburners!

Marsh grass spread for miles on the river banks. The sun did a great job keeping everything toasty on a December day. I even took my shirt off, just in case the chicks wanted to check out my guns. Just kidding. I didn't see a single babe, just a bunch of greasy looking dudes, deck hands on huge barges and cargo ships. They hardly noticed us as we zipped by.

Boat docks and flat buildings started popping up along the shore. Later, this big, grassy hill rose up and followed the river. Salt said it was the levee, a long dam that kept the river from flooding when the Mississippi rose after rain or snow upriver. Weird thing, that levee. Kind of sucked, too, because it totally blocked my view. Those lucky guys in the big ships probably saw right over the top of it.

So, thanks to the levee, the rest of the way to the city of New Orleans passed by uneventfully, massive ships, massive barges, and a massive dirt wall. We hauled butt right on by.

Must have been after lunch before we finally arrived in town because my belly let me know about it. Salt tied the

Donzi off at a wharf next to a big warehouse. Our boat floated so far below the top of the dock we had to climb a ladder to get to shore.

Salt told me to wait outside as he marched off in the direction of an office. A couple of guys were standing around yakking when Salt walked up. After he went inside they quit talking and stared at me. I felt kind of out of place, that, and hungry.

A couple of minutes later, Salt came out of the office with some fat guy. The guy was laughing and joking with Salt. They shook hands and Salt motioned for me to catch up to him as he started down the wharf. I don't know how he does it, but that old sailor either has friends or makes friends every place we go.

The fat man pulled the two dudes into his office as I made my way to Salt.

"Told him something funny about his boss," Salt said. "They'll keep an eye on our boat for us. Hungry?"

"Stomach's about to digest itself."

"Ever have a beignet?" he asked.

"Saw one of those silly things in the bathroom at a fancy hotel once," I told him, "but didn't know how to use it."

Salt looked puzzled, then he said, "No, *beignet,* not bidet. Oh, kid. You crack me up sometimes. A beignet is kind of like a square donut without the hole, covered in powdered sugar."

"That sounds better, man," I said. "I could deal with that."

"I know just the place," Salt said. "Follow me."

He went around the end of the warehouse, down a parking lot, and over a couple of railroad tracks to a gap in a wide concrete wall. A seriously large steel door stood on rollers to the side of the gap.

"They take their security for real down here," I said as we cruised by the door.

"It's a floodgate," Salt said. "A lot of this town's below sea level. They've got to do what they can to keep the water out."

We turned left and headed down North Peters Street. Before long, shops popped up. We crossed over to a sidewalk that ran under the awnings. One of the shops looked pretty awesome. It sold clothes, but not every day, normal clothes. The stuff in the windows had clearly been sewn together for rock stars. After the beating I had taken the night before, my clothes had seen better days. I persuaded Salt to stop.

Let me tell you something. If you're ever in New Orleans you need to find this place. That store totally rocked! They had big, stacked boots with enough leather and buckles all up and down them to make Gene Simmons want to buy a pair. Their shirts looked more like snake skin than cloth. And, gargoyles covered everything. Wicked cool! I took a black shirt with a massive dragon design and a pair of black jeans into the changing room.

Yep. As I stared into the mirror, I knew if I threw on a little makeup I could pass as a member of KISS, especially with my hair hanging to my shoulders. I just threw my old rags in the can and strutted out of there like a dude from an 80's hair band. Rock on!

"Why don't you complete your act by setting your head on fire?" Salt smirked.

That old fart was always crackin' wise.

"That's okay," I told him. "You'll be begging me to bring you back here when you see all the chicks flocking in."

"The only thing's going to flock to you will be the fashion police."

New Orleans had very different buildings than Florida, old places with red brick, and balconies with black metal railings. Salt called that part of town the French Quarter. Well, Napoleon must have built the place. It was ancient.

We crossed the street to a crowded, open air restaurant with a sign above it that read "Café Du Monde – The Original Coffee Stand." Inside, people sipped coffee and wiped powdered sugar off their faces with napkins.

Must be the home of the famous square donuts with no holes, I thought.

The place was packed. Salt and I grabbed a small table just inside the railing by the street. I remembered from school that "monde" was French for "world." The sign didn't lie. There were people in there from every corner of the planet. We were swimming in a sea of tourists. Oh well, I guess we were tourists, too. I didn't care at that point. I just wanted something to eat!

Keeping my voice down low, I asked Salt, "So, what's our plan?"

"Get some grub, sonny," he whispered.

"Stop it, Salt. I mean here in New Orleans."

"Like sea shanties, kid?" he asked as he pulled off his shades.

Salt loved to mess with me. Sometimes it was irritating. That was definitely one of those times.

"We came to New Orleans to listen to a bunch of old sailor songs? Seriously, Salt."

"Figured, what with you all duded up like one of them rocky-rollers, you'd appreciate a little music. That's all."

"Come on, dude! You're killing me!"

A waitress walked up to our table, wearing a little white hat, carrying a notepad and a pencil. She barely noticed Salt, but eyeballed me like fresh meat on the grill, smiling and smacking gum the whole time. She was cute, but *way* too old, probably thirty at least.

"Hi y'all doing, honey?" she asked.

"Good," I said.

"I like your shirt, sugar," she said. "Y'all with *ZZ Top*? I heard they're in town." She giggled.

"Yeah, that's it," I said, "We're playing in the Astro Dome tonight."

She let out a laugh with a little snort at the end.

"Well, y'all better get going," she said. "Houston's a few hours from here – or are you taking your jet?"

Salt got a kick out of that. Without the sunglasses, I could see the lines crinkling up around his eyes. For him, that was practically rolling on the floor with laughter.

"It's been a long tour," he said to the lady. "He meant the Super Dome. Coffee, please. Black. My guitar playing friend here will have two orders of beignets and a chocolate milk."

"How about a burger or something, man?" I said. "I need some real food."

"Sorry, sugar," the waitress said, pretending to pout. "You're going to have to dial up your chef back on the G5. We only have one item to eat on our menu – biegnets! But, I'll be happy to bring some chocolate milk to the airport if you have your crew cook us up a few lobster tails. I bet that plane's nice and cozy."

She shot me a sassy wink before strutting away like a runway model. I heard her snort again as she went.

"Appears your flock has arrived," Salt smirked.

I gave up and looked out to the street. I was in no mood.

"Listen. We'll get some decent grub in a minute," he said. "Just wanted you to know a little something about the next place I'm taking you into, okay?"

I turned back to Salt.

"First of all, it's a bar," he said. "They don't allow minors, but keep your cool and I'll figure it out. Once we're inside, don't say nothing. The place is full of thieves and snakes." He stopped and thought for a second. "But... the food's pretty good."

"Why would we ever go into a place like that?"

Salt leaned over the table close enough to see the blood vessels in his eyes.

"Cause there's a fellow in there that might be able to shed a little light on the Lafitte brothers."

"Why would he help us?"

"If the price is right, anybody'll help anybody," Salt said.

Out on the sidewalk, the shadows were getting long. The sun had already dipped behind the buildings.

Across the street next to a park, a vendor sold paintings stacked along a fence. She was old and wrinkled, a face like a fish with a scarf wrapped around her head. The lady stared at the tourists like a witch. Most folks gave her lots of room as they walked by.

As I was wondering if she ever sold anything with looks like that, the old lady slowly turned her head and stared directly at me, *like she knew I was sitting there thinking about her!*

The hag didn't just notice me. She lasered holes through me. I looked away and looked back. Her shark eyes were still locked onto me. A big group of people on the sidewalk moved between us blocking the sight of her. I was relieved. When the street was clear again, she was gone. Good.

"Ready for chocolate milk, sugar?" the waitress cooed into my ear.

I jumped so hard that my shoulder hit her tray and the milk went flying, glass tumbling through the air in slow motion spewing a tsunami of brown liquid in a perfect arc, most of which splashed down harmlessly between our table and the next.   Most, not all.   About a quarter of it landed on the waitress's feet.   Luckily, the glass was plastic and bounced harmlessly a few times before rolling under a nearby chair.

Salt calmly picked up his coffee.   He sipped it without a word.

The other customers stopped their conversations and spun around in their seats to gawk. I felt like a first-class dork.

"Well, what's your next act, rockstar?" the waitress asked. "Gonna lick it up?"

I looked at the milk slick spreading across the floor.   There was no way I'd be going after that, even with a straw.

"No.   My toes, dummy.   I don't care about the floor," she said.

I followed the chocolate river to her sandals, and, like a suckerfish, I swallowed her bait.

"I can't do that," I stammered.   "I...I have a girlfriend."

She took one look at me and busted out laughing, I mean high-pitched squeals followed by *two* snorts after each set. Every other customer in earshot joined in.   Welcome to New Orleans.

"Don't worry about it, sugar.   You're so sweet," she told me.   "I was just teasing you.   It was an accident.   My fault.   I spooked you.   Shouldn't have done that.   *Earrrrrrrrl!!! Get over here with a mop!!!!!*"

Wow! She had a set of lungs on her. If anyone in the restaurant didn't already know about the situation, they did then. I glanced at Salt. He still hadn't said anything. He just slowly bit into a beignet – but those eyes, oh, those eyes of his. They said it all.

I leaned back in the chair watching Earl hustle through the tables with a mop. I pushed my sleeves up and laid my arm on the metal railing trying to look nonchalant, though I knew my face had to be red as a sunburn.

A cold hand clamped down on my arm.

"Want to hear your fortune, boy?" a voice croaked next to me.

I whipped around. It was the witch from across the street. She was even more hideous close up. And, she sounded, like, a thousand years old.

"I...I...I don't have any money," I said.

"Oh, I'll do yours for free."

She smiled and I saw exactly three teeth. I don't think she flossed them, either.

"Might be very *interesting*, boy," she said. "Might be something you want to know."

"Turn him loose, you crazy, old woman!" a man's voice boomed.

It was Earl. He was a big, black man with a bald head covered at the top by one of those little white hats all the employees wore, and he was waving the stick end of the mop at the old lady like he had no problem smacking her in the head.

"You ain't got no business over here," he warned her. "Now you get back over on the other side of the street and quit pestering our customers, or I'll read *your* fortune with this here broom stick!"

She scowled at him like a cat. When she opened her mouth I thought she was going to hiss, but instead she spoke to me again.

"Remember, boy, for free."

She released my arm and hobbled to the street.

"Durn old fool," Earl said. "She hurt you, boy?"

I rubbed my arm. The skin felt cold where she had touched me. I pulled the sleeve down.

"No," I said. "I'm good."

"You're right about that outfit, kid," said Salt, eyes crinkling. "Got 'em flocking out of the woodwork."

"Try a beignet, baby," said the waitress. "I'll be right back with another glass."

Earl mopped up my mess at our feet. I knew we'd have to leave those guys a good tip.

The café crowd went back to their conversations and Salt and I finished all six beignets. I had four. He had two. We left Earl and the waitress a great tip, but she wanted more. Much to Salt's delight, she hassled me for backstage passes and the phone number to the jet. Very funny.

We took the sidewalk between Decatur Street and Jackson Square. The creepy, old lady had returned to her spot beside the paintings. I watched her as she watched me. I wasn't about to back down from her, no matter how creepy she looked. I'd give her one thing, though. The woman could win a staring contest. She didn't blink once.

"This is the original part of the city," Salt was saying like a tour guide. "Started by the French in 1718, a bunch of fur traders. That's why they call it the French Quarter. But, most of these buildings went up after the French gave the town to the

Spanish. In 1801, they gave it back to the French who sold it to the United States a couple of years later. That was about the time Jean Lafitte moved to town. By then, people from all over Europe, Africa, North America and the Caribbean lived here. Lafitte's brother Pierre, who was just as cross-eyed as our pal Skeebo, had already been doing business on these streets as a smuggler and slave trader.

There. Now, you've had your daily history lesson."

"Didn't the British want the town, too?" I asked.

"Yep. The Brits went to war with the United States in 1812. One of their goals was to win this territory for themselves. Our country sent a general named Andrew Jackson to stop them. Got a statue of him in that park over there."

At Iberville Street, we let a horse drawn carriage clop by in front of us before crossing Decatur. The French Quarter crawled with people. Men, women and a few kids swarmed the streets in every direction. It reminded me of Key West. Christmas decorations hung all over the old buildings. We walked down Iberville, past Royal, until we got to Rue Bourbon.

"What's 'Rue' mean?" I asked, pointing at the street sign.

"French for street," Salt said. "Let's turn here. It'll give you an education."

We turned right. Bars, restaurants and shops covered the street on both sides. I saw a few places with very friendly women hanging around the doors, too. They weren't wearing much.

"Hey, Salt," I began.

"Don't even think about it, kid," he said without even turning around.

I guess Skeebo's not the only one with eyes in the back of his head. Regardless, I made a mental note to come back some day and check out one place where a mechanical lady glided in and out of a window on a swing. Cool town.

The further up Bourbon Street we went, the less action I saw. Buildings were shuttered. Many places had street people sitting on the stoops. I was a million miles from Palmetto Cove.

Salt and I pounded the pavement a few more blocks. Without warning, he ducked into a narrow alley between two lonely buildings. The ground was well worn, like it had seen a ton of foot traffic. Halfway down the alley, Salt stopped.

"Remember," he whispered, "just keep quiet and follow my lead. Once we get in let's stay to ourselves for a spell. We can order some chow and see what's what."

I nodded.

The alley seemed to narrow the further we went, felt like the buildings were closing in. As I started to get claustrophobic, it opened into a dingy courtyard, small, with no plants or anything, just dirt. Over to the left stood a tiny frame house that hadn't seen a drop of paint in centuries. No sign hung over the door to give us the name, but the door was open and music poured out.

"Wait here," Salt said.

He left me there, walking straight up to the porch and dissolving into that black hole of a door.

The Pirate Bar

So there I was, standing in front of some weird, nameless bar in the middle of some big, strange city, all by my lonesome.

I wasn't alone for long, though. A couple stumbled out the door and down the porch steps, laughing, talking to each other. The woman winked at me as they went by. I just shoved my hands into my pockets and looked the other way. Finally, Salt came out.

"Alright, kid," he said. "They ain't going to let you in here. Underage. Not so sure I want you in this cesspool anyway. So here's what you do. Go down that alley on the side of the building. You'll see a door at the end. It leads to the backstage area. Knock on that door three times and they'll let you in."

The alley looked like a garbage chute, trash stuck all over the place, narrow, dark, scary.

"Can't you go with me, Salt?"

"I need to sit in the bar for a few minutes."

"Salt, you don't drink," I reminded him hoping I could get him to walk with me down that spooky alley.

"Not drinking," he said. "Plan B. I'll be a spyin' them roughnecks in there. See if I spot any Lafitte employees."

"How you going to know who they are?"

"Trust me. I know a few of them. If Petey don't tell us what I want him to, one of those roustabouts might."

"Who's Petey?"

"Plan A. Now git!"

He turned and went back inside. I didn't wait around. I made a beeline down the trash chute for the back door. It was dark down there. At the end, a bare light bulb stuck out above the door Salt had said to knock on. I hustled along in my borrowed boots, crunching broken glass and kicking empty beer bottles out of the way. To make matters worse, a rat running from a cat shot across the dirt just ahead of me. Oblivious to my presence, and completely in my way, the two of them almost took my legs out from under me. I put on the brakes just in time to feel the pitter-patter of tiny feet run across my toes. I thanked Red again for the boots.

And, yes, the cat was black. Just my luck. Ever since that hurricane showed up on Friday the 13th last summer, I've been a tad superstitious. I told myself to forget the black-cat thing, ignore it, just a coincidence. And, as usual, I didn't listen to myself.

As I continued down the alley, I wondered if I'd get hit by a stray bullet from a drive by, or get bit by some rattlesnake I'd missed in the shadows, or if the entire sky would just quit floating, fall to earth, and crush me like a bug. But fortunately, none of those things happened.

I made it to the door and raised a fist to knock when a hand shot around the corner and grabbed my arm.

At first I thought it might be a cop arresting me for sneaking into the bar. Then, I recognized the witch.

"Dolphins," croaked the old hag from the café.

Her eyes fluttered shut, as if she could see stuff on the backs of her eyelids.

"Dolphins…and waves…and…something else."

I tried yanking my arm away, but it was no use. The old bat had a grip stronger than superglue.

"Let me go!" I shouted at her.

She held tight and grinned, baring those three nasty teeth, stinking like low tide on an oyster bed.

"Oh, yessss, yessss…I see it now…"

A little cackle slipped out of her, a crazy chicken laugh.

"*Fire on water.*"

Her eyes popped open.

"Yessssss! Fire on water. Out in the swamp, boy. Out on the sea."

"You want money? Is that it?" I asked her. "Here. Take it! Let go of me!" I handed her one of the twenty-dollar bills Salt had given me at Café Du Monde.

"No money, dolphin boy," she hissed. "Future's not for sale. Can't buy a fire. Fire is given. Fire is coming. Your fire. Death fire. Burn, baby, burn."

Great. The woman was seriously deranged, still pinching my arm with her claw. I reached out and banged on the door three times with such force I ripped the skin off my knuckles. The possibility of a bar employee coming to the rescue didn't faze the wrinkled up hag one bit. Instead of running, she started singing… and chicken-laughing.

"Twinkle, twinkle little star… Heh, heh, heh, heh…"

Only when the door finally opened and light fell across her face, did she hiss like a vampire at the break of day and drop my arm.

I turned to face my savior.

"Yes?" said a big dude standing in the door.

The man seemed large enough to crush the old woman with his pinky. Sensing that he would also enjoy doing me that small favor but unable to form the words to ask, I simply stabbed a finger at the witch. Expecting lip-snarling, mouth-foaming bouncer rage, I was perplexed when the big guy's face curled into a question mark.

My finger pointed at empty air. The witch had vanished. Creepy.

Then, anger did screw up his face, anger directed at me. I noticed the twenty still in my hand, so I quickly held it out for him, and smiled. He snarled, stuffing the bill into his pocket without a word.

"Um...I'm here to see Petey?" I said before he could slam the door in my face.

The gorilla looked me up and down, like he was trying to decide whether he should crush me first or just swallow me whole, alive and kicking. All at once, his face relaxed, like the big doof just remembered something. He almost smiled.

"Oh, yeah," he said. "Come on in. Petey's expecting you."

I moved fast, shooting in under his arm before he changed his mind.

"Park your butt here," the dude said pointing to a chair. "He's almost done."

He walked off down the hall and pushed open the door at the end. After a burst of bar noise, I found myself all alone again.

The chair he had motioned to sat way close to the exit door. The other end of the hall looked a whole lot friendlier, so I picked up the chair to carry it down there, you know, closer to the people noise. And, if that old hag planned another sneak attack, I figured I'd see her coming.

I passed three doors on the right. Two of the doors looked plain and normal, but the middle door sported a blood-red, burning star – rising out of the sea!   Yellow-red flames scorched up the wood off a five-pointed star that seemed to float on the water. Coincidence? I thought not.

I told myself to calm down before I started overreacting.

Myself said, *You better run, son!*

I told myself it was probably just a dressing room.

Myself said, *Yeah, right. A dressing room for Satan!*

My feet didn't hear me either. They gave the fire-on-water painting a wide berth as I passed the middle door. My hands held the chair legs out like a weapon. My brain screamed at me to leave town immediately.

Man, I did *not* want to be there.

At the end of the hall, I slowly set the chair down, keeping my eyes on the exit door the entire time. Music and singing, and people hooting and hollering, pounded against the door. I loved every decibel. Given the choice between a demented fortune teller from hell and a crowd of music loving rednecks, I'll choose the rednecks every time.

I leaned the chair back on the door and sat through two or three songs with my eyeballs locked onto the exit, almost giving up on the idea that the witch might fly down the hall and attack me on her broomstick, when the door behind me suddenly swung open. I fell backwards, thumping my head on the floor. I just about pooped my pants, too. Flat out on my back, but still in a sitting position, I stared up towards the ceiling into the eyes of a cocktail waitress.

She was laughing. I had bad luck with waitresses that day.

"Your buddy'll be back here in a couple of minutes," the young woman said. "You need anything, sugar?"

She wore a tiny skirt and held a small, round tray.

"He said it's on him. Say, you're cute upside-down," she said.

She smiled and winked. They all smiled and winked - must be why they call New Orleans the Big Easy.

"Coke, please," I said without bothering to move.

"Sure, baby. I'll be right back."

She winked again and left.

I rolled out of the chair onto my belly so I could see into the bar. Mostly, I saw the stage. It was really close. A guy sat in the middle of it on a stool with his back to me playing some kind of miniature accordion and singing to a crowd of folks sitting at tables. The tables had lava lights which made the customer's faces glow red. The crowd looked about as friendly as the bouncer who let me in. The red lava lights didn't help, just made them seem like a bunch of demonic barracudas in the devil's saloon.

I thought of the burning star again.

The singer kept time by tapping his toes on the wooden stage. Something about his foot drew my eye. When I looked closer I realized he didn't have any toes, or a foot for that matter. His leg was a peg!

Then I noticed his hand holding the accordion - a hook! The guy rolled his head back as he belted out the song and – I swear – there was a patch on his eye. The man looked just like the buccaneers you see in the movies.

The song ended. A few people clapped. One guy stood up and cheered way too loud and way too long.

"Thank you, thank you," pirate-man said. "Now, you all know sea shanties were sung to keep time amongst the sailors as they worked together haulin' ropes. But did ye know they also told of news in far away ports?"

The crowd mumbled. Most people weren't paying any attention. A girl jumped into a guy's lap at one table, a dude punched his buddy in the arm at another.

"Well, sailors didn't have newspapers aboard," continued the pirate-man. "Not that they could read anyway."

A few people laughed.

"These songs sometimes gave the swabs vital information about their impending port o' call. This next shanty is one of those. And, you all know it by heart. So raise your voices high!"

He started the accordion again. The melody kind of sounded like that old song, *Blow the Man Down*.

> *Oh, down by the seashore a bonny lass lived.*
> *She gave away kisses, more'n any girl gived.*
> *And I saw her each marn-nin' and each evenin' too.*
> *A deep-water sailor knows just what to do.*

Then, on cue, like they had each heard their instructions perfectly clear, every voice in the room started booming away.

> *Hold her real tight! An' hug her real hard!*
> *But never ye take her down to the shipyard!*

Once again, pirate-man sung alone.

> *I went by her cottage one fine summer day.*
> *She said she had seen me tall ship in the bay.*
> *With lips like a cherry, so tender and sweet,*
> *She asked for to board her, me ship in the fleet.*

Then the crowd.

> *Oh, hold her real tight! An' hug her real hard!*

But never ye take her down to the shipyard!

Her arm in mine, we stepped down the path.
The neighbors were lookin', but no care I hath.
My heart was a thumpin' so ever so hard.
Away we both skipped down to the shipyard.

The waitress brought me my soda.   Even she was singing.
Well, I guess that's better than laughing at me.

Oh, hold her real tight! An' hug her real hard!
But never ye take her down to the shipyard!

The shipyard was busy way down by the sea,
With more men and PIRATES than you ever did see.
They all saw the damsel what served them up tea.
I knew there be trouble 'ere their eyes turned to me.

Oh, hold her real tight! An' hug her real hard!
But never ye take her down to the shipyard!

Ye sailors twarn't happy, the punches did fly.
A boot in me belly. A fist for me eye.
The lass, she was laughin', enjoyin' the fight.
She had taken us all, just not all in one night!

Ye can hold her real tight! An' hug her real hard!
But don't never take herrrrrrrr... down to the SHIPYARD!

When the song ended, most of the guys busted out with an
"Arrrrrrr!" or just yelled something.   The few women

scattered around clapped their hands. One of them put her fingers in her mouth and whistled.

Another woman, at a table close to my door, jumped into a guy's lap and kissed him.

"Tell me *you* ain't never done nothing like that," he said to her.

"I'll never tell," she laughed, then threw another lip lock on the dude.

Salt was right about that place. It *was* full of a bunch of thieves; at least they looked that way. One nasty dude had a huge tattoo of a skull on his arm. Another man, sucking on a cigarette, wore a muscle shirt and a doo-rag. None of them believed in shaving. All of them looked plain mean.

I spotted Salt at a table near the back. And, I've got to tell you, he fit right in. He caught my eye and got up.

Pirate-man thanked the crowd and left his stool for the bar. Salt walked around the stage to the door and joined me in the hall.

"Trying to sneak in on your belly?" he said. "Get up. Got some grub coming for you."

"I bet it's awesome," I said sarcastically as I picked myself up off the floor.

"You'll be pleasantly surprised," he promised. "Besides, you've got to be gnawing at your stomach lining by now. You won't care what it is."

I was hungry, no doubt, but I figured any meal I ate in that stinking place might be my last.

Salt went past me down the hall, stopping at the door with the flaming star. I hung back a couple of steps, trying to decide if I should tell him about my little incident in the alley.

"Petey's room," he said. "He'll be along directly."

While we waited, I heard pirate-man come limping down the hall like a clock that had lost its ticks, his peg-leg tock-tock-tocking its way on the plank floor as he came.

"Well, blow me down!" he bellowed when he saw Salt. "The scurvy dog has returned!"

"Harley, meet Petey," Salt said.

I didn't know which hand to stick out. I just went with the right, hoping that Petey's shiny, and very sharp looking, hook wouldn't give me my first body piercing.

"Good to meet you, sir" I said.

"Shiver me timbers!" he said. "Don't call me sir. You make me sound old."

He spared the hook, gripped my hand and pumped it, seeming happy enough, for a pirate anyway.

"Come in, come in," he said. "Me cabin's a might cozy, but we'll manage."

Petey opened the fire-on-water door and we followed him inside. I still had doubts about going into that room, but this guy seemed more like Santa Claus than Satan.

"Sit down old man," Petey chuckled. He pointed at Salt and said, "Now there goes a 'sir.'" Then, to Salt, "Judging by that big bandage on your ear, old man, you look like you're starting to fall apart, too. Pray tell what hath transpired. Skin cancer?"

"Mosquito bite," Salt said as he pushed past Pirate Pete.

Salt and I sat on a pair of rickety ladder-back chairs that, by the looks of them, had sailed around the world several times on Petey's ship – if he ever had a ship. The pirate took a seat on a stool at a makeup table, one of those contraptions with a mirror and a bunch of bare light bulbs around it. The only other furniture in the room was a four-foot stack of drawers in the corner and an old chest next to it on the floor. And, yes, the chest looked like your typical treasure chest. This guy was into it all the way to his eye patch.

The walls were covered with all sorts of pirate photos. When I looked closer, I realized the pirate was the same in every picture – Petey – only, in some of them he still had all his body parts.

"You haven't aged a day, Pete," said Salt. "I see you're still sticking to your diet and exercise plan."

"That's right," said Pete patting his huge belly with his hook. "I *diet* on a gallon of gumbo every day and I *exercise* my right to be a couch potato." More laughs. "Son, a wise man once told me, 'Don't run when you can walk. Don't walk when you can sit. And, never sit when you can lie down.' Served me well ever since. Keeps me out of trouble, it does!"

You couldn't help but like the guy, corny jokes and all.

"So, what brings you two scallywags to The Big Easy?"

Salt motioned to me. "This little hitchhiker's from down around my neck of the woods. Found his way into my boat – and my business."

Petey gave me the once over with his only eye.

"What's your name again, son?" he asked.

"Harley Cooper," I said.

"Not Harley *Davidsen* Cooper?!" he said.

"Yep."

"Not *the* Harley Davidsen Cooper," said Pete, his eye widening to porthole size. "Why, you're famous, son. *You* ought to be out there on that stage. Not me. Your picture was splashed all over the news up here after that god-awful hurricane."

"You'll have to talk to my agent," I grinned.

"Blimey!" he said laughing. "Well, yo ho ho and a bottle of well done, me little swab. Heard you saved a couple of lasses from that storm."

Somebody knocked on the door.

"Arrrrr?" said Petey.

"Got some dinner for your guests," said a girl's voice.

"Well, bring it in, honey," said Petey. "This boy here looks like he's about to gnaw his own boots."

The waitress carried a tray holding three plates of food and three glasses of iced tea. She set everything down on Petey's makeup table.

"I'll take that empty Coke glass, sweetie," she said to me and winked for the third time. Maybe she liked me, or maybe she just had a nervous tick. I don't know. I just thanked her and handed over the glass. Salt gave her some cash and she was out the door.

"Here, Mr. Harley Davidsen Cooper," Petey said handing me a plate of steak and potato. "Allow me. I never served a hero before."

"It's going to go to his head if you keep that up, Pete," said Salt. "And, he'll become even more unbearable."

"Aw, I can tell he's a humble lad, Joe," Pete said grinning at me. "Reminds me of me at that age – minus all this extra jewelry, of course." He waved his hook.

I accepted the steak, set the plate on my knees and went to town with a knife and fork. Not bad, or maybe I was just starving.

"What are you eating there, Petey?" I asked him, pointing at the third plate still on his table.

The plate was piled high with super-red, heads-on shrimp, except these shrimp had claws.

"You mean these crawdads?" he said looking sideways at me with one eye. "They're for you, son. Believe me, I've had my share tonight." He sipped his tea.

"What are those things?" I asked.

"Crawdads? Think of them as freshwater shrimp."

"Heads on shrimp? Reminds me of bait," I said.

"I'll demonstrate," said Salt.

Salt picked one off the plate and ripped its head off. He pinched the meat out of the tail and cleaned the guts off with the tail flukes. Then, he popped the meat in his mouth and picked up the head.

"Gotta suck the head," he said. "That's where the flavor is."

He put the gut end of the head between his lips and slurped the juices down. Yuck!

"Man, I'll try the tail," I said. "But there ain't no way I'm sucking anything!"

The tail meat was decent, full of whatever spices they used to boil the crawdad. You had to work at it, though, not much meat on those things. Petey laughed some more as he watched me fumble through them.

"So, Joe," the pirate-man said. "Just what *is* your business, here in New Orleans? Or did you stop by just to grace my humble presence with an overdue visit?"

"Well, Pete, now that you ask, it's pirates," Salt said.

"Pirates, you say," said Pete as he swivled on the stool to check his outfit in the mirror. "You come to the right spot. This place is full of them."

"The ones I want to know about aren't currently in the bar."

"And just which ones might those be?" asked Pete as he patted powder on his nose with a small puff.

"The Lafitte brothers," said Salt.

Pete missed his nose and accidently covered his eyepatch with flesh colored powder.

"You join the Air Force, Joe?" Pete said, looking at Salt in the mirror. "Cause you're aiming awfully high, partner."

Pete started to laugh at his own joke but his smile faded like the sun behind a thunderhead when he caught the look on Salt's face.

"You're serious, huh?" Pete said.

"'Fraid I am, Petey. They done run off with a girl that's as close as family and a bundle of loot that don't belong to them neither."

"Alright, Joe, the money I get...but you...but this girl, what's so special about her?" Pete said. He dabbed the powder puff once or twice and went back to work on his face. "Unless you've changed your spots, I remember you as a lone wolf, Mr. Gaspar."

"I'll get to the point here, Pete, because my schedule's kind of tight," Salt said. "I'll pay you a grand now and another thousand on the other side if you help me find them."

Pete stopped working the puff and swiveled around on his stool to face Salt directly.

"You're starting to speak my language," said Pete with a sly smile.

"Well," said Salt, "let me have it then."

"I said 'starting to speak my language.' I can't quite tune in everything you're saying. These are big fish, you realize."

"Will five thousand do it? Half now, the other half if we find them."

"Twenty-five in cash now?"

"Yep. And, like I said, I'm in a hurry."

"Done and done," said Pete, his eyes gleaming like he'd struck gold.

He hoisted himself onto his peg leg and limped over to the chest in the corner. The lid creaked when he cracked it open just long enough to pull out a map. He unfolded the big sheet of paper on the makeup table, smoothing it out under the lights.

"Across the river there's a canal," he said.

"The Harvey. I see it," said Salt.

"Go through the lock and take your boat down that piece of water," said Pete. "Keep a going along this water here until you get to this little burg – Jean Lafitte."

"They named a town after the guy?" I asked.

"Not the psycho you're after. His ancestor. Named more than one town, son," said Pete. "A whole lot of people liked the guy, war hero and all."

"I thought he was a pirate," I said.

"That he was, that he was," Pete continued. "But, he also bailed out a guy named Andrew Jackson once upon a time. Ever heard of him?"

"The guy on the twenty-dollar bill?" I joked.

"Well, yeah…uh…that happened later, after he was president an all. At the time, he was a general.

Jean Lafitte and his brother Pierre were pretty powerful in the day." Petey looked over at Salt. "The Lafitte's still are." He paused a moment. "Tell you what, son. Since your still working on that feast I'll tell you a little tale about those two privateers."

Salt rolled his eyes, holding up a hand to stop him.

"I'll be quick, Joe," Petey promised.

Petey told a diddie as well as Salt, maybe better. By the time he finished, my plate was empty except for a bunch of crawdad heads, guts still inside.

"And beyond all their lawlessness, beyond all the guns, the boats, the money, today's two Lafitte brothers are very different and infinitely more dangerous than their forebears in one very important regard," Pete said.

The stage pirate leaned in and hushed his voice to a whisper.

"They are both completely insane."

"We go way back," Salt replied. "Known them for years."

Now we were getting somewhere. Salt had only given me bits and pieces. Here was a man who seemed ready to spill the whole story.

"I don't go way back with them," I said. "What do you mean 'insane'?"

"Spare the boy, Pete," Salt said. "He doesn't need to be bothered by other people's opinions."

"Opinions?!" said Petey as if the word had stung him. "Ha! Is keel hauling a man's bare back over razor sharp barnacles opinion? Is hunting down a runaway employee's family for sport opinion? No, my friend, these are facts. And the boy needs to know what he's getting into."

Salt stood up and threw his hands in the air. Pirate Pete wheeled his stool over to me.

"Listen, son," he said. "The Lafittes are both completely off their rockers."

"He's met Skeebo," Salt said from the other side of the room.

"Skeebo? Heh, heh. He's just your average, run of the mill crazy. Somebody you'd meet living under a bridge on I-10," Petey said. "Wants to be a tough guy. Thinks the world's out to get him.   And, at the same time, thinks it owes him everything.   Prone to irrational violence.   Etcetera, etcetera. The type you can see coming.   Looks the part, too, I might add."

He paused to gulp his tea, wiping his mouth with the back of his sleeve when he was done.

"But br'er John?   He's a breed I ain't never come across before or since."

"Since what?" I asked.

"Since I trained him," said Pirate Pete straightening up on his stool.

"Trained him for what?"

"To become a pirate, of course," he said proudly.

"Here we go," said Salt.   He stood in the corner with his arms folded, watching us.

"Never mind him, sonny.   It's the truth," said Petey. "Lafitte came to me to learn how to be a stage pirate.   Or so I thought.   The first thing I noticed?   He was wicked smart.   Like a photographic memory.   Show him a thing once, and that's all it took.   The perfect student.

Then, I saw his true nature."

"Opinions," said Salt.

Pirate Pete wheeled on him, his face flushed red.

"You weren't there, Gaspar!" he yelled.   "You have no idea! Look at my arm! Is that one of your opinions? Huh?!"

"Lafitte did that to your arm?" I asked him.

He rowed the stool back to me with his peg leg.

"Aye.   And the leg," Pete said sadly.   "He severed them both in separate mock-swordfight incidents during a couple of shows.   I thought it was honest mistakes both times."

"Oh my God!" I said.   "And your eye? He did that, too?"

"No. Bird poop. Whole different story," he said regaining his composure. "Look, the point is – he's a very dangerous man with a very serious disease. I was only the beginning of his cruelty. After me, he moved on. Left the stage to take his act to the world. Says he must fulfill the Lafitte destiny."

"Wait a minute. Back up," I said. "Disease?"

Pirate Pete became very still. Instead of answering my question he polished his hook along the puffy material of his pirate pants.

"Go ahead, Pete," said Salt. "Tell him. You've come this far."

Petey looked over at Salt, then to me.

"People laugh, Harley," he said, "when I tell them what the disease is. I've told Joe, here. He laughed. He doesn't believe me. Maybe it's because I came up with the name, because I'm not a medical professional."

"Well, what do you call it?" I asked.

"Pyratosis," he said gravely, "an affliction which causes you to truly believe…you're a real pirate."

"Look, Pete," said Salt. "I told the kid he's dangerous. I told him he's a lunatic. I know that from dealing with him years ago."

"You don't know this, Joe," Petey said over his shoulder. "He's a hundred times worse than when you last saw him." Then to me, "He dresses like a full blown buccaneer from the golden age of piracy. He talks like a pirate. Thinks like a pirate. Acts like a pirate – at all times! Pyratosis."

His face became all twisted and pain with fear like just talking about Lafitte made him hurt.

"Me? I'm a showbiz pirate. I know the jokes, the songs. I know when the curtain goes up and when it comes back down. This guy? He's always on. Always plotting, deceiving, conniving. Always one step ahead of the law, too. It's like he's made some sort of pact with the devil."

He thought for a moment.

"Or... maybe he *is* the devil," he said quietly, almost to himself.

Salt just closed his eyes and slowly shook his head.

"Five thousand dollars?" Pirate Pete said to Salt.

"Five grand," said Salt.

"Well, okay then," said Pete. "I can see you're serious about this. That's a lot of crackers for me parrot.

Okay. So what you do in Jean Lafitte is look up this fellow named Skeeter Leblanc. Skeet knows every inch of those bayous. He can get you there."

"Can't you just point to their place on the map and we can get ourselves there?" I asked him.

"Not that simple, son," Pete said. "They've got one location back down off Barataria, but it's said that their main place is in the bayou up here." He drew a circle on the map with his finger in an area that had no roads. "Not many folks know that swamp...or care to. Mysterious place. Indians think it's haunted. They call it the *Burnin' Bayou.*"

"Burning? As in *fire*?" I asked.

"Uh huh. Something about fire on the water."

Chills shot up my spine. I felt a cold claw pinching my arm. The old hag's face popped into my mind. I even heard her chicken laugh echo through my head.

Fire on the water.

"Can I trust him to take me to the right spot?" Salt was asking Petey.

I tried to compose myself in spite of wet palms and a hammering heart.

Just a crazy old lady, I told myself. Did I listen? What do you think?

"As much as you can trust anybody down there," Pete said with a smile that he directed at me. "But you'll know you're getting warm when Skeeter starts stuttering. Does that when he's nervous."

Trusting a stuttering swamp-rat named Skeeter didn't do much to make me feel better. Louisiana was getting way too weird. My friend Bill once told me, in a very spooky voice, that the swamps around New Orleans were full of voodoo worshippers. I was beginning to believe him.

"But, the way I see it, partner," Petey was saying to Salt, "you ain't got no choice. Skeet usually hangs out by the store next to the payphone in the mornings." Petey snapped his head around and winked at me. "That's his private line."

"Number?" said Salt.

"Twenty-five hundred," said Pete.

"That's no phone number," I interrupted, trying to get my head off of zombies and back in the game.

"He wants his money," Salt told me.

Pete smiled and held out his only hand. Salt reached into his jacket, pulling out a wad of bills. He counted a bunch of hundreds and gave them to Pete, who, in turn, gave us Skeeter's private payphone number. He also described what Skeeter looked like, waving his hook around in the air as he talked. He noticed that I was staring at his metal hand.

"Yes, son," he said to me. "What I just told you is fact, not opinion."

I didn't doubt it. But, I did have one question left.

"Bird poop?" I asked him.

"That's right," he said. "Bird flew right over and crapped in me eye."

That didn't seem right.

"Bird poop wouldn't put out an eye," I said.

"Aye. But, it was me first day with me new hook!" he said waving his prosthetic device at me. "Har, har, hardy har, har! Gets 'em every time!"

Salt just shook his head. "Let's go, kid."

"I'll be waiting," said pirate Pete.

"I'll send you a money-gram if it all works out," said Salt as he shut the door behind us.

Harvey Canal

Bourbon Street had come to life.

Like they say in New Orleans, *Let the good times roll.* They were rolling alright, at least with the sidewalk crowd, not with me, though. As I kept pace with Salt, my eyes searched every porch stoop, every side street, and every shadow for that crazy, old witch.

The party faded behind us as we walked to North Peters Street. Down by the river, the city got lonely, and dark. Something had stolen the music, the bright lights, the party of the French Quarter and replaced it with something that felt like a grave yard.

At the gap in the wall, the huge flood gate stood ready to slam shut. On the other side of that, the big warehouse sat there, like a tomb, waiting. Salt kept going around the end of the massive building to the wharf. The river flowed black between the lights on the wharf and the lights on the far bank. I couldn't see the water, only a few lights reflected off the void. But, I sure felt the presence of the Mississippi River as it rolled by. Even invisible, it was a giant, alive, watching us.

No one greeted us on the wharf. If the pier had a night watchman, he was taking a nap. Heavy machinery rumbled down the river somewhere. Our footsteps made the most noise of all as we walked over the boards.

The Donzi bobbed in the river current just where we left her. Amazing. I half expected the boat to be gone, just like the party in the Quarter.

Suddenly, Salt waved a hand to stop me. He peered carefully down into the boat.

The cabin door was open and a light burned inside. Shadows moved across the cockpit deck, human shadows. Someone was in the cabin!

Salt drew a pistol from behind his back, where he got it or *when* he got it I didn't have a clue. There it was, though, in his hand as he descended the ladder to the boat.

The person inside moved around some more. Shadows hit the deck outside the door. Salt eased one foot on the boat, then the other. He crept over to the cabin door and waited.

A ship's horn sounded somewhere far down the river. Before the sound of it had faded away, Salt jumped down in front of the door and shoved the barrel of that pistol into the cabin.

A moment later, he dropped his arm. Crouching, he stared at something I couldn't see.

"Somebody left you a present, kid," he said.

"What are you talking about?"

"Come on down," Salt said. "It's a seeing, not a telling."

I scrambled down the ladder and onto the Donzi, joining Salt by the cabin door. At first, I didn't know what I was looking at. Then, it clicked.

"Is that me?" I said.

"Well, a pretty good replica of you, anyway."

Someone had made an exact scale model replica of me, right down to the long hair and rock-and-roll t-shirt. The three-foot figure turned slowly on a cord hung from the cabin roof, like a piñata. Freaky. I wondered if I was full of candy.

"Better copyright your face, kid. Next thing you know they'll be turning you into bobble-head dolls.'

The figure only differed from my current appearance by the addition of one, small detail – the mini-me wore a leather necklace with some kind of pendant dangling down its chest.

"Santeria," Salt said.

"Sante-who-a?"

"Voodoo," he said.

"Voodoo?!"

Bill, my friend back home, the guy who had warned me about the spiritual preferences of the bayou people, didn't seem like such a kook anymore.

"Somebody cursed me?" I asked Salt.

"Well, not necessarily," Salt said. "There's bad voodoo and then there's the good kind."

He leaned into the cabin and snapped the cord off the ceiling.

"What's that?" I said after spotting something else.

A folded piece of paper had been taped to the doll's back.

"Somebody send you a love letter?" asked Salt.

While Salt removed the paper and unfolded it, I gave him the details of my second encounter with the old hag back at the pirate bar.

"Interesting group of women you're attracting with that shirt of yours," he said after I ran out of breath. "Let's see what we got here."

He held the paper under the light.

"Looks short and sweet," he said. "Here. I'll read it to you. *'When fire meets water, blood will flow. Protect the boy when this is so. Papa La Bas gives wishes three. Trick the future and it shall be.'* That's it. That's all it says."

"That's all?"

"That's all."

"What's it mean?" I wondered.

"Don't sound like no curse," said Salt. "Sounds more like a blessing, like you just got three wishes." He tossed the doll to me. "Hang onto this thing. Might bring you some good luck."

I caught it with both hands. It felt lighter than it should have. Maybe it was filled with voodoo marshmallows.

The pendant looked homemade, hand carved, out of wood. The edges were rough, but I made out the shapes of two animals, a monkey and a chicken. I knew next to nothing about voodoo, really didn't take it too seriously, but something made me take the necklace off the doll and slip it over my head.

I stowed my short twin next to the life jackets in a compartment under the cushions. His eyes never blinked.

"Well, let's git," Salt said. "Will you please do the honors?"

The motor rumbled to life as I hopped up and walked over the length of the Donzi's long bow to unhitch the boat.

Using the map on his GPS to locate the Harvey Canal, Salt motored across the Mississippi, under a big bridge, and to the canal Pirate Pete had pointed out. The black water tugged at the Donzi's hull as we went, pushing the boat up and down, and I imagined huge, slimy eels had surfaced, bumping us along on their backs. The mind is full of tricks, especially at night in a town crawling with voodoo.

Petey's canal led us away from the flow, and the eels. The boat settled down and glided up to a seriously huge wall.

"Harvey Lock," Salt said. "This canal runs all the way out to the Gulf."

Street lights on both sides of the canal gave off just enough light to see black current swirl in and brush up against the enormous metal doors. Somebody must have seen us down there because machinery started to whir and the lock's gates rumbled open.

As the gigantic gates opened, their motion made them seem even bigger. I was mesmerized. Salt, on the other hand, barely noticed. He just nudged the go-fast boat forward and we drifted in.

"This lock'll take us down a few feet to sea-level," he said. "Then, those far gates over there'll open up and we can head down to Jean Lafitte."

The second pair of gates opened, just like Salt said, and we floated down the Harvey Canal. I was kind of hoping the other side of the lock would open into a more natural place, you know, trees and wetlands. No such luck. More industry slid by, complete with rusty barges, warehouses, and plain, old junk. The air stunk with fuel, chemicals, grease, and low tide.

I figured it would be a good time to get some rest. I crashed on the couch behind Salt's chair.

When I woke, the air smelled different, earthier, muddy, swampy. I figured we had worked our way out of the city and into the wetlands south of New Orleans. I felt better. Big cities made me uncomfortable. Nature was my home and I was glad to be back in it, even if that nature was different from the nature I was used to in Florida. Petey had mentioned Indians in his pirate diddie. I wondered if any were still around.

"Where are we Salt?" I asked.

"Still in the Harvey," Salt said. "A lot further south, though. You winked out. Missed all the scenery."

"Sorry, Salt. I was drowsy or something," I said.

"Maybe that old lady put a nighty-night hex on you," he said.

"Hex? You mean cursed?" I said. "You think I'm cursed, Salt?"

"Just joking, dude. Calm down. I think you cursed yourself the moment you put on that silly dragon shirt."

There must have been a road running alongside the canal because every now and then I'd see a car go by. Docks connected backyards to the water. Most of the homes had been decorated with Christmas lights, many of the docks, too. Occasionally, dogs barked at us when they heard our big motor chugging along. After a while, the number of houses grew. Salt pulled out his GPS to check our position.

"Coming into Jean Lafitte now," he said. "Need to find a quiet spot."

When Salt judged that we were even with the heart of town he pulled the boat over to an old dock on the west side of the canal, the side opposite town. The house up from the dock appeared to be rundown and abandoned. No one was likely to bother us.

"Got a few hours 'til dawn," Salt said to me. "If you're not too sleepy, I'll put you to work – since you insist on coming along and helping out. You've got the first watch."

"What am I watching for?" I asked.

"Anything that tries to mess with this boat," he said. "I'm going to get some shut eye."

Salt disappeared into the cabin. He left his phone sitting on the steering console. I grabbed it and sent Eden a text. The hour was late, but I took a shot. Salt's phone rang a few seconds later.

"Make it to New Orleans, crab boy?" Eden said after I answered.

"Been there. Done with that," I said.

"You didn't stay long."

"Nope. Crammed a lot in, though."

"Like?" she asked.

"Like sightseeing, shopping, a little voodoo...you know, stuff like that."

"Voodoo?"

"Yes. I met several interesting people. One was kind enough to give me a special present. Can't tell you what it is, though. I'm going to re-gift it to you for Christmas."

"So you're doing good?"

"Good," I said.

"That's good. Harley? I was wondering..."

"Yes?"

"What do you think will happen to Isabella?"

"Now you're worried about her?" I said. "We're going to find her."

"No. I mean now. What do you think those guys are doing with her?"

"Well, I guess they could have let her go when they got here like they said, but I doubt it. More likely they'll hold onto her."

"Why?" she asked.

"That's the thing," I said. "She's unaccounted for. Officially, she's not in this country. The authorities don't know about her. That means the Lafitte's can keep her indefinitely."

"For what?"

"That's the scary part. They could keep her for anything, you know, like their own slave," I said. "Or, they could even sell her as a slave to someone in some other country."

"People get away with that?"

"Yep. Salt says it happens. That's why we've got to get her back...and fast."

"She's really pretty," Eden said. "Don't you think?"

"Yeah, I guess so."

"Come on, Harley. You know she is. I saw the way you were looking at her back on her dock."

"I was concerned about her."

"I know the things that concern you."

"Eden. Stop it. She was getting kidnapped! I was worried about her!"

"Hey, calm down," she said. "Why so defensive all of a sudden?"

"Cause you're making something up that doesn't exist."

"You sure?"

"Sure."

"Hey, security guard," Salt called from the cabin. "Mind letting an old man get a little rest? You're supposed to be watching, not yakking."

I moved to the very back of the boat, letting my feet hang over the edge.

"I've got to be quiet," I whispered to Eden. "Salt's getting fussy."

"Harley?" she whispered.

"What?"

"I do trust you," she said. "I just get paranoid sometimes."

"Don't we all?"

"Tell me a story."

"Are you serious?" I asked her.

"Yes. I want to hear a story."

I racked my brain. The first one that popped into my head was the diddie about Lafitte that Petey had just told me.

"Okay," I said. "But, it's going to be a pirate story."

"Is there any other kind?"

"Hush," I told her. "This is a new one. First, some background. In late 1814, the privateer and pirate, Jean Lafitte and his men, had been pardoned for all their crimes in exchange for helping the American general, Andrew Jackson, defeat the British at New Orleans. But, Lafitte was told that he could not return to his pirate kingdom on Grand Terre Island in Barataria Bay. So, he set sail for Texas.

Back then, Texas was still controlled by Spain as part of its colony, Mexico. The Mexicans, however, were at war with their mother country fighting for independence. The war kept most of Spain's military busy further south, stretching it too thin to guard the spot of territory Lafitte had turned into his new headquarters – Galveston Island.

Lafitte built a compound on Galveston and returned to his old pirate ways. He plundered ships and towns around the Gulf of Mexico bringing the merchandise back to Galveston and living like a king. From there, his brother, Pierre, smuggled stuff into New Orleans and sold it to merchants they had dealt with before.

The U.S. government had passed a law banning the importation of slaves into the country. But, that didn't stop the Lafittes. They sold thousands of captured slaves to slave traders and also began selling directly to wealthy plantation owners.

One slave was an African named Wash. Lafitte sold the guy to a farmer in Kentucky. Wash worked the fields in Kentucky until he escaped and found his way down to Louisiana.

And that's where the story begins."

"Nice," Eden said. "You sound like a college professor. Is there a quiz after this?"

"Dude! You said you wanted a story."

"Okay. Okay. I'll behave."

"Anyway, the story came directly from this guy, Wash, when he was an old man many years later.

One day Wash was fishing on the banks of the Calcasieu River in southwestern Louisiana when he saw a schooner sail up and drop anchor just upstream. The men on the ship were in a big hurry to unload their cargo, and that made Wash curious enough to sneak through the woods and hide in the bushes to watch. Men rowed ashore in longboats to dump heavy sea chests onto the sand. Wash recognized their captain. He was none other than Jean Lafitte, the man who had sold him into slavery.

Lafitte ordered his men to dig a large pit and bury the chests. When the job was complete, Lafitte took a pistol and fired it into the air. Minutes later, Wash heard something coming through the woods behind him. Fearing for his life, he hid next to a log and covered himself with old branches.

From under the branches, Wash watched as many sets of bare feet passed by to join Lafitte at the shore. Lafitte had called his allies, the Atakapa Indian tribe.

The Atakapa helped the pirates build a crude wall of clam shells and sand along the water's edge. Then, the warriors brought the ship's guns ashore and set them along the new fort, aiming them towards the river. When the last cannon had been unloaded, Lafitte gave the order to scuttle the schooner. She sank to the bottom of the river.

Wash waited by the log through the night, too amazed by the strange actions he had just seen to leave. The next morning, Wash watched a long boat crew row up the river in a big hurry. As the new boat pulled to shore at the fort, the men jumped out and ran to Lafitte. Immediately the pirate captain gave a command that sent the buccaneers and Atakapa to battle stations.

Wash crept away from his log to a better position downstream. Once on the shore of the river, he spotted a third vessel sailing upriver – a United States warship.

Lafitte had planned an ambush.

As the U.S. ship drifted past the clamshell fort, Lafitte opened fire. Wash held his ears when the pirate guns exploded and the Navy cannons returned fire. Lafitte's first volley found its mark. The warship began taking on water. Her men dashed around on board desperately trying to stop the river from pouring in.

During the confusion, Lafitte sent a bunch of his men, along with the Atakapa warriors to attack the vessel in longboats. Indians and pirates swarmed the deck with knives and swords. The Navy guns stopped firing, but Wash had to cover his ears again to block the horrible screams of dying sailors.

After the fight, Lafitte sunk the navy's ship beside his own and set out on foot to the town of Lake Charles up the Calcasieu River. Days later he returned to the clamshell fort in a new vessel, dug up his loot and sailed away.

The Atakapa returned to the forest with new guns and other booty Lafitte had paid them. And Wash, fearing for his life, kept his mouth shut almost until the day he died…the end."

"Nice," Eden said. "Salt tell you that?"

I heard her yawn.

"No, this pirate dude in New Orleans."

"Sounds like these Lafittes haven't changed their ways much."

"Pirate Pete says the one you met, and his brother, sure haven't," I told Eden, not really wanting to scare her with all the "pyratosis" stuff. "We're meeting a guy tomorrow who's going to help us, though." I tried to sound positive.

"I'll help you, right now," she said. "Just get me a plane ticket and I'm there. I'm still mad at you for sneaking away like you did."

"Salt and I can handle it," I said. "Besides, I don't want…"

"Don't want what? Don't want me to stop you from doing the Salsa with your Cuban chica?"

"No, Eden. I was going to say I don't want you to get hurt. I thought you said you trusted me." I groaned. "Look, I've got to get off Salt's phone. I'm burning up battery."

"Just make sure you don't burn your tongue on any Latin hot sauce!"

"Eden."

"Sorry. *Sorry.* I'm just jealous and protective."

"You have nothing to worry about."

"So you keep saying," she said. "Call me tomorrow?"

"Okay."

"Harley?"

"Yes?"

"I want you back."

"I want me back, too."

I hung up.

The sky over my head was clear. Orion's belt stood out like a three diamonds. I can usually pick out those three stars in about five seconds. The one on the right is called Mintaka, my good luck star. In school, I learned it's actually a two-star binary system. One star circles the other about every six days. Pretty cool.

From his belt, I outlined the rest of Orion. I like Orion because he's got a club raised over his head like he's about to give someone a serious smack-down. If you can find his club, you can also locate the zodiac constellations, since the club hand is just below the feet of the twins in Gemini. Then to the left of Gemini you can see Cancer and Leo, to the right, Taurus and Pisces. On that transparent night, I saw them all.

There are millions and millions of stars in the sky. They probably go on forever. But, we humans are lucky to see two thousand, and that's on a clear night, away from the lights of town. Good thing, I guess. If we saw them all, the sky would be so bright that we wouldn't have any night. And, with all that light, I certainly wouldn't have been able to see what happened next.

Mintaka erupted – just flared to life! – and streaked across the other stars above the water until it blew up over the horizon northwest of us. I checked Orion's belt again. Oddly, Mintaka still twinkled in the trio. It had been a meteor, not a runaway star. But the weird part was that it had come from my good luck star, Mintaka.

Isabella's face popped into my mind. An odd sensation swept over me. I felt sure, beyond a shadow of doubt, that the shooting star had just showed me the direction where the Lafittes were holding Isabella – northwest.

Fire is coming...your fire...death fire.

I shut the old hag's voice out of my head. I refused to believe those words. Salt talked about faith. That's all well and good, but to me it means you have to sit back and rely on things working themselves out. A better way is action, doing what you know is right. I intended to find Isabella. And, I intended to set her free. I had faith in that. And, that's all I needed.

Skeeter

I woke up to the putt-putt-a-putt of a passing outboard and a flock of sea gulls screeching in the sky. The sun had risen. And, so had Salt.

"Rise and shine, mornin' glory," he said standing over me.

I was stretched out on the back seats of the Donzi.

"What say we get this show on the road with a cup of coffee," he said.

"Sounds good," I answered between a stretch and a yawn.

I hopped up on the dew-slick fiberglass to untie the forward line. Salt fired up the Donzi.

"You're a pretty good actor, kid," Salt said after I got back to the cabin. "Had me fooled."

"What?"

"Your eyes. You had them closed like you were sleeping," he said. "If I was a crook sneaking on the boat, I would have never known you were awake. Good thinking."

"Leave me alone, man," I said. "We're in the middle of nowhere. Nobody's going to sneak up on the boat."

"With a name like Jean Lafitte, this old town might have a pirate or two."

Salt didn't play baseball or football or basketball, or even watch sports on TV. No, I think needling me was probably all the sport he needed in his life. He was good at it, too, enjoyed every minute.

Salt idled the Donzi across the canal to town. We eased along until we came to a small store with a dock.

Each of the store's glass front doors had fake snowflakes and a paper Santa Claus on their panes. A bell rang when I pushed one open for Salt to walk in. It smelled good in there, like fresh donuts or something. Salt went for the coffee pot and I tracked down that delicious aroma.

"Can I help you?" said a sweet looking old woman from behind the donut case.

"Yes, ma'am," I said. "I'll take a dozen."

I picked out a dozen, six different flavors, and the woman closed the lid on my breakfast. She wore a permanent smile as she went about her work, seeming to enjoy it all.

"Someone's awful hungry first thing in the morning. Is that it?" she said.

Her voice sounded like music.

"Um, no," I said. "We're getting something to drink, too. Say, do you know a guy named Skeeter?"

The smile slipped off her face like a turtle diving off a log.

"What do you need him for?" she asked me sourly.

"Well, we're supposed to meet him."

"You are, huh? Well, you better buy yourself a pair of them white rubber boots over there. You're going to need them. That boy ain't nothing but a knee-deep pile of poopie-doo! Excuse my French."

"Is this the store he comes to?" I asked her, although I would have preferred to drop the subject.

Her sweet face had gone ugly in a heartbeat.

"This is the *only* store, son. And I run him away from here ten times a day. He ain't no good. You hear me? You and your friend best stay away from him. You look decent to me. No reason to screw that up."

I noticed Salt behind me.

"The coffee and these drinks, please ma'am," he said to her, then shot me a look that told me to keep my mouth shut.

The old woman eyed him suspiciously. I just picked up the donuts and headed out.

I sat on a bench overlooking the dock and the water. A great blue heron walked up the seawall towards me. The dude was looking for a handout. I wasn't about to share one of my precious donuts with him. He just shook his beak and stood there waiting for me to give in. When Salt crunched up on the gravel, the bird squawked and flew away.

"This store got a pay phone?" Salt asked.

"Over there," I said.

To the left of the doors on the corner by the parking lot, a payphone hung on the wall. Someone had taped an oversize candy cane to it for the season. Salt checked his watch.

"Eight bells," he said referring to the hour. "Reckon what time our guide arrives?"

"That lady in there didn't make him sound too trustworthy," I said. "Do you think Petey knows what he's talking about? Is this guy cool?"

"No swamp rat who knows where that cock-eyed fellow and his brother live is going to be the chummy type," Salt said, sipping his java. "Like old Petey said, though, we ain't got much choice."

Tires rolled over gravel in the parking lot as a pickup truck coasted to a stop. We watched the driver get out. She turned out to be a plump lady in a red Santa hat carrying a very large, black leather purse down by her knees. A Yorkshire terrier's head stuck out the top of the purse, bouncing along with her steps. The lady noticed us staring.

"Merry Christmas!" her voice rang out full of cheer.

"Merry Christmas," I returned.

The Yorkie yapped a couple of times before they entered the store.

"When this guy gets here," Salt told me, "play it cool. Let me do the talking. And, don't give him any information he doesn't need to know."

"You're going to get him to just drive us right up to their house?" I asked, wanting to know what Salt had in mind.

"Something like that," was all he said.

No wonder Salt's single. He's got real communication issues.

We sat there chit-chatting and growing old for another hour or so. I almost told him about the shooting star from the night before, but in the light of day I didn't feel nearly as sure about its meaning. Plus, I'd told him about enough weirdness lately. So instead, I called home and let my mom know everything was cool. After a while, I left the hard bench for the soft boat cushions. Salt kept his post by the store, holding his second cup of coffee.

Close to nine o'clock, I checked on Salt and saw him punching numbers into his phone. The payphone started ringing. This gnarly looking dude, walking across the parking lot, went straight to the phone and picked it up.

Salt spoke into his phone and the guy at the payphone looked his way. The dude set the handset on the cradle and headed towards Salt. I hopped off the boat.

"Well, then, a friend of Petey is a friend of mine," Skeeter was saying to Salt as I came within earshot.

The problem was, the man didn't look friendly at all.

He had longish black hair sticking out from under his New Orleans Saints ball cap, and from what I could see, he didn't wash his hair or the cap very much. His face sprouted a patchy black beard and, just above it, his green eyes darted around like a weasel's. They fixed on me as I approached.

"Travelling companion?" he asked. "Another friend of Pirate Pete?"

"Uh huh," said Salt. "He's coming with us."

"And where're we headed?" Skeeter said. "Ol' Pete didn't say."

"Fishing. Back in the bayou. Lake Cataouatche," Salt told him. "Petey says you know your way around."

"How come you don't take yourself?" Skeeter said. "That your fancy boat down there?"

"That tub won't fish," said Salt. "Draws too much water. We want to get way back in there. See some real back country. Cypress and all."

"That right? Okay, alright. No harm in that. Petey tell you my rate?"

Salt shook his head.

"I'm not cheap," Skeeter said with a slick smile. "Especially if I'm toting young'uns." He cut his eyes back over at me.

"We need two boats," Salt said.

"Two? You got more coming?"

"Once you get us in we can find our way back," said Salt.

"Two boats?" Skeeter repeated. "That raises the ante. Yes it do. Yes it do." He stroked his chin whiskers with two fingers and a thumb.

"Too much for you?" Salt asked.

"Oh, no. No, not at all, mister...ah."

"Salt. Folks just call me Salt."

"Well then, Mr. Salt, for a day of sightseeing with two boats, I reckon you'll be ponying up two thousand smackers."

"What? Are you insane?!" I said before I could stop the words from flying out.

"Sounds like Salt junior would rather go to the playground," Skeeter said.

"Fifteen hundred and you got a deal," Salt said without batting an eyelash.

Skeeter seemed to think about it for a moment, rolling an old toothpick over his teeth with his tongue.

"Fine. Fine," he said. He pointed a finger at Salt. "But fuel is extra. Got that?"

Salt nodded.

"Gonna take me a little time to round up the boats," Skeeter said.

"You're a tour guide with no boats?" I asked.

Salt glared at me.

"Guess I'm gonna have to change your name to Pepper," Skeeter laughed to himself, "on account of you're so hotheaded. Hee, hee. Salt and Pepper. Don't you worry none, Pepper. I'll be back directly, to pick you up." Then to Salt, "And, the downpayment. That's half the fare. The rest when we get there - cash. I don't mess around with no credit cards."

"Fine and dandy," Salt said.

"By the way, Mr. Salt, what in the world happened to your ear?"

"Caught a fish hook in it," said Salt.

"Got to watch them hooks," Skeeter said.

"Was the last guide's fault," Salt said. "I *fired* him."

"I s-see," said Skeeter and walked off across the parking lot.

"Hey, Pepper," Salt said. "Thought I was the one that was going to do the talking."

Great. That was just the kind of nickname that stuck. I couldn't stand that Skeeter guy. I needed to think of some awful nickname to give him. Then, it dawned on me that "Skeeter" *was* an awful nickname.

"Might as well grab a few provisions," Salt said reaching for his wallet. "Here, Pepper. Take this and get some vittles in the store. I think I see a hardware store down the street. I'll be right back."

I took the cash from Salt and walked back to the store. I bought peanut butter, jelly and a loaf of bread. Oh, and these things called "Moon Pies." They looked pretty tasty. I also got some drinks, cans of sardines and a box of crackers for Salt. The old lady at the counter scowled at me again. I guess she had seen us talking to Skeeter.

Down by the boat, I noticed the sun was doing a good job warming up the day. I pulled off my long sleeve dragon shirt to catch a few rays.

Salt returned about a half hour later. And we sat around another hour or so before Skeeter rounded the canal towing another skiff behind his boat.

"Salt?" I said watching Skeeter drive up to the dock. "What do we need two boats for?"

"Our friend here doesn't need to know our agenda. He'll get us close, then, we can send him home."

"How will you know when we're close?" I asked.

"I'll know," was all he said.

"Hey, Pepper," Skeeter shouted, "do me a favor and grab this line."

He threw a rope and I tied it off next to the fuel pumps. Skeeter topped off the tanks, reminding Salt to go inside and pay for it. I loaded our supplies into the second boat. Salt had brought back some fishing poles and a bag of stuff from the hardware store. We stuck that in the boat, too.

"Sorry it took me so long, Pepper," Skeeter said smoothing back his greasy hair. "Had to get my hair done."

He put his Saints ball cap on backwards.

I didn't even look at him as he spoke to me. But, I did make sure to flex every muscle from my waist up as I took the gear and stowed it on the boat.

"What y'all want to fish for?" Skeeter said as he eyed the poles.

I didn't even know what kind of fish they had back in the bayou. I didn't want to say anything stupid. Luckily, Salt arrived just in time.

"Anything that bites," he said to Skeeter. "And here's your change." He handed our guide a wad of bills.

Skeeter's fingers ripped through the money, counting it faster than a bank teller.

"Pot's right," Skeeter said. "Let's get this picnic moving."

Salt climbed down and sat by the motor.

"Just stow those rods under the seats next to the oars," he said.

The boat was your typical eighteen-foot aluminum skiff with three flat benches running across and a forty-horsepower outboard hanging on the back. I sat on the middle bench. Salt pulled the cord on the motor and it fired right up. We unhitched the lines and backed out into the main canal.

"We're gonna run across Salvador before we get up in Cataouache," Skeeter called to us. "Try and keep up."

He punched his throttle and we left the good town of Jean Lafitte behind us.

The Bayou

I couldn't tell you how I appeared outwardly. Inside, I was a bundle of nerves. Riding along on that boat I had too much time to think. I knew we were getting into the thick of things, and when that happens to me, my mind starts racing, imagining all kinds of crazy stuff.

For starters, I saw us pulling up to the Lafitte's dock in front of their cabin. That old hag was sitting on the porch in a rocking chair, waiting for me. I saw John Lafitte, Skeebo's big brother, in the backyard sharpening his sword on a big grinding wheel, Pirate Pete walking around the corner with his squeeze box, playing a version of *Blow the Man Down* that echoed like music through an airplane hangar. I had to stop it, think about something else, watch the scenery go by, anything.

Salt turned our boat out of the straight, man-made canal, into a more natural looking waterway.

"We're crossing the Intracoastal," Salt yelled to me above the noise of the motor. "That's Lake Salvador up ahead."

While we had been sitting around waiting for Skeeter to come back with the boats, I had gotten up the nerve to tell Salt about the meteor, how it showed me where Isabella was being held. Salt hadn't laughed, or even batted an eyelash. He just said that was the general direction of Lake Cataouache, the place he told Skeeter to take us. His reaction, or lack of one, made me feel better, like I wasn't going crazy after all.

A few minutes later, we popped out into Lake Salvador, a pretty wide body of water.

"Now we're into the freshwater zone," Salt yelled.

Several boats had anchored around the lake. I figured the water must hold some type of fish worthy of catching, redfish maybe. As if to confirm my thoughts, an osprey fell from the sky and struck the surface. When the bird flapped off, its talons held a squirming fish. The osprey shook the water off its feathers and flew away with its new breakfast guest.

We followed Skeeter out of that lake and through a creek to the next big body of water. When he slowed down, we did, too, settling into the dark water next to him.

"Well, here you have it," Skeeter said with his arms stretched wide, "Lake Cataouatche, in all its glory. A sight to see, huh?"

Calm water surrounded our boats. An awesome forest of cypress formed the shoreline.

"Sure is beautiful," I said.

"That's right, Pepper," said Skeeter. "But, that there bayou will swallow you whole if you let her."

He stared at me like a snake. The guy was filthy and no good. The sooner we got rid of him the better.

"Looks like a pretty good creek coming in over that way," Salt said pointing east past a stilt home perched half over the lake and half over the shore.

Skeeter glanced over his shoulder at the mouth of the creek. His eyes darkened as he swung back around to Salt.

"Naw," he said. "It might look good f-f-f-from here, but there ain't nothing worth seeing, or catching, b-b-b-back up in th-th-th-there."

Skeeter had suddenly started to stutter. He didn't look so good either, scared and nervous.

"That's okay," said Salt. "If there's not much back there then it should be nice and secluded."

"Th-th-th-there's a m-m-m-much better creek j-j-j-j-just up the lake."

"Peaceful," Salt said smoothly, looking Skeeter directly in the eye. "Quiet and peaceful."

"L-l-l-look, Mr. S-s-s-salt. Just p-p-p-pay me the rest and I don't c-c-c-c-care where you go."

"Sure thing, Skeeter," Salt said reaching into his pocket. "Here you go. The other half."

Salt tossed the bundle of bills over to Skeeter. The nervous guide's hands shook so much that he almost fumbled the money overboard. He got control of the wad just in time, though, and drew it in close to his body with both hands. Skeeter was breathing hard. I almost felt sorry for him. The dude was seriously spooked.

Skeeter took another look at the stilt home and then the creek.

"Steer clear of that c-c-c-creek," he said. "You hear? Ain't nothing f-f-f-f-f-for you there." He started his motor. "Bring back the b-b-b-boat!"

With that, he blasted off the way we had come.

"Didn't even say good bye," I said.

"Would've taken him too long," Salt said. "I don't think he wanted to stick around."

"What if he warns the Lafittes that we're coming?"

"Always a chance of that, I suppose. But, with all that money burning a hole in his pocket, I don't think the payphone back at the store's going to be his first stop. Besides, they already know we're here," Salt said nodding at the house. "I'm sure that place has eyes."

"The stilt house?" I asked.

"Yep. Early warning system. Guy with a pair of binoculars and a cell phone. Probably checking us out right now. But, even if the Lafittes are expecting me, they think you're fish bait out in the Gulf. They'll be looking for one of us, not two of us."

"So what do we do?" I asked him.

"We fish," Salt said in that raspy voice of his. "Hand me a rod. We'll convince that swab in the house that we're just two dumb tourists fishing for bass."

Salt held a fishing pole with one hand. He pulled out his GPS with the other.

"You got a fish finder on that thing?" I joked.

"No," he said. "But, I do have satellite photos."

I watched as Salt zoomed in on our location and followed the creek back into the swamp. The screen showed a lazy black line snaking back into the swamp – but no hideout.

"Don't see a house," Salt said. "That doesn't mean it's not there."

"Wouldn't a house show up on that thing?" I asked.

"Lafitte bragged to me years ago that he was working on some sort of camouflage system," Salt told me. "Might explain why my boat disappeared from that whirly bird camera down on Barataria Bay."

Salt squinted at the GPS as he dragged his finger on the touch-screen to slide the satellite photo up the creek.

"Bingo," he said, finally. "Pretty clever, but very unlucky."

"What do you see, Salt?"

"Look here," he said holding the GPS out for both of us to see. "Here's the creek. Here's a boat's wake showing up white. Here's where the wake stops as it curves in to a side channel."

"No boat," I said.

"Boat disappeared," he said. "Sound familiar? When the satellite snapped this shot, they had just driven that boat under their camouflage. Snug as a bug in a rug – so they think."

"You think they brought Isabella *and* the treasure?" I said, remembering the other reason we were hunting the pirate brothers.

"That's a whole lot of loot," Salt said tipping his cap back with the corner of his phone. "I doubt they brought it all the way up here. But if they did, there'll be a boat at this place capable of taking it back. Let's just drift around and fish for a while until that lookout forgets about us. We can ease back in there after sunset."

So we fished. Lake Cataouache is known for bass, redfish and the occasional walleye. We flipped spinner bait out for largemouth bass hiding in the snags along the shore. We caught a few, too. Of course, it turned into a competition between me and Salt to see who caught the most.

After the sun settled down across the lake and the sky had gone from yellow-orange to deep purple, we got moving. The boat had an electric motor mounted on the stern. Salt used that to silently slip past the house guarding the entrance to the creek.

"This creek was one of the routes Jean Lafitte used to smuggle cargo, and slaves, into New Orleans in the early 1800's," he told me under his breath. "Makes sense that these bozos wanted to set up shop on it."

"How do you know all this stuff, Salt?"

"I've heard a lot of sea shanties," he said from the darkness behind me.

Even though I couldn't see them, I knew his wrinkled eyes were twinkling at that one.

The cypress trees had lost their needles for the winter. That didn't mean the swamp was hibernating, though. In the clumps of Spanish moss that hung from their skeletons and under their bony limbs, the night buzzed with life.   Frogs croaked. Crickets chirped. A night heron barked like a dog with a sore throat as it fished along the water plants. And, if you listened really closely, every now and then a gator would let go of his log and softly plop into the water. Those splashes washed goose bumps over my arms. Alligators and I don't mix.

We kept quiet, listening to the night, as the electric motor pushed us along.

Then, I heard something.

Coarse laughter echoed through the swamp. I recognized that demented cackle, too, as it floated in ahead of us – Skeebo Lafitte.

"Alright, kid," Salt whispered. "That's him. We're getting on it now, so listen close and pay attention. I want you to drop me off and stay in the boat."

"But, Salt -" I started.

"No, buts! I'm running this thing and I want you to stay in the boat. Whole lot less for them to see if only one of us goes. I'm going to slip in there and see what's what."

The cackles came again, louder this time, and deep voices followed. We weren't close enough to tell what they were saying yet. Salt slowed the boat to a crawl.

"If there's any sign of trouble, Harley, you fire this thing up and blaze a trail out of here. You got me?"

"Yes, Salt."

"But, in the meantime be ready. If I luck up and grab Isabella we'll need to bolt."

"Got it."

The chatter got louder. I searched the darkness for lights or the outline of a cabin, trying to force my pupils to grow. The only light came from the dark, purple sky beyond the maze of cypress limbs. And, it was barely bright enough to be called light. No moon had risen and only a few stars slid through the branches.

"Man, we done good!" It was Skeebo. "I'm telling you, dude, we need to hit the Quarter tonight."

Skeebo sounded drunk. Another voice, stone-cold sober, with a creepy edge to it, answered.

"Mayhaps ye *needs* to curtail ye drinking," the voice warned. "The morrow brings a day o' toil hauling the spoils from Barataria. Harrrrrrr!"

"C'mon, bro. Have a little taste with me. Huh?" said Skeebo.

"And I'll give ye a taste o' me whip in exchange! Would ye likes me to loosen the cat from the bag?"

The voice didn't sound so brotherly.

"Lighten up, man. You're going to give yourself a stroke, Boudreaux."

The conversation got stronger, clearer, and then oddly, began to fade off. We still hadn't seen any sign of a dock or a boat or a house. When the voices had become mumbles again, Salt spoke.

"Couldn't see anything on shore. Must be camo," he whispered. "Saw ripples on the water coming towards us, though, out of that cove we passed. Should have been calm."

He shoved the electric motor's tiller to the left and our little boat circled to the right. We backtracked a ways, then I grabbed tree branch to hold us steady as Salt brought the boat to the side of the creek.

"That tree's an oak," Salt said. "Means the house is up on higher ground. I'm going to ease along the edge of the swamp and come at them from the back. Stay here. Don't talk. And get ready."

Taking only the canvas bag he had brought from the hardware store, he slid off the boat and slipped quietly into the woods. Salt could walk through the woods as quietly as an Indian. In a few seconds, he had blended into the night completely. The crickets and other creatures didn't seem to mind their new guest. They went right on chirping.

The Lafittes seemed just as oblivious. Skeebo sounded like he was singing some kind of a song, not too well either.

Waiting in that boat about killed me. But, I had given Salt my word, so I sat there feeling helpless.

A dog started barking. By the sound of it, the mutt was enormous.

Skeebo stopped singing.

A man yelled something, though with the dog getting louder and more excited, I couldn't tell what he said. The dog shut up and I noticed the whole swamp had fallen dead silent.

"It's him!" I heard Skeebo say. "Joe Gaspar."

My heart sunk into my stomach.

"On your feet, Gaspar," said Skeebo. "I thought you might try something like this. But, you just slithered into the wrong hole, my double-crossing friend."

More silence, then, "Looky what we found. Come up here to shoot somebody, José? We don't look too kindly on gun toting trespassers around here, Gaspar!"

I heard a thud and a grunt, like someone had kicked the wind out of Salt.

"Please escort our guest to the big house, Bubba. I'm sure my brother would love to see who's come to visit."

I didn't hear much else until boots hit the wooden planks of a porch. A door opened and closed, and that was that. The sounds of the night critters faded in again as if nothing had happened.

But, something *had* happened, something bad. The swamp had just swallowed my friend Salt, whole. Cutting him out was going to be like gutting a live barracuda with one hand tied behind my back.

The Pirate's Lair

My plan was simple. I aimed to take the fastest, most direct route to the house while they were still focused on Salt - I'd drive straight to their front door.

As quietly as possible, I moved to the back of the boat and took a seat next to the tiller. The electric motor hummed no louder than an aquarium pump as it pulled the boat backwards away from shore.   Still, to my ears, it sounded like a commercial jetliner. I was so paranoid the dog would sense me.

He barked a couple of times, and I knew from the tone that the thing was still on alert. I'd have to be extremely quiet. The problem was, I couldn't control the direction of the wind. He might smell me at any moment.

The moon had risen enough to shine on the cove Salt had pointed out. Ripples spread out from darkness on the far side. I spun the johnboat around and headed in.

The cove narrowed to a creek size channel and curved to the left.

Just when the trees got thick enough to blot out the moon, the boat hit something, not solid like a rock or a tree, spongy, like grass. I re-aimed the bow and tried a different spot in the creek. I hit the stuff again, and as before, the obstacle was just springy enough to bounce the boat backwards. I twisted the motor control to bump the boat forward, then let go and crawled to the front.

As the boat drifted in, I stuck out my hand. My fingertips ran into some kind of barrier, a heavy material stretched tight. It felt like the stuff they put across a trampoline, that synthetic, black fabric. My hand ran over the texture until I hit a seam stretching vertically from the water higher than I could reach. In the center of the seam I felt the teeth of a huge zipper. I traced my hand along the zipper down to the water, then under the surface. The barrier ended about a foot below and right in the middle was a big zipper pull tab.

I didn't know what in the world I'd be facing if I pulled on that zipper. I knew one thing, though – I'd be a sitting duck in that boat. So, I decided to go in ninja style, without the boat.

I backed the boat into a bush, took off my boots, and slipped into the bayou.

December weather had cooled the water. The stuff was pretty chilly as I ducked below the surface and felt my way under the camouflage barrier. I opened my eyes underwater. Points of light filtered down from above. I swam away from them until I ran out of air.

I popped up to a strange sight.

The mesh material had prevented the scene from passing through to anyone observing from the creek outside. But, on the inside, the woods were much brighter and I saw everything clearly. Unfortunately, the view was not cool at all.

The place looked like something out of a bad dream.

Light flickered from torches stuck in trees. They began at the docks and continued around a frame house into the cypress beyond. I saw a skull spiked on a stake. A hatchet had been driven into the bone so hard that it still stuck there. Slick and shiny, another skull stared out at the water with hollow eyes. Well, one eye wasn't exactly hollow. The shaft of an arrow had taken care of the eyeball.

Flames mixed with swamp water, creating crazy reflections that ran across the surface all the way to my face. Wet hairs raised on my neck when I noticed the combination.

When fire meets water, blood will flow.

Words from the note pinned to the piñata-me were coming true! Dude, I was so freaked, I half-inhaled the water.

I had to get out.

I kicked towards the docks. Two identical eighteen-foot Carolina Skiffs were tied to one dock and a twenty-foot bow-rider with a jet drive floated next to the other. I swam under the dock next to the jet boat.

I hadn't been there long enough for my ripples to die down, when the front door of the house opened and two guys walked down to the skiff dock. I held my breath.

"I'll bet you a week's pay that the old fool came alone," said a gruff voice. "We'll find his boat out in the creek."

I eased around the bow to get a good look at them.

"Well, he sure didn't swim here," the other guy said.

"Got that right," the first man snickered. "Swamp's so full of snakes and gators you'd have to be nuts to get in that water."

They both laughed as they climbed down into a skiff.

"They know this clown?"

"He's the one we jumped down in Florida two days ago. That's his boat down in Barataria."

"No way."

"Way, dude. Skeebo said they go back a ways."

"Well, I'm sure brother John'll roll out ye old welcome mat for him."

"Got that right."

They laughed again, mean and low. The motor started and their boat eased off the dock towards the barrier. The zipper buzzed and I watched the skiff putt off down the creek. I hoped our boat had floated out with the current to give me time to get up to the house.

I scrambled up to shore on my hands and knees. If anyone else happened to be outside, they would have spotted me. The torches made it that bright. But, the yard looked empty, so I sprinted to the house in a crouch-run, diving belly down into the crawl space. Above me, footsteps knocked against the floor boards towards the back of the house. I crawled to them on elbows and knees.

The crawlspace stunk like dead rats and rotten fish. With each foot I crawled, more mud caked on my shirt sleeves. When the boots stopped clunking, I stopped to listen. The muffled conversation came through the floor well enough to hear words. I recognized the two voices. It was the Lafittes.

"Can't believe the fool came all the way up here," Skeebo said.

"The hornswaggler be wantin' the girl, not the money," his brother replied.

"Money. Girl. What's the diff," said Skeebo. "He's a fool just the same."

"Aye, mayhaps a useful one."

"That girl sure is sweet," said Skeebo changing the subject.

"Arrr. That wench, she be worth harrr weight in gold amongst the landlubbers of Guatemala, by gad," the darker voice said. "I know just the gentleman, devil a doubt."

"Aw, man," Skeebo whined. "I was hoping we'd keep her."

"Avast! Stint this foolery and forget the lass! She sails in the morn. We have more pressing concerns. Where be the rogue Gaspar presently?"

"Tied to a chair in the dining room," said Skeebo.

"Cast off then, mon frère, let's not be keeping the good swab waiting."

If the guy really had pyratosis like Petey said, then the corny pirate voice had to belong to John Lafitte. I crawled after their footsteps until they stopped.

"José Gaspar! We be meeting again! What say you?"

"Good Lord. Look at you," Salt said. "You been travelling outside the country? Sounds like you picked up an accent."

More footsteps sounded quickly across the planks.

"Sink me in oil and burn me with torches! No one sneaks aboard me ship to foul me ears as the likes o' ye. Fling another filthy warrrd, Spaniard, and, on me soul's salvation, I'll carve ye gizzard and fry it for me breakfast."

"Chop his head off now, dude!" Skeebo said.

When Salt spoke next, he sounded like someone had a chokehold on him. "Hard…to…say…much of anything…with that blade…on my neck."

"Thar! Breathe freely, mackie. But, mind yer tongue, lest ye be cravin' a date with the earthworms. Harrrrr!"

More boots scuffled the floor over my head, then someone clapped their hands twice.

"Wharrr be that hunk o' dogmeat with me dinnarrrr?!" Lafitte demanded.

"You told the boys to search the creek for Gaspar's boat," Skeebo said.

"By the devil's twisted teeth! Does a chore like that take half the bloody night?"

"They've only been gone a few minutes," Skeebo said.

"Well then, shake a leg and fetch us drinks whilst we wait," Lafitte said.

"The usual?" said Skeebo.

"Aye. The same."

Skeebo walked off.

"So, Spaniard, yer debt to me be finally settled. Why risk the whip and pickle by showing yer face here?"

"Sell her to me, Lafitte."

"Shiver me sides! That be a good one. Ye fails in ye rescue so ye figures to buy what ye can't take. Harr, harr, harr."

"I'm serious, John. You're going to sell her anyway. Sell her to me."

"Ye be one sick urchin, Gaspar. That wench be less than a third ye age."

"I'll take her home to her parents."

"Bless me guts. Near be float a tear from me eye."

"Cash money. And you won't have to bother with shipping her off to some other place."

"What maggot burrows ye brain? Take me for a fool, do ye? Attack me home? Steal me hostage? You've the tongue of foul bilge water. Ye will run straight for the cops."

"You know I can't do that, Lafitte. She's got no papers. They'll take her back."

"No," Lafitte continued, "Make no mistake, Gaspar. Ye both be sailin' the morning's tide...unless."

"Unless?"

"Aye, me Spanish son of a tavern hag, thar might be a way."

Footsteps clunked on the wood again, showering me with a dry, stinky mist.

"Here you go," said Skeebo. "One for you and one for you."

"Ah, me hearty. 'Tis time for a toast. Raise yer tankards high," said Lafitte. "Here's to ye and here's to me, and if ever we disagree I'll blow ye down and drink to me! Bottoms up!"

Someone choked and spit.

"Good Lord," said Salt. "What is that?"

"Why it's his favorite," laughed Skeebo.   "Tang and Mountain Dew."

"Keeps the scurvy at bay," Lafitte said.

"Awful," mumbled Salt.

"What say ye, scupperlout?!"

"Awfully good…Look, Lafitte, you were saying there might be another way?"

"Aye, pirate. 'Tis rumored ye had a map? Certe?"

"What kind of map?"

"Don't toy with me knave, or I'll bash yer loaf!   The treasure map ye used to find the loot in less than half a day! By Blackbeard's burnin' whiskers, I know ye has more!"

"More maps?"

"The treasarrrr book, ye dullard.   Many a story has been told about the blessed records kept by the scum, Gasparilla. Many a tale o' how they passed from hand to bloody family hand.   And now, you black-hearted crab hauler, ye be the last in that line o' misfits. The book for ye freedom. That be me offer."

It got really quiet. I hoped Salt wouldn't give up the secret book. Finally, he spoke.

"I have no idea what you're talking about, Lafitte."

"Wrong answer, swab."

A door opened and closed.   Boots pounded through the house to the room above me.

"We found his boat, boss," a man's gruff voice said. "Empty, except for a pair of boots and some fishing tackle. I guess he brought the shoes for the girl to wear."

"No other rable-rousers?"

"Nope. Searched up and down the creek. Nobody."

"Arrrr. Take hold me guest and bind him to the post, then fetch me cat-in-a-bag. He has tarnished me belly's desire. Perhaps the language o' lashes persuade me hunger to return... and this swab to a healthier reply."

I heard Salt struggling as the guys dragged him out towards the back of the house.

I started crawling again as fast as I could, and didn't stop until I had reached the back porch. Torch light fired up the small yard behind the house, but I stayed just out of its reach, hidden in shadows under the porch.

Two guys the size of gorillas pulled Salt down the porch steps and into the backyard to a telephone pole. They forced his arms around the pole and tied his hands together. One of the guys ripped the back of Salt's fishing shirt wide open.

The big dorks walked over to an old log and sat down. Salt stood at the pole looking at the house.

I was about to get his attention when the back door opened and two more people walked out onto the porch above me. One of them continued down the step into the dirt yard. Tattooed eyes on a bald head stared straight back at me. It was Skeebo Lafitte. He carried something in a grungy, cloth sack.

A dog whined across the yard in front of a small out building, a shed maybe, to the right. A huge Rottweiler strained against a chain.

"Easy, Polly," one man said to the dog. "You'll get your chance."

"Couldn't leave well enough alone, could you?" Skeebo said to Salt poking him in the ribs. "Couldn't let bygones be bygones. Well, now you're going to wish you had! Uh, huh."

Boots clunked down the steps and a buccaneer straight out of the 1700's walked slowly over to Salt.

He looked to be about six-foot-four, black hair to his shoulders under a black hat as big as a sombrero. One side of the brim had been folded up to the top and had an ostrich feather sticking out the back. He pushed up the ruffled sleeves of his puffy, oversized shirt. Baggy, black pants, stuffed into black boots, ended just under his knees. To top it all off, a sword in a scabbard hung at his side off a wide belt.

The dude looked ridiculous. It had to be John Lafitte. I prayed to God that pyratosis was not contagious.

"What me dear brother is trying to say, Mr. Gaspar, is that we had considered our score settled," Lafitte said.

Salt's eyes narrowed to slits.

"I owed you nothing, Lafitte," Salt said.

"Arrrrrrr, but ye did!" said Lafitte. "'Tis beyond doubt me family suffered long e'er since ye Latin baboons denied us our spoils."

"Jean Lafitte didn't even have a family," Salt shot back.

"Jean Lafitte had no family that history knew of, Mr. Gaspar," Lafitte said taking a couple of steps toward Salt, close enough to wipe his nose on Salt's collar. "But, I assure ye," he spoke to Salt's ear, "we do live and breathe."

Lafitte turned abruptly to face his brother and I saw his face for the first time. Dark eyes sank into his skull below angry eyebrows. A scar ran down his left cheek. Greasy hair spilled out of a black bandana under his hat. The man looked pure evil.

Grinning, Lafitte reached into the sack Skeebo held open. Taking his time and smiling, he pulled out an ugly whip that split into mini-whips at one end. The other end, the handle, glowed in the torch light. Its leather handgrip disappeared into the midsection of a snarling panther. The cat shined as if made of pure gold and, in its fangs, it held a huge, red ruby.

"Ye know this piece," Lafitte said to Salt while holding the whip under his nose.

"Where'd you get that?" Salt asked.

"Aye, ye know it," sneered Lafitte. "It be the very cat-o-nine what served the dog Gasparilla. The very one what scarred me blessed forefather after *yer* yellow blood *stole his booty!* Tore the flesh from his hide, they did, and left him for dead in the briny sea! A-harrrr!"

"You're insane, Lafitte. Gasparilla took that with him when he fled the royal prison before sailing to Florida. He kept it as a reminder of their brutality, but never used it himself."

"I give ye an 'F' on ye history, Gaspar," Lafitte laughed. "And, tharrrr be no make-up exam! For ye see, the cat be out o' the bag."

Lafitte handed Skeebo his hat, adjusted the bandana he wore underneath, and prepared the whip, untangling the rawhide strands with his fingers.

He calmly took aim.

I thought my heart was going to rip out of my chest when that whip smacked Salt's skin. The leather opened bright red slashes, like a cat claw, onto his back, but my friend barely made a sound.

"So, Gaspar," said Lafitte, "I be making me-self clear? Does ye remember the book?"

I knew Salt wouldn't say a word, and he didn't. I had to do something. I had to act. I couldn't just wait around, be patient, let things work out. No one else was going to rescue Salt. It had to be me.

Lafitte let the whip fly again. Another claw mark appeared, crossing the first. Salt grunted a little.

"Nice, bro," Skeebo said with one eye closed. "You done made a pattern!"

Lafitte lashed Salt's back again.

"I'll buy the girl," Salt said through his teeth. "Where is she?"

"Cease yer prattle, swab! Or, so help me, I'll sew shut yer lips!"

I had to do something. But what? They outnumbered me four to one. They had all kind of weapons. I was just a kid.

The whip cracked against Salt's skin once more. I had to move. As I rose up to get going, the weird monkey-chicken pendant bounced off my throat.

...Protect the boy when this is so. Papa La Bas gives wishes three...

Now, honestly, up to that point, I was not a big wisher. I was in a jam, though, and figured it couldn't hurt. I held onto the pendant, closed my eyes tightly, and tried to make it count.

A moment later, I moved.

Like a mouse on a mission, I scrambled out from under the house into the light of the flames. I didn't know what I was doing, but I was doing it.

"Hey, jerkwad!" I screamed at Lafitte.

It surprised him so much he actually jumped. When he whirled around to face me, I got a sense of how big he was. The man was huge, I'm talking NFL defensive lineman big.

"Well, bleed me dry," Lafitte said quickly composing himself.

"That there's Gaspar's sidekick," said Skeebo, staring like he'd seen a ghost.

"Harrrrr?" said Lafitte while slowly drawing his whip. "Did ye not cast him to the sharks?"

"I did. But, he keeps coming back," said Skeebo, whining out the words like a little kid. "Like…a boomerang."

"Well, two scurvy dogs for the price of one sounds good to me," said Lafitte as he wound up and slashed at me with the cat.

Sometimes, being young has its advantages. I moved faster than he did. I dodged the leather and jumped over to the nearest torch, ripping the thing out of the ground, stake and all, and waving the burning end towards him before came out of his lunge.

Lafitte straightened up and smiled.

"Git, boy!" Salt yelled at me. "You can out run them."

"That's it lad," Lafitte sneered. "Run! Polly wants a cracker."

When she heard her name, the big dog barked.

"Bite me, Lafitte," I said.

He tried to whack me again, but I was ready for him. I blocked the whip with the stake and, after the braided leather tips had wrapped around it, I yanked back with all of my 160-pound frame. Lafitte wasn't ready for that. The thing popped right out of his big, hairy hand.

Skeebo, who wasn't doing anything to help his brother, broke out into a fit of hysterical laughter. This infuriated Lafitte. His face got seriously red and he charged me like a bull.

Now, the Lafittes would surely be classified as bona fide, backwoods swamp men by any civilized person who met them. But, I noticed they shopped at Target like everyone else. At home, my mom had the same kind of torches they did. Their flames burn at the end of a wick shoved down a can of lamp fluid.

When Lafitte was almost on me, I cracked that can right on his bandana, drenching his head in hot, flammable liquid. A second later, he burst into flames.

Skeebo screamed like Little Bo Peep when he saw his brother's head on fire. He ran over and tackled him to the ground. And, while they were rolling around trying to put out the inferno with Lafitte's black hat, I got over to Salt.

"Salt! Hold your hands still. I'll untie them," I said.

"Run, kid," he told me. "You got them to stop, now run while you can. Those other two are getting up."

"I'm not leaving you again, Salt!"

"I'm sorry, kid. This is has gotten away from me. It's more than I can handle. Get the cops."

A shotgun blast almost took my head off. I looked around the pole. A guy near the log was pumping another round into the chamber.

The gun went off again. This time Salt yelled out. Some of the shot had ripped open his pant leg.

"Go, kid!" he yelled. "You got no choice."

I took off towards the swamp faster than a cartoon mouse, running blind straight into the Louisiana night, hauling butt. I zigzagged around cypress trees. The gun boomed again. Tree bark exploded next to my head. I cut over, putting the shed between me and the gun. That Rottweiler went nuts.

Out of the corner of my eye, I saw Lafitte still burning on the ground, Skeebo trying to beat the flames to death with the hat. After that, I didn't look back.

Queen Anne's Revenge

I don't know if you've ever been shot at. Before that night, it had never happened to me. Let me tell you, though, when you hear a bullet fly past your head, or as in my case a whole bunch of buckshot, you understand right away that your ears are directly connected to your adrenal glands. Dude, I was covering some serious ground.

Plus, they had Salt. They had Isabella. If they got me, that would be the end of it. Some way, somehow, I had to reach the cops. That much was doable. We weren't that far from town. When I had looked at the aerial shots on Salt's GPS I'd seen houses to the east. All I had to do was figure out which way was east and get there. In the meantime, I was *running*. My feet barely touched the ground.

Because of the darkness, trees seemed to come at me from nowhere. I couldn't see their trunks until they were a foot or two in front of my face. At least the full moon had risen. Without it I would have been totally blind. Palmetto fronds whipped my arms and legs. New cuts burned as their teeth sawed my skin. I was making a ton of noise in the underbrush. I really didn't have much choice.

The big dog started barking. I figured they had set her on my trail and that worried me even more. There was no way I could outrun that thing. I had to get clever, and I had to do it quick.

Immediately after hearing the dog, I hit another snag. My feet began splashing through water. I made even more noise. The water also seriously slowed me down. In a few strides, it was up to my knees, then my waist. I just kept chugging along, like an escaped convict, hoping the water wouldn't get any deeper.

The underbrush didn't grow in standing water, but cypress trees stuck up everywhere, and not only their trunks. Cypress trees grow these things called knees that stick up out of the swamp like little fence posts. I don't know what they're for, but they sure got in the way. Since I really couldn't run anymore, I decided to go into silent evasion mode. I slowed down and zigzagged around the cypress as quietly as I could.

The dog closed fast, probably still back on dry ground following my scent. When her bark became more of a yelp, I figured she'd gotten to the edge of the water. I stopped just long enough to hear her paws rustling around in the dry leaves. I had time to put a little distance between us. I prayed that Rottweiler's were afraid of water. I prayed a lot that night.

I used my hands to pull myself through the swamp. The cypress knees had smooth, rounded tops that actually turned out to be useful in deeper water. I grabbed one and pushed off, making a turn so that I headed directly towards the rising moon.

I upset something big to my left and the animal splashed away from me. I couldn't see what it was, but the creature made plenty of noise. I stopped for a moment to listen and to let the animal's splashing have a chance to lure the dog off my trail. The dog had fallen silent, too, probably listening to the same animal. Shortly, she began to whine.

Next, I heard the dude.

"Get in there, Polly! Get 'im! Go! Go on! Go!"

The dog barked again and, when I looked over my shoulder, I saw the beam of a flashlight slicing through the cypress. The mutt kept barking as she and the man waded in. The flashlight tracked off to my left, apparently following the animal I had spooked. I turned and eased off in the opposite direction.

With those guys going the other way, I felt a bit better about the situation - until the shotgun went off. The boom echoed through the night like rolling thunder. I instinctively checked my body. I was very relieved not to find any holes.

"Aww, man!" the dude said in the swamp somewhere behind me. "Polly, that ain't nothing but a nutria, dog. Now, *get* the boy!"

I had no idea what a nutria was. All I knew was that the dog was coming again. Somehow, that overgrown canine sensed where I was and came straight at me, barking like she had rabies or something. I started hauling butt again, not caring how much sound I made.

Before I had gone ten feet, I stepped off a ledge and went completely underwater into a sinkhole. The sound of barking dissolved into a liquid rush of bubbles and gurgles. I popped my head above the surface and treaded water. The dog sounded even closer. As I frantically pumped my arms and kicked my feet, the dog broke through to the edge of the sinkhole, foaming at the mouth to get me. I dropped below the surface and kicked like a frog.

Blind, swimming like a mad man, I waited for a blast of lead shot to rip me apart. Five seconds. Fifteen. Twenty. Nothing happened. Thirty. Forty. And then, the pain began – in my lungs. I was running out of air.

I surfaced, or tried to. My skull crashed into something hard, pinning me under. I reached up and felt slimy wood. I had gone below a root or something. I kicked forward to get away, my lungs on fire, bubbles coming out my nose, stroking, stroking, until I cleared the root. My head shot to the surface and I sucked in air like a vacuum cleaner.

On hands and knees, I pulled myself up a short, muddy shore, not crawling more than two feet before slamming into something else.

I tried to get my bearings. The moon was gone. The night had suddenly gone pitch black. I couldn't see a thing, just had to feel. Maybe the lack of oxygen had affected my vision. My fingers became my eyes. With an arm stretched out in front, I found rough bark. I explored the darkness above my head and discovered it was clear. Slowly, I rose to my feet.

The dog still barked somewhere, distant and muffled, like someone had shut a door and locked her inside a doghouse. I stretched out my arm and found the tree again, following the wood with my fingertips. I needed to get past the thing and keep going, but the bark curved the wrong way, around me instead of around the tree trunk. I stepped back into the water and held out my other arm, touching more bark on the other side.

I had surfaced *inside* a tree!

I was trapped and, as soon as that realization hit me, I started to panic. The dog-in-a-box barking got closer and closer as the Rottweiler ran around the sinkhole pond. I had no choice but to stay put. I had no time to escape. If I swam out, Polly would likely bite my head off when I crawled up to shore.

So, there I stood, in a vertical coffin maybe four feet wide, waiting, listening. A cool breeze tickled the back of my neck and, after repositioning to locate the source, I noticed a head-high slit an inch or two wide passing through the living cypress trunk to the outside world. The inside of that tree was so seriously dark that this tiny window opened to a night outside that seemed as bright as day.

At first, I was glad because the knothole meant I wasn't completely cut off from the outside. Also, I might be able to see my pursuers as they came around the tree. That small ray of hope got shot down with my next worry - the dog might catch my scent through the hole and bay up like she'd treed a raccoon.

I certainly didn't have much time to fret about it. A moment later the dog appeared in the moonlit swamp. I pulled back from the spy hole and froze like a tree within a tree. The dog's nose worked the ground and I heard her paws shuffling around the leaves. She stopped, listened and stared directly at the knothole like she had the ability to see through cypress wood. Figures. She was a Louisiana dog. She was probably equipped with voodoo powers to read my mind. I held my breath.

Something tickled my ear. I ignored it, not wanting to give the dog any help in locating me. It didn't matter. The x-ray eyed demon-dog started to go off, yapping full throttle like she'd discovered a nest of mailmen.

Then, the flashlight beam came into view, dancing across the ground. The bubba with the shotgun couldn't be far.

The tickle on my ear turned into a cool, smooth sensation down the side of my neck that felt kind of like I had leaned into a garden hose filled with cold water.

The flashlight got brighter and the mangy mutt was soon joined by a shotgun barrel and a pair of muddy boots.

"Where is he, girl?" Lafitte's gunman asked the dog. "Is he behind the tree? Huh, girl?"

The gun barrel lifted up and leveled at my chest.

"Well, let's have a peek. Boy? You back there?!" the man demanded.

The end of the garden hose thing slipped into my field of view and a forked tongue flickered out tasting the air. Perfect – I had a snake slithering down my neck while Bubba and his dog planned their next trip to the taxidermist. Some lucky charm around my neck!

"Come out, come out, wherever you are," the guy sang like a kid.

Caught between a 12-guage and a set of fangs was almost too much to bear. I simply closed my eyes and hoped for the best, as a bead of water trickled down one side of my face and some kind of serpent slid down the other...and, I started to shake.

Fortunately, the snake didn't seem to mind. He extended himself off my shoulder and stretched for the knothole. The brightness of the flashlight beam didn't slow him down either as Bubba splashed it through the crevice.

"Make it easy on yourself, boy," the dude was saying, "and just come out from behind that – what the?! Holy crap! A cottonmouth! Get back dog!"

I heard the dog yelp when the big guy stumbled over a root or something and went down on top of him. As they hit the ground, that gun went off at the sky. BLAM!! Even inside the cypress, it made my ears ring.

Snakes must not have ears, though, because this one didn't stop, or even slow down. It sped up. The crazy thing shot through the knothole and made a beeline for bayou boy and his swamp dog.

"Aiiiiiii! Get back! Get back!" he screamed at the snake.

When the tip of its tail had cleared the hole, I leaned forward and stuck my eye in there for a better view.

The man left his flashlight burning on the ground as he backstroked across the cypress needles like a human crab to get away.

"Dumb dog!" he swore. "You done treed a snake!"

He scrambled around to his hands and knees, and kept going in the opposite direction right behind the dog's butt.

"Dumb dog!" he repeated from the forest. "Lost my light!"

The dog whined.

"I ought to make you go get it – snake and all!" he said from further away. "Come on. Get back on the trail. That boy's getting away."

They crunched off into the night as I resumed breathing.

I ran a hand over my wet hair and down the side of my neck where the cottonmouth had just slithered. I tried several times to wipe away the feeling of the reptile. It didn't work. The shaking didn't stop either.

I hid in that hollow cypress another thirty minutes making sure the dynamic dumbos didn't double back. During that time, the swamp outside slowly chirped and croaked back to life. I figured the coast was clear.

Feet first, I re-entered the water and slid out of the cypress and under the roots. Nobody shot at me or shined a light into my eyes as I crawled up on shore. I didn't even get snake bit. Bubba's flashlight was still on, shining away into the forest floor. I picked it up and switched it off thinking it might come in handy.

By then, the full moon had risen pretty high in the sky. I had a hard time figuring out which way was east. And, I couldn't see enough of the constellations to find the north star. Using my internal sense, I picked a direction and struck off. If I was right, the road to town, and to the police, couldn't be very far off.

The whole ordeal felt similar to being lost in the Gulf two nights before. I was alone, cold, wet and exhausted, not to mention lost in the dark. The more I thought about it, the more discouraged I became. I even had thoughts of lying down and going to sleep.

What kept me going? Salt and Isabella. They were the ones truly suffering. And, they were counting on me, and running out of time. That reality gave me the strength I needed to keep moving. As long as my feet kept walking, I was certain they'd take me to someone who could help.

It's kind of funny how life shapes a person. Sometimes what happens to you in a previous situation affects how you think and react later when you face a similar situation, especially if those situations are traumatic.

Here's what I mean.

One of my earliest memories came from an experience I had when I was lost. I was really small. My mom and dad were still happily married and we hadn't moved to Palmetto Cove yet. We lived in a trailer in a small fishing village called Matlacha.

Mom was off at her job as a clerk at the Super Value store. And my dad was out fishing for mullet. I was staying at a daycare center, and I use that term very loosely, set up in one of the other trailers. The lady in charge had more kids than she could possibly watch, even if she wasn't constantly on the phone.

Well, I got bored, squeezed through the pallets she used as a fence, and wandered off. I think it was my first big-time walk through the neighborhood alone. At first it was pretty cool. I got to pet dogs I had only been able to wave at before. I climbed around on a couple of swing sets that I had worshipped from afar, you know, stuff like that. Then, I turned a corner and saw that gi-normous, old shrimp boat tied up at the dock on the edge of the trailer park, the *Thelma Mae*.

I guess I had seen the boat plenty of times, because whenever my mom tells this story she always says how much I pestered her about getting on that boat. Well, that day, I got my chance. I walked right up, jumped right on, and nobody said a word to slow me down – the dock and the boat were deserted.

Instantly, I had left Matlacha for a voyage on my very own pirate ship. She was no longer the *Thelma Mae*. She had become *Queen Anne's Revenge* and I was Blackbeard, running around her rusty hull waving a broken gaff through the air like a sword.

Of course, a pirate captain was most at home at the helm of his vessel, barking out orders to his crew. So, eventually, I found my way to the wheelhouse and managed to pry open the squeaky door.

The place was cooler than I ever imagined. Not only did it hold an actual ship's wheel and all the controls, it also had bunks as well. That made it the captain's quarters, too! On the other side of the wheelhouse, I found a stove and a sink, my galley. I was in pirate ship heaven.

I had made my break from the babysitter that morning. By the time the midday sun climbed high in the sky, the bridge of *Queen Anne's Revenge* was getting pretty hot. I kept playing and imagining and plundering until sweat rolled off my face like rain. I got real thirsty, too. And, as much as I hated to, I needed to go find a drink. Well, when I tried to open that big rusty door, I couldn't get the thing to budge. Not panicking, remaining calm, I tried each window. Unfortunately, none of them opened either. I was stuck.

I looked out towards the trailers of my neighborhood and saw a whole bunch of people walking around. They seemed to be searching for something, treasure maybe? It didn't dawn on me that they might be looking for a lost little boy.

I yelled, hollered, screamed, waved my arms. Nothing worked. No one even glanced over at my sweat box on the shrimp boat. Gradually, I ran out of steam and got real sleepy. I laid down on one of the bunks and passed out, my clothes drenched.

If it weren't for my dad, they would have found my pirate skeleton in there.

Working on a hunch, he had thought to search the old boat when he came back from fishing that day. You see, I had mentioned that shrimp boat, no, I had *begged* him forever to give me a tour of the *Thelma Mae*. He knew I had a fascination with the shrimper. That didn't stop him from getting really mad with me, though. He didn't let me go fishing with him for a month!

Anyway, the point is, my dad rescued me from terrible danger. One of the best things he ever did for me, by the way. And, that rescue set the stage for how my mind always worked when I wedged myself into one of those predicaments. In the back of my head, I always had this feeling that somebody's going to bail me out.

Maybe that's what Salt means by faith. I couldn't tell you. But, I can tell you that it gives me the will to keep going a little longer, to hold out, to stay positive. Thanks, Dad. For all the things you did really wrong, you got it right that day.

And, that night in the *Burnin' Bayou*, I needed every ounce of it.

Swamp Music

Franklin D. Roosevelt, the 32nd President of the United States, was one of Ms. Corley's favorites. Ms. Corley was the best teacher I ever had in middle school. She was also the only one who ever paddled me. I deserved it, I suppose. Anyway, she was always spouting out quotes from FDR. That night in the swamp, one of those quotes popped into my head.

The old president had said, "To reach port, we must sail – sail, not tie at anchor – sail, not drift."

You hear that stuff in school and it kind of rolls in one ear and out the other, until it applies to you. Then, it pops up like a sign on the shoulder of the road at night.

So, I listened to President Roosevelt and kept sailing along. I fought through scrubs. I waded across channels of black water. I bumped along over countless cypress knees. And when I could barely walk, because the ground became so spongy, I pulled myself through Jean Lafitte Preserve with my hands.

It was exhausting.

I tried not to take breaks. I had to get to the cops as quickly as possible. The worst part was that, in the darkness, I had no idea if I was going in a straight line or in a big circle.

It seemed like hours. Except for the position of the moon, I had no way to tell how much time had passed. My rubber watch had snapped off. I had no cell phone, only my shirt, pants, socks, and the dude's flashlight.

My feet were killing me. They weren't so much sliced as they were bruised. Each step was pure torture.

During a break to pull a thorn out of my toe, I heard music.

The tunes floated through the air like smoke, fading in, and fading out again. I cocked my head to the left and right but couldn't really pinpoint where the music was coming from. I figured it best to keep going in the direction I had been travelling. The song faded in again, upbeat, happy, fast. I caught a bit that sounded like an accordion, not like Pirate Pete's, different. The notes slowly drifted away until the song faded out completely and I thought I'd lost it.

All at once, the music started up again, louder than before. I moved faster, though I had to stop splashing from time to time in order to follow it.

I spotted a light low in the trees.

I took off, running through shallow water down a trail. After three or four steps, something grabbed my ankle, ripping my leg out from under me. In one bone wrenching jerk, the thing yanked my ankle up, pulling me skyward until I hung completely upside down by one leg, dangling like a rag doll in the air.

I thought I must have banged my head on something, too, because bells rang in my ears.

The accordion music stopped in mid-song. A few moments later, a spotlight clicked on as I struggled to free my foot.

"Basco!" boomed a voice.

I froze for a second to listen and the bells stopped ringing.

"Baaaaasco!" the man called again from the direction of the light.

I climbed my leg up to my ankle and the ringing started up again. I had been snared in some sort of trap. The bell was there to alert whoever had set it. The thing had done its job. Someone was coming!

I held myself in place with one hand and felt around my ankle with the other. A wire noose bit into my sock – and my ankle – and the force of gravity cinched it tight. I needed a pair of pliers or wire cutters. I didn't even have a pocket knife. Friend or foe, I was about to make a new acquaintance.

"Come on, boy" the trapper said. "Let's get 'im."

Great. Another backwoods dork and his dog. My life could not get any worse.

Soon, feet splashed through the swamp, heading towards me. At least the trapper was nearby. My ankle was already starting to ache. Hanging that way for a few hours really would have been tough. I was getting ahead of myself, though. I didn't know for sure if this dude was *going* to cut me down. Maybe he was related to the sadistic Lafittes. Maybe he'd just set up a camcorder to video tape me squirming for hours. Maybe he liked tiny bell music a whole lot better than accordion music.

"What in God's creation do we have here, Basco?" the man said as he and the dog approached. He carried a flashlight in one hand and a large caliber handgun in the other. "Some kind of animal has crawled into our backyard. Not gator. Too big for one of those rats."

The dog barked.

"Well, I don't know if it's edible or not, Basco," he said. "Hey. You edible?"

I hung upside down like a mute opossum.

"I'm talking to you up there. You edible or not?"

"Not edible, sir," I said. "You mind cutting me down?"

"It can speak, Basco. Let's see what it's doing in our trap," the man said to the dog. "Before I decide to let you go or not, I need to know what you're doing in my back yard?"

Wonderful. Backwoods *and* paranoid.

"Sir," I told him as I squinted into his light, "I had no idea this *was* your backyard. I'm lost."

The dog stepped forward and sniffed my head. I braced myself, but he didn't bite. In fact, his tail wagged back and forth in front of the flashlight. He went a step further, confirming his friendliness by slobbering a wet tongue down the side of my face.

"Okay," the man said. "Tabasco says you're telling the truth. I guess we get you down."

He shoved the pistol into a holster and grabbed a rope hanging off the sapling that had snatched me off the ground. Before I knew it, my ankle came free and my head hit the swamp, followed by my shoulders and the rest of me, of course. I righted myself, shaking the mud out of my ears.

"You got the reflexes of a dead cat," he said.

"I'm tired."

He laughed to himself as I got to my feet. It wasn't the least bit cruel, though. There was something warm in it.

"Let's get you up to the house, boy. You're a mess," he said.

The dog splashed off back the way they had come and the man motioned with his flashlight for me to follow. I picked up my own borrowed flashlight and went.

His house, more of a cabin actually, had been built on a small rise of dry land. Around front, camp fire flames danced on the ground outside a ring of stones. A single rocking chair waited by the edge of the fire.

"You take a seat by the fire," he said. "I'll be right back."

He was an odd looking man, and big. I watched him bypass the steps to reach the porch in one giant stride.

Basco laid down by the fire in a spot he had hollowed out, head on paws, watching me. One of his eyes was blue. The other looked like a marble with streaks of blue and swirls of brown.

I checked out the grounds around the cabin, no cars in range of the fire light. There was a canoe or something down the hill. Beyond that, things got too dark to see.

"Here we are," the man said as he came back. "Wrap this around you while you dry out." He handed me an Indian blanket.

His skin was dark and his black and gray hair was pulled into a pony-tail. The corners of his eyes wrinkled when he smiled.

"Oh, almost forgot," he said. "My one luxury out here."

He returned to the porch and switched on a boom box. The accordion music started again in mid-song.

"Zydeco blues," he said. "Never gets old."

He carried a chair from the porch and joined me by the fire.

"Billy Joe Eagle-Feather," he said extending his hand. "But, folks call me Frenchy."

I shook his hand. It was big.

"Pardon me for saying so, sir," I said to him, "but that name doesn't sound very French to me."

"Mom was African. Dad was Choctaw. The Frenchy part got thrown at me because we're down on the bayou and most folks have no idea what pigeon hole to stuff me into. Somebody at work called me Frenchy years ago and it stuck. Easier for people, I suppose. You?"

"Harley Davidsen Cooper."

"Well, pardon *me*, but you don't look like a biker."

"Mom's a Floridian and Dad's a drunk," I said. "He wanted a biker son, I guess, but he screwed up the spelling on the birth certificate so I'm closer to being Norwegian."

His eyes crinkled again as he looked me over. The man seemed very calm, very sure of himself.

"Well, Harley. How'd you get lost in this swamp in the middle of the night?"

My gut told me I could trust him, besides, I needed his help, fast. The truth had to be the best approach.

"Mr. Eagle Feather," I began.

"Call me Frenchy, son. I've gotten used to it."

"Frenchy, I'm going to give you the condensed version because I'm short on time."

I hit the high points and Frenchy listened. He raised his eyebrows a time or two, but he let me go on without interruption.

"So, as you can see," I said, getting ready to make my pitch, "I could really use a ride to the police station. You'd be doing me a huge favor if you gave me a ride. I can easily repay you anything you want when I get back to Florida. You have a car around here?"

Frenchy stared into the fire without a word. The Zydeco music played on in the background.

How hard could it be, I thought. A simple yes or no would be fine. If he didn't want to take me there he could at least point me in the right direction. Finally, he broke out of his trance.

"You know these fellows, these Lafittes," he said still gazing into the fire, "they've been around these parts for a long time." His eyebrows pushed up a set of lines on his forehead. "And, so have my people. Both sides of the family."

Frenchy lifted his gaze off the fire and settled it down on me, his eyes pinning me to the chair like two weights.

"That's an interesting story you just told," he said. "And, I heard those gunshots, just like you said…I believe you, Harley. Now, I'm going to tell you a story. One that's been passed down in my family for over two hundred years."

The dude was heavy, as in serious and intense. I felt his power. That encouraged me to keep my mouth shut and let him continue, even though I didn't have the time for any long winded explanations.

I fidgeted in the rocker.

"Don't worry. Don't worry. You'll get the short version, too. But, you need to hear it in order to understand my answer to your question.

You see, Harley, my ancestors were slaves. Again, both sides. And they were turned into property by that very same Lafitte family and other folks just like them."

Frenchy turned his attention back to the fire.

"Now, on my mom's side, they kept track of things through the women. That family tree stretches way back to San Domingue. That's a place that doesn't even exist anymore. Today, we call it Haiti."

He focused on me again. Man, those eyes were major league. I'd like to see him and Salt in a staring contest.

"They don't teach this much in school, but Haiti was the second republic in this hemisphere after the United States. The slaves there in San Domingue revolted. Overthrew their wealthy French owners and declared themselves free. They kicked out most of the white people who had survived the revolution. Jean Lafitte was one of these.

Lafitte must have been some guy, ruthless enough to be hated by all the black folks down there, but charming enough for my great, great, great, great grandmother to fall in love with. He was a sea captain, a slave trader and a pirate. And his butt was between a rock and the hard hatred of a group of people he had not treated very kindly. They wanted him dead.

Well, my grandmother, she felt different. She intervened. She explained that Mr. Lafitte was her husband, talked up his good points, and arranged safe passage for both of them off the island on a ship bound for Cuba in 1803. They lived a good life together there for a few years until the Spaniards got restless and started kicking the French out and it was time to leave again. This time, Lafitte sailed a boat-load of refugees to New Orleans to meet his brother Pierre.

That boat made a pit-stop on the island of Grand Terre at the mouth of Barataria Bay, and Lafitte built a house for my grandmother. He made trips into New Orleans. She stayed there. A few months later, after he had established himself in the town's social scene, he sold my grandmother and every other black person on that island, into slavery."

Frenchy paused for a second. By the fire light, I saw his eyes working over some thought running through his head. The Zydeco music had taken a break as well. Then, as the tunes got cranking once more, Frenchy continued his story.

"I suppose that Lafitte and his brother did well for themselves in these bayous. Built a big smuggling empire. Had big parties in New Orleans. Eventually helped Andrew Jackson and all that.

He may have even met some of my father's relatives in the fighting. Jackson and the government used a bunch of

Choctaw warriors to repel the Brits, too. Promised them land and peace. That didn't last, though. A few years later, soldiers marched the Choctaw to Oklahoma and forced them into a different type of slavery.

My great grandfather on my dad's side emancipated himself and led a small group of Choctaw back down here to their homeland. Their descendants still live together not far from here. One of them, my father, met my mom and here I am.

You see, Harley, I know these guys. And I'm not talking about Skeebo and John themselves. I'm talking about their kind, the kind of men they are.

Now, I've considered them both crazy for years, crazy but harmless. Then I start hearing the rumors, the ones about them acting like pirates, smuggling people up from Cuba, and worse. I figured live and let live, none of my business, you know.

Now, when I hear first hand from you what they have in store for your friend and that girl, the blood in my veins begins to boil. It's one thing to be born a pure idiot, stumbling along from one screw-up to the next. But, *choosing* a life of crime, preying on others and their misfortune in the name of misguided ancestors who did the same, well, that fits the definition of evil. And, I can't abide by evil."

"Then you'll help me get to the cops?" I asked him as a rush of enthusiasm straightened me to the edge of my chair.

"Cops'll take forever. No, son, we have to act tonight. We're going to help you get your friends back. Right now."

"We? Who's we? You got more people around here?"

Maybe it was a reflection, but I thought I saw a fire spark to life in Frenchy's eyes.

"Basco!" he said to the dog. "We got business tonight. Let's get packing."

The dog lifted up from his snooze and cocked his head at Frenchy. As if he understood English, Basco jumped to his feet, ready to go.

"What kind of dog is that Mr. Frenchy?"

"Just Frenchy, son. And, that's a Catahoula."

"Cata-what-a?"

"In the 1600's, the Choctaw around Lake Catahoula domesticated the red wolf. Mixed it with a trapper's dog and came up with that. You sure you're a Florida boy? Tons of them down there."

"Hog dogs?" I said.

"Good hog dog. Fearless. They'll bay up a boar hog for an hour until a hunter shows up."

Basco wagged his tail.

"He doesn't look so vicious to me," I said.

"Trust me," Frenchy said. "When Tabasco gets hot, he's got a side to him that'll make you lock all the doors and turn out the lights."

Basco chuffed and smiled.

Frenchy walked back inside his cabin. When he came back out a minute later he wore a buckskin jacket, the pistol in the holster and a big knife in a sheath that hung down almost to his knee. He threw a pair of old boots down in the dirt at my feet.

"These'll probably fit," he said, "unless you like being barefoot."

"Thank you," I told him.

They did fit. I made a silent promise to hold onto that pair.

"Where's your car?" I asked him.

"No car, Harley," he said walking past the fire down the hill. "No roads out here. We'll take my yacht."

"Yacht?"

"Pirouge, actually," he said. "Kind of an old timey dugout canoe. Follow me."

Frenchy clicked on a flashlight as we got away from the flames. I saw it then, the pirogue pulled up on the shore by the water. I flipped on the flashlight Bubba had left at the hollow tree, hitting the water with a second beam. Light reflected onto a stand of cypress thirty yards away on the other side of a black pond. Lilly pads spread across the lake where the trees met the water.

"We're going to paddle there?" I asked.

"Son, we're only fifteen minutes away."

"Oh."

"You took the long way here," he laughed. "Get in."

Son of a Sea Hag

Frenchy's pirogue did look sort of like a canoe, one small seat in the back, no seats in the middle. Basco pushed past me and took the bow. His super short, golden coat had been stained with a mixture of different colored spots, like Frenchy had flicked paint at him off a brush.

Frenchy shoved the pirogue into the lake and took the rear seat.

"Let's save these lights," he said. "Might need them later."

"Are they somewhere on this lake?" I asked.

"A creek leads out of here, winds around, and passes very near their backyard. Grab that paddle and dig. We're going to the left."

As my eyes adjusted to the night, the cypress swamp showed more detail. The full moon followed us along branches draped with Spanish moss. Frogs and insects chattered away all around. My paddle slurped as it dipped in and out of the water. I couldn't even hear Frenchy's paddle. I felt its power, though, as the dugout heaved forward with each stroke.

"When we hit the shore in a few minutes," said Frenchy, "I want you to be quiet as a mouse. There's a shed out back. Chances are, your friends are locked inside. With any luck, the bozo brothers and their little thug-lets will be asleep."

"Yeah, I saw the shed when I was there. They had that big dog tied up in front of it."

Frenchy stopped talking and kept paddling. In fact neither one of us said anything else until we slid up on the mud behind the Lafitte's place.

"Tabasco," Frenchy said in a low, firm voice. "Hunt."

Basco silently hit the ground, crouching immediately. He waited until Frenchy and I were out of the pirogue before inching forward up a trail to the Lafitte's compound. The path must have been fairly well used because very few leaves from the tupelos and scrubs had settled onto it. Basco and Frenchy made no sound at all as they crept towards the yard behind the main house.

All the torches had been put out. However, the moon shined brightly enough to make out the shed and the Rottweiler sleeping on his chain at the shed door. A man, slumped over with a shotgun on his lap, slept in a chair on the back porch of the main house across the yard. Basco stopped at the edge of the yard and looked back at Frenchy for instructions.

Frenchy leaned over to my ear.

"I'll take care of the guy on the porch," he whispered. "Basco's got the dog. When things start happening, you move from here to the shed and get them out."

"What if it's locked?" I said under my breath.

"Improvise," he said.

Frenchy got Basco's attention and pointed at the sleeping Rottweiler.

"Tabasco. Heat's on that dog," he whispered.

Basco locked onto the Rottweiler, tensing for the command to attack.

Frenchy pointed to the ground at Basco's paws and said, "Hold."

I stood next to the Catahoula watching Frenchy sneak up to the porch tree by tree. Polly's chain jingled as the dog shifted positions. Luckily, the mutt didn't wake up.

Frenchy made it up on the porch undetected. I watched him slide out that big blade and hold it to the man's neck. He eased the gun off the sleeping guy's lap and leaned it against the house before checking on us.

"Tabasco! Skit that dog!" he yelled.

Everything happened at once.

Basco shot across the yard at Polly. The Rotty lifted her massive head just in time to see the Catahoula launch himself like a missile, teeth first.

The guard on the porch jerked awake. Frenchy held him in place with a fist full of hair and that huge knife on his neck. The slacker didn't move an inch.

The Rottweiler lumbered to her feet too late. Basco smashed into her shoulder and knocked her back to the ground. The two animals snarled and snapped in one big ball of fangs, paws and fur.

When I started for the shed, the back door of the house burst open. Frenchy was ready for it, his leg stretched across the opening. Skeebo led the way. He tripped over Frenchy's leg and went airborne.

The dogs broke apart and Basco circled Polly. The Catahoula faked a lunge and fell back, testing the larger dog's reflexes. Polly jumped to the side, obviously a lot slower than the muscular hog dog.

Skeebo nailed the hard packed ground at the bottom of the steps, crumpled in a heap, and didn't move much. Frenchy dumped the other guy out of his chair down the steps to join Skeebo at the bottom. When John Laffite stepped out on the porch, the Choctaw calmly stuck the barrel of his pistol into the smuggler's neck.

"Down the stairs and on the ground," Frenchy commanded.

Meanwhile, Basco and Polly faced each other in a standoff, just growling, waiting for the other to make a move. That's when Basco made a transformation that literally caused goose bumps to rise on my arms. That *barely* domesticated cousin of the red wolf – and I do emphasize the word 'barely' - got back to his primal roots with a snarl so nasty the devil himself would have stopped dead in his tracks had he heard it. The Catahoula's face wrinkled up to his ears baring a set of fangs, white as the moon, sharp as broken glass. Maybe I imagined it, but his eyes seemed to turn red and his teeth seemed to grow a few inches just before the dog sprang off the ground. I almost felt sorry for the Rottweiler. The big, dopey dog was frozen and helpless as those demon jaws landed squarely on her neck and took her down. Basco pinned Polly on her back and all the Rotty could do about it was whine like a puppy.

A man burst out of the shadows on the far side of the shed. It was the Bubba who had hunted me. He held a 2-by-4 high over his head as he rushed Basco from his blind side.

With a whole lot of instinct and hardly any thought, I made a beeline for Bubba. He never saw me coming. On the run, I gripped the D-cell flashlight like a baseball bat. Bubba reached the dogs before I did, but not by much. As he began to swing that board at Basco's skull, I reared back and nailed him in the head with that flashlight like I was swinging at a fastball.

He went limp before his body hit the ground. The 2-by-4 bounced off the dirt beside him.

I tossed the flashlight onto his belly as the dork rolled over groaning.

"Here's your light, dude," I said.

"I got him covered," said Frenchy. He held the pistol on Bubba and the shotgun on the others. "Go get your friends out."

Basco had Polly by the throat. The Rottweiler wasn't going anywhere. I stepped past them to the shed and, as I got closer, I noticed something on the ground in the weeds. It was the bag Salt had carried off the boat. I picked it up and looked inside.

"Nice going, Salt," I said to myself when I spotted the pair of bolt cutters.

I snipped the lock and pulled open the door. The shed was dark inside.

"Salt?" I tried.

Much to my delight, my old friend came limping out using Isabella under his arm as a crutch. He looked okay, just beat up, not about to die or anything.

"You okay, Salt?" I asked.

"Seen better days, kid. I'll make it though."

Isabella spotted Bubba on the ground, then looked up and met my eyes. Her expression said it all – surprise, relief, thanks.

"That the cops?" Salt asked looking over at Frenchy.

"No," I told him, "That's a neighbor."

"Billy Joe Eagle-Feather," Frenchy called over.

"Ye be the son of a sea hag," said Lafitte. "And, a right dead one at that!"

"Shut your mouth, Lafitte, before I shut it for you," Frenchy said. "You're done. Don't make me stick a fork in you to prove it."

Bubba rolled around and sat up.

"Take this, Harley." Frenchy tossed the shotgun over. "March him into the shed and, if he takes a step in the wrong direction, blow his leg off."

I caught the gun and leveled it at Bubba.

"In the shed, mister," I said.

He got off the ground holding the side of his head and shuffled into the shed.

"Why don't you guys keep him company, Lafitte?" said Frenchy. "At least until the cops arrive. I wouldn't want the guy to get lonely."

"You're dead meat, Frenchy!" said Skeebo as he checked for broken bones. "You done crossed the Lafittes for the last time."

"Shut up, cross-eyes," said Frenchy behind his pistol. "I ain't never messed with you guys at all. Just stood by, year after year, while you and the rest of your criminals messed with everybody else. About time I did something.

And if you want to go around whining about what this man's relative supposedly did to your long lost grand-pappy, let's talk about what Jean Lafitte did to *my* family.

Now get your sorry butts off the ground before I sic that dog on you!"

That did it. All three of them got moving towards the shed.

"Me dear, half-breeded neighbor," Lafitte said while doing his best to smooth back what was left of his burnt up hair, "surely there be a way to ye heart. We've a pile of doubloons at me vessel?"

"Basco!" Frenchy said pointing at the pirate.

The Catahoula kept his grip on the other dog's throat but locked his blue eyes on Lafitte.

"Quite so, me hearty," Lafitte said. "In the shed we go."

Frenchy covered their backs with his pistol and I kept the shotgun on them as they filed by. Skeebo tried to look scary and mean, giving me a cross-eyed squint as he went. He just looked funny to me, though, like a cartoon character.

"I know where you live, boy," he said to me.

"That's great," I told him. "Be sure to send me a post card from prison, *freak*."

"Oh, I will, boy. I will," Skeebo said, trying his best to sound like Clint Eastwood. "And when you open it – BOOM!"

"You don't open post cards, idiot."

"Well, maybe it ain't no postcard," he said losing the tough-guy tone. "Maybe it's a fancy package. Yeah, a package. And when you open it – BOOM! – right in your face."

"Just get in the shed," I said, pushing him along with the barrel of the gun.

"BOOM! Check your mail. Special delivery!"

I shut the door and wedged one of the bolt cutter handles through the padlock holder, locking them in.

"Let's get down to the boat," said Frenchy. "Tabasco. Release."

Basco relaxed his grip on Polly's neck and slowly backed away growling. The Rottweiler had no fight left in her at all. She retreated towards the swamp as far away from the Catahoula as her chain allowed. If she had had a tail, it would have been between her legs. I saw her working her stump in that direction.

"How's the leg, Salt?" I asked as I shouldered Salt's other arm to help him walk.

"Get this shot out and it'll be good as new," he said. "Stings a bit right now."

For Salt, admitting any pain was huge. It had to hurt.

"Who's your friend there?" he asked.

"Found his cabin back in the swamp," I said. "He likes to be called Frenchy. He's lived here forever, Salt. His family goes way back, as far as the Lafitte's people. And, the history isn't good. I think what they did to us was the last straw for Frenchy."

"Lucky acquaintance," Salt said.

"Just got to have a little faith," I said grinning at him. "There's our boat," I said to Frenchy when I spotted Skeeter's rental tied to the other dock.

"I thought I'd take you back to town in this one," he said pointing at the jet boat. "More comfortable, and a wee bit faster. I'm sure the Lafittes won't mind if we borrow it for a while. The police can bring it back to them."

Isabella and I helped Salt down into the jet boat. The keys were in the ignition and, after a couple of tries, the motor kicked over and fired up. I unhitched the ropes and took the front seat across from Frenchy.

"Come on, Basco," Frenchy called to his dog. "Unless you want to stay."

Basco leapt onto one of the bow couches and walked through the windshield door to Frenchy whipping his tail back and forth the entire time. I could tell that dog enjoyed a boat ride as much as my dog, Hammerhead, maybe more.

When we drifted up to the camo material that hid the Lafitte's compound from the outside world, I went to the point of the bow. The zipper slid up easily, opening a big split for the boat. Frenchy eased us through.

Funny, as soon as we were back on the outside of that camo, the air smelled sweeter.

"Frenchy," said Salt from the backseat, "know anything about their hideout down in Barataria?"

"Mr. Gaspar, I presume?" Frenchy asked Salt.

"Call me Salt."

"Well, Salt," said Frenchy, keeping his eyes on the creek as he navigated a turn, "I've heard about one, but where it is, I don't have a clue."

"They got my boat down there," said Salt.

His head was leaned back on the cushion and his voice sounded weak. The gunshot wound must have been taking a toll.

"That's what Harley told me. Look, Mr. Gaspar-"

"Salt."

"Salt. Truth is, I could have blown the whistle on these guys years ago. Should have, too. But, I suppose I became a one man island back here in the bayou.

Tonight, your young friend here opened my eyes. I-"

"Listen, Frenchy," Salt said, "no apology necessary. Sounds like we're cut from the same bolt of cloth. I've had plenty of chances over the years to stop these looney tunes, too. I knew full well what they were up to. And, I just let them go. If anyone owes an apology it's me."

I guess Frenchy felt responsible for the whole mess. But Salt did, too. I think Frenchy rescued Salt in more ways than one. Heck, they rescued each other, a little bit. The unexpected rewards of truthfulness and unselfish actions, as Salt has explained to me on more than one occasion, can be surprising. Good fortune comes from good living. I just hoped our good fortune would last all the way back to Florida.

Not everyone on the boat appeared so positive, though. Isabella stared off into the darkness looking uneasy.

"Isabella," I said, "how're you doing?"

"I'm okay," she said, "just worried."

"I think the worst is over," I said trying to convince both of us.

"No, I'm worried about my parents," she said turning to face me. "They don't know whether I'm dead or alive. Do you guys have a phone?"

"Never got around to one of those," said Frenchy.

I shook my head.

"We'll call them soon as we get to town, Izzy," Salt said. "Promise."

Basco turned around and, after licking Isabella's arm, laid his head in her lap.

"Those people are sick," Isabella said. "I thought you were dead, Harley."

The moon slipped out from behind a tree, highlighting the puddles welling up in her eyes.

"Lucky my dad taught me how to swim," I joked.

"Quiet, guys," Frenchy said holding up a hand.

"You hear something?" I asked him.

He cut the motor and I heard it, too. In the night behind us, a pair of outboard motors had cranked up.

"Hang on," said Frenchy. "We can outrun them."

Sunrise

Two flat-bottom skiffs exploded out of the side creek before Frenchy even found the throttle. They were on us in a hurry.

"Go! Go! Go!" I yelled.

Our hull shook as the motor revved and we accelerated, though not nearly fast enough for me.

"Frenchy!" I said, trying to get him to go faster.

"Hang on. She'll get there," he said calmly.

With four people and a dog, we had a lot of weight in the boat. It took a few seconds to get up on plane. Frenchy was right, though, when she finally got there, that jet boat was flying. In fact, we were hauling so fast, I had no idea how the man was going to handle all those sharp turns at night, even with the moon's help. He seemed to steer the boat by sense of feel.

"We're losing them!" Isabella yelled from the back.

I saw a flash and heard a pop.

"Get down everybody," I shouted. "They're shooting."

Frenchy leaned the boat into a hard turn and the skiffs vanished behind a wall of trees.

"Woo Hoo!" I hollered.

"Oh, it's not over," said Frenchy. "There's a channel back there, a short cut to the lake. Those skiffs can squeeze through it."

He cut the wheel and the bow-rider banked hard the other way, as we rounded a bend. After straightening out, Frenchy reached down between the seats and picked up the shotgun I had used earlier.

"Take it, Harley," he said. "It'll give us some breathing room if they beat us to the open water."

I took the shotgun and laid it on the side rail barrel out aimed at the cypress.

"Look out!" shouted Frenchy as we rounded another bend.

I looked ahead of us just in time to spot a big branch hanging low over the water on my side, directly in our path. The limb struck the bow before ramping up the windshield. I had to raise the shotgun up before I could snatch it into the boat. I was a fraction of a second too late. The branch ate me up and tore that gun right out of my hands.

The impact spun the boat across the channel. Thank God those jet boats are built to slide. Frenchy quickly regained control and punched the throttle again.

"Everybody okay?" he asked over his shoulder.

"We're good," answered Salt.

"Frenchy, I lost the gun," I told him. I felt like an idiot.

Frenchy didn't waste any time fretting about it. He simply reached under his jacket and pulled out that big pistol.

"Take the revolver," he said. "Keep it down unless we need it. Then, be careful. It kicks."

The thing felt way heavy. I gripped it with both hands and aimed it at the sky.

"Salt, can you handle this thing?" I asked.

"No can do, kid. Can't turn around with this leg all banged up."

"Give it to me," said Isabella.

"What?! You can shoot?" I shouted over the noise.

"That's a Smith and Wesson .44 caliber, is it not, Mr. Frenchy?" she said.

".44 Magnum. That's right," Frenchy said.

"Give me the gun, Harley," she said holding out her hand. "I shoot with my dad all the time."

Behind us, the white wake of a skiff ripped around the bend.

"Harley, now!" she yelled.

I handed the butt of the big revolver to her. Salt hunkered down as Isabella immediately rested the gun in both hands on the padding covering the back of the boat. The skiff came out of its turn leveling off about fifty yards back. In the limited light I couldn't see faces, but it looked like two guys sitting in the boat. As their boat steadied, one of them raised a gun to his shoulder.

Isabella didn't hesitate. The .44 exploded, spitting thunder and fire into the night. I couldn't tell if she hit anything or not, but the skiff slowed to a crawl.

"They backed off!" I shouted.

Isabella still faced our wake, gun in both hands, ready.

"That's only one boat," Frenchy said.

"But, they'll stop the other," I said.

"Not if they took the short cut," said Frenchy.

Basco put his front paws on the seat next to Salt and rose up for a look at the water behind our boat. The dog barked a couple of times into the wind.

We rounded a corner and burst out of the swamp into the open waters of Lake Cataouatche. The moon hung over the far western shore, blasting out of the sky like a flood light. To the east, cloud bottoms had been brushed with a trace of fire. Frenchy leaned the boat and aimed us south.

Though we ran dark, without navigation lights, I knew the boat's bright yellow paint job shined like a beacon to anyone in our immediate vicinity – and I had no doubt that there were people in our vicinity.

We bounced across another boat's wake just before a gun boomed out of the house at the mouth of the creek.

Basco dove for cover on the deck between me and Frenchy as the fiberglass exploded just forward of the windshield. Frenchy yanked the boat to the right and, after following that course for a moment, swerved back to the left.

I heard another boom, but this time the blast was much closer. I whipped around and saw Isabella settling the .44 back on the cushion. She'd just bought us enough time to get out into the lake, and out of range of the gunner in the house.

Just when my hearing started to return, Isabella's cannon blew a hole in the night once more. Man, that thing was loud. My ears were ringing worse than at the end of a *Metallica* concert!

The other skiff had taken the short cut and was closing fast across the lake. To make matters worse, the first boat skidded out the mouth of the creek, hauling butt across the chop to join the other skiff forty or fifty yards off the edge of the lake. We were zigzagging to avoid bullets. They flew towards us straight as an arrow, gaining fast.

Frenchy saw them coming and straightened out while ramming the throttle forward until it hit metal. The jet-boat hesitated – then, the motor shut off!

"*Frenchy!*" I screamed.

The skiff's, running side by side maybe seventy yards back, closed the distance much faster. Isabella took aim again and fired. The massive gun recoiled off the cushion, but the Lafittes kept coming.

"Frenchy! Do something!"

Of course, he wasn't waiting for my encouragement. He already had the lever back to neutral and the starter turning. It fired and he gradually fed the thing fuel. The boat creeped ahead, plowing the water about as fast as a duck with a broken leg.

Our motor coughed, sputtered, and shut down again. I heard a crazy rebel yell coming at us from one of the skiffs. The pitch of their motors fell as the Cajun's boats settled into the water on either side of us.

Their four guns threatened to end things right there. I heard Isabella drop the .44 on the deck.

"Aharrrrr!" Lafitte cried out. "Caught you, you sawed off runt!" Silhouetted against the rising sun, the pirate pointed a finger at me. "Blaze me curly locks, did you?! Free me swabs, eh?! Pay ye now with ye hide, boy!"

I watched the gun come up level with my head as if I was watching TV. I heard him cock the trigger. And, just as the flash and boom filled the air, a blur of fur and fangs flew off the floor to the pirate's throat.

Basco took the slug in his chest. The dog went limp in midair and his body splashed into the small piece of lake separating our two boats. He did not even cry out or whimper. And, dropping into the water like a stone, he was gone.

The recoil of Lafitte's gun caused their boat to drift to one side. That uncovered the sunrise behind his back. The top of the sun had just begun to ripple streaks of fire over the water towards our boat.

I remembered the charm around my neck.

... Papa La Bas gives wishes three. Trick the future and it shall be...

It worked before. Why wouldn't it work again?

I grasped the pendant into the palm of my hand, closed my eyes, and wished my heart out.

After, I cautiously raised my lids. The sky had darkened. The sun had not begun to rise.

The skiffs were still seventy yards away. Frenchy worked frantically to start the boat. Basco sat panting with his tongue out, watching his master.

I checked the sky to the east. The leading edge of that big, beautiful, blazing ball sizzled into view like an instant replay.

The motor caught. The tachometer redlined. The impeller shot a column of water into the lake. And, we took off like a fighter jet.

"Everyone hit the deck!" Frenchy commanded.

We all dropped down, including Basco, and as Frenchy steered the boat blind with a single hand at the bottom of the wheel, a gun rocked the air behind us. Simultaneously, the windshield exploded. Bits of safety glass blew all over us, but the engine kept making a most excellent noise and we kept flying forward.

The next time they shot at us, their gun sounded much farther away and disturbed nothing on our boat.

"I think we're good," Frenchy yelled as he came out of his crouch to check on the position of the lunatics behind us.

From my spot under the console, I watched the sky grow brighter. Finally, like an old turtle, I stuck my neck up and looked to the east. The sun had popped up, a big, beautiful circle of light. We had made it to the next day.

I relaxed my grip on the monkey-chicken pendant.

The skiffs had shrunk to dots behind us. Up ahead in the distance, vegetation outlined both sides of the pass to Lake Salvador on the horizon. A white pinpoint of light, probably the stern light of some fishing boat, emerged into the open water and travelled along the western shore of the lake.

We were getting back to civilization. I felt better.

"Everybody doing okay back there?" I asked my friends in the backseat.

"Fine as frog hair," Salt said.

Isabella finally turned around towards the front, dropping the pistol into her lap.

"How long to town?" Isabella asked Frenchy.

"Twenty-five minutes or so," Frenchy said, "if this motor holds."

She looked over at Salt, wind in her hair and tears dried away.

"How's the leg?" she asked him.

"Well, missy, I hate to say it, but it might need a band-aid," he said. "Got any?"

I found a first aid kit squirreled away in a console compartment. The plastic wrapping still covered the case like it had been bought the day before. I guess Lafitte and company didn't waste any of their corporate healthcare benefits on gunshot victims. I pulled out a roll of gauze and bottle of antiseptic making an exception to their business plan.

Salt's leg looked bad. His skin had been peppered with bird shot. Each and every hole oozed blood. A couple bled more than the rest, like the lead had severed veins or something. I didn't even attempt to tweezer out any pellets, especially while scooting across a lake in a jet-boat. I just doused everything with antiseptic and tied him up tight with gauze and bandages.

"Any tighter and my toes are going to go to sleep," Salt said.

"Sorry, Salt. I figure the pressure will keep the bleeding to a minimum," I said. "But, really man, you need to see a doctor."

Salt didn't disagree. He just let his head fall back on the cushion behind him. He stayed that way, too, across the rest of Cataouatche, through the channel, and during the trip over Lake Salvador. The motor did shut down a couple of more times on the way. Isabella got the pistol ready each time, but didn't have to use it.

As we crossed the Intracoastal Waterway, the sun burned red in the clouds above the town of Jean Lafitte.

"Harley," Frenchy called over, "you say you left the boat at the store?"

"Yep. Tied to the dock. Skeeter said it would be safe to leave it there."

"I bet he did," said Frenchy. "I'll take you back there. Miss Lapointe can call the sheriff for us."

"You mean that old lady in the store?" I asked.

Frenchy cocked an eyebrow. "Don't let her hear you say that. That woman can turn on you."

"Seriously," I said.

The small houses that lined the canal through Jean Lafitte grew larger as we approached and I tried to remember how far down the seawall the store had been. Its roof and gravel lot soon came into view.

I saw the Donzi, just where we had left it. That boat knew how to stay put. Then, I saw the police car. As we got closer, a greasy looking guy in a Saints ball cap came out of the Donzi's cabin.

Miss Lapointe

"That's them, sheriff," said Skeeter pointing to our boat as we reached the dock, "the ones that done stole my boat." He turned to Salt. "Hey, loser. Where's my boat?"

"You already drink that fifteen hundred I gave you to rent it, Skeeter?" Salt replied, sliding his eyes over to the man in the uniform standing on shore.

The sheriff's deputy pretended not to hear what Salt had said.

"I'm going to need for all y'all to step out of that boat," the sheriff commanded.

"I'm afraid that's going to be a little tricky, officer," Salt said showing the man all the blood-soaked bandages around his leg.

"What in the tarnation happened to you?!" the sheriff said.

Before Salt could reply, two buzzing-bee outboards answered for him. We all watched as Lafitte, his brother and the two henchmen drove their boats full tilt down the middle of the main canal. At the last instant they spotted us at the dock on the side canal and swerved over to hem in the jet boat.

"These guys pumped me full of lead," Salt said motioning to Lafitte with his thumb jabbing the air over his shoulder. "And in case you hadn't noticed, they also shot up this boat."

"Ye mouth be spewing bilge once more, Gaspar," said Lafitte, his black hat burned and crumpled on his head. Then to the sheriff he added, "Yonder scurvy dogs plundered me vessel, they did."

Lafitte tapped the jet boat with his hand.

"That's just what I figured, John," said the cop. "Got ourselves a bunch of boat rustlers."

"Aye," said Lafitte. "Sneaked into me camp in the wee hours, his course set for loot and booty, devil a doubt. 'Twas me dog raised the warning. Then, chased them off we did. Har!"

"You know this is our boat, George," Skeebo told the sheriff, though his twisted eyes seemed to be talking to his nose.

"So you shot him while protecting your own property, did you?" George asked. The policeman pinched his face at Salt. "Doesn't surprise me one bit that you're mixed up in this, too, Frenchy. Just like a thieving Indian to hook up with some out of town boat gang."

"Ain't against the law if they's on your property, stealing your stuff, is it?" Skeebo shot back.

"Har," said Lafitte.

Frenchy rolled his eyes and shook his head. "You know you better get your facts straight before you start making allegations, George. Lawyers love facts."

"I got all the facts I need, half-breed! Now, everybody out of that boat!"

Isabella and I did our best to help Salt out of the boat. The bleeding hadn't slowed down. When he got him off the cushions, the middle of the back seat was smeared with something that looked like dark, red finger-paint. Salt groaned when we heaved him up on the dock. At the bench, he fell more than sat.

"Deputy," Frenchy said speaking slowly, "Obviously, you're going to find a great difference of opinion here. Judges and attorneys can straighten it all out later. But one thing's certain – this man needs a doctor, and he needs one soon."

"Needs to hang from the yardarm, what's he needs!" yelled Lafitte.

"Where's my b-b-b-boat, you no g-g-g-good galoot?" sputtered Skeeter.

"Your boat?" said Skeebo. "Let's talk about *our* boat! You got them all red-handed, George!"

Frenchy's calm, confident approach had gotten to George. He was less sure of himself, shifting around on his feet. He even looked a little confused.

"Okay, okay," he said. "Everybody simmer down a second. Let me think."

The deputy took off his hat and scratched his head before continuing.

"Stay put!" he warned Salt with a finger. "Nobody move. I'm going to call this in. Then, we'll sort it all out."

He walked a few yards away and spoke into the radio microphone on his chest. Something drew my eyes to Lafitte's boat. Isabella had punched a hole the size of a fist through the bow with Frenchy's .44. I wondered if anyone had hid the gun. Unfortunately, both Skeebo and his lunatic brother seemed to be perfectly intact, so did the other thugs in the next boat. Skeebo stood there in his johnboat, both hands on his hips, glaring at us with one eye open and the other eye shut tight as a clam.

"Think you can just come up from F-f-f-florida and muh-muh-mess with these guys, Pepper?" Skeeter sneered at me.

He was obviously trying to snuggle up to the Lafittes and save his own hide. Who knew what lies the loser had told the sheriff.

Basco growled at the dude and bared his teeth.

"Better keep that muh-muh-mutt tied up, half-breed," Skeeter said to Frenchy. "I know lawyers, too. And my lawyer'd love a little dog bite case."

Frenchy just waved his hand at Skeeter. "You don't even know how to spell lawyer."

Miss Lapointe walked back into her store, ringing the little bell on the door as she went. I guess she'd been standing there the whole time. Deputy George ended his radio chatter and waddled back over, one hand resting on the butt of his pistol. He stopped short of us, keeping to the higher ground, and, without taking his eyes off Salt, yelled to the store.

"Miss Lapointe! Would you come back out here and join us for a moment?! And bring Bessie!"

The lawman looked down at Salt's wound.

"Guilty or innocent, I reckon you do need medical attention," he said. "Ambulance is tied up with an accident over in Estelle. Going to be there a while. I got another deputy coming, but this looks pretty urgent, so I'll carry you over to the doc myself."

"Wise decision, sheriff," said Frenchy.

The bell rang again and Miss Lapointe came back out. She carried a 12-gauge shotgun with her. Did everyone around the bayou pack heat? Man, I felt like I was in the wild west or something.

"Ellen," George said to the shopkeeper, "mind making sure nobody wanders off? I'm going to run this fella down to the clinic."

Miss Lapointe's face was bitter and hard as a rock. Her shotgun looked pretty mean, too.

"No problem, George," she said. "I got them."

"You two, help me get him into the squad car," the sheriff said to me and Isabella.

"Uh, sheriff?" said Skeeter. "If I may? I have an appointment that I need to attend to..."

"You keep your butt parked right there, Skeeter," George growled. "This whole thing smells different from how you explained it. I got questions for all of you as soon as I get back."

Salt managed to get his good leg under himself as we helped him to the squad car. George opened the back door and we slid him in. While I was still hunched over with my head inside, Salt spoke to me.

"Trust your ticker, kid. You got a good heart. It'll lead you down the right road."

"But, Isabella," I said. "What do I tell the cops?"

"Do the right thing, Harley. Have a little faith. It'll work out. You'll see."

I didn't see how it could possibly work out, not in a good way.

The deputy waved me off and shut the door. I watched the squad car crunch gravel on its way to the street.

I worried about Salt, but I also worried about Isabella and her family. I guess they were illegals, though they seemed innocent to me, just caught up in things out of their control, both in the U.S. and down in Cuba. They were good people. There had to be a way to resolve it.

I felt Isabella standing close to me. She turned and took my hand.

"Do not worry, Harley," she said to me in a calm voice. "He will be alright."

"Salt's a tough one," I said. "He'll do fine. It's not him I'm worried about."

Isabella squared her body to me. Her mouth curled into a small smile. She dropped her face for a moment before meeting my eyes again. She let my hand go to bring her fingers to my cheek.

"The world should have more Harley Davidsen Coopers walking around on it," she said softly. "You came back. You saved us. You're so brave. I want to thank you."

Her other hand came up and pulled my face towards her lips.

I couldn't say a thing. A tingle had found its way to my brain and pulled the plug on my vocal cords.

But, Miss Lapointe wasn't at a loss for words.

"Get your happy butts back over here, lovebirds," she cawed like an old crow. "I've got a bone to pick with you, boy!"

Isabella had cast a funky girl-spell on me. The world, the problems, even Eden, were all, like, a million miles away. I was in la-la land, enjoying the vacation. With just two sentences, though, Miss Lapointe's voice had managed to pop all that like a needle on a soap bubble.

Isabella took her hand away and followed me to the dock.

Lafitte and company had tied their skiffs to the jet boat where it floated just behind the Donzi and joined Frenchy and Basco on the dock in front of Miss Lapointe, and Bessie. The pirate looked mad enough to rip off my arm and beat me to death with it.

"I'm highly disappointed in you," Miss Lapointe began.

"Aye, grubby, little swabs they be," Lafitte chimed in.

"Put a lid on it, Lafitte," Miss Lapointe said as she swung the shotgun and aimed at his gut. "You're about as worthless as anyone I've ever met. And, considering your present company, that's saying a lot."

"Point well taken, me lady," Lafitte said showing the palms of his hands.

Miss Lapointe continued.

"When you walked in my store yesterday, I said to myself, 'Now here comes a good egg.' I can tell these things," the lady said. "Good, kind-hearted kid. Wasn't so sure about the other guy. But you? 'Bright future,' I thought. Then, you asked me about dipstick here."

She motioned to Skeeter. He averted his gaze and stared at the ground.

"What's your name, honey?" she asked Isabella.

"Isabella."

"You look just as sweet. How in the world did you two get wrapped up with these swamp rats?"

"I can explain," I said, remembering what Salt had just told me.

"Uh-uh. Nope. No time for that now," she said stopping me. "I just want to tell you this, son. You got your whole life ahead of you. Make it good. Make it count. Don't waste your time on worthless junk like these guys."

"Uh, Ellen," Frenchy said tapping a finger on his wrist.

Miss Lapointe winked and nodded.

"I've known Frenchy forever," she said tossing him a plastic grocery bag. "With him, it's more than a hunch. I've seen his true colors many times. He's one of the best. And it's only because of him that I'm doing this. You see, he just told me the truth. A condensed version I'm sure, but truth just the same." She took her hand off the gun and patted her heart. "You feel that here," she said with the first smile I'd seen on her face since the day before.

She locked her eyes on me for a second.

"Now, I'm going to give you a choice," she said. "Either you stay here and dig your hole even deeper, telling George some crazy story...or you go. You get on that big boat and you go make things right by playing it straight and doing your best."

I couldn't believe it. She was giving us another chance!

"Well, son? It's up to you," she said.

Of course, the last thing I wanted to do was disappoint a lady with a shotgun – twice. And, I didn't waste any time trying to make her understand. Time was short. We had to go.

"Thank you," I said. "I agree one hundred percent. And, I promise."

"See that you keep all your promises," she said.

"Harley! Let's go," said Frenchy. "The clinic's only a couple of doors down. The deputy'll be back any minute."

Basco and the Choctaw jumped down into the Donzi. I grabbed Isabella's hand and pulled her after me. Miss Lapointe suggested with the tip of her gun that Skeeter untie us. He did, without a stutter of complaint.

"My good lady," said Lafitte, "might we be permitted to pursue our quarry?"

"Take it up with George," she said. "Here he comes."

Sure enough, the cop car was coming down the street with lights flashing.

"I'll drive," I told Frenchy.

The go-fast boat was docked nose out. I rolled the key over and the twin motors ignited. Frenchy shoved us off the dock and I kicked that thing hard. She blew a whole in the water behind us and we exploded into the channel.

"Which way?" I yelled to Frenchy.

"Left," he called. "Let's get you south."

Out of the corner of my eye I caught Isabella waving goodbye to Miss Lapointe. I turned and waved, too. She waved back, though no one else did.

"Where we going, Frenchy?"

"Away from this mess," he said, "as fast as we can."

I turned left and we headed south.

Barataria

The town of Lafitte, not to be confused with the town of Jean Lafitte, sits about five miles down a curvy canal from Miss Lapointe's store. The Donzi made it there in just over four minutes. If that boat could have somehow sprouted wings, I'm sure we would have flown. We practically did.

As I dodged docks and other water craft, Frenchy explained that he could get us to Grand Isle on the Gulf coast. There, we could lay low with friends until Salt got patched up.

The buildings of Lafitte zipped by as I kept the tip of the bow aimed at the center of the canal. After that town, we left civilization behind. The canal lost its natural turns and became a man-made straight line with dredge piles on both sides. I pushed the Donzi even faster.

The boat jumped a wake forcing us airborne for a second. When we splashed down, the old rum bottle rattled across the deck.

"What's that?" said Frenchy.

"Wow! It's the map that led us to the La Paz treasure," I explained.

"Really?" he said. "Never seen a real pirate map before."

He grabbed the bottle off the floor and popped the cork.

"Careful," I said. "I'm sure it's still worth something."

Shielding it from the wind, Frenchy spread the map across the front seat while I steered the boat.

"Thought you said the treasure was in Florida," he said.

"What?"

"This map, you said it's supposed to show the way to a treasure in Florida. But, it doesn't. It's a map of Barataria Bay."

I pulled the throttles down. The Donzi settled into the water.

"Let me see that," I said.

He handed the map to me. It looked the same, but different somehow. The symbols were still hand-drawn, old looking, the words still in Spanish, but I didn't recognize any of the waterways or islands.

I checked the bottle. It was the same one I had pulled out of my crab trap that day last August, the same one I'd tucked the map into a couple of days before. I'd recognize the old bottle anywhere from its stains alone.

"I don't get it Frenchy," I said. "It's not the same map. I don't know that water."

"Maybe it changed," said Isabella.

"Now how could that happen?" I said.

She shrugged her shoulders. "I don't know...voodoo maybe?"

I knew that was impossible, but hairs rose on my neck just the same. Louisiana was a strange place indeed. I checked the compass in case it was spinning in circles. The float sat perfectly still, pointed to the south.

"You might not recognize it, but I do," said Frenchy. "That's definitely Barataria Bay." He pointed to the open water on the map, then to the big X. "And, *that* looks like a pirate's symbol for treasure."

He was right about the treasure symbol. It was the same one that had marked the spot before. I did not see the tiny hand holding a plant, however. Occupying that spot, I saw a small, hand-drawn image of Salt's sportfisherman.

"What? They didn't even have sportfishermans back then," I said.

My neck hairs refused to back down.

"Call me crazy," said Isabella, "but looks like your map has the ability to morph and follow the location of the treasure."

Another old pirate trick? Salt had some explaining to do.

"Didn't you tell me the Lafittes took your gold and your friend's boat into that bay?" Frenchy asked me.

"Uh-huh."

"Well, I don't know what or how or why or who, but it seems we have a map to both," he said. "So I have a question for you, Mr. Cooper."

"What's that?"

"Do you want to get them back?"

That was a no brainer.

"You bet I do!" I said.

"Then let's go."

The Donzi flew south once more. While Isabella napped on the seat, Frenchy shared what he had heard over the years about the Lafitte's Barataria Bay operation and his thoughts on how we could take back Salt's boat and the gold. I learned something else – Frenchy was one smart guy. The dude thought of everything. I liked him even more.

A little later, Frenchy tapped my shoulder so I'd slow down before Mud Lake. Once we'd entered the open water, he checked the map and pointed to a cut on the eastern side. I banked the 38-footer left, avoided a slow moving dredge, and gave her the juice again, crossing the lake in less than a minute.

"This channel runs for miles to the northeast," Frenchy explained, after the hull settled. "The map shows it passing right by their canal, but my guess is, you won't even see it."

"What do you mean you can't see it? Vegetation?" I asked.

Isabella yawned and stretched behind me.

"Way more advanced," Frenchy said. "You remember the zipper material back at their cabin?"

"Yep."

"That's actually a piece of fiber-flage," he said.

"Fiber who?"

"Military grade. Hi-tech stuff. Has fiber optics woven through it to project an image."

"Like a picture?" Isabella asked, leaning forward, throwing an arm over my shoulder.

"Try High-Def video," Frenchy said while scratching his dog between the ears. "On the side panels, they project video of the surrounding grasses. It moves with the wind just like the real thing. It gets dark at sunset and brightens with the rising sun. On the overhead layer, they project a scale image of a satellite photo taken before they built the place."

"They have a layer of that stuff *over* their buildings?" said Isabella.

Frenchy nodded. "I heard one of their guys bragging about it once," he said to her. Then to me, "I'm sure they'd be using it down here, too."

I remembered the helicopter video of the Hatteras vanishing. Military stealth technology would explain it.

"Isabella," I said, "What can you tell us about this place?"

She closed her eyes recalling the memory.

"They had me blindfolded, but I peeked through the edges," she said. "From what I saw, it was kind of dark, like we were inside an airplane hangar. One other big boat and a couple of smaller ones." She opened her eyes. "They put me on that jet boat and we left."

"So, Salt's Hatteras is still there?" I asked.

"As far as I could tell, they left it tied to the dock."

"Other people?"

"I only heard one new voice inside that place," she said.

"I'm pretty sure he keeps a minimal crew," said Frenchy. "If we get in there undetected, we may luck up and find the treasure still onboard Salt's boat."

"How do we get in?" I asked him.

"Same way you snuck in before," he said. "We swim."

The green grass slid by for a mile as we carefully checked out every blade. I didn't see anything out of the ordinary, just marsh and sky. Frenchy, on the other hand, must have eaten his carrots because he spotted something invisible to Isabella and me, and casually tossed the empty rum bottle into the weeds at the water's edge.

"That's it," he said. "That's the entrance. I saw the seam. Keep going, and act natural, in case anyone's watching. We'll stash the boat up a ways and swim back to that bottle."

"Can't we just cut across the marsh and come in through the side?" I asked.

"Sensors in the mesh," he said. "They have them in their other place. We'd probably trigger alarms."

Shortly, a small creek opened to the right. I backed the Donzi into it and cut the motors. Frenchy took off his jacket exposing the big knife on his belt.

"What happened to the gun?" I asked.

He reached behind his back and pulled out the pistol.

"She's right here," he said. "Only two shots left, though."

"Can I borrow your knife?" Isabella asked.

Frenchy unsheathed it and offered the handle. Isabella stuck the blade tip into the fabric of her jeans up around her thigh – way up – and ripped a hole with the steel.

"I can't swim in these jeans," she said.

She kept cutting until her pants had been shredded into a pair of skin-tight cutoffs. And the whole time, that chick made sure to work her legs into the most provocative positions possible. When she was all done with her performance, she handed the knife back to Frenchy with a smile.

"Thanks," she said. "That's better."

Of course it was better – for me. And that, I'm sure, was her point. Why do girls pick the craziest times to do that stuff? Well, two can play at that game. I stripped off my dragon shirt and tossed it over my shoulder, carefully aiming at her face. Score! The cloth completely wrapped her head.

"Oh, sorry," I said sarcastically. "That shirt really slows down my butterfly stroke."

She peeled off the shirt and glared at me.

"Ah, if you kids are finished playing, we can get moving," said Frenchy as he stowed the treasure map in a compartment below. "If we want to surprise them, I'm guessing we don't have much time."

We followed Frenchy to the swim platform at the stern. He hopped in the water first. Next went Basco.

"It's not deep," Frenchy said as he found his footing. "Bottom's a little soft."

The water came up to his waist. Basco swam to shore. I guess he preferred picking his way through the cordgrass. Isabella hopped in, going completely under. She surfaced with both hands pulling her long, black hair into a ponytail.

I said good-bye to the Donzi and got wet.

We waded most of the way, going slow to keep from splashing so much. The whine of an outboard faded in from the direction of Mud Lake. We froze, listening as the sound grew.

"Coming this way," said Frenchy. "Tabasco. Down."

The Catahoula dropped to his belly and hid in the weeds. The boat sounded really close.

"Here it comes," said Frenchy. "Get under until it passes."

I took a deep breath and squatted down to get my head under water. The boat sounded different down there. The prop, not the pistons, made the noise. I heard the high-pitched rotation of the blades slice past like a torpedo.

I waited for the wake before standing up again. After the turbulence shook me, I raised my head slowly just in time to see a flats boat vanish around the bend.

"Just a fisherman," I said to Frenchy when he surfaced.

Basco rose up on all fours when he saw his master stand up. He grinned at us with his tongue out. I wondered if I could train Hammerhead to be that disciplined.

"Shouldn't be too much farther," Frenchy said as he scanned the grass ahead of us.

We found the rum bottle right where he tossed it. The bottom dropped off. While treading water, I stared hard at the windblown grass on the shoreline, trying to force my mind to accept that what I saw was actually a projected image. It looked absolutely natural, nothing but ordinary grass swaying in the breeze, under blue sky. I swam closer. Only then did I spot the woven fibers of the material. The stuff was just a foot from my nose. I reached out, running my fingers down the synthetic fabric, following it underwater. The trampoline material felt identical to the camouflage around the Lafitte's place on the bayou except for one thing. I couldn't find a zipper.

"It stops about two feet under water," I whispered to Frenchy and Isabella.

Frenchy made a dive-under motion with his hand and we felt our way below the hi-tech camouflage system like a bunch of crabs. I opened my eyes on the other side and watched Isabella, Basco, and Frenchy pop up one by one.

The scenery had changed completely, like switching channels on the television. Marsh, sky and sun had been replaced by big mercury-vapor lights hanging from metal trusses high above. Not a single blade of grass remained in sight. The water rippled ahead for the length of a football field before lapping against a concrete seawall. At the far side of the man-made cavern, tied at the seawall, the *Florida Blanca* floated like a white ghost.

Salt's new Hatteras wasn't the only vessel. Another boat, black and just about as long, had been moored to the same seawall just ahead of her bowsprit. That boat looked fast and sleek, with a high bow made for heavy seas. But mostly, it looked mean, the way a naval warship looks mean.

"I don't see anybody here," said Isabella.

"Doesn't mean we're alone," said Frenchy. "Let's get to cover. Harley, that Salt's boat?"

"Yep. The white one."

"Follow me," he said.

That man swam as silently as he walked. So did Basco! The dog paced his master perfectly, always staying a couple of feet off Frenchy's shoulder. I brought up the rear, keeping Isabella between me and the two Louisiana natives.

The seawall bordered the water on three sides, forming a square, U-shaped mini-harbor. A couple of smaller fishing boats bobbed against a floating dock connected to the nearest seawall. We aimed for them.

Basco popped out of the water like a seal onto the floating dock and stood there waiting for Frenchy without even shaking the water off his fur. Amazing. I hauled myself out the same time Frenchy did and we each grabbed an arm to pull Isabella up.

We were in.

Nothing moved except the water dripping off our clothes. Nothing made a sound. It was as if the place was deserted. Frenchy motioned for us to stay silent while crossing the floating dock to a short ladder that led up the seawall.

Basco leapt to the top, waiting for us as we climbed. A flat concrete floor connected the seawall to a single story building fifty feet away. The boxy building had no windows, as far as I could see, only doors that were spaced at regular intervals twenty or thirty feet apart. Some were normal doors for people. Others were overhead roll-up doors large enough to drive a truck through. But, the only vehicle around was a lone forklift parked in the corner where the building made a right angle turn following the dock. And follow the dock it did, all the way around to the other side of the square "U."

Except for an occasional cardboard box, we had no cover at all. Frenchy drew his pistol and moved over to the building. Isabella and I followed, hugging the concrete block structure as Frenchy and Basco led us down to the corner.

The doors emitted no sounds, no hints of what they held. We passed several before stopping at the forklift. Frenchy waved us close.

"The place could be deserted, but I don't think so," he whispered. "Rumor has it that, between human trafficking and contraband smuggling, this place stays pretty busy. We'd best keep on our toes."

On our toes? I was already so tense I couldn't feel my toes.

"Let's just get to the *Blanca*," I said.

"What about the treasure?" asked Isabella.

"We'll check the boat for it," said Frenchy. "If it's not there, we can decide to search for it or hit the trail and get out of here."

"Sounds good to me," I said.

Staying low, we skirted the edge of the building towards Salt's boat. As we passed by the windows of an office, I noticed a fat guy slumped over in a chair sleeping. Frenchy saw him, too. He put a finger to his lips and motioned us forward. When we were even with the stern of the *Florida Blanca*, we crossed over the loading dock to Salt's boat.

"The barrel was back here next to the fighting chair," I whispered. "It's gone."

"They could have moved it inside," said Frenchy.

We hopped onboard.

I put my ear to the sliding glass door and listened. Nothing stirred inside, so I slid it open. The salon looked pretty much the same as the last time I had seen it. The kitchen was a mess, food crumbs, dirty dishes, and empty cans and boxes all over, but not a scrap of gold.

"Come inside," I told them, "and I'll check the cabins."

I figured that was a dead end, but I had to see. Strong odors of diesel and fiberglass filled the air as I went deeper into the sportfisherman. One by one, I checked all four cabins. No treasure. And, thankfully, no bad guys.

"It's not down there," I said as I reached the top of the stairs. "No way they'd drag it all upstairs."

The Cajun Pirate   267

"Probably right," said Frenchy. And after a moment, "Still quiet out there. What do you guys think?"

"Let's do it," I said. "Let's go to the warehouses."

"Might want to check that other boat first," Frenchy suggested.

I nodded to him as I walked over to the slider. The dock remained as gray, silent and motionless as a tomb. I opened the door and led the way out.

We crouched and hustled to the black boat in front of the *Blanca*. On our way past the lettering across the back of the Lafitte's trawler, I read the boat's name and almost tripped over my own feet. In huge letters across the stern were the words *Booty Bandit*. Now, there's a name that's so ridiculous on so many levels, I just won't even go into it.

The boat had an open pit in back, like a fishing boat, its steel hull ending at a wooden rail three feet above the deck. No barrel of booty waited for us on the *Bandit's* metal deck, however. A third of the way up the boat's length, doors led inside. A passage on the starboard side cut around the cabin to the bow. Stairs rose from that passageway up to the bridge. More stairs descended below decks. The hull curved up sharply at the bow to give the vessel a real ocean-going appearance. A line of portholes level with the top of the seawall flanked the boat's side. And, curiously, the forward-most porthole had been covered by a round steel plate, black like the rest of the boat, with a hinge at the bottom.

I let go of Isabella and swung my leg over the rail. No lights burned on any of the three decks and she felt dead in the water. If anybody had been onboard I would have felt or heard or seen something. I didn't, so I walked to the cabin door and entered the ship.

The room was dark and kind of short, like, four feet deep. A workbench ran along the far wall broken up in the middle by a door. Two computer workstations flanked the door on the workbench counter. Those systems, which seemed to be powered down, were the only objects in the room.

Isabella stuck her head through the door. When she spoke I felt her breath on my ear.

"What is this place?"

"Maybe they like to play video games," I said.

A couple of steps away, the *Booty Bandit's* next door opened into a room even dimmer than the first. I fumbled around for a light switch. When the lights came on, I didn't see any booty, but I did meet the bandit.

Pirates

After his service to the United States in the war of 1812, Jean Lafitte received his pardon from Andrew Jackson as promised. A year later, he returned to the life of a smuggler and pirate. The government chased him out of Louisiana, so he set up a new base on Galveston Island off the coast of Texas where he got rich all over again selling stolen merchandise to the citizens of New Orleans with the help of his brother Pierre.

Eventually, the U.S. Navy persuaded Lafitte that he should leave Texas. The pirate agreed, burned all his buildings and left. That's where the story gets murky. They say he sailed to Panama or the Yucatan or Cuba. They don't know for sure where, or how, or when, he died, but they do agree he was nowhere near Louisiana.

That's what they say. But, I learned that day that "they," whoever "they" are, can sometimes be quite wrong. Because when those lights came up on the *Booty Bandit*, I found myself face to face with Jean Lafitte. And, it scared the crap out of me.

Two inches from my ear, Isabella screamed like a stuck pig. An ice pick to the brain would have been less painful.

"WHAT *IS* THAT THING??!!" she yelled.

"A statue or something," I said.

Towering over us like a stuffed grizzly bear, a man with the hideous face of a rotten skull stood ready to chop our heads off with an enormous sword. His flesh had dried into beef jerky.

His eyeballs had rotted away. His teeth were exposed, both between his curled up lips and through gaping holes in his cheeks.

The guy was very dead.

His clothes, however, looked like they had been delivered from the dry cleaners that morning. He wore a clean white shirt with elaborate ruffles on the chest and a bright red-velvet coat with gold embroidery, black pants and shiny black boots. A big black hat covered the top of his gnarly head. One side was turned up and fastened to the top part. A couple of ostrich feathers stuck out the back.

A cheesy, self-stick nametag had been stuck onto the breast of his coat. I leaned over to read it. The machine printed part said "Hi, my name is." Below that someone had written by hand *Jean Lafitte.*

A door shut behind us.

"What is going on in here?" said Frenchy.

"That's totally sick," I said. "They've got a mummy in here dressed up like Jean Lafitte."

And, that wasn't the half of it. I looked past the Lafitte mummy and saw something worse. The room was deep, continuing forward all the way to the point of the bow. Sitting in a triangular cluster at the far end like coiled snakes, were three massive guns. One pointed to port, one to starboard, and the third, at the tip of the bow, connected to a scissor lift. Above it, a hatch provided access topside.

"Ho-ly smokes," said Frenchy. "I hadn't heard any rumors about this."

They weren't so much big guns as they were small canons. They looked wicked, capable of inflicting some serious damage. Ammunition, big shells, filled rack after rack along the curved walls.

"Who do these people think they are?" Isabella mumbled slowly.

"Pirates," I said.

The frozen grin on the Lafitte mummy's face seemed to agree.

A voice echoed across the dock outside. Frenchy ran to the computer room, cracked the door for a peek.

"It's guy from the office," he said. "Heard the scream. He's searching the docks with a flashlight."

I put an eye to the door. A large man, waddling like a penguin, slowly approached the *Bandit*, splashing the hull with a bright beam. The dude went 350 pounds easy, all blubber. Then, I saw something else mixed in with the flashlight's dancing beam, a shaky pinpoint of red light.

"He's got a gun," I said. "I see the laser sight."

The bright red dot jumped spastically over the metal deck and landed next to my face on the door jamb. I shrunk back and waited.

"Who's there?" the guy growled.

I thought he was coming aboard, but his feet shuffled along the seawall instead, going past the bow towards the other end of the dock.

"He'll be back," said Frenchy, "and when he comes, we'll be ready."

He checked the .44 revolver, making sure one of the last two bullets lined up with the barrel.

"I'm going to sneak up to the front of the boat," Frenchy said. "When you see him again, give this command to Basco - verbatim - in a calm, firm voice."

Frenchy spelled the command for me so his pooch wouldn't spring into action. He instructed Basco to wait and slipped out the door. I lost track of him as he rounded the corner, sneaking up the walkway to the front of the boat.

Isabella and I waited forever before the sound of penguin feet returned. A few moments later, the big guy came into view. I knelt down to the patiently waiting Catahoula.

"Tabasco. Tackle. Teeth on. *Skit him!*," I told him.

Quick as lightning, Basco shot out the door and over the boat's rail. A moment later, he was all over the rolie-polie, close to his throat, fangs bared like some sort of rabid wolf.

"Oh, Jesus!" the fat man burst out before tripping backwards over his own feet.

The guy had a gun in his hand. After he hit the deck, his elbow made contact with the ground and the gun fell out. Basco laid his ears back, inching forward.

Marshmallow man forgot about his flashlight, even his gun. He just heaved over on his hands and knees, trying to scramble away from the insane dog as fast as he could. It worked, until his forehead ran into Frenchy's kneecaps.

"Tabasco. Sit. Teeth off," Frenchy said.

The demon dog transformed himself into man's best friend, plopping down on his haunches his tongue hanging out.

"Shouldn't play with guns, mister," Frenchy said to the dude at his feet. "Sooner or later, someone's going to put an eye out." Without taking his eyes off the guy, Frenchy called to us. "Come on out guys!"

Isabella and I left the *Booty Bandit* computer room to join Frenchy on the dock. I leaned over and scooped up the man's handgun. I had never pointed a gun at another person in my life, but I figured if anyone deserved to look down the wrong end of a laser sight it was that pirate. I put the bright, red dot on his big, round belly.

"Where's the gold?!" I demanded.

"Bite me," he said. "I'm just a security guy. I don't know anything."

"Hmmm. That sounds good. Tabasco. Dinner time," said Frenchy. "Teeth ON!"

Basco sprang to his feet, wicked fangs and growls, and slowly advanced on the guy.

"I haven't fed the poor thing in three days," Frenchy chuckled.

The plump man was clearly concerned. Fear screwed up his face as he tried to shuffle backwards from his seated position. Basco was much faster. In a flash, the dog pounced on his chest, forcing the guy to the ground while snarling in his face like a junkyard dog on a cornered rat.

"Call him off! Call him off!" the security man blubbered.

"You ready to answer the young man's question?" Frenchy asked.

"Yes. Yes," he cried. "Just get the mutt off! I hate dogs!"

"Too bad. Looks like he loves you. Off, Tabasco. Sit. Teeth on."

Basco sat down as before, except he kept his fangs exposed, and his eyes riveted on the quivering tub of goo.

"Let's have it," said Frenchy.

"It's right there," the big guy whimpered. "Right behind that door." He pointed to the nearest roll up door. "But it's locked and they didn't leave me the key."

"I got a key," Frenchy said.   "Keep an eye on him, Harley."

"I've got him covered," I said. "But, I don't know how long I can keep Basco from digging in to dinner."

Frenchy walked over to the door and tried the padlock. When it didn't open, he stepped back a couple of paces, took aim and blasted it off with a round from the .44. Man, that thing was loud!

The door rolled up easily and there it was – a wooden barrel stuffed with pirate's treasure sitting all alone in a dark, empty room. We had found it, the hope of a whole town. Man, that felt good.

Frenchy walked over to check out the gold. Hey reached in and removed a single doubloon, holding it up so it would catch the light from the mercury vapor fixture. The coin shimmered, golden and sparkling.

I had to see it up close.

"Hey, Frenchy," I called over to him. "Mind if we swap places."

"Sure," he said still holding the piece. "Come on over. Tabasco. Hold."

The gravity-challenged warehouse guy brought his hands up to cover his face as Basco leaned a bit closer and let out a menacing growl. Isabella and I walked over to join Frenchy in the vault. Isabella picked up the guy's flash light on the way.

"Here, dive in," Frenchy said. "I'll hold that."

I handed the pistol to him and leaned over the barrel. Isabella waved the flashlight over the mound of loot splitting the beam into a thousand shimmers. Golden coins, gold rope chains that had no beginning or end, rings with emeralds and rubies the size of grapes, a metal drinking cup studded with jewels, all of it sparkled with a million pinpoints, like sunlight on the sea.

"Wow," Isabella said, her face glowing gold, her eyes dancing with treasure light.

I eased my hands into the massive pile. The pieces felt cool, heavy to the touch. My hands swam like fish in a sea of gold, very happy fish. I brought them up, letting doubloons and chains spill off my fingers and clink back down like a jackpot in Vegas. The sound was pure magic. Money, dude.

"On your feet, fat boy."

Frenchy pointed both guns at the watchman. Basco had risen and now stood by the Choctaw's side. The man on the ground rolled over to his stomach and pushed himself up.

"Get inside," Frenchy told him, motioning to the room where we stood.

The expression on Frenchy's face had gone cold.

"What's he doing?" Isabella asked me.

"Taking care of business," I said.

"Tie him up, Harley," Frenchy said as the watchman came into the room.

I made the big guy sit on the floor and tied his hands and feet with some old bailing wire.

"Now, get to the back of the room! Both of you!" he snapped at me and Isabella.

"Frenchy," I said, "what's going on man?"

When Frenchy smiled, it wasn't a happy one. The dude looked like an angry opossum. "Think I'm gonna just let you walk out of here with all this loot? Think again."

"I don't believe it," Isabella said. "He's stealing your gold, Harley."

The dough-boy on the floor started laughing.

"Frenchy," I said, "of all the people…I thought-"

"Oh, save it, Florida boy," he said. "You thought what? That the world is sprinkled with goodness like sugar on a donut? Everybody running around doing their good deeds, doing their best? Well, news flash, Miss Lapointe – it ain't! Money makes it spin. Always has, always will. I've waited a long time for mine. Watch your toes!"

BAM! He slammed the door down and locked it from the outside. The cargo bay went dark, Isabella and me on one side and big boy on the other, a barrel full of gold somewhere between us.

"He left the treasure," I said to no one in particular.

"Oh, he'll be back," the watchman chuckled. "He's going to get the fork lift."

"Harley, I'm sorry," said Isabella. She flipped on the flashlight and took my hand.

"*Harley, I'm sorry,*" a voice mocked her from the far side of the room. "Oh, *please* shut up. It's every dog for himself in this world. You're an idiot for trusting that guy."

Not too long after, I heard Frenchy start one of fishing skiffs we had seen tied to the dock. The outboard revved for a several seconds before slowing down to a crawl. The whir of big machinery filled the air. I figured that must have been the main door sliding open. The outboard wailed again, slowly fading away.

"He's getting the Donzi," I said.

Thankfully, the watchman stopped laughing. I had to think of what I needed to say when Frenchy returned. I planned on hanging onto that gold. I needed to be more convincing than ever.

A few minutes later, the noise of the rumbling Donzi filled the air in the Lafitte's artificial cave. The sound came closer and seemed to pause directly outside the door. Then footsteps. Then, a smaller motor. When the door rolled up once more, Frenchy faced us in front of the fork lift, both guns pointing in our direction, one at the fat guy, the other at Isabella and me.

"Tabasco. Ready. Teeth On," Frenchy told his dog.

The Catahoula bared his fangs and growled.

"Frenchy, look," I said. "That's a lot of gold there."

"You bet it is," he said. "That's why I'm taking it."

"No, what I mean is, there's way more in that barrel than you can even spend."

"You want to split it with me?" he asked.

"Well, yes," I said.

"Now that's funny!" Frenchy said laughing out loud. "That is truly hilarious. Oh, man, you Florida boys are a riot. That's the best you can come up with?"

"A lot of people are counting on that money to get their lives back!" I shouted at him.

"Well, I got a bunch of people living in a swamp near here who've never had a life to begin with," he shot back. "In fact, their lives were stolen by these folks and the government generations ago. Now who do you think deserves it more? Huh?"

"Tee, hee, hee," laughed the fat man. "Looks like we got ourselves a little Mexican stand off."

"Shut up!" we both yelled at him.

"Frenchy, your whole life you've played by the rules. That's what you told me. You really want to throw that all away now? You want to stoop to their level?" I jerked a thumb at blubber-head.

"Hey, I just work here," the watchman said.

Frenchy climbed up onto the forklift.

"Just cut the small talk, son, and hook up them chains," he said as he drove the lift to the loot.

With both a gun and a dog poised to do some serious damage, I went over and looped the chains over the fork lift's hook. The Lafitte's security man watched from the floor. Before moving away I found Frenchy's eyes one last time. They were cold as grapes in Greenland.

"Back off, boy," he told me. "Don't want to roll over them Florida toes."

I stepped back a little and Frenchy hoisted the barrel out to the dock. He hopped off the lift and, without a word or even a glance, shut us in the dark once more.

We listened as he worked to load our treasure into the boat. When he was done, the Donzi, which was still running, left the dock and screamed back to the bayou.

"So what now?" said Isabella. "We just sit here and wait for those creeps to come back?"

"I'm not waiting for anything," I said.

I found my way to the chain that operated the door and pulled on it. A crack of light appeared at the bottom. Frenchy had left it unlocked. I worked the chain as fast as I could.

"Come on, Isabella," I said after it opened a few feet.

"Where're we going, Harley?"

"After him!"

We slid under the door out into the open.

"Let's get to Salt's boat," I said. "We might be able to catch him."

Unfortunately, getting a seventy-seven-foot sportfisherman off a dock doesn't happen instantly. First, we had to untie all the lines. Next, I had to run up the ladder to the bridge and start her up. When I got there, I discovered the key was gone.

I was not in the mood for guess work. I ran down, jumped off the boat and found the watchman rolled over on the floor.

"Where's the key, fatso?" I said as I wrapped the back of his collar around my fist.

"Office," he squealed. "Key rack on the wall. Don't hurt me."

I let go of his shirt and sprinted down to the office. The key rack held all sorts of keys. It took a while, but finally I spotted the set bearing the Hatteras logo. I grabbed them and locked the office door behind me to slow down the security guy in case he got loose and tried to follow us.

Turns out, it didn't matter all that much. We had company.

"While the cat's away," Skeebo said backing Isabella and me against the wall with his pistol. "Hey, bro. Caught a couple of mice over here. That big, ol' swamp rat's got to be around somewhere."

John Lafitte, still decked out like Captain Morgan, hauled himself out of their yellow jet boat and up onto the concrete. He straightened his scorched hat and his ruffles before walking over.

The watchman, who had rolled out of the storage room while we were looking for keys in the office, didn't look either of them in the eye.

"Ahoy, bilge rats," Lafitte said. "Thought ye'd plunder me loot, did ye? I be likin' yer style. Too bad I have to kill ye." His eyes searched up and down the dock for a second or two. "Where be the worthless half-breed what brung ye here?"

I said nothing. Isabella pulled close to me. Her whole body shook. Lafitte slid his sword out of its scabbard and held the tip to my throat.

"Mayhaps a taste o' me steel might help ye with yer memory," he said.

"The black feller took the gold already, sir," the watchman said face down on the floor.

"What's that, Junior?" said Skeebo laying his double vision on the watchman for the first time.

"I'm sorry, Mr. Skeebo. They surprised me, over-powered me and forced me to take them to the treasure," he stammered on his belly. "Then that one double-crossed this one and took it all away in his go-fast boat."

"Arrrr. The Donzi," said Lafitte.

At that instant, the Donzi shot by the opening to the Lafitte's lair going about a thousand miles an hour towards Mud Lake. The noise was incredible.

"Thar she blows!" yelled Lafitte. "Keep a close watch on these scallywags, me brother. I shall return with the treas-arrrr!"

Moving faster in fluffy, women's clothing than I ever thought a man could, Lafitte ran across the dock and jumped onto his black boat. For the first time, I noticed the jolly roger flying over the bridge. We watched as the pirate untied his ropes, flew up his steps, fired up his motors, and sped away from the place like a demon on a mission.

The metal key in my hand reminded me that Isabella and I had our own ticket out of there as well. Skeebo had not noticed that Salt's Hatteras had been unhitched, and fatso seemed too flustered under his boss's crossed-eye to bring up the subject. All I needed was an opportunity.

That's when I saw the shovel leaning against the building.

"So, Junior," Skeebo said as he walked over to the watchman, "how *did* you let this thing happen? Huh?!"

The big guy started shaking like a bowl of gelatin. Isabella and I stood to one side of Skeebo as he lowered his head to the security guard. We were probably still in his field of vision, well, a normal person's field of vision. I had no clue what Skeebo's world looked like.

"Like I said," the big man tried to explain, "they jumped me. It happened so fast."

"They just *materialized* in front of you out of thin air, did they?" Skeebo said, getting more and more angry.

I took a half step towards the shovel.

"I guess that explains how they slipped past the surveillance equipment you were supposed to be watching!" Skeebo said as he moved even closer to the guy.

I inched over to the shovel a little more and waited for Skeebo to notice. He did not.

"I *was* watching the screens, Mr. Skeebo. *Honest!* Oh, please don't hurt me, Mr. Skeebo."

"So they materialized and then what?" said Skeebo gritting his teeth.

I took another step. That put me only an arm's length away from the shovel handle.

"They had a dog – no – a wolf, or something," Junior whimpered, trying to work his hands free of the bailing wire. "It was awful mean. Big ol' teeth and everything. You know I don't do well with dogs, Mr. Skeebo."

Skeebo raised a fist up in the air. "*Junior!* Give me one good reason why I shouldn't knock you into next week for being so stupid?"

Junior shut his eyes and cowered like a frightened elephant seal. Skeebo cocked his fist back and shifted his weight to deliver a blow to the watchman. Both of the blind, tattooed eyes on the back of his bald head glared straight at me. I reached over, grabbed the shovel like a golf club, and nailed that sucker in the skull.

Thwack!

I was getting good at that. The shovel rang like a bell and Skeebo dropped like a sack of manure.

Junior pushed one eye out of his blubber like a snail to see what had happened.

"Oh…my…*gawd!*" he said with a trembling voice.

Skeebo lay sprawled on the deck next to Junior's cheek.

The watchman's eyes went to the shovel in my hands. "Please don't hurt me, mister. Y-you can just go now."

"Get on the boat Isabella," I said.

As she ran over to the Hatteras, I carefully kicked the gun away from Skeebo's open hand. It spun around on the concrete towards the water, then dropped over the seawall and plopped in. Skeebo appeared to be out cold.

I kept the shovel until I got to the boat. Only then did I toss that into the water, as well.

"Let's get up to the bridge," I told Isabella as I came aboard.

We took the ladder to the fly bridge deck. At the console, I shoved the key in and twisted. The motors rolled over, but didn't catch. I backed off, waited a moment, and tried again. Nothing.

"What's wrong, Harley?" said Isabella.

"Give her a second."

I waited longer and turned the key a third time. The motors still did not fire.

"Harley?!"

"Seriously, Isabella."

The fourth time turned out to be the charm. The motors blasted to life and I revved those suckers in neutral just to make sure. The boat had a bow thruster to make docking and departure easier. I leaned on that thing hard. The tip of the bow responded as a jet of water pushed us off the dock. I gunned the motors and headed for the bayou.

Isabella ran back to the door behind me at the end of the fly bridge.

"Skeebo still down?" I called to her as the boat picked up speed.

"I don't see him!"

Panic shot through my system like a jolt of electricity.

"Look down the dock," I shouted. "Is he at the other fishing skiff?"

There was an awful moment of silence. When she spoke again, I knew from the fear in her voice.

"Harley. We've got a problem."

"What is it?"

"He's on the boat."

Bassa Bassa

"Skeebo?"

"*Yes!*" she screamed. "*Harley!* He's coming up the ladder!"

"Lock the door!"

I needed more time. We hadn't even made the hangar door yet, and to my horror, the huge door was closing. I shoved the throttles forward until they wouldn't go any further. Unfortunately, a seventy-seven foot boat doesn't respond immediately. The gap between the door and the wall shrunk way fast. It was going to be very close.

Skeebo reached the flybridge door and pounded on it with his fist.

"He's trying to get in!" shrieked Isabella.

The big sportfisherman picked up speed just before we shot the gap. The massive, fiber-flage door came at us with a metal I-beam on its leading edge. The bow made it through to daylight, but the I-beam struck the boat on the starboard side and rocked us to port. The door kept coming, raking down the fiberglass, a screeching trash compactor, pushing the stern to the left as the sportfisherman powered through.

As the battering-ram door forced the stern left, the nose of the boat went too far right. I fought to keep control of the wheel, to swing the bowsprit back to the left. It was useless. I tried hitting the bow thruster to straighten her out. When the

Blanca finally cleared the building, she fish-tailed out of control, almost to the marsh.

I backed off the throttles. Our momentum sent us skidding sideways into the creek. I gunned the motors again. The tide gods were with us. The only thing that kept me from sticking that boat in the mud was a high tide. I got the thing headed in a straight line down the creek towards Mud Lake.

That done, I turned to check on Skeebo. He had left the fly bridge balcony. With any luck he'd fallen overboard when the door smashed into us.

"He's coming in downstairs!" Isabella yelled.

I guided the boat around a bend, leveled her out, and aimed the bowsprit down the barrel of the channel.

"Isabella! Get up here!"

She ran up to the captain's chair.

"Take the wheel," I told her.

"What?! I can't do this!"

"You can do it. Just go straight! Keep her in the middle."

I shoved her into the chair and wrapped her hands around the wheel. Boots pounded up the stairs.

"You gave me a nasty headache, boy!!" Skeebo yelled halfway up.

I darted over to a position at the top of the stairs just out of sight and waited. The stairs turned at the very top so that the last couple of steps squared up to the room. When Skeebo rounded that corner his ugly head was about the same height as my knee. I let him have it, square in the nose, with the best karate kick I could muster. His head snapped back and down the stairs he went.

"Harley! There's a turn coming up!" Isabella shouted.

"Just steer it like a car. Pull back on the throttles a little."

I vaulted down the stairs expecting to find Skeebo on the floor. But, when I got to the salon, he was gone. The slider to the aft deck had been left open. As soon as I turned my back to check the deck, Skeebo launched over the kitchen bar and tackled my legs from behind. I rolled, kicking my legs free and in the process managed to nail him in the chin with my heel.

I scrambled to my feet and looked for some kind of weapon. Skeebo found one first. He ripped a fire extinguisher off the wall and swung the canister at my head. I ducked. The extinguisher shattered a window.

Suddenly, the boat rolled hard to port. Skeebo had raised the extinguisher high for another attempt at crushing my skull. Top heavy from the weight of the container, he lost his footing and fell over.

I ran outside to the fishing deck. The floor was at a crazy angle as Isabella horsed the boat around a bend in the channel. A channel marker came out of nowhere and raked the hull on the starboard side so hard that I had to grab the rail at the very end of the boat to keep from falling overboard.

Isabella finished the turn and the boat leveled out again. Skeebo charged out of the door like a crazy bull, yelling and screaming. He had completely lost his mind.

I'll never forget that sight. His tattooed scalp gushed blood on the side where I had lit him up with the shovel. His hands clawed the air like a monster. His furious eyes bulged in at each other like he had a gnat on his nose.

I stood there, frozen, like a deer in the headlights and let him come. He leaped over the fighting chair as agile as a tiger and covered the distance in one stride, clawing for my throat when he reached me. I dropped to the deck, letting him whiff empty air.

The rail caught him just below his waist and the sucker went right over the transom – sploosh – into the prop-wash.

I stood up and waved good bye, remembering when I had been the one to fall overboard.   Funny, what goes around comes around, I suppose.

Although the gouges from the fiber-flage door and the marker looked wicked bad on the starboard side, the damage didn't seem to have compromised the integrity of the hull.   Salt was sure to flip out, though.   I worried about the integrity of my hull.

Across Mud Lake, channel markers formed a straight line as far as the eye could see down to Barataria Bay.   Isabella was weaving around between them like a drunk driver.

Even so, I couldn't resist checking one more thing before returning to the helm.

The teakwood fishing deck of the *Florida Blanca* had a large access hatch cut into it.   Even though the hole was large enough for a mechanic to get big parts down to the engines, the seamless construction made it hard to notice the hatch as you stood on the deck.   You had to look for it because the cuts in the wood lined up perfectly with the grooves in the deck.   The tell-tale giveaway was the brass pull ring.

I bent over, popped the ring up, and pulled open the hatch. My heart thumped faster than the diesels' pistons.

There it was, right where Frenchy had put it, the sweet barrel of shiny gold.

The boat, the girl and the gold, we had done it!   I howled like a Choctaw warrior.

As I said before, Frenchy's plan was killer.   He figured there'd be at least one person at the Lafitte's Barataria hideout, somebody to keep an eye on things.   So, he cleverly devised a way to mislead that somebody into chasing him, or at least giving others a reason to chase him, instead of Isabella and me.

We didn't expect the Lafittes to show up so quickly, but Frenchy's plan also included a contingency for the unexpected. After loading the gold onto the *Blanca*, he took the Donzi up the creek, instead of out across Mud Lake. There, he turned the boat around and watched the entrance to the hideout. If I wasn't out of there with the Hatteras inside of fifteen minutes, he would come back to the rescue. He must have seen Laffite's jet boat go in. Baiting Lafitte out in his gunboat was pure brilliance, and a little lucky, too, of course.

Isabella had no idea. We couldn't take a chance on her accidentally spilling the beans. Salt always told me, as far as treasure is concerned, the fewer people that know, the better.

I closed the lid on the gold and went back up to the bridge.

"Oh, Harley," Isabella said. *"Dios mio!* Am I glad to see you. What happened?" She took her hands off the wheel and flung herself around my neck.

"Uh...the boat," I said, angling around her to regain control.

I told her how Skeebo had opted for a midday swim. I didn't mention our cargo...yet. I had bigger things to worry about at the time, like trying to drive a giant boat down a tiny channel without hitting anything. Salt had let me take the wheel a couple of times while we were out to sea, but that was months before, and we were, well, out to sea. There's not much to run into way out in the Gulf. A narrow channel is a different story.

The *Florida Blanca* felt clumsy in the water, kind of like driving a house. That's probably because she was so much bigger than my boat. I figured the best thing to do was just focus on making it to the next marker, then the next and the next. So, that's what we did, from Mud Lake down to Barataria Bay.

Isabella kept an arm across my shoulders as I drove.

"Harley Davidsen Cooper?" she cooed in my ear. "Did you know you're my hero?"

"Um, thanks, Isabella. But, believe me, I was just as freaked out back there."

"You never show it, handsome," she said, laying her head on my shoulder.

I think the girl was coming on to me. I needed a diversion before I got into trouble.

"Hey, Isabella, I know. Would you mind going downstairs and finding something for us to eat? I'm starving."

"My pleasure, sweetie," she smiled at me. "And if you eat it all, you can have dessert. Something sweet...and Cuban. You like Cuban?"

"Sure. Heh, heh. Cuban's great," I managed.

It worked. She peeled herself off and headed downstairs to the galley. If I could just keep her busy until we met up with Frenchy I had a chance.

Think about Eden. Think about Eden. Think about Eden!

I have this picture of Eden that I took at the beach one day. She didn't even know that I took it because I shot her from behind. She's sitting cross-legged on the sand in a bikini with the wind blowing her hair around, just sitting there with her blonde head up high taking in the air, hands on knees. She's all alone in the photo, surf, sea, sky and Eden. *Eden and the Sea*, that's my private name for it.

The picture was at home in my room. I keep another copy in my head, just about as clear. Focusing on that picture always worked. It worked that day as well. It got my mind, and my hormones, off Isabella.

However, I just about crashed the boat.

I caught myself nodding off. My head snapped back up just in time to avoid the next marker. The near accident jump-started my heart with a dose of adrenaline. Wow! I was suddenly *very* awake.

The channel ahead remained virtually free of boat traffic. I saw one center console boat coming towards us. That was it. The boat looked to be out in the open water of Barataria Bay. Frenchy said he'd be waiting a little further down the channel in some place he called Bassa Bassa. From there, I'd follow him to Grand Isle and we could call Salt. Hopefully, I could get some sleep as well. I was exhausted.

I scanned the water behind us. No evil, black pirate gunboats in sight. I brought the Hatteras over to the right side of the channel to let the oncoming center console pass on the port side. A couple of fisherman waved to me as they cruised by. Their wave was friendly, normal. It was very nice to get back to friendly and normal.

Isabella brought some food up and served it with a smile. The steak tasted great, cooked to perfection. I detected a Cuban flair. I guess she was trying a new tactic – win me through my stomach.

Fortunately, about the time we were finished, I spotted the Donzi anchored near the channel. Isabella started to freak when she spotted Frenchy, so I filled her in on what had happened. The explanation just proved to be another excuse for her to throw her arms around me, declare me her hero once more, and, of course, kiss me. Dude, I'm not even bragging. The chick would not leave me alone!

"Looks like things worked out on your end," I called to Frenchy once I had stopped the Hatteras.

"Just got here. Left him lost and lonely back in the bayou," he said. "Lafitte's not the only one who knows the short cuts around here. Hi, Isabella!"

"I knew you were no bad man," she smiled and waved.

Tabasco barked. I guess he wanted to make sure his good name had been cleared as well.

"How'd you dump Skeebo?" asked Frenchy. "I checked their warehouse and the big guy told me he'd hitched a ride on your boat. Had to take the skinny water to beat you here."

I told him "dump" was a very appropriate word to use. Then, I told him the rest.

"Well, the best thing for you to do is put some miles between you and this place," he said.

"Couldn't agree more," I said. "Phase two?"

"Yep, follow me," he said. "Grand Isle's not far. You can call your buddy and fuel up there."

I waved to him to take the lead. Isabella wiggled around me to the ladder, making sure I got a good look at her cut off shorts on the way up to the bridge. I detoured through the salon, grabbed a t-shirt, and took the stairs.

"Harley, what's phase two?" she asked when I reached the helm.

"A marina in Grand Isle. Fuel. Phone calls. Supplies."

"Supplies?"

"Yeah," I said. "Salt and I are taking you back home."

"You mean you and I are taking a tropical cruise," she said with her eyes sparkling.

Silently, I prayed for strength. If I could just keep her occupied with conversation until Salt got back I had a chance.

"Boat ride. Not cruise. Boat ride," I told her while keeping my focus on the Donzi in front of us.

I kept her talking about all kinds of stuff as we rode to Grand Isle. Man, my tongue and brain were worn out by the time we got there. I'm just not wired for so much talk.

Frenchy pulled into a fishing marina on the west end of Grand Isle just past a Coast Guard station. I thought hard about turning into that station. I decided to talk to Salt first. We could always go to the Coast Guard later.

Docking wasn't the nightmare I had worried about. The bow thruster definitely made things easier, so did the shrimp boat berth at the end of the t-dock. It was unoccupied. All I had to do was slide her up against it slowly and gently. The dock hands did the rest. I found the fuel credit card still in the slot above the wheel where Salt always stuck it.

The guys on the dock were a bit shocked when they saw Isabella and I were the only ones on the sportfisherman. I nonchalantly handed them the card and told them to fill her up before striking off down the planks to join Frenchy at the store.

Isabella was already talking to her parents on the phone.

First, I had to find out about Salt. Frenchy said the doctor would probably have to operate in order to remove all the shot from Salt's leg. That meant he'd be in a hospital, of course. Frenchy gave me the name of the most likely one. I found a payphone and dialed.

"One moment, sir. I'll connect you," the hospital operator told me.

"Y-ello," said a groggy voice a couple of seconds later.

"Salt!"

"Harley!" He cleared his throat, perking up a little. "Is that you?"

"Right here, man. How's the leg?"

"Leg's fine," said Salt. "How are you, kid?"

It felt great giving him the news. He laughed as he listened, must have been the anesthesia. Salt never laughs.

"You done good, kid," he said after I'd finished. "You done good."

"When can you get your butt down here so we can go home, Salt?"

"Well, I got a couple of problems, kid. One, there's a cop stationed outside my door. For my own protection, they say, but I get the feeling they don't want me going nowhere. I've got an attorney headed down from New Orleans to fix that.

And, the doctor says I shouldn't be taking any boat trips across the Gulf in the next week or so. Something about damaged arteries and rough water not mixing so well.

But, you need to scoot. They're looking for you and that Donzi." He paused for a second, then added, "You think you can manage my boat down to Cayo Costa?"

"Sure. I guess so."

"If I can arrange an escort then that's what we'll do. Put Frenchy on the phone."

"He wants to talk to you," I told Frenchy.

Salt hired Frenchy to drive the Donzi back to Florida. We would have to bring extra fuel. No big deal, the marina had plenty, and the containers to put it in. I felt a whole lot better having Frenchy and Basco along for the ride, even if they were in a separate boat. The weather report looked fine, but this was my first solo run across the pond.

After we said goodbye to Salt, I called Eden. Isabella got real quiet on the phone next to me. I knew she was listening to every word. I couldn't really go anywhere more private, though. I was stuck using the pay phone.

"Oh, my God! Harley! Are you okay?! I've worn a hole in my brain worrying about you!" Eden said on the other end.

"Everything's cool, babe."

"You haven't called in two days, dude!"

"I didn't have a quarter," I said hoping the lame joke would lighten her up.

She sounded a tad angry.

I gave her the high points and told her I would soon be on my way back.

"I'll give you all the details when I get there, Eden," I said.

"Promise?" she said.

"Cross my heart," I told her.

"So, this guy, Frenchy, and his super dog are in that Donzi," she said. "Where's the Isabella girl riding?"

"With me, I guess."

"You and her. In the same boat. For hundreds of miles? Alone?"

"Look, Eden. You have absolutely nothing to worry about. Okay? Besides, I'll have my hands full, I'm sure."

I tried to sound as convincing as I could. I knew girl's had this sixth sense, this weird radar that can tell when another female is trolling around.

"You better keep an eye on them hands and make sure they don't get full of the wrong thing, Harley Davidsen Cooper. Don't think I've forgotten about how she looked at you back at César's place. Or, what she told me."

"Seriously. It's cool. You're over-reacting."

"That's just because I know how *you* react around hotties. Oh, Harley, be careful. I want you back here." She eased up a little there at the end.

We said goodbye and I made one more call to my mom. She was freaked, too. But, then again, she's always freaked at me. I worked it out and she promised not to call the Coast Guard if I was home inside of two days.

I hung up and stared at a Christmas decoration hanging down from the ceiling of the store, a big, cardboard snowflake slowly spinning on a string. As I followed it through two revolutions, I felt hypnotized. Cops or no cops, I had to get some sleep, at least a couple of hours, before we took off.

The dock hands loaded fuel and supplies into the boats. I signed the credit card slip after adding a pair of walkie-talkies so Frenchy and I wouldn't have to scream at each other. And then, we walked back down the dock to the *Florida Blanca*.

I spotted some dude checking her out as we approached, a cell phone to his ear. He moved to the other end of the dock by the time we got there. I didn't hassle him, or blame him, for that matter. She was one fine looking ride…on the port side at least. A sense of pride swelled up in me just knowing I'd be the one to take her back home.

We went aboard, cranked the air and crashed. The couch felt sweet as a marshmallow. It had been the longest day of my life, probably because it had really been two. What a way to spend Christmas break.

Out to Sea

When Frenchy shook my shoulder, I woke up from a dream where I was lost in a cypress swamp, hiding in the trees from a patch of fire burning on the water. My heart was still racing.

"What time is it, man?"

"Four in the morning," he said.

I sat up and stretched.

"Isabella?" I asked.

"Still sleeping. We probably ought to move."

"Yeah," I said. "I only meant to sleep a couple of hours."

Basco licked my hand. That earned him a scratch between the ears.

"You sure about driving this thing?"

"Yep. I got it," I said. "I'll just keep it slow in shore. She'll do 28 knots in fair seas. That won't be a problem for you."

"Not in that hotrod, it won't. Over to Tampa?"

"Anna Maria, at the mouth of Tampa Bay. We can pick up fuel near there, then head south down the Intracoastal."

"Gotcha," said Frenchy. "I'm following you."

"And, I'm following the navigation computer. Should take us between 16 to 18 hours to cross the Gulf once we get out to sea. Maybe we can grab some more shut-eye when we hit Florida." I yawned. "This vacation is wearing me out."

"I know the feeling," said Frenchy. "And, I haven't even left my backyard yet. Fair winds."

He patted my shoulder and took the stairs down to the main deck with Basco in tow.

"I've got the walkie-talkie," he said as he went down.

"Maybe I can find you on the VHF radio," I joked.

I hit the head downstairs and, after relieving myself and splashing a little cold water on my face, returned to the bridge. The motors fired up instantly, vibrating the hull enough to feel them. Satisfied that everything seemed to be running properly, I went aft to the outside balcony.

Frenchy stood below on the dock under a light with Basco by his side.

"Got all the lines but one," he said. "You ready?"

"Ready," I replied. "Let her go."

He saluted me and untied the last rope. As he threw the line back to the boat, a shadow crossed my mind. For a brief instant, I doubted that we were going to make it. I'm not sure why, but I wondered if that was the last time the *Florida Blanca* would ever set sail, you know, leave the dock. A tiny voice, quieter than a whisper, told me that would be her final voyage. Butterflies? Paranoia? Unease because I was about to embark on a journey practically solo across seas a thousand times wider than anything I'd ever faced before? Or a gloomy premonition. I had no idea. I suppose I could have easily explained it away if I thought about it. I could've chalked it up to nerves, a hundred things.

I'll never be able to explain what happened next.

I looked up into the night just in time to spot another crazy shooting star. Before its trail of brimstone had even left the sky, goose bumps had already run up my back to my neck. Freaky, man.

I thought of the witch. She felt near.

Frenchy waved and turned to walk down to the Donzi. I waved back, too late.

One shooting star would have been a coincidence. But how many had I seen? One a night? It had to be some kind of record. All the rest seemed to be good omens when I had spotted them. Not this. This one felt bad. I walked back inside the bridge with a sinking feeling in my stomach. And, a sinking anything is always trouble on a boat.

The thruster shoved the Hatteras off the dock and the diesel motors spun her around towards the pass between Grand Isle and Grand Terre. The Coast Guard station still slept as we passed by. Again, I almost turned in to their docks, wanting to shed my burden, just dump it in their hands and be done.

It seemed wrong to break the law, and by harboring an illegal alien on the boat I'm sure I'd be guilty of something. The thing was, protecting Isabella seemed so right. My mind said one thing. My heart said another. And, I had no one to decide it for me.

Meanwhile, as I fought myself over what to do, the big sportfisherman kept going. Before I knew it, we had left the land, and the Coast Guard, behind altogether. Score one for the heart.

The bridge of the 77C is high tech. All the compasses, meters, gauges and other electronics normally found on larger vessels had been replaced by computer screens. Five of them glowed in the dark in front of me. The second from the left displayed an electronic chart tied into the navigation system. I plotted a course Tampa and watched it appear on the screen. All I had to do was stay on course. And if I didn't? Well, Mr. Technology would let me know.

A few miles offshore the boat fell into the rhythm of gentle swells. The sky over the eastern horizon grew brighter and I forgot all about falling stars. Actually, I started thinking about tunes and how I needed to hear some. Salt didn't have any cool mp3's on the computer, or anything, but he did have satellite radio. I found the alternative rock channel and cranked the snot out of some Linkin Park.

That music suddenly made my whole experience twenty times cooler. Sweet. Soon the sun popped up over the water, and it was calling my name. When I heard my name a second time, I lowered the volume and turned around. It was Isabella.

She was wearing a t-shirt, and, from what I could tell, that was all. Even first thing in the morning, she was hot! I was so in trouble.

"Morning, hero," she smiled as she slowly covered the distance to the captain's chair. "We must be on our private cruise now."

"Uh...this is your captain speaking," I said into my fist. "All passengers must return to their cabins immediately. Rough seas ahead!"

She looked out the window, then back at me.

"Smooth as glass out there, captain," she said. Then cocking her head to one side, "But I know a way to get this boat rocking..."

Oh, man. I had to think – quick! My defenses were weakening. *Eden and the Sea. Eden and the Sea.* I tried to will the image into my mind. The picture barely materialized, a ghost of itself.

"Isabella," I started.

"Call me Bella, Harley."

"Look...I, uh..." I couldn't think! I wanted so bad to say no, to tell her to back off. Problem was, my mouth wouldn't cooperate, at least not fully. "I...have to drive the boat right now."

"Doesn't it have auto-pilot or something?"

"No! Definitely not. Salt's old school. Doesn't...uh...believe in all that stuff." I let out a very weak laugh.

"Oh, come on," she said. "What are all those computer screens?"

I turned to look at them, like I had never noticed them there before.

"These? Um, other stuff. Weather conditions, information about the boat, the engines. Definitely no auto-pilot here..."

She came closer. Her arm slid over my shoulder. She smelled sweet.

"So? Pull over," she breathed into my ear.

T-shirt material. That was the only thing protecting my relationship with Eden, so thin, so filmsy, so easy to rip off and throw on the floor.

Eden and the sea!

Her fingers went for my hair, getting tangled in the curls, pulling me towards her. Her skin was perfect, so smooth, so tanned. Her lips parted just enough to show white teeth and the tip of her tongue.

I pulled myself away, forward, pretending to check the course and controls.

"Listen, I've got to put some mileage between us and Louisiana. Okay?" I said. "Let's cruise for a while."

"You mean later?"

"Sure."

What was I doing? I was a complete robot and she had the controls. How do chicks do that?

"Great," she said happily. "I'll go cook us breakfast."

She gave me a smooch on the cheek and bounded off to the stairs.

"But, Harley," she said turning back at the top of the stairs. "You *are* my hero. And I *will* repay you...whether you like it or not. But...you're going to like it. Then, who knows? You might forget all about her."

Thankfully, she went down to the galley, humming all the way. I breathed a sigh of relief and took in the view of the rising sun.

"Harley. Y- there?" Frenchy's voice crackled with static on the walkie-talkie.

The sound of it just about made be jump out of my skin. The Donzi bobbed up and down behind the *Blanca* in her wake.

"I'm here, Frenchy. Go ahead."

"Jus- ch---ing to --- if this thing w--ks. How's it sou--?"

It sounded horrible. I could barely understand him through the cheap thing.

"Not so good, Frenchy. Let me see if I can find you on the VHF."

"Roger that."

The back panel of the walkie-talkie had some small print. It said the device transmitted on channel 14, so I rolled the *Blanca's* radio over to 14 and clicked on the mic.

"Okay, Frenchy, I'm talking on the main radio now. Can you hear me?"

My voice came through all screechy on the walkie-talkie in my lap, lots of feedback. I switched it off.

"That's a hundred percent better," Frenchy said clearly through the overhead speaker.

"Awesome," I said. "I hear you great, too."

"What's our position?"

I checked out the nav screen. "Looks like we're due south of the Mississippi. Straight shot to Tampa from here."

"Any weather out there?"

"Nope. Clear. Just loads of sunshine ahead of us."

"Well, Merry Christmas," he said.

"About time something went right on this trip."

"Okay, then. I'll holler at you later."

"Roger, that," I said. "*Florida Blanca* over and out."

Isabella served breakfast on the flybridge while I continued to drive Salt's boat. I must admit, the girl knew how to cook. It was delicious. And to top it off, she didn't throw herself at me one bit. To tell you the truth, I missed it a little. My fourteen-year-old ego enjoyed her sixteen-year-old flirting techniques – whether I wanted to or not.

But, it turned out that she was just switching tactics again. Instead of using words or food, she must have decided to use her body. A little while later, the girl walked out onto the front of the boat, the part just below my window, spread a towel on the deck, stripped down to her underwear and proceeded to work on her tan. As much as I tried to force my eyes to the horizon or onto one of the oil platforms in the distance, they darted back down to that sun deck with a will of their own. I was in hot water and it was beginning to boil.

The show lasted for over an hour, then she got up and walked back towards the stern without bothering to wrap up in the towel. I had no idea what to expect next. I thought she'd come right up the steps behind me. Minutes ticked by and nothing happened. I had calmed down a little, just about let the whole thing go, when I heard her call my name again.

I turned around to see her coming towards me in a towel, her hair wet, combed back like she had just taken a shower. She settled onto one of the couches next to the captain's chair.

"Harley," she said again, "I really like you. I know I've only known you for a few days, but it started before this whole mess, when I first saw you in my yard."

"Isabella, please," I tried.

"Please, Harley, I have to tell you this stuff. It's in my heart. It needs to come out." She looked out the window. "The Lafittes taught me something, or at least reminded me of it."

She stopped and waited for me.

"What's that, Isabella?"

"Please. Call me Bella. They reminded me that life is unpredictable, unpredictable and short. You never really know what's going to happen next. Or…if this is your last day on earth."

She got close to me, her voice lower, breathy.

"You know, Harley Davidsen Cooper, we must grab our chances while we can. They may be the only ones we have."

I looked over at the sea. She put a hand on the side of my face, five hot fingers, and pulled me around to face her.

"I know this boat *must* have an auto-pilot," she said to my mouth.

I could smell her shampoo or whatever chick lotion she had found to put on her skin. The scent drifted into my nose where it immediately mixed with testosterone, changing my blood chemistry into a fluid more combustible than the diesel fuel in the motors below. Any more pressure and I was going to explode.

She leaned forward so her lips brushed my ear.

"I've seen the way you look at me, Harley," she whispered.

That was it, ignition, not so much *what* she said as how and where she said it. My hands came off the wheel and onto her bare shoulders.

I know I was an idiot, a complete fool, but I had to do what I had to do.

I gently pushed her away.

Summoning every fiber of willpower in my entire being, I spoke the following words: "Isabella…I have a girlfriend."

"She wouldn't have to know," she said quickly.

"That's not the point," I said. "Look. You're right about that seize the day stuff, a little dramatic, but right. That's what makes it so awesome when you do connect with someone like my girlfriend, like Eden. In my crazy life, she's a constant in all that uncertainty, someone I can count on. I know she feels the same about me, too."

Isabella sat down, frowning at her hands, picking at them.

"You know what that is?" I asked her. "Do you know what we have?"

She looked up at me, her eyes watering.

"Trust," I said. "Eden and I trust each other. We trust each other to be there when things in our lives get really hard… I trust her and she trusts me – totally and completely. I can't diss that."

She was crying, not sobbing or wailing, just sitting tall letting the drops roll down her cheeks.

"You *are* amazing, Isabella. You're smoking hot, for one thing. Oh, yeah. I *have* noticed. And, sixteen? That's a total boost to the ego. But, you're totally cool, too. If it weren't for Eden…"

She stood up.

"I am such an idiot!" she said.

"No, you're not. You took a chance, a very brave chance. I think that's totally cool."

"No, I'm not brave at all." Lines of pain wrinkled her face. "I'm just a liar."

I was confused. So, she *wasn't* coming on to me?

"I thought guys liked that stuff, all that hot, sexy stuff, you know, what you see on TV. Isn't that what you like?"

"Yeah," I said, "on a TV show. Not in real life. Not at fourteen. Not yet."

"I just want you to *like* me, Harley." She wiped her face. "I've never done any of that stuff before. It was all an act. I am sooooo stupid!"

"No, you're not."

"Yes, I am."

"No," I said picking up her hands. "You're not. Know why? You were honest just now. That's the smartest thing anybody can do. *That's* what makes me like people. To tell you the truth, I don't really care about all that other junk. Just be yourself. You're beautiful."

She cracked a tiny smile.

"You mean to tell me," she said, "that none of the moves I made today had any effect on you whatsoever?"

"No comment," I told her. "But, I will say, that with a girlfriend like Eden, I wouldn't let myself fall for it. Wouldn't want to risk it."

"You love her, don't you?"

I didn't know what to say to that.

"I meant what I said to you, Harley. Life *is* unpredictable."

"You don't have to tell me."

"If anything ever happens between you and Eden, you let me know," she said.

"Okay, Bella," I said. "Just be who you are."

"Sure, I guess," she said. "Can we at least be friends?"
"We're already friends," I said.

With the tension gone, with the air clear between us, we sat there on the bridge and we actually became good friends. We talked for hours, about all kinds of stuff. It was cool. Then, we noticed she was still wearing a towel. She ran downstairs to change.

I enjoyed the sea air, reflecting on what I had said to her about Eden. Where did that come from? I'd never said that kind of stuff about Eden before, or even thought it. When I'd finished replaying each sentence in my head though, one fact stood out – it was all true. We got paranoid about things every now and then, but we did trust each other.

Maybe when we're backed into corners, when every defense has been cut away, the only thing left to bleed is the truth.

In regard to my relationship with Eden, I had just seen what pumped inside my veins. Bella had forced me to express it in terms so clear that not only did she get it, I got it, too. That moment changed me, I think, and definitely for the better. Not only did I feel closer to Eden than I had ever thought possible, I also felt stronger in my core, more solidified, more *Harley*. Weird how a thing so wispy, so not even a thing at all, can come out of nowhere and change you.

Ahhhhhhhhh. Life was good out to sea.

That all changed in less than an hour.

Wakes in the Water

"Hey, Harley. You there?"

It was Frenchy on the radio.

"Yep. Go ahead."

"I think Basco has to go. I've got no room with all these extra fuel cans all over the deck. Mind if we stop and put him on the back of the *Blanca*, put down some papers or something?"

"No problem," I said. "I've done it before with my dog."

I gradually backed off the throttles and the boat slowed, sliding into the calm Gulf of Mexico like a pelican coming in for a landing. Frenchy idled up in the Donzi just as I flipped a fender over the side, not that I should've even worried about new scratches with all the fresh gouges on Salt's boat.

"Throw me a line," I called over.

Bella came out into the sun on the stern deck to see what was happening.

"Hey, Bella," I said. "Mind grabbing some newspapers or paper towels or something? Basco's got to go."

Frenchy scooped up his dog, lifting him over the gunnel into our boat. Bella returned and covered the far corner using a roll of Christmas wrapping paper. Basco promptly walked over to do his trick. I turned to Frenchy to give the pooch some privacy.

"Nice day for a boat ride," said Frenchy.

"Or for a poop," I laughed.

"Take your pick, I suppose," he said.

The Gulf spread in every direction as far as the eye could see, deep, blue, and tame. The small swells drifted by like smooth, glass domes, raising us less than a foot as they passed. The sun had long since burned off the morning chill. The scene could have passed for a gorgeous December day miles south back home.

"What's that?" Bella asked.

I looked over and saw an oil rig not too far away. The outline looked familiar. I recognized the Petronius Tower.

"That is the world's tallest, free standing structure," I said like a tour guide.

"No, that," she said pointing to the open sea.

I followed her hand and saw nothing but rolling blue. Basco started growling. Then, I saw it, a single wave, a two-foot tall crest of white water, breaking the slick surface of the gulf.

"Rogue wave?" I said. "I don't know."

"Yeah, but it's coming towards us."

"Bella, it's only a couple of feet tall," I said. "Probably came from a passing ship."

Basco started barking.

"A ship leaves a bunch of waves in its wake," she said. "Where are the others?"

"Basco, be quiet," I said. "Dissipated maybe? How should I know?"

As the whitecap approached, I did see other ripples trailing off behind it, parallel to it, like the wake of a boat.

"Harley. We need to go," said Frenchy with a sense of urgency.

"Frenchy," I said. "There's nothing to it. It's just a harmless, little wa-"

I never finished that sentence. That's because, my insides turned to water. The wave was no longer alone in the sea. The Lafitte's gunboat had materialized directly above it. The main gun on the tip of the bow was out and aimed directly at our Hatteras.

"Too late," said Frenchy.

I didn't even answer him. The gunboat was at least a hundred yards off when it uncloaked. I had a chance and I took it.

I unhitched the Donzi and threw the ropes overboard. Frenchy had tied up on the side of the boat opposite Lafitte. He could easily turn and outrun them.

I bolted up the ladder to the fly bridge. The motors were still running. All I had to do was shove the throttle forward.

The *Booty Bandit* closed faster than I thought, its big forward gun staring at us like a one eyed dragon.

The Hatteras began to move.

Maybe the gun was a big bluff. Surely he'd hold his fire. Even crazy people had to be concerned that the folks in the oil rig would report a canon blast. That was my thinking. My thinking was dead wrong.

A deafening boom shook the insides of the *Blanca*, rattling windows and the very frame of the boat. The hull, however, remained unharmed.

I checked on Frenchy. He had not moved. Why didn't he run?

Lafitte could not have followed us both. Suddenly, I understood – Lafitte had sent a warning shot across my bow. The side gun hatches were also open. Another gun pointed directly at the Donzi.

A shot of adrenaline scrambled my thoughts and I started to freak. But, I *had* to think! Run or stop? Run or stop?

I pulled the throttles back and the sportfisherman settled into the water once more. I smacked the wheel a couple of times hard enough to sting my palms.

"A-harrr!" a voice blasted through the speakers. "Harrrrley Cooper! Did ye think ye could escape the likes of me? Did ye suppose ye could traipse away with me treasarrrr? Cut yer engines or I'll cut yer boat in two!"

"What are you doing, Harley?" Isabella cried as she ran up onto the bridge. "We can outrun him! Go!"

"We might be able to outrun his boat, but not those guns," I said, forcing myself to calm. "Sorry, Bella. We've got to go deal with this guy. Don't worry. It's three against one."

Once outside, I saw the most terrifying thing of all. It wasn't three against one. Skeebo was standing on the bow of the *Booty Bandit* with a vicious grin across his face. He raised his arm and pointed a finger at me, an awful look in his cross-eyes, like he wanted to tear me apart one piece at a time – with his teeth.

"Cut yer motors, swab, or I'll blow ye to the fishes!" Lafitte commanded over a loudspeaker.

I reached over to the auxiliary control console and switched the engines off. The *Florida Blanca* gave a final shudder, then floated like a dead fish.

Frenchy pulled up again, tying the Donzi to our stern. He cut his motor as well, so I heard him clearly when he spoke.

"Cooperate with them," he said quietly, "and wait for an opportunity. It will come."

The pirate ship rumbled closer. Out in the bright sunlight, I saw the fiber-flage material covering her hull and superstructure. Skeebo threw a line as soon as they were within range.

"Make fast ye barge to our vessel, swab, and be making it quick! And you, wench! Stay where I can lay eyes on ye!" Lafitte instructed through the loudspeaker.

Isabella and I went down the ladder to the stern deck. I shimmied forward around the cabin and tied the line to a cleat, then returned aft to tie the second line. Once the two boats were joined by the ropes, Skeebo jumped over onto our deck. He carried some sort of wicked looking automatic weapon. I expected him to spray us with bullets, but he didn't.

Isabella backed off into a corner. Her eyes looked spooked, like a wild horse. She probably expected Skeebo to come after her. Instead, the jerkwad yelled at Frenchy.

"Get them hands where I can see them, injun boy!"

The Choctaw raised his hands.

"Now get on over here," Skeebo said, "slowly. Tie that mutt to a cleat."

Frenchy did as he was told.

"Now sit your black butt down! And don't move a muscle," Skeebo told him. "Think you're pretty smart, don't you? Tried to trick us back there. You'll see who's got the brains around here, boy!"

Frenchy sat down a couple of feet from Basco. Lafitte walked out on the bow of his boat to stand over us with another gun. He wore the long, red coat from the mummy and its hat as well. Pyratosis? No. Freak-a-tosis.

"Where be me loot?!" Lafitte bellowed.

"A moment, dear brother," Skeebo said. "I want to reacquaint myself with someone."

The tattooed freak walked over to where I stood and punched me square in the gut. I went down.

"That's just the beginning, punk!" he yelled. "Got greedy, didn't you? Should of gone to the cops."

"Coast Guard's on their way," I said gasping for my breath.

"Lies!" he screamed and kicked me in the ribs. "We monitored your radio, boy! Hell, we even had a stooge on Grand Isle keeping track. You folks were running for home. Tried to trick us. Throw us off your trail. You think we was just a bunch of dumb Cajuns, huh?"

My belly hurt like fire. I balled up expecting him to kick me again. He had worked himself into a rage.

I heard Isabella whimpering from her spot on the couch above me.

I remembered the charm around my neck. According to the note, I had one wish left. I reached up to my throat and grasped the pendant.

Skeebo ripped my hand away.

"What you got there, boy?" he said leaning over me. "Why that looks like one of them voodoo luck charms, now don't it?"

I was too weak to struggle. He snatched it off my neck.

"Well, the old Papa La Bas," he snickered. "Hey, boy, this here's Louisiana property." He kicked me in the gut again. "Not only that, seems your luck's getting worse while mine just got a whole lot better. I think Papa's gonna feel more at home around my neck."

He tied the ends of the leather together and slipped the pendant over his head.

I wished anyway. I wished for him to die. I wished for him to have a heart attack, a stroke, get hit by lightning, anything. I wanted to see him suddenly reach for his chest and fall to the deck gasping for air. And, die!

He didn't.

Instead, he kicked me in the stomach for the third time.

"Avast, dear brother!" Lafitte said from his boat. "Remember. If they fork over the gold, they may weigh anchor and depart the realm."

Skeebo regained his composure, somewhat, stepping back. Cross eyes still burning at me, he cracked his vertebrae by snapping his neck from side to side at extreme angles.

"Yeah," Skeebo said. "I almost forgot. We ain't going to hurt you none if you hand over that there treasure. In fact, you can keep this whole stinking boat and get out of here. We don't even want the girl no more."

"Harley, just give it to them!" Isabella blurted out, her voice shaking with fear. "Give them the gold!"

I groaned. We had just lost the treasure. Isabella had told them what they wanted to know and, partially, it was my fault. I had violated rule number one – tell as few people as possible about the gold. I had confided in Isabella, and now we were going to pay for it.

"A-ha!" said Skeebo. "I knew it! You *do* have the loot. And, it's on this boat somewhere."

"Arrrrrrr!" said Lafitte.

Skeebo came back to where I laid and leaned over me.

"Now tell me where it is," he said, "or I'll enjoy beating it out of you."

I looked over at Frenchy. He closed his eyes and nodded.

"It's under your feet," I mumbled.

"What's that boy? Speak up!" said Skeebo.

"I said it's in the engine compartment. You're standing on it."

He spread his feet and looked at the deck below him. After spotting the pull ring, he grabbed it and yanked open the hatch. For a moment, his eyes un-crossed completely. Skeebo fell to his knees so he could reach down and touch the treasure.

I half expected Frenchy to rush him from the side, to tackle him, take away his gun. But, I checked on Lafitte. He held his gun on us with one finger on the trigger. Frenchy would have been sliced to ribbons and he knew it.

"It's here, brother! It's here!" Skeebo squealed.

"Shiver me sides," Lafitte exclaimed. "'Tis music to me ears! Now bind them, hand and foot!"

"But...I thought you said we could go?" cried Isabella.

"Oh, ye be sailing, indeed," Lafitte told her. "Just as soon as the booty's aboard. Harrrrr!"

Skeebo used dock lines to tie our hands as we sat on the deck with our backs to the transom. He also bound our feet. When he finished, the slug kicked me in the ribs hard enough to roll me over to Basco. The Catahoula consoled me by licking my forehead.

Lafitte, meanwhile, worked a cargo crane into position.

"Brotharrrr!" he said to Skeebo. "Make fast me chain to yonder booty barrel! Arrrrr!"

Skeebo hooked the chain to the barrel and gave his brother the thumbs up. Lafitte's crane switched on, pulling the chain tight and slowly lifting the treasure out of the engine compartment.

I wished hard for something to come along, a rogue wave, a whale, anything that would rock the boat enough to spill the treasure all over the deck and dump them in the water. But, nothing happened. Oh, the sea did rock us a bit, but only enough to slam the barrel into the fighting chair and scratch up one of its arms pretty good.

"Oops!" Skeebo said sarcastically. "I'll pay for that. Lord knows I got the dough!"

Laffite hoisted the barrel onto his boat and secured it to the deck while we sat there, tied up and helpless. When he had finished, the lunatic came over to the rail so he could see us.

"Au revoire, me hearties," he said with a smile. "It saddens me soul to say that this time, we be meetin' no more."

"We'll visit you in prison, you sick moron," I told him.

"Such language!" Lafitte said with mock surprise. "No, wee swab, yer only visitation will be amongst the fishes at Davy Jones' locker. Fair winds and followin' seas, all!"

Laffite nodded to Skeebo before moving to cast off from our boat.

Skeebo started motors from the *Blanca*'s aft control station. He nudged the throttles forward and straightened out her course, then tied the wheel down so the Hatteras maintained that heading by herself.

"I hope you losers enjoy your final cruise as much as I do," he said to us, then, laughing like a hyena, he shoved the throttles forward as far as they would go.

The motors wailed as the sportfisherman began to gain momentum. Skeebo jumped over to the Donzi and cut the lines with a knife. I heard its motor fire and he raced away.

"What are they doing?" Isabella asked. She didn't look so good.

"We've seen their Barataria hideout," Frenchy said calmly. "My guess is, they're getting rid of us."

"You mean sending us out to sea?" she squealed.

"I'm afraid it's going to be a little worse," said Frenchy.

The radio blared through the speakers.

"Arrrrrr! This be yar captain speaking," Laffite's voice boomed above the motors. "I regret to inform ye that today's weather repart has changed. Instead of fair skies and light breezes, ye may expect partly scattered explosions and occasional burnin' hellfire...NOW!"

A tremendous boom rocked the transom against our backs. Simultaneously, high atop the *Florida Blanca,* the tower blew apart sending metal and junk crashing down to the deck around us. Another ice pick from Isabella's terrified throat pierced my eardrums.

"Harley," yelled Frenchy. "There's a knife by your foot!"

I looked towards my toes and saw a fillet knife with a white, rubber handle pinning my jeans to the deck.

"He's got to reload the gun himself," shouted Frenchy. "Use the knife."

That was easier said than done. Not only were my hands and feet tied, now my legs were held in place by the knife. I jerked my knees to my chest. The blade sliced cleanly through the jean fabric and remained embedded in the teak deck. I scrambled around and did my best to get my wrists to the blade.

The radio blared again. Basco barked at it, but that didn't stop Laffite's horrible singing voice from coming through the speakers.

"There once was a sorry sailor," he sang, "who sailed upon the sea! His head rolled off one marrrnin', cuz he sailed too close to me!"

BOOM!!! The *Booty Bandit* thundered off another round. The shell streaked by somewhere very close overhead, but hit nothing.

I worked the rope up and down the knife blade as fast as I could.

"Bella, help me out here," I said. "Is the rope in the right spot?"

She was the closest to me, with the best view. I needed her eyes. And, more than anything, I needed her to stop screaming. It was driving me crazy.

"To your right a little," she said. "There. That's it."

"Keep your eyes on it and let me know if I need to adjust, okay?"

"Okay."

"Took him about forty-five seconds to reload last time," Frenchy said. "You've got about thirty left."

One of the ropes snapped free lessening the tension around my wrists.

"Back to the left some, Harley," Isabella said. "Yes, that's it. You only have two to go. *Hurry!!*"

I did hurry. And, I sawed. And, I hurried some more. None of it was half as fast as I'd liked.

Something gave way in the rope. The last piece fell off and my hands sprung free. I spun around, snatched the knife out of the deck and went to work on my feet. In seconds, the rope fell off.

Popping up like a jack in a box, I checked the position of Lafitte's boat. He appeared to be lining up on our port side, aiming his starboard gun. The s-curved wake trailing out behind his vessel told me that he had fired his center cannon the time before. Contrary to what Frenchy thought, he didn't have to reload each time. He had three guns, so he had three shots – one from the port side, one from the top gun and one from the starboard side. He was lining up his third shot. More than likely, he intended the next round to sink us.

The Donzi trailed Lafitte's boat a half-mile or more back.

The radio clicked on.

"Ye best be ducking yer pumpkin, swab," Laffite's voice crackled over the airwaves. "This next one's liable to sting yer arse! *Booty Bandit* over and out!"

"*Harley! Get down!*" Frenchy yelled.

I hit the deck just as Lafitte pulled the trigger. The round caught the flybridge squarely in the side and the whole boat heeled over to the right with the impact. I thought it might flip us. The *Blanca*, or what was left of her, had different thoughts. She fought back, rocking over to the right and leveling out.

Laffite had to reload.

I dove for the steering wheel at the aft controls. With the boat plowing the water at over thirty knots, I cut the wheel free of Skeebo's ropes, and turned to starboard, away from Lafitte's boat.

The Petronius Platform slid into view on my left. We were amazingly close, maybe less than a mile. We must have been running straight at it. I could have made a run for the oil rig. And, I would have, except for one small problem. Lafitte had charged forward to take a position between the Hatteras and the tower.

I didn't get a chance to see the pirate vessel for long, though, because Lafitte engaged his fiber-flage system and, just like that, the *Booty Bandit* melted into the waves.

"What's he doing?" Frenchy asked.

"He just cloaked himself somewhere over there," I said pointing to the empty water on our port side. "There's an oil rig over there but I can't risk it. Skeebo's trying to pin us in from the other side."

I watched the Donzi veer off with a burst of speed to track us off our right side. We were trapped.

The fly bridge was shredded. Fiberglass, shattered windows and twisted metal supports bounced around up there at crazy angles. Bits and pieces showered down on us each time the boat took on a swell. The damage extended into the salon as well. It didn't think the boat could take much more. But as long as those engines were humming, I did my best to get away from those creeps.

My mind raced. What would Salt do? He had always told me to have faith. Well, the way I see it, faith opens a door. It's up to us to walk through it. A knife had been provided to free myself. The rest was surely up to me. I needed to make a move. But what could I do? Then, it hit me.

I turned the boat and ran directly at Skeebo.

Would Lafitte fire at me with his brother in the way? I had no clue. One thing was for sure, though. I was going to take that cross-eyed sucker out once and for all.

Enough of the structure in front of me had been blown away to give me a partial view ahead. I punched those throttles full blast and took aim at the Donzi.

Skeebo did the craziest thing possible. Instead of trying to run, he turned the speed-boat towards us. Suddenly we were playing a game of chicken on the Gulf.

I did not care one bit. I was sick of those guys. That, and the fact that the Hatteras was well over twice as big as the Donzi, kept me on a straight track.

"Hang on guys!" I called back to Frenchy and Isabella. "We're going to run over Skeebo!"

Frenchy had cut Isabella loose and she was working on his ropes. Once free, he grabbed the rail and braced himself against her.

I glanced over towards the Petronius Platform just in time to see a burst of light flash just above the water. Lafitte had reloaded. The shell landed wide right and exploded, sending a shower of spray in all directions. I wiped saltwater off my face and checked on Skeebo's boat.

The red Donzi still raced directly at us on a crash course. A moment later, the boat shot under the tip of our bow and I lost sight of it. I heard the boat scream by. At the last instant, Skeebo had veered to the side. The Donzi tore through the sea just feet away with Skeebo doing his best to pepper us with lead.

It was time to make another move. I slowed the Hatteras and brought her around, hard. Laffite had two shots left before reloading. His aim wasn't so good if I was maneuvering against him. With any luck, I'd evade those last two rounds and make it to the Petronius before he had time to reload again.

Laffite could hide his boat, but not his wake. I spotted it after I made the turn towards the oil rig. He was trying to come about to line up the sights of his forward gun. I leaned into a turn forcing him to go farther to take aim. When he took the bait I switched course and turned to opposite way.

Skeebo had made a big arc to take a distant position behind me. Lafitte countered my tactic by continuing his turn so that he came in line between us. I shifted course again and gunned it straight for the tower.

I knew we had just seconds before he lined up for another shot. To my surprise, the flash came earlier than that.

This blast looked different, though, brighter, more intense. And, instead of a quick burst that came and went in a split second, it grew, getting even brighter. I wondered if he'd changed ammunition. No thunder followed, either, just a dot of fire growing larger. Then, I realized that the light originated from a point in the sky much higher than Lafitte's boat.

Silently, the ball of fire exploded into the sea behind Skeebo's boat.

Actually, the impact was more like a crash landing. Something very large and very fast tore a hole in the Gulf of Mexico behind the Donzi. At the time, I had no idea what it was. But, I did see enough to know that it had kicked up a nasty wave.

Next, the shock wave hit.

We felt it before we heard the thunder, powerful enough to thump my chest like a bass drum. The boom that followed contained enough bass to power a dozen hip-hop concerts.

Skeebo must have felt it as well. The Donzi changed course as he tried to outrun the growing wave. He didn't stand a chance. The monster wave ate him up, flipped the stern over the bow and the whole boat went down under a mountain of water, but not before all that extra gasoline burst into flames.

After the boat had been sucked down, the fire spread on top of the water at the crest of the surge.

The wave kept coming.

In front of us, the Petronius Platform rose out of the water less than a quarter mile away. It was going to be close.

"You feel that rumble?" Frenchy asked as he and Isabella came up behind me.

I just pointed at the wave. The wall of water had risen to fifty feet. Flames had formed a ridge another fifteen feet high.

"What in the world..." said Frenchy.

"Out of this world, dude," I said. "I think it was a meteorite."

Ghost breath sent shivers up my spine. A cold claw gripped my arm. The witching time had come. Fire had connected with water.

A detail stood out at the base of the wave. It looked like water, but not like the water behind it. Lafitte's hi-tech fiber-flage system simply could not reproduce the image of a tidal wave. The outline of the *Booty Bandit* appeared in the hues of a calm sea.

The radio crackled to life on a busted speaker somewhere aboard the *Blanca*.

"*By the devil's whiskers, I'll skin ye alive, swab, down by Davey Jones locker!*" Lafitte screamed at me over the airwaves.

The watery ship rose up the gigantic wave and teetered for a moment on the top of the whitecap, catching fire instantly as its synthetic skin connected with the flames.

"*Ye better pray ye perish before ye hits bottom! Arrrrrrrrrrrr-*"

Static hissed, cutting him short.

Then, just like his cross-eyed brother a minute before, the burning sea swallowed John Lafitte, boat, treasure, and all.

Tsunami

Indifferent to who it killed, the monster wave charged across the Gulf like a liquid locomotive. We were next in line to die. Our only chance to survive was to reach the Petronius Tower and climb it before the wave hit. I figured that chance was very small. I didn't want to think about how all the oil and natural gas flowing into the rig would react to open flame. And, even if we managed to make it up the ladder unburned, who knew if the platform could even survive the impact of that much water?

We did the only thing we could do – we kept going.

Apparently, the folks on the oil rig knew the wave was coming. As we approached the base, sirens filled the air. The screeching alarm added another layer of panic.

"I'm going to pull up to the floating dock and hold her there while you guys jump off!" I yelled to Frenchy and Isabella over the blaring sirens. "A ladder goes straight up!"

But, a weird thing happened as we got near the Petronius. The sea turned into a rushing river. We were headed upstream. The tidal wave sucked up water ahead of it, pulling the Gulf into itself. As the scorched tsunami drew closer, the Hatteras slowed down.

I jammed the throttles for more speed only to find out the engines were already turning as fast as they could. The levers did not move an inch.

We slowed even more. The massive girders loomed overhead. The dock floated only yards away.

The boat stopped moving forward. We began slipping back. We weren't going to make it.

"Look," yelled Isabella behind me.

"A basket!" said Frenchy. "Keep her here Harley!"

I looked up and saw that the workers had lowered a rescue basket on a rope. It hovered directly over our heads like a metallic angel. Frenchy grabbed it and pulled it down to the deck.

Isabella and Basco jumped in.

"Harley!" Frenchy yelled. "Get your butt in here!"

That was an eerie moment, dude. White water rushed around the Hatteras and through the steel tower. The motors wailed away at top speed. Yet, the sea was pulling us back.

I let go of the wheel and hopped into the basket as it began to lift off the deck. Frenchy stood on the other end. They must have had the cable connected to a super-winch because we shot to the sky faster than an express elevator.

I looked through the chicken-wire at my feet to check on the poor *Blanca*. She was no longer there. The tidal wave had sucked her backwards and turned her sideways. She looked an awful mess as she slid backwards up the enormous slope of water, her side raked with gouges, her top half blown to pieces. But, she still fought to escape. I heard her props scream when they lifted out of the water.

Then, a miracle occurred.

At the top of the wave, just below the crest and the flames, the *Florida Blanca's* props bit into the water again, just partially in the water, not enough to move her. For a few seconds, the spinning blades spewed a massive curtain of seawater over the wave. That did two things. One, it doused the flames with such a huge amount of water that it put out the fire. And, two, it created an enormous and perfectly formed rainbow that covered the wave like a crown.

With zero gratitude, the monster wave sucked the Hatteras down and she was gone before I could blink. The rainbow faded away as a shadow passed over the sun.

The wave had arrived.

As the crest came crashing through the tower's steel rigging, it became painfully obvious that our basket dangled below the water line. Just how far, I didn't have time to judge.

One thing was clear.

We were about to get wet.

"Hold your breath!" "Hang on!" Frenchy and I shouted at the same time.

The very last sight I saw before closing my eyes was Frenchy reaching for Basco.

Then…the monster swallowed us, too.

News Flash

In a million years of writing, Harley Cooper could not possibly have come close to describing how terrible I felt as I watched that TV news story.   It ripped my heart apart a thousand times.

I was waiting under the pine tree at the dock for him to call and tell me everything was alright.   Instead, it was my mom who ran out to give me the news that an asteroid had crashed into the Gulf of Mexico somewhere southeast of Louisiana.

"Eden, it's on the television," she told me.

I ran past her to the trailer like I was running through a nightmare.   My feet were in quicksand, my tears blurring the steps so badly I missed the first one and crashed down on my knee.   I didn't even feel it until the next day.

Inside, she had left the news on.

"A meteorite, that scientists estimate may have been the size of a softball, struck the Gulf of Mexico one-hundred-twenty miles southeast of New Orleans at 2:06 this afternoon. The impact occurred very near a working oil platform where witnesses report seeing a fifty-foot wave generated by the meteorite's collision with the sea."

The reporter stood on a helipad high above blue water.

"Workers also say a Hatteras sportfisherman was swept away and sunk by the massive wave just minutes after impact. The incident took place there, west of this rig."

The camera zoomed out to show the patch of sea the lady motioned to. A small group of people milled around on the edge of the platform behind the reporter. I was out of my mind as I scanned their faces looking for him. The camera zoomed back in to her before I had finished.

"When we come back," the reporter continued, "we'll speak to one witness who came up close and personal with the monster wave and lived to tell about it."

A commercial advertising a pill that made other pills work better popped onto the screen. I scraped both sets of fingernails up the sides of my legs. My mom walked in.

"Mom! Did they say anything about Harley? Did you see him?"

"Calm down, Eden," she said in her I'm-sure-he's-dead-but-I'm-here-for-you voice. "What are the chances of him being involved in this thing? Needle in a haystack."

"But, Mom, you were watching! Did they?!"

"No, Eden, they didn't."

"The boat. How'd they know it was a Hatteras?"

"Eden, you know these news shows. Takes them an hour to spit out the details. They drag everything out. Don't show anything but commercials."

I was going nuts! I couldn't take it! I jumped up, ran into the kitchen, walked in circles, and ran back. When I got to the TV, a commercial advertising a pill for cat indigestion was finishing up.

The news came on again – not from the oil rig, from the studio!

"And, we're back. I'm Josh McFarfield and this is NewsTeam Live. All afternoon long we've been hearing reports of a killer tidal wave lurking in the Gulf of Mexico, but where did it come from? Was this a natural phenomenon, or was it something else? We go now *live* to Ashley Unger, a cosmologist with the Huntley Space Institute in New Orleans, Louisiana.

Hello, Ms. Unger. How are you?"

"I'm fine, Josh. Great to be here."

The scientist stood before a large crowd. The people behind her definitely wanted to be seen. They were tripping all over each other to get on camera.

"Ms. Unger, does the Huntley Space Institute have any idea what happened today?"

"Well, yes, Josh, we actually have a pretty clear picture of what took place. We've been following the situation for days."

"Exactly *what* situation are you referring to?"

"The Copernicus Meteor Shower. Small bits of space debris, rocks if you will, that originated from an ancient collision between two asteroids, which happened over 25,000 years ago, bombard our planet about this time every year."

A scary, old woman, who looked like a witch, fought her way to the front of the pack to stand next to Ms. Unger.

"Good Lord," said Josh. "You mean this type of thing could be a yearly occurrence?"

"Well, I guess that's a possibility, but usually the bits of rock that enter our atmosphere are no larger than a grain of sand. They pose no real threat to those of us on the ground."

The strange lady held a canvas in one hand, a painting maybe.

"And the one in question today?"

"Yes. That was R-7452. We noticed it for the first time yesterday. At the time it was as large as a human head. We thought it would probably expire completely before impacting the planet due to the enormous friction and heat created during a high-speed trip through our atmosphere. Even so, we plotted the course, you know, where the meteorite might hit."

"And?" asked the newscaster on the edge of his seat.

"And we were off less than a quarter mile, I'm happy to say."

Ms. Unger did have quite a large smile on her face. The weird lady beside her smiled, too. She was missing teeth.

"But, of course," she added seriously, "we notified all parties in the potential impact zone as quickly as possible."

"Nice work, Ms. Unger. Thanks for joining us."

"Thank you, Josh. I love you."

"Uh...how's that, Ms. Unger?"

"I...uh, love your work, Mr. McFairfield...your work," she stammered. "The good reporting you do."

"It's McFarfield, and...uh...thank you for that...Ms. Unger."

In the crowd behind Ms. Unger, the creepy looking old woman raised her painting to the camera, a sign, actually, that said, "Fire On Water!" in flaming letters over a calm sea. Under that, smaller letters said, "Told you so, dolphin-boy!"

The news guy quickly turned to another camera and straightened his tie.

"She's obviously one very excited scientist," said McFarfield. "Anyway, when News Team Live returns, we'll speak *live* to a survivor of this deadly outer space attack. Back in a moment."

If I had had a gun within my reach I would have shot myself. No, strike that. I would have shot that idiot news guy, then I would have turned the gun on myself.

"MOM! He said 'deadly'! As in people *died*. You'd tell me if Harley called, right?"

"Yes, dear. Haven't heard a word. The boy's still at sea, I'm sure. He'll call tonight."

I checked my phone for the thousandth time even though it had been glued to my hand all day. No calls, no messages, no texts. I was going to throw up if I had to sit through another set of stupid commercials.

I threw open the door, instead, and ran outside to the canal. My dad's boat, and his gun, was gone so I just tossed little pine cones into the water until I thought a minute and a half had elapsed. After that, I sprinted back home.

Josh McFarfield was already talking when I returned to the TV.

"Now we take you *live* to Trina Perkins with this report. Trina?"

"Thanks, Josh. We're here on the Petronius Tower, site of the asteroid bombardment with a young man who had a close brush with the killer tidal wave."

I knew it was him when I saw the first lock of his shaggy head.

"Harley Davidsen Cooper, the Florida fourteen-year-old who piloted a fishing boat crew to safety just ahead of the huge tsunami."

Listen, I'm not going to stand here and criticize her looks. I mean, granted, she was hot. But, I could have killed him. He was staring right at her butt! On national TV!

"Mr. Cooper...ah, Mr. Cooper?   Mind telling us what happened?"

"Dude, is that a phone?" Harley asked pointing to the gadget on her hip.

"Uh, yes, Mr. Cooper. That's my phone."

"Does it work?"

"Yes, of course. It's a satellite phone. It works from anywhere. Now, Mr. Cooper –"

"Cool. Can I borrow it?"

"Um, yeah, I suppose…but first -"

"No. Now."

He picked the phone right off her belt and started punching in numbers.

"Well, apparently…uh…Mr. Cooper has more important things to do right now…Um…while he's doing them…ah…Josh? Are you there?"

"News Team *Live* is standing by, Trina."

My phone rang in my hand and scared the buh-jeezus out of me.

"Hello? Harley?"

"Eden! Oh, God, I'm so glad to hear your voice. You won't guess what happened."

"Harley. Are you okay?"

I'm sorry. I started crying. Honestly, I would have liked to keep everything we said to each other private, but there was no chance of that. Our conversation became part of News Team Live when Josh McFarfield sniffed out what was happening.

"I'm okay now," Harley said. "Eden? I've got to tell you something, something that became real clear to me out here. Eden…I lo-"

"Harley Cooper?" The anchorman's voice cut in. "Josh McFarfield here. News Team *Live*. Tell me. How did you feel knowing you were on the edge of *death* when that wave hit?"

I knew what he was going to tell me. I cried even harder. I just wanted to be there, to hold him, to bury my face in his messy hair.

We both ignored the news people.

"Why didn't you call me?" The question just popped into my head and out my mouth before I could stop it.

"The rig's communications were down. These guys just flew out."

"How's everyone else?"

"They're all fine. Frenchy, Isabella, even Basco, the dog I told you about. He made it, too."

"Harley?"

"Yeah?"

"You're on TV right now," I told him.

"I am?"

He was. And, he looked more beautiful than any movie star I'd ever seen. He turned to the camera and blew me a kiss.

"That's for you, baby," he said over the phone *and* the TV.

"Go do your interview," I told him. "We'll talk later."

Shortcut Home

"Okay! Talk at you later!" I said.

I had a lot to tell Eden, things I had never told her before, couldn't tell her before. Some things seemed way more important after the last few days, worth saying, you know?

Weird talking to Eden through a TV camera, though. She could see me, but I couldn't see her. The reporter chick seemed ticked at first. She calmed down, though. She even became genuinely interested when she finally got to ask me a few questions.

I told her how the boat belonged to a friend of mine but that he was in the hospital so I had to take it home for him. She asked me about the other boats, the ones others said had been chasing me, shooting at me. I told her I didn't know what she was talking about. I was too shell-shocked to remember that part.

You see, I've done TV interviews before. Those guys don't have very long attention spans. They jump to the next question in a heartbeat, especially if it's live.

She got to questions about the wave. After all, the water was really the big, scary villain in this whole thing, and TV folks love big and scary. I described how we made it to the rig, how the real heroes, Red's crew, had plucked us up in the nick of time.

"And you were actually struck by the wave?" she asked.

Wilson Hawthorne

"Yes, ma'am," I said. "But, it was just the top. Hit us hard, though, knocked us out into the air like a pendulum. Then, we watched it go out to sea. What happened to it?"

"Luckily, it dissipated before landfall. Mr. Cooper, one last question, if I may."

"Sure."

"What were you thinking when you knew the wave was going to hit? What got you through it?" she asked me.

I didn't even have to think about that one.

"Well, Trina, it's simple. A friend of mine once told me, 'You just got to have faith. It'll all work out.' I guess it did."

Her time was up and I was glad. I left her and News Team Live on the helipad and went downstairs to find everybody. They were all in the dining room.

Red was waiting for me. She pulled me aside as soon as I'd stepped through the door.

"I know I heard guns out there," she said, her eyes nailing me to the wall. "Joe filled me in on the first part of your little adventure when you guys passed through. Mind explaining what happened after that? And while you're at it, tell me the real reason he's laid up in the hospital?"

Afraid she'd read the truth in my eyes, I looked away.

"Listen, son, Joe Gaspar and I go way, *way* back," Red said. "There ain't much I don't know about him. Get my drift? Lord knows, as far as he's concerned, this red head can keep a secret."

The lady had been so nice to me. Heck, she saved our lives. Plus, she did seem genuinely concerned about Salt, almost like she was family. I hated to keep anything from her. So, I told her everything, out of earshot from everyone else, of course. But, I left out the treasure part. Sorry, rule number one. In return, she promised to pull some strings with the

Coast Guard. Turned out she was on a first name basis with a Coastie who happened to be very high up on the food chain. Her efforts saved my butt a second time when the Coast Guard did finally track me down.

Exhaustion had definitely taken its toll on my body. I couldn't imagine what Frenchy felt like. I think the three of us, and Basco, too, were too pooped to be anything else but numb. After a few hugs, and a couple more calls on the reporter's sat phone to my mom and Isabella's folks, we all hit the sack.

Just as I settled in and closed my eyes, someone knocked on my cabin door.

"Come in," I mumbled.

"Hey...oh, sorry," a guy in a jumpsuit said. "They said you'd be in here. Just wanted to catch you before you fell asleep. I work here on the rig."

I blinked my eyes at him trying to focus. "Okay."

"One of the guys found this floating in the water." He held up a three-foot doll that looked like me. "Kind of favors you. Figured it might be yours. A souvenir from New Orleans, or something?"

"Yeah, that's it. Thanks," I said.

"You're welcome," he said. "We thought you'd want it back."

He set the piñata me on the floor next to my bed face down. There was an old map, in Spanish, stuck to its back. I knew that if I had the energy to look at it, the map would probably show the La Paz treasure sitting a half-mile away on the bottom of the Gulf.

The guy turned to leave.

"Oh," he said just before closing the door. "Those boots...the ones Red gave you when you were here before?"

"Yeah?"

"They were mine. Just wanted to let you know you could keep them."

"Thanks, man" I told him. "I think I will."

I fell asleep before he shut the door.

I woke in the dark. The room had no windows, no clocks either. I didn't know if I had slept two hours or two days. I even thought it all may have been a dream. I fumbled around, found the door and opened it. The tight, steel hallway told me where I was.

My body ached, but my mind was more refreshed than it had been in days. I remembered my way back to the dining facility. The strong smell of coffee hit me as I got close. Frenchy sat at a table drinking a cup, Basco curled up on the floor at his feet.

"They got communications back," he said as I sat down.

"Any word on Salt?"

Basco stood up wagging his tail. He put his head in my lap.

"I think they said he was the first call," Frenchy said. "He's on his way out on one of the company choppers right now."

The wall clock read 1:20. I assumed that the brightness outside meant p.m.

"Awesome," I said perking up. "They released him from the hospital?"

"Not only did the doctors release him, the cops did, too," he said with the cup raised to his mouth. "Seems the Lafittes, and all the evidence, disappeared. They couldn't find anything Salt had done wrong. Had to let him go."

"Isabella?"

"Still sleeping, I suppose. I got up a few hours ago, haven't seen her yet."

"What's the plan?"

"Well," he said as he stretched back in his chair and set his cup down on the table, "I don't reckon there's a need for a boat driver anymore. Red said I could hitch a ride back to Grand Isle. We can make it home from there."

I felt a sudden twinge of sadness knowing I'd have to say good-bye to the old Choctaw and his dog.

"But," he continued, "we'll wait until your buddy gets here, of course."

That brought a smile to my face.

The door swung open and Red walked in.

"Sleeping Beauty is awake!" she said. "Get your beauty rest, handsome? How were the accommodations at Che Petronius?"

"Thanks, Red," I said. "You guys have been great."

She plopped down a piece of paper on the table in front of me.

"Thought you might want this," she said. "It's the coordinates of Lafitte's boat when the wave took her down. Fifteen-hundred feet of water. She's down there somewhere."

Red glanced over at Frenchy, then back at me.

"A salvage crew with the right submersible can reach that easy," she told me, cupping a hand to the side of her mouth. "You know…in case you had any valuables on board." She winked. "Now you owe me – twice!" She laughed.

Well, it wasn't me who violated rule number one that time.

Salt limped out onto the helipad an hour later. By then, Isabella had gotten up. She was anxious to get home. To tell you the truth, so was I. Red sent us back in style. After we all said our good-byes, me, Salt and Isabella boarded one of her corporate helicopters and flew all the way back to southwest Florida. Thanks, Red!

Salt pointed out Isabella's yard to the pilot once we crossed the Peace River and he set the bird down right there. Ana and César poured out of the house with tears pouring out of their eyes.

"*Dios mio!*" cried Ana. "*Isabelita!*"

They didn't even wait for the guy to stop the chopper blades. We'd just opened the door and they ripped her out. I've never seen so many kisses in all my life!

Using their land line, I called Eden while César exchanged a thousand thank you's for a thousand of Salt's *de nada*'s.

Isabella grabbed my hand and turned me around just before I boarded the helicopter.

"I want you to stay in touch, Harley Cooper," she told me, holding my hand. "You're still my hero."

"Look," I said. "I did what anybody else would have done to help somebody."

"No, not for that, silly." She searched my eyes. "For showing me what it is to stay true. She's so lucky. And, so am I. Friends?"

"Forever."

Backing away from the chopper, she blew me a kiss.

We flew over Charlotte Harbor, then Pine Island Sound. The hundreds of mangrove islands that dotted the waters below looked even more beautiful from the air. I felt lucky to live down there, and lucky to be back.

As the helicopter slowed to a hover over Cayo Costa, the island where Salt lived, the sun bounced off the Gulf of Mexico far to the west, filling the cabin with shades of gold.

Funny, I thought. You can hope for something, wish for it, pray for it, and it will arrive. You just never know when. And, sometimes, the form it takes when it shows up may surprise you. I guess at the moment, that golden light was all the gold I needed in my life. The universe works in mysterious ways. I was fine with it.

The pilot set down in a grassy field south of Salt's house. From there, it was a short walk up the fire break. Before we had even seen the first leaf of the oak trees that cover Salt's property, a black blur rounded the corner, nailed my chest, and knocked me to the sand – my dog, Hammerhead.

"Hey, boy," I said as his tongue slimed my face. "How ya doing? Huh? Good to see me? Good to see you."

Hammerhead barked hello about an inch from my ear.

"I'd say the mutt missed you, kid," said Salt.

At the sound of Salt's voice, Hammerhead jumped off me to sit obediently at Salt's feet, looking up at him, licking his chops.

"Yeah. I've got something for you," said Salt reaching into his pocket. "Here."

Hammerhead snagged the cracker in mid-air, happily crunching it down and forgetting all about his poor master lying in the dirt. Some dog.

A few more turns of the trail brought us under the oaks to Salt's funky cabin, round, green, and covered in moss just like we'd left it.

"Mother of pearl," Salt said with amazement.

344   Wilson Hawthorne

I followed his eyes and saw her, too. Aruba, Salt's scarlet macaw, sat on the porch on top of a chair. The old man didn't run, but he limped pretty fast to his favorite bird in the world.

"Just look at you, bird," Salt said as the parrot wrapped his talons around Salt's finger. "Like you're all dressed up waiting on the Sunday church bus."

"Hello, *raaawwwwk!*" Aruba replied.

Salt examined the feathers on Aruba's wing. I saw the hole Skeebo's bullet had burned between them.

"Well ain't you some kind of magician," he said.

Eden appeared out of the cabin door holding a sprig of mistletoe over her head.

"Welcome home, crab boy," she said to me.

I held out the very carefully wrapped scale model of myself. It even had a fancy bow.

"Merry Christmas."

Epilogue

All the coolest books have an epilogue, so I decided to put one here. Plus, I figured you'd want to know what happened to all that treasure on Laffite's boat.

Well, a month after we got home, Salt located a salvage operator with all the right toys. Salt and I flew to New Orleans and met the guy at his boat. Frenchy joined us, too. We all headed out to that patch of sea next to the Petronius Platform with the salvage submersible, a sweet, underwater metal detector, Red's coordinates, and, of course, a two-hundred-year-old treasure map that had mysteriously transformed to show the gold's new location.

I asked Salt how his grand-pappy's treasure map did that. He said it was "an old pirate trick." I don't think he knew.

Finding Laffite's wreck was easy. Finding the barrel didn't take much longer. It was lying on its side exactly fifty paces from the *Booty Bandit*, where the map showed a big X.

Some of the gold had spilled out of the barrel. No problem. The salvage crew worked the arms on the remote controlled submarine to move the barrel into an upright position. I got to watch it all on a monitor.

They used the metal detector to scour the area for scattered pieces. We found a bunch of those. The little sub brought them all back and stuck them in the barrel, too. Then, we hauled the whole thing up.

Salt amazed me again with his generosity. He gave the captain and crew a few pieces. I guess that's standard practice on a treasure salvage.

And, he offered Frenchy a really nice chunk on the condition that he use it to make things better for his people, the descendants of the Choctaw and slaves who scratched out an existence back in the bayou. Frenchy proudly accepted, saying that he'd love to build a new school.

We stopped in on Red at the Petronius Platform on the way back. She was happy to see us, but she was happiest to see Salt. I thought there may be something going on between those two. When Salt pulled out a gorgeous, 200-year-old gold rope and wrapped it around her neck, I knew there was.

Later, at home on Pine Island, the news people made a big deal out of our donations to rebuild Palmetto Cove. Salt didn't give a toot about any of that. He just got a kick out of seeing the smiles as people arrived from the FEMA trailers to move into their new homes.

We even rebuilt Smitty's place. Okra promised me a lifetime supply of her famous peanut butter cookies. I proudly accepted.

I even took her to the movies.

About the Author

Wilson Hawthorne lives on the Gulf coast of south Florida with his favorite treasures: his wife, five kids, and one very crazy Catahoula. When he's not writing books, you'll find him on the waters of Pine Island Sound thinking about pirates when he should be catching fish.

Please send correspondence to:
Wilson@TheLastPirate.net

The Cajun Pirate is the second book in the pirate series. Visit www.EyelandTelemedia.com to hear about the third book: *Curse of the Pirate*.

Join The Last Pirate on FaceBook for updates and info. Fair winds and keep reading! Arrrrrrrrrrrr!

Made in the USA
Middletown, DE